Duncan Lay is the author of two best-selling Australian fantasy series, the Dragon Sword Histories and the Empire Of Bones. He writes on the train, to and from his job as production editor of The Sunday Telegraph, Australia's biggest-selling newspaper. He lives on the Central Coast of NSW with his wife and two children.

Twitter: @duncanlay
Website: www.duncanlay.com
Facebook: www.facebook.com/duncan.lay

I0662187

Also by Duncan Lay

The Last Quarrel: The Arbalester Trilogy 1
The Bloody Quarrel: The Arbalester Trilogy 2

The Poisoned Quarrel

Duncan Lay

First published by Momentum in 2016
This edition published in 2016 by Momentum
Pan Macmillan Australia Pty Ltd
1 Market Street, Sydney 2000

A CIP record for this book is available at the National Library of Australia

The Poisoned Quarrel: The Arbalester Trilogy 3 (Complete Edition)

EPUB format: 9781760302511
Mobi format: 9781760302528
Print on Demand format: 9781760302535

Cover design by Xou Creative
Edited by Tara Geodjen
Proofread by Chrysoula Aiello

Macmillan Digital Australia: www.macmillandigital.com.au

To report a typographical error, please visit momentumbooks.com.au/contact/

Visit www.momentumbooks.com.au to read more about all our books and to buy books online. You will also find features, author interviews and news of any author events.

To Belinda, Gabriella and Shaun.

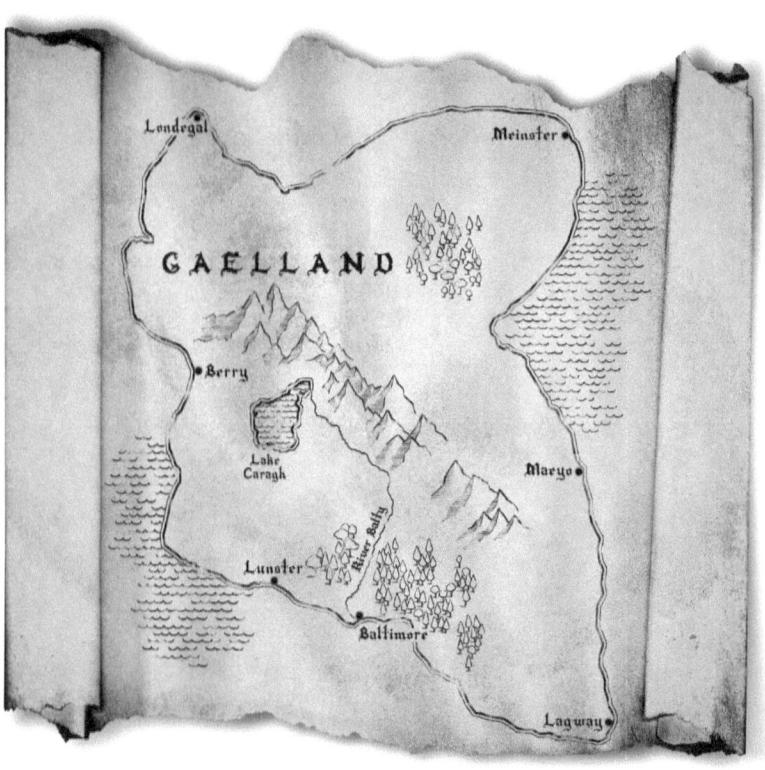

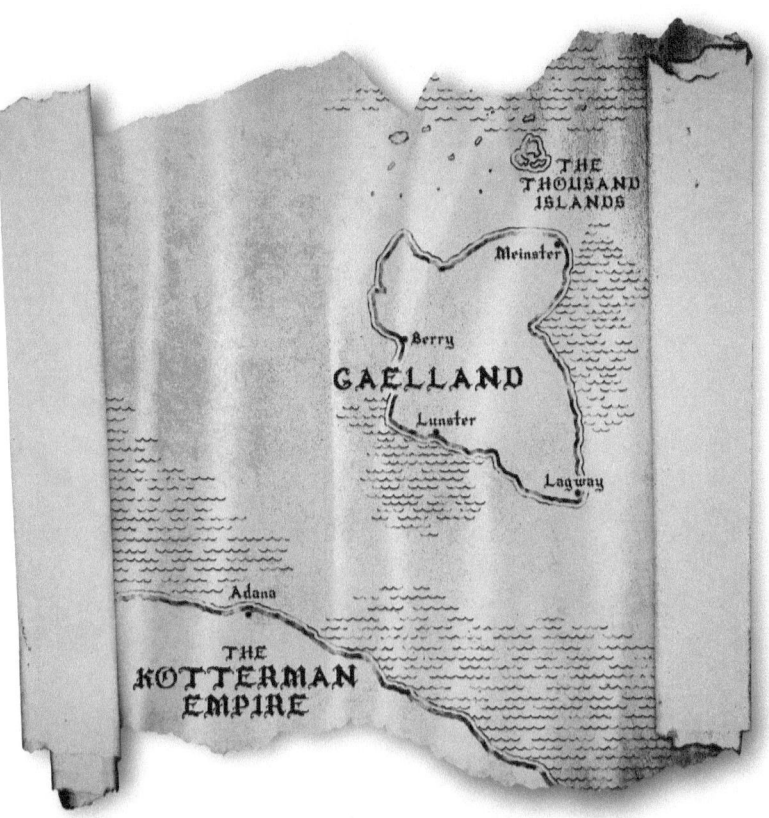

THE
THOUSAND
ISLANDS

Meinster

Berry

GAELLAND

Lunster

Lagway

Adana

THE
KOTTERMAN
EMPIRE

CHAPTER 1

Swane pointed a dripping finger at the single candle that stood on the altar and willed its flame to grow, to become something he could use to burn Fallon and the rest of the bastard rebels out of his father's castle.

The candle's flame expanded, lighting the room as if the sun had just come up, then it spluttered and died, turning to a wisp of smoke.

"This isn't working. Why isn't it working?" Swane complained angrily, his face spattered with blood. In frustration, he hurled his shining knife across the room, where it struck the wall with a metallic clatter.

"Sire, you have to give it time. If it was easy, then anyone could do it," Ryan said soothingly, from the other side of the makeshift altar. In between them lay the corpse of a serving girl. Her face, still locked in its expression of terror, gazed up at them. Swane felt no guilt looking into her unseeing eyes. Instead, to him, they only seemed to mock him.

Swane ground his teeth with anger. It should be so simple. He had watched Brother Nahuatl many times. Make the blood sacrifice and offer the heart to Zorva, then enjoy the power. But all he could get was enough for a simple trick, nothing he could use to terrify the world. He could not remember the right words, or maybe he had them in the wrong order. Or was there something else he was missing? It was all in the Fearpriest's book, which he had been forced to leave behind when he fled Berry, just ahead of Fallon's vengeance. He had thought to experiment until he found the power of Zorva but his host, the new Earl of Meinster, said this had to be his last sacrifice for now. While the ordinary people were cowed by years of the old Earl's rule, who knew what would happen if word got out they were worshipping Zorva in the castle?

"Well, how am I going to get my throne back without the power of Zorva? You and Meinster sit around all day telling me all the things I cannot do," Swane whined. *It isn't fair! It isn't my fault I didn't pay enough attention to Brother Nahuatl. After all, who could have expected the Fearpriest would be slaughtered by that bastard Fallon?*

"Sire, we shall get your kingdom back. You just need to have patience. Something will happen to change our fortunes," Ryan said.

Swane laughed harshly. "You think someone will just walk through that door and hand me the key to winning back my kingdom?"

"Of course not, sire, that is ridiculous," Ryan said, but then was interrupted by someone thumping on the door.

They exchanged a look, then Ryan tossed a cloth to the Prince, who hurriedly cleaned the blood off his face and hands, while Ryan covered the corpse of the serving girl and their makeshift altar.

"Who is it?" Ryan asked loudly.

"It is I, Meinster. Open up," the new Earl called. He had not long taken up his title but already he was using that instead of his birth name, Swane thought sourly. Still, at least he was nothing to fear. Swane relaxed, tossing the bloodied cloth down and Ryan unlocked the door with relief, to reveal the young Earl.

"Any luck?" he asked.

"Nothing," Ryan said.

"Perhaps you need to use the rite to call for a Fearpriest. Bring a replacement for Brother Nahuatl here," Meinster suggested.

Swane shook his head, holding back his frustration only with great difficulty. "First it would take moons for them to arrive. And second, I want the power, I don't want someone else taking it from me." He rubbed his hands distractedly through his lustrous hair, anger and spite fighting for victory across his magically-enhanced face.

It was the one time he did not resemble his murdered brother, Prince Cavan. "My father was going to have to rely on Nahuatl as well as Fallon to win him an Empire. I want it all for myself. I shall be King, Fearpriest and General and all shall bow before me."

"Of course, sire. But we need to get the power first, before we begin to plan what to do with it," Ryan said.

That was exactly the sort of good sense that was driving Swane mad.

"To that end," Meinster said, before Swane could say anything, "the Duchess Dina is here, pleading for an audience and promising that she can restore you to your throne."

"Well, sire, maybe the solution to our problems has just walked through the door," Ryan said lightly.

Swane wiped the last of the blood from his hands. "She had better have something good to say or she'll go on this table and we'll have one more try at summoning Zorva's power."

*

"Give me one reason why I shouldn't kill you for helping that bastard Fallon," Swane growled.

Dina gave him her most winning smile, which had always brought men around to her side. It had not been a long trip north to the county of Meinster – where Swane held sway, thanks to the help of the Guild of Magic – but it had been a nervous one. She much preferred to deal with men such as Fallon and her late husband Kinnard. They were so much easier to manipulate. Yet she was getting a good feeling from Swane. For all his bluster, she suspected he was delightfully uncertain and controllable. Even better, he was obviously blessed with a complete lack of conscience, which had been the main flaws with Fallon and her husband. In Kinnard's case, it had been a fatal flaw.

"I can't give you just one," she said. "There are so many."

"Humor me. Give me something because, Zorva knows, I grow sick of waiting here while Fallon sits on my throne."

"Well, perhaps I should just say I want to see Fallon dragged out and executed and you triumphant on the throne and I have the way to do it," she said with an easy smile. The fact he was still talking was a good sign.

"I have heard much in the way of promises from people but little in the way of action."

She held up her fingers and counted.

"I have your father's network of informers in my hands and head. Get an army to Berry and I can get you inside. Meanwhile, I can tell you exactly what Fallon and his friends are doing and where his army is, not where he wants you to think it is. Then I can sow unrest in Berry, so the people will turn from Fallon and welcome you with open arms. With me I also have the leaders of the major Guilds from Berry, bringing you not just the money you need to take back your country but the magic to get you over the Spine, through the frozen mountain passes and into the west of Gaelland, before an unsuspecting Fallon knows you are there."

Swane leaned back in his chair. "Why are the Guilds not here with you?" he demanded.

She bowed her head slightly. "They can be here within the day. They wait because, like me, they were forced to help Fallon or face death at his brutish hands. Yet they know that your father would have seen them as traitors and punished them accordingly. Your father, for all his talents, was a hard man to predict. They hope you will combine his best qualities with that of trust. They beg for the chance to make amends and restore you to your throne. As soon as I give them the message you will welcome their aid, they will rush to your side."

She saw his face darken at her words and wondered, for a moment, if she had overplayed her hand.

But then Ryan, Swane's silver-haired companion, leaned in and whispered into Swane's ear. That was the role she wanted, she decided, watching Swane reluctantly nod. The trick was to get the hook in and then work it until it was set so deep he could not escape. Before coming here she had questioned the head of Regan's informants, Munro, about Swane and all the stories swirling around him. It had been fascinating. There were all sorts of rumors about the real fate of Swane and Cavan's mother, as well as tales of how he took his pleasures from the servants. It made for an interesting mix and certainly opened a door for her. After all, everything was a weapon. And, although Swane was young enough to be her son, that was merely an advantage. He had not met anything like her before.

"So you threaten me?" Swane asked, breaking the silence.

"Of course not, sire!" she said, putting all the hurt she could muster into her voice. "I merely seek to show you that I am your most loyal servant and, unlike the others who have given you false promises, I will have you outside Berry within another moon. Just say the word and it is yours."

"And if you cannot deliver on your promises?"

She walked swiftly across to him, falling to one knee and taking his hand in hers. She slipped her other hand onto his inner thigh and angled her shoulders so he had no choice but to stare down the top of her low-cut silken dress.

"Then you may do what you wish to me, sire," she said in her throatiest voice.

She felt his leg tremble slightly and knew he had taken the bait. The hook was set. It took some effort not to burst out laughing. Men were so stupid! They thought they were in control but they knew nothing.

"Send word to the Guilds. Your time starts now," he said.

She looked up. "I swear I will see you rise," she said huskily and saw the flicker on his face and the corresponding response in his trews. All too predictable. After all, that was where men's brains were really kept. Within a moon, he would be doing whatever she wanted. Killing Fallon, for a start.

CHAPTER 2

Fallon looked out over the wreckage of Berry. On the horizon, huge columns of smoke showed where other towns burned. Gaelland was a charnel house and Berry was mere rubble. In between the smoldering houses, bodies choked the streets, the wreckage of what had been Gaelland's biggest city. Dead faces stared up at him: men, women and children, all accusing him. Worse, they all seemed to have Prince Cavan's face. It was all his fault. He had doomed them all. He had killed Cavan and unleashed horror on this land. The dead faces that did not look like Cavan haunted him even more. His friends and family. All dead. All had died in agony. He was the last one alive and he longed to join them in death, for the guilt and pain to be over. Behind him he could hear the slow footfalls of the men coming to kill him. He wanted to draw his sword and at least take some of them with him but it was jammed in his scabbard and the noise of boots on the stone was getting closer ...

Fallon jerked awake and sat up, feeling his heart pound. He looked over to where Bridgit was returning to bed, a cup of water in hand, her soft boots scraping on the stone floor.

"What is it?" she asked, sitting down on the bed. "The dream again?"

Fallon nodded. "It gets more real each time. Berry is destroyed and the rest of the country is aflame. It is my fault, because I killed Cavan."

Bridgit kicked her feet out of the boots. "You have to put that aside. You cannot let Cavan's death destroy you."

"But if I had not killed him—"

She grabbed his arm. "You cannot think like that. You have to put it aside."

"That's all very well to say," he said, reaching out for her water. "But we are the ones who have to make the decisions. Gaelland stands or falls on us."

She took a sip and then handed the cup to him and he drained it before passing it back.

She inspected it with a sigh. "Do you want me to make more of the decisions? Take that fear away from you?"

"I can't put that on you. And you have the baby to think about," Fallon said. "No, it has to be me. There is nobody else."

"Our friends," she said simply. "We always ask them for advice anyway. That way we can discuss things and vote, if necessary. It won't be just your choice or mine."

Fallon liked the sound of that the more he thought about it. "It works, because there will be seven of us, so we cannot be deadlocked."

"Only seven? But who are we leaving out?"

"Padraig and Rosaleen. We can't have a wizard or a priestess in there. It would look like magic or like the church is being used to rule Berry. Of course they can advise, but they can't vote."

She nodded. "Well then, it is settled. Will that make you feel better?"

Fallon chuckled. "Not completely but it might stop some of those dreams."

"Good. Now perhaps we can go back to sleep?"

Fallon smiled and lay back down. But he could feel the dream waiting for him. He would never be rid of the guilt for killing Cavan. Nor should he. He deserved to suffer.

CHAPTER 3

The castle was filled with the sound of music, laughter and cheering, just as it had been so many times before. But, unlike those times, there were no frightened servants rushing in and out, and the private banquet room was closed – it was far too small. Instead the throne room itself had been filled with a variety of mismatched chairs and tables and the women of Baltimore, Killarney and other small hamlets along the Lunster coast had done the cooking; family favorites and traditional recipes were being passed up and down the table. Lamb and potatoes made many tables creak, while there was also an astonishing array of creamy treats – honey cakes and the like – everything the women and children had been deprived of during their time in Kotterman. Friends and family shared plates, stories and embraces as they celebrated both their return from slavery and surviving the battle of Berry.

Fallon used a throwing knife to bang on a goblet but it was lost among the hubbub and he finally had to get Padraig's attention to nearly bring down the roof with a magical bellow for quiet.

Even then, a score of children led by Devlin's cheeky young son Will still scampered under the tables, playing a complicated chasing game and making people laugh.

"Welcome home to those who escaped the Kottermanis, but let us all remember those who lost their lives along the way," Fallon announced. "They will not be forgotten and their families will be cared for."

Heads bowed across the huge room as they acknowledged the likes of Murphy, killed by Swane and his Fearpriest. In one corner, women reached out to embrace Ena and her children, as well as the other grieving women.

Gallagher surged to his feet.

"Here's to Fallon, who led us through dark times and risked his life and soul to not just get back our families but defeat the Kottermanis!" he shouted, raising his glass.

At this most of the men in the room stood, also holding up their drinks.

Dermot, the farmer whose dog had escaped the Kottermanis and adopted Kerrin, while he himself had helped Bridgit's escape plan, was the first to finish and raise his drink again. "And here's to Bridgit, who rescued us and led us back from Kotterman and then tricked the Kottermani Prince to win the battle!"

At this the women and children and the rest of the men leaped to their feet and the two cheers merged into one. Fallon leaned over and lifted Bridgit up, so she also stood and acknowledged the cheers. He put his arm around her.

"Who would have thought we would see this day?" he whispered in her ear.

"I would have said you were mad as a spring hare had you suggested it," Bridgit muttered back, holding her fine silver goblet high. "I never dreamed of eating from these plates, nor drinking from these cups, while the throne of Gaelland waited behind us."

Fallon kissed her forehead. "Many's the night I tried to tell you that things would get better, that our luck would change. And now look at us, living in the King's castle, Kerrin strong enough to wrestle a bear and a second child on the way."

She chuckled and smoothed down her dress. It hung loosely after her time on the ship escaping from Kotterman, except where it clung because of her pregnancy. "I don't recall you ever talking about being made a slave, sailing across the ocean and executing the King for worshipping Zorva among all that!"

He grinned. "You would never have believed me if I had, so I kept quiet about it."

The people had long since sat down and gone back to their own conversations and food, so they flopped down and surveyed the remains of the plates before them.

"Aroaril, we ate a lot tonight," Bridgit said with a burp. "I feel guilty eating so much when winter's on the way."

"You have to have one last feast night before the cold closes in," Fallon said. "And Aroaril knows, you all deserved it after what you've been through."

"I can't help thinking about all the families out there that will be going to bed hungry, while we stuff ourselves silly."

He leaned in and kissed her again. "You think too much. We've earned this. And it's not like we have made three score of servants cook it and serve it to us. We did it all ourselves."

"We?" she said with a smile. "I don't recall you slaving over a hot oven!"

He winked and pulled a plate of lamb chops towards him. But he didn't get the chance to eat any of them, because Brendan got there first.

"So what do we do now?" the big smith asked as he sank his teeth into the meatiest chop.

"Right now, or when you've finished an entire sheep?" Devlin asked.

"Dev, you're making jokes again!" Gallagher grinned as he and Rosaleen joined them.

"Well, one of us has to. And it'd be a mortal sin for you to be doing it now," the farmer said, with a pointed look at how close Gallagher was sitting to Rosaleen.

The priestess pursed her lips as she looked at Devlin.

"You know you can't say that sort of thing," she warned. "I will have to give you a penance. Perhaps a whole night praying for forgiveness in the cathedral."

"What? It was just a silly jest!" Devlin cried, then caught sight of the way Rosaleen was winking at Gallagher. He pointed at them both. "Now that's just evil!"

Fallon led the laughter around the table. Bridgit was right; of course they could all rule Gaelland as long as they worked together.

Riona pushed away the remains of an enormous plate of chops and mash. "So what happens now?" she asked.

"Well, we have to clear up this mess," Nola said, looking around the room. "And we'll have more luck of getting some selkies to help us than we will some of these menfolk."

"Never a truer word spoken in jest!" Riona said. "But I meant, do we go home or stay here?"

"We don't have to do either. Prince Cavan had a secret island, far to the north of here," Brendan said. "We can pack up and go there and never have to worry about anything again."

Fallon shifted in his seat. "We can't leave the people. If we do, Swane will come in here in spring and start sacrificing to Zorva."

"But we're not nobles. How can we rule the country?" Riona asked.

"You never saw the nobles in action. I've scraped things off a sick sheep's arse that could do a better job of ruling," Devlin said.

Riona leaned in and kissed him. "You always know how to say the most romantic things."

"But who said we have to be the ones to stop Swane?" Nola asked.

"Nobody. But neither can we walk away," Bridgit said quietly. "No more than we could walk away from a sick child. We have to get Gaelland healthy again and back on its feet before we can worry about ourselves."

"How do we do that?' Brendan asked.

"We talk about it and then decide what to do next," Fallon said. "All of us, except Rosaleen."

"And why not Rosaleen?" Gallagher asked hotly.

"Because she is the head of the church now."

"Well, don't you want her there then? She will make the rest of us look good," Gallagher growled.

"Because the church cannot rule the people and make decisions."

"Who said?"

"Well, it was Duchess Dina, but that does not make it wrong. She was right about some things," Fallon said. "Putting the church in charge might look like a good idea but it'll make some people nervous and give others ideas."

"Fallon is right," Rosaleen said firmly. "If we say that being head of the church grants you a seat on Gaelland's ruling council, then every bishop and senior priest angry that I am running the church will redouble their efforts to get rid of me and get their fat backside onto the council."

"If they did that, we would throw them into a cell,' Gallagher declared.

"And then you'd have the ruling council controlling the church. We need to pick our fights, not go around looking for more trouble," Bridgit said.

"But how are we going to be taken seriously as the rulers of Gaelland?" Riona asked. "We're just ordinary people from Baltimore."

"Because we'll come down like a hammer on anyone who questions us," Brendan snarled, snapping a chop bone in his hands.

Nola laid a hand on his arm and he subsided, but Fallon could feel the awkwardness around the table.

"This all sounds very noble but will we really have a say? I mean, the boys have been letting Fallon do the leading, while Bridgit has steered us right," Nola said, breaking the silence.

"Of course we shall listen to each other. And you know I have always listened to Bridgit," Fallon said.

She snorted. "That's not quite the way I remember it," she said.

He laughed. "I have learned my mistake."

Bridgit gave him a nudge in the arm. "Well, I hope that does not come back to bite you."

"Don't worry, I'll bite it first," Brendan said, sinking his teeth into another fatty chop.

CHAPTER 4

The throne room was cleared and empty after the feast. Protesting children had been put to bed but, in many rooms, the adults were still talking, trying to make sense of what had happened over the last few moons.

"The families are all back together. Just as we vowed," Rosaleen said.

Gallagher felt his heart beating faster. He had sworn not to even think about her until everyone else was happy. But now he could think of little else. For years, all he had to sustain himself was the memory of his wife but now, when he looked at Rosaleen, he could not see his wife's face anymore.

"I am hardly a fit consort for the Archbishop of Gaelland," he said hoarsely. "A country fisherman who is losing his hair is not the right companion. And the things I have said about Aroaril—"

Rosaleen stepped closer and ran her hand down his face. "Those were said out of your pain, not because you are evil. I know your heart and I know Aroaril will forgive you. Besides, much of what you claimed about the old Bishops was right."

He could smell her hair, a faint scent of mint and he wanted to breathe more of it in.

"Are you sure?" he asked. "You could do so much better—"

She raised herself up on tiptoe and kissed him and all his excuses melted away.

"I was lost without you. It is terrible to say, but I am almost glad we have been through so much, for it brought us together," he said, brushing her hair away from her face.

She smiled gently. "It is true. Aroaril works in mysterious ways."

Gallagher looked up at the ceiling and felt the truth of that sink into his bones. Maybe it was all for a reason. He had loved his wife but there had not been the same all-consuming passion he felt for Rosaleen. Perhaps he was meant to be with her and this had all been part of a test, to see if he was worthy.

"I see now," he said. "Aroaril meant us to be together. It was ordained. You have a task to tackle, to bring this country back to Aroaril. And I am here to help you. I was a doubter and a sinner and you have converted me. I can help you convert others."

"Our lives can take strange paths, that is true, but He lets us choose which direction to go. He never forces us down a path," she said.

Gallagher was not really listening. It was all so clear to him now. Aroaril had chosen him for a special task, had tested him but now he had come through the fire and he had been rewarded with Rosaleen's love.

"Do you understand, my love? Do not read too much into—"

He rolled over and kissed her, enfolding her in his arms. This was not a time for talking.

*

"You don't need that horrible hammer anymore," Nola said, patting Brendan's hand.

He recoiled from her touch. "Are you mad? Do you know how many people out there want to do us harm? You and the girls have just come back from a nightmare. I will not let that happen again."

"And it won't. We are safe now," she said. "We have stone walls around us and our friends beside us."

"And it is my hammer that will keep you safe. I left you alone and let you be taken. Nobody will hurt any of you again," he swore. His huge hands wrapped around her gently. He was twice her size but he had never raised his voice, let alone a hand to her. She was small but had a big voice and a core of iron harder than anything he had worked with at the smithy. When the Kottermani slavers had taken her and his girls, it felt like they had taken his heart.

"But you could not have stopped them that night. You would have been taken too, or, worse, killed," she said gently.

Brendan felt his fury bubbling over at the thought. "I would have stopped them," he swore. "I would have smashed their heads in until they begged for mercy!"

Lost in the thought of crushing Kottermani raiders, he jumped when she grabbed his arm.

"Please don't talk like that," she said. "Fallon has a whole army now. He does not need you to fight. You can do more for him as a smith—"

"I will not risk it!" he growled.

"My love, please, do you not want to go back to what we once had—"

"What, people laughing at me? No, I would rather they fear me!"

The door banged open and he surged up from the bed.

"Ma, can we go into town?" their eldest daughter Mildrith asked.

"No!" Brendan thundered. "Are you mad?"

Shocked, Mildrith fled.

"Oh come now, you didn't need to yell at the poor girl," Nola said.

"Yes, I did!" Brendan bellowed at her, throwing his arm out as he turned around. "You don't know what I saw out there and what lurks in those streets!"

He turned away again, clenching his fists. How could he make them understand about the child snatchers, men who could only be killed by crushing their heads with his hammer?

"They worked every day in the fields and then nearly starved on the voyage home," Nola said quietly. "You should go after her and apologize."

"What?" Brendan roared and swept around again and this time caught a jug of water, which flew across the room and smashed against the wall.

"I'll go and talk to her, because it's not safe for me in here," Nola said fiercely and stormed past him.

"And what does that mean?" he yelled.

He reached out for her and she dodged away, a strangely familiar look in her eyes. It took him a moment to place it, then he realized it was fear. He had seen it in so many other eyes, yet never in hers.

"Wait!" he cried. But she was gone.

He picked up the pieces of the jug and felt like he needed to put himself back together as well. It always felt as though he was going to fly apart. He hated seeing that look in Nola's eyes but neither could he give up that hammer. It wasn't safe. She would understand, eventually. He would never hurt them, just protect them.

*

"Did you hear that? Sounded like something broke," Riona asked.

Devlin patted his stomach. "Yes, it did," he said with a smile. "Just some wind."

She pulled a face. "How many times have you told that joke?" she asked.

"I couldn't tell a joke when you were gone," Devlin said, looking up at the ceiling, his smile gone.

Riona leaned over, running her fingers through his chest hair. "Are you sure?" she teased. "I've never known you not to make a jest about something."

He did not smile. "Truly. I could not bring myself to laugh when you and the kids were gone. Aroaril knows the others tried. Padraig was forever giving me lines about Brendan. But it would have felt wrong."

"And now?"

"Now I cannot stop myself from laughing and jesting," he said, then winked. "And that is not all I can't stop myself doing."

"Eating, it looks like," she said with a grin, poking him in the stomach.

He laughed. "And do you feel like a nibble?"

"Will you be serious for a moment?"

"Whist, I cannot be serious now, woman!" Devlin said, running his hand through her hair. "Seeing you and the kids come back was like lifting a weight off me. I have to laugh about things, jest and

16

quip, because otherwise it will feel like it did when you were gone. Every time I jest, it reminds me you are home."

"Is that the only thing you remember?" she smiled.

"Well, now that I think about it, there is another thing," he said, kissing her ear.

"And what is that?"

"I can't get to sleep for all your snoring!"

She slapped him on the chest as he roared with laughter and he pulled her down to him. When he was with his family, when he was laughing, the dark memories of those terrible days without them vanished. But they always lurked there in the back of his mind, ready to steal out of the mists. Only jests could keep them at bay. Jests, and other things. But you couldn't be doing this around the kids, or out in public. More was the pity ...

*

"What's that noise?" Bridgit asked.

"It's just the castle. Nothing to worry about," Fallon said, kissing his way down her neck.

She restrained him with a little difficulty. "It doesn't sound right."

"Let's worry about it later," he suggested, slipping his hand down her body. She caught it with the ease of long practice.

"If you won't go and see what it is, I will," she warned.

Fallon sighed grumpily and rolled out of bed, grabbing a robe and wrapping it around himself.

"I hope you are happy. This floor is freezing and my feet will be like ice when I come back," he grumbled.

Bridgit sat up carefully, keeping the blankets high so as not to let the warmth out.

Fallon opened the door and disappeared into the corridor. She heard him talking softly to someone. She was about to see what was happening when he came back, dropping his robe on the floor and diving under the woollen blankets.

"All fine," he said happily.

"Not yet. Who was it?" she asked, deftly slapping his roaming hands.

"Kerrin."

"Kerrin! What was the matter? Is he sick?" She began to wriggle out of bed but he grabbed her arm.

"He's fine. He wanted to patrol around the corridors for a bit, to make sure we were safe. I sent him to bed. He's fine," he said again reassuringly.

"Patrol?"

"He thinks we can't look after ourselves now." Fallon chuckled. "But it's all safe now. He's gone back to bed." He reached out for her again but she grabbed his hand.

"How long has this been going on?" she asked.

Fallon shrugged. "Not every night," he said finally.

"So most nights then?"

"Not that many. Anyway, can we talk about that later?"

"Oh, I'll talk to him right now," she said.

"Oh no," he protested. "It can wait until tomorrow. You don't want to upset him and have him up all night."

"Are we still talking about Kerrin?" she asked archly.

"Well, it applies to us both."

"All right, I shall wait until tomorrow to talk to him," she said. He reached out again, only for her to intercept his hand.

"You had better make sure that door is shut properly first," she said firmly.

Fallon groaned, but this time he raced across to the door and back again.

*

The morning was cold, wind whistling around the castle and making everyone pull on an extra jerkin, but it was warm by the fire. "Kerrin, come sit with me," Bridgit invited.

Her son hesitated in the doorway. "But mam, there is training on. Dad is recruiting another army and he will need me there. I have to show the men how to loose a crossbow."

Bridgit felt her mouth harden. Fallon had suggested, and the others had agreed, that they begin forming a larger army to firstly stamp out Swane and then fight the expected Kottermani invasion.

The idea was that Fallon's former recruits would train the new men and over the course of winter they would have enough men to turn back the Kottermanis. Progress had been slower than expected, with a trickle rather than a flood of men coming forwards, but Fallon was confident of turning that around.

"Now then, young lad. You will come and sit with me. Your father has any number of soldiers to help him and he has been doing this sort of thing for more years than you have been around. It is time for you to put away the crossbow and stop patrolling around the castle."

Kerrin, who had been walking into the room, froze in horror.

"Mam! I can't put away the crossbow," he said, his face stricken. "How can I protect you?"

She stood and walked to his side, enfolding him in her arms. "I am so sorry," she said, pressing her face against the top of his head. "You have had to go through things that no boy should. But it is over now. We are back together and there is a castle around us and an army to protect us. It is time for you to put away the crossbow and get back to a normal life."

He lifted his head. "But I like the crossbow. I am good with it," he protested.

"I know you are. Just like your father. But you need more in your life than that. You could do anything. I just want what is best for you."

"And I just want to keep you safe, mam!"

She kissed his head. "I know, and I love you for it. But it is my job to keep you safe, not the other way around. I don't like you going out in this weather. And I don't want you catching your death of a cold in this draughty castle of a night, either."

"But I don't cough anymore. And I don't feel the cold like I used to," he insisted.

She dropped down to one knee. This was not going how she planned and it broke her heart to see him like this. It was as if all the gentleness had been hammered out of him, like iron in Brendan's forge, and the little boy she had hovered over for so many summers was running away from her.

"I want to spend time with you," she said. "I missed you so badly when I was in Kotterman and now there is so much for us to do here, and a new baby brother or sister on the way—"

"I'd rather a brother," Kerrin said immediately.

"That's good! Someone to play with?"

"I can teach him the crossbow and he can help me protect you," Kerrin said.

Bridgit took a deep breath. "Give me the crossbow," she said firmly.

"Mam, I—"

"No excuses. The crossbow. Now."

His mouth twisted downwards but he handed it over and she took it from him after only a moment's wrestling.

"Now, we are going to sit here and do some reading, sing a few songs and spend the day just the way we used to, before all this happened," she said firmly. "You will see this is for the best. We are safe here and tonight you are going to stay in bed. If you come outside then you will be in big trouble. Bigger trouble than even your father will be."

Kerrin's mouth twitched upwards into a slight smile and he nodded.

"Good!" she hugged him close. "Aroaril, I missed you so much!"

He held her back, his arms tightening powerfully around her. "I missed you too, mam."

*

Kerrin walked back to his room happily. It had been a good day with Mam, the sort of day when he could imagine they were back in their cozy home in Baltimore. Except he could never forget what happened. She had taken his big crossbow, but he had a secret weapon. He took out the small Kottermani crossbow that his dad had given him, as well as the quarrels that Brendan had made. He swiftly loaded the crossbow and sent a quarrel punching into the straw target on his wall, then practiced loading and loosing until the target was riddled. Then he pulled open another drawer and took out a pair of throwing knives. Mam had said nothing about them. They joined the quarrels in the heart of the straw target and he nodded in satisfaction.

Mam might think there was no danger here and she might be right. But he would be prepared if things went wrong. His parents were trying to pretend everything was the same but he could see that was not true. They were only fooling themselves, not him. He would give it a few days and then start his patrols again, when he was sure they were asleep. He could not trust them to keep themselves safe. He had to do it.

CHAPTER 5

"We're in for a storm, Highness," Gokmen said grimly, knocking on the cabin door and entering in one movement.

Feray looked up from the map of Gaelland she was studying. The former slave master's swarthy skin was looking sallow and his eyes were wide.

"Why do you tell me this? Do you wish to scare my children?" she asked sharply.

Asil and Orhan were reading one of their father's books, Asil helping his younger brother with some of the words, but now they were both staring at Gokmen.

"I did not intend offence, Highness." Gokmen bowed his head. "But Prince Kemal charged me with keeping you safe and you ordered me to get us back to Adana. The sailing master wants to turn around and run before the storm, back towards Gaelland. Whichever choice I make, I break one of my oaths."

Feray slammed down a paperweight on the map and pointed at her sons. "Stay here. I shall be right back," she told them and followed Gokmen out onto deck.

They had made good speed away from Gaelland over the past three days and the weather had been kind. With each passing turn of the hourglass, her hopes had risen that they could escape the cold north and make it back into warmer, calmer seas.

But one glance at the sky told her that was a forlorn hope. The clouds sat across the horizon like a bruise, forbidding and ominous.

Already the wind had freshened and blew her hair back from her face. The sailing master, a tall, lean man with a leathery face, hurried to meet her, bowing briefly. She had little to do with him on the way out but he was the most experienced of the sailors Kemal had brought with the fleet, a man from her own part of the Empire. She did not know his real name and would not dream of asking it, for all on board merely called him Gemici, which meant sailor.

"Highness, we must run before this storm. To sail through it would be the greatest folly," Gemici said.

"And what if there is another storm behind this one? We shall never get back to Adana," she told the sailor. "We have no time for this. If the Emperor arrives in Gaelland next spring to find my husband a prisoner, we are all dead. So we have nothing to lose. We go through the storm."

"Highness, the sailors are scared. They will not do it," Gemici said.

"Really? Then summon them. And quickly, for the storm approaches," she said angrily, her eyes flashing.

Both Gemici and Gokmen were far larger than she was but they bowed and hurried to obey.

The crew was larger than normal, because she had combined the men left behind on the two ships that had escaped the disaster at Berry. The others had all been lost when her husband's surprise attack on Berry had failed. She had reproached herself bitterly since that day. There had to be something else she could have said to persuade Kemal not to attack. He had ignored her warning to him that the Gaelish in Berry were not to be underestimated. It was a mixture of luck and skill that all her ships had not been taken as well. They had sailed into Berry – as Kemal had instructed – in the morning. The curtain of rain had lifted at a critical point and they had seen the other Kottermani ships crawling with Gaelish. Instantly she had ordered the ships to turn around and sail away, before the Gaelish could snap them up. Unfortunately her husband wasn't so lucky.

Once in the open sea and clear of any pursuit, Princess Feray had come to a hard decision. Neither ship had enough men to handle the rough trip home, so she had combined both crews on the best ship and sank the other. Now they had extra sailors but she feared they would need them to defeat the storms they would surely face. Of course the storm they would face back in Kotterman if the Emperor learned his oldest son was a prisoner of the Gaelish would be even worse. But Feray was descended from a line of kings and not about to let fear stop her. Not just Kemal but her own sons depended on her being strong. The Emperor's other sons would seek to use this as an excuse to supplant her husband. If that were to happen, then Asil and Orhan's lives would be in danger. The new Crown Prince would not leave nephews behind who could one day challenge him.

Still, one danger at a time, she told herself, watching the sailors assemble in the belly of the ship. Kemal would not have needed to speak to them, of course. They would have obeyed the Crown Prince without question. But she did not have that luxury and neither did she have any guards to enforce her will. Gokmen was an imposing presence but he was only one man.

"Men of Kotterman!" she cried. "I need your help to face and defeat these storms to return to Adana. I know it will be hard. But if we flee before the storms, we shall die. If the Gaelish do not kill us, the Emperor will, for not having the courage to do our duty. So, you see, there is not a choice at all. We either embrace death, or we fight for life, and for a safe and rich future for all your families."

She paused and looked around at the sailors, whose faces were betraying a mix of emotions and uncertainty.

"I swear to you that every man who steps ashore at Adana will never need to work again," she said. "I am entrusting you with not just my life but the lives of my sons, the Emperor's grandchildren to you. I need to save my husband, the Crown Prince, but I cannot do this without you. Will you stand with me?"

For a few moments nobody moved, then Gokmen took a step forwards and roared his agreement, raising his meaty right fist and spinning around, looking at the others. A heartbeat later, the others joined in.

"You will not regret this," she told them, hoping silently that proved true. "Now, to your places. Obey your officers and we shall all come through this. We sail in the best ship, with the best crew. We have nothing to fear as long as we stand together!"

This time the roar was much louder and then Gemici took over, rattling out orders and the men raced off in all directions. Most raced up the ropes to the masts, and out across the sail lines, hauling in the thick linen sails and tying them down, while others hurriedly lashed down anything on the deck and the rest disappeared below.

"Highness, you should also go below,' Gokmen advised. "The storm will be upon us soon and you should make your cabin ready, as well as be with your sons."

She smiled at him. "My husband will not forget you."

He bowed again and she left it there. She knew he had only been brought on board because Kemal wanted him to be desperately grateful. When Bridgit and the other Gaelish slaves had escaped, Gokmen should have paid with his life for allowing it to happen. Ironically, as Kemal had helped them escape, it had not been Gokmen's fault. But, by sparing his life and bringing him along, Kemal had wanted to secure Gokmen's absolute loyalty.

The storm was coming upon them at a frightening speed. The waves were now tipped with white and the clouds black, while the wind was whistling through the masts, catching the small sail that Gemici had left up, normally scarcely enough to move the big ship but here it would be vital in giving them enough speed to tackle the waves.

She slipped down the ladder, feeling the instant relief of being out of the wind. But that was short-lived, as she felt the motion of the ship change as the bow plunged into the big waves. She heard Orhan cry out in fear and she raced back into their cabin, to see the boys trying to stop their books from flying in all directions.

"Come here," she ordered.

"I want Baba!" Orhan wailed.

She gathered him to her chest. "As do I," she said softly. "But we shall need to be brave and clever to get him back again."

She wondered where he was and how he was being treated. Fallon was not a monster but Kemal had lied to him, then attacked his city, killing many of Fallon's friends and people.

"Be safe, my love. Pray for us," she murmured, and the ship shuddered as it slammed into a bigger wave.

CHAPTER 6

"Will you not stop this and leave me alone? Have you no mercy?" Kemal cried.

"I thought you would be glad of the company," Bridgit said, settling herself down on a chair.

"I would be glad of the company of my family. Or a regiment of my finest soldiers. Not you," Kemal said angrily.

Bridgit shook her head slowly. "You were the one to attack us. We would have been happy had you held to your deal and left us in peace."

Kemal just glowered at her. Before attacking Berry he had been haunted by dreams of Fallon and the night he had been tortured and broken. Now he was tormented by the way Bridgit had tricked him and forced his men to surrender, when he'd had Fallon surrounded and beaten.

His sleep was not made any easier by the fact he did not know what had happened to Feray and his boys. They were not prisoners but where would they have gone? He had not left enough men aboard the last two ships to make a rescue possible, nor could they risk sailing back to Kotterman with the winter storms raging out there on the seas. Yet if they stayed around Gaelland then they were risking capture by Fallon's men or, worse, by Zorva-worshippers.

Of the two, Fallon was the better option, he had to admit.

He had been given a set of rooms in the castle and, although there were guards outside the door, he was not chained up or denied anything. The rooms were beautifully furnished, every piece a fine example of Kottermani workmanship. He was also eating well. King Aidan had demanded his kitchens be able to produce Kottermani food and, although it was not quite the same as Kemal would choose at home, it was close enough that he could not complain.

His men were nowhere in sight and his questions about their whereabouts were ignored. Not that he expected Fallon to keep so many soldiers in the castle but he worried about what had happened to them, not to mention what they had done with his wounded. He had given orders for the Gaelish wounded to be left alive but he dared not trust Fallon to do the same.

Apart from Bridgit's regular visits, he was left alone. He had thought there might be the chance to grab her and then turn the tables on his captors but she was too clever for that. The wooden door of his sleeping room had been replaced by a barred iron door. Usually this was kept open but when she arrived, it was swung shut and she sat outside, able to talk, but safely out of his reach.

"You seem to have taken to power well. That is a rich dress," he said sourly.

She brushed the skirt. "I am wearing this because today I attended the wedding of our Archbishop to her husband, our dear friend Gallagher. And tonight it will be put away, once I have finished my duties."

"Duties? Talking to me? Why do you come here, if not to gloat?" he asked.

She smiled briefly. "Why did you want to speak to me, when I was your slave?"

"I had to speak to one of your people. You were the obvious choice," he said wearily.

"Well, your people are our prisoners now and perhaps I need your help to get them to work," she suggested.

"They are warriors. They will never slave for you!" Kemal growled.

"Maybe they just need the right motivation. What if we told them you would die if they did not work?"

"I would never order them to do that. No matter what you did to me," he declared. He had taken more than enough from these accursed Gaelish. He would not give them anything else.

And yet, he was afraid. Feray, Asil and Orhan were still out there. Even if they were not prisoners of the Gaelish, they would need his protection. His brothers were always looking for a way to be Crown Prince. And they may be fighting for the Elephant Throne but his family was like a pride of lions. If a new lion fought his way to the top with tooth and claw, the first act would be to kill the old leader's cubs.

He hid these worries behind a sneer. He would give Bridgit nothing.

"Then let us talk about your father and the rest of your family. Do you have brothers and sisters?"

"Why do you persist in asking me about this?"

"Because I wish to know. What will they do when they learn about your capture, do you think?"

Kemal glared at her. "You seek knowledge that will help you defeat them. I will not help you."

"What if they arrived to find you on the throne of Gaelland, and Fallon and me gone? What would happen then?"

He smiled thinly. "You seek to trick me into talking. Well, that will not happen."

She gave no sign that she was upset by his words but turned her head at a commotion somewhere else inside the castle.

"What is it?" Kemal asked, unable to stop himself.

"Perhaps you will find out. But for now, I have to go," she said, standing and turning away.

"Wait! We are not finished!" he cried, not wanting her to talk but not wanting to be left in silence either. But she did not turn back and he sank onto his bed. How had it all come to this?

*

Bridgit hurried across to where Padraig was beckoning to her. "You have to talk to Fallon. He's planning to march out now," the old wizard said warningly.

Bridgit sighed. She was getting nowhere with Kemal but planned to keep persisting. The problem was, Kemal had shown himself to be a consummate liar in pretending to sign a new treaty and then returning in the dead of night to launch a vicious attack. How could she believe anything he said now? But, plainly, Fallon was going to get nothing from him and at least there was a hope they could, if not gain his trust, then at least gain information from him by the spring. They had plenty of time. Although, perhaps not as much as they hoped if Fallon did not come to his senses.

"I'll talk to him," she said, clasping her father's arm.

"He's going to take some convincing," Padraig warned. "And I'm afraid some of it is my fault. After all, I was the one to tell him all those stories about the evil Guilds. He just keeps telling me this is what Cavan would do."

Bridgit squeezed her father's arm and hurried off to find Fallon organizing several companies of men. You could not call them recruits anymore. All of them had lived through the brutal battle of Berry and although none were over twenty summers, there was something about them now that seemed far older. Their numbers were shrunken – for hundreds had been killed or wounded – and while most of the wounded would recover to rejoin the ranks, thanks to the work of Rosaleen and the other priests, they were still recovering.

As soon as the recruits saw her, many of them gave a cheer, for it was she who had saved them when all seemed lost. Besides, while they were under Fallon's command, some of these men were hers. Gannon and the Lunster guards – the ones she had freed from the cells during the battle of Berry – owed their loyalty to her first, Fallon second. She smiled and waved back at them, although her smile wavered when she saw a small figure striding behind Fallon. She thought Kerrin would not want to leave her side after all they had been through, but her son was still following Fallon and the recruits around at every opportunity. She was sure he was still loosing a crossbow and throwing knives when he thought she wasn't watching. After what had happened to them she could understand why he was obsessed with weapons, but it felt like he was not the same son she had left and seeing him eagerly chase after Fallon rather than sit with her never got easier.

"Fallon!" she called, waving.

He was talking with Devlin and Gallagher, Caley at his side. He broke off to walk to her, Caley trotting beside him.

"What is it? We need to be away quickly, before word spreads," he said impatiently.

"Do you think this is wise?" she asked pointedly.

Fallon stopped and stared at her. "Even if you forget how they have terrorized men like your father for more summers than I can count and stolen from the people, the Guilds have been in league with Zorva, helped Aidan and now they helped Dina escape from the city. So we might as well do what Cavan and I intended all along and crush them. With their leaders in cells and their money in our hands, the city will be safe and we can turn our attention to getting rid of the back-stabbing nobles."

"But all the guilty ones are gone. They have left with the Duchess. All that's left are the ones who knew nothing or were too insignificant to be part of Aidan's plans," she argued. "If we were going to do this, we should have struck earlier. Now is too late."

"That is what they want us to think. But they will have left behind a few spies, ready to betray us at the first opportunity. Well, I am not going to give them a chance. We shall crush them, once and for all."

"And how will we deal with the merchants then? They will not trust us and we'll end up paying more for everything, for the Guilds hold them to tight contracts."

"The merchants shall deal with us fairly, or they will regret it," Fallon said flatly. "I hear what you are saying—"

"Are you? Because it sounds like you are doing what you want. Or rather, what you think Cavan would want," Bridgit said. "I thought we'd decided that we would leave them alone until spring, so we're free to concentrate on destroying Swane?" She raised her eyebrows at him, the way she always had when she was trying to warn him he was doing something foolish. But he merely rolled his eyes at her.

"You don't understand what Cavan and I went through with these Guilds. Helping Dina escape is the last straw. Besides, we need their money if we are to make it to spring. Now, I don't have time for this. We have to strike before they know we're coming and they have time to hide their money."

"At least let me come along."

"Too dangerous," he said with a shake of his head. "For you and the baby."

"For Aroaril's sake, Fallon, I am not made of glass!" she snapped.

But he merely leaned in and kissed her cheek. "You need to stay safe and not get too excited," he said. "I shall be back by noon and we can talk more then." Before he could say anything more he turned away, waving to his men, Caley barking, as if she was giving them orders as well.

Bridgit bit her lip to stop herself shouting at him. Then she saw Kerrin and pointed at him. She could not stop Fallon from going but there was no way she was letting Kerrin go.

"Kerrin! Here. Now!" she snapped.

For a moment he dragged his feet but then he slouched over.

"Mam! I want to go!" he protested.

"Not happening," she said firmly. "You're coming with me."

She did not look over her shoulder as Fallon's men began to march out in tight ranks.

CHAPTER 7

Swane sat, brooding, in his room in Meinster castle. So many things needed to happen before he could return to Berry in triumph. He was under no illusions as to how dangerous Fallon was. He had seen what the man had done in Berry castle, after all. Unarmed and surrounded by twenty of his father's most loyal men, he had somehow turned the tables on them and slaughtered them. All his life, his father had been telling him what to do. The only time he had tried to strike out on his own and listen to Brother Nahuatl, it had ended in disaster. He had laid a trap for Cavan, only for his brother and that accursed Fallon to destroy their plans and not only capture them but drag them before Father.

Swane felt a pulse of satisfaction as he remembered seeing Cavan's corpse and helping Nahuatl cut out his brother's heart. Although it had not been claimed in a sacrifice, the heart of a royal prince had enormous power and he still had it, in a sealed box, hidden in his old room. If he could but get his hands on that, as well as Brother Nahuatl's book, surely he would unlock all the power he would ever need. The first sacrifice you made brought you a surge of power but, after a few, just a simple sacrifice only brought you a little power. He hated the way Zorva drew you in like that. The first sweet taste of power was so intense, everything else was just not as good, so you kept searching for a way to restore that perfect sensation as raw magic surged through your body. Ultimately the only way to find it was to summon a Fearpriest, or become one.

But while he could feel the tug in the back of his mind to call another of Nahuatl's people, he wanted all the power for himself. And that could only happen if he got the book back. But that might as well be at the bottom of the sea.

He rang the bell for more wine. The serving girls were becoming reluctant to bring anything into his room, despite Meinster's threats of death for anyone who spoke of what was happening here. He waited irritably, thinking he would have to go and find some wine and hating the fact that this would never have happened to his father, when the door opened.

"I hope I am not disturbing you," Duchess Dina said, carrying a jug of wine and a platter.

She was wearing a warm fur coat around her shoulders but a whispery silk dress underneath and he could not stop looking down at her body.

She was old enough to be his mother but that only made things more interesting. His first memories of sex were tied up with his mother, usually of his mother tied up. Sex and violence, violence and sex, they were inseparable, but Dina seemed to offer something else.

"The servants were dithering about and I knew your father would not want to be kept waiting and nor should you. The rightful King of Gaelland has worries that ordinary people do not understand," she said warmly, deftly setting the jug down and pouring him a goblet.

She handed it to him, leaning forwards as she did so. He tried to look at her eyes but failed miserably. He took the goblet and she poured another for herself and then sat on the edge of the bed.

"To your return to the throne!" she toasted him.

He drank deeply, feeling the wine rush to his head, although, strangely, her perfume seemed to be intoxicating him even more.

"Tell me, sire," she said gently. "What are your biggest worries?"

He drained his wine. "That Fallon will never be removed from my father's throne!" he snarled.

"That will not happen, sire. But there has to be more than that," she said, taking his goblet and refilling it, handing it to him in exactly the same way as before.

"How do you mean?" he asked, his mouth suddenly dry.

"You are a king but you are also a young man who has been ripped from his home and lost his father in the most brutal way. Your family has been riven by tragedy as well, losing your mother at such a young age. There must be something you miss."

He looked at her uncertainly and she smiled and toasted him with her own wine, shifting closer to him on the bed. Her face was made up artfully, shining faintly with Kottermani powders, her lips stained a vivid red, standing out against her pale skin in the candlelight. It made him think of blood and he glanced down into his goblet to see what lay there.

"Sire, you can trust me. My only thought is to see you on the throne and Fallon brought to a screaming end. I am here for you, to do anything to make you happy."

He took another gulp of wine. She offered him the platter, holding the last of the season's pears.

"I find the ripest are the sweetest, don't you?" she said softly, taking one herself.

He shook his head wordlessly. Sex had always been about taking his pleasures, just as his father had done, and he felt completely lost here. He had met Duchess Dina many times before at his father's court, but she had not seemed anything like this. He had noticed her, as the wife of the King's cousin, but he had not lusted after her, the way he had many of the nobles' young mistresses. Up close, feeling as if he was the only man in the world for her, it was very different. As a deposed king he needed her, as a man he wanted her. Her less than subtle suggestions, coupled with the wine and the perfume, had his head spinning as to what he should do. He had just decided to reach out when she replaced the pears and broke the thick silence.

"Perhaps you can tell me one thing though, sire. I thought you might have tried to use Zorva's power to stop Fallon."

Swane choked a little on his wine.

"If only!" he said bitterly.

"What happened?" she asked sympathetically.

He found himself spilling out his fears and frustrations about the lost magic and how he could not generate the power he needed. She listened carefully, nodding thoughtfully.

"There must be some way of unlocking this power."

"There is one thing I need from my father's castle," he blurted. "I have hidden items in my room. A box and a book that could help me."

She flicked her hair back from her face. "Then we may well be in luck," she said. "I know that, as of a few days ago, your rooms remained empty. I should know, as I spent quite a few days in the cells before I escaped."

"Fallon kept you there?" Swane growled.

"You see why I long for him to be destroyed, sire," she said, pressing her hand across her mouth, then surging to her feet.

"Wait, where are you going?" he asked.

She turned away from him. "I am sorry, sire. The memories of those days haunt me still. I was living one day at a time, always afraid that I would do something to anger the brute and he would have me dragged out and murdered in front of a baying crowd, just like your father."

"He will pay for what he has done," Swane vowed.

"We shall destroy him, and then you will unlock the power you were always meant to have. I shall be proud to serve under you," she said. "Then perhaps I can put this nightmare behind me." Her shoulders hunched and she appeared to sob.

Swane stood, wobbling a little, but before he could hurry to her side, she strode towards the door. "Forgive me, sire, I am not fit company for you tonight. But I shall be better in the morning."

Swane watched her go, unsure of what to think or feel and tantalized by the scent she had left behind.

*

Dina shut the door and leaned against it for a moment, smiling to herself. The little fool was hooked and she just had to play him skillfully for a day or two longer before bedding him. Then he would be hers and there would eventually be but one real ruler here. Best of all, she had just learned the secret to gaining Zorva's power. With that in her hands, Swane would be even more dependent on her. Just the way she wanted. She only had to send some messages to Berry.

Dina pushed away from the door and hurried off, just in case Swane's lust got the better of him.

*

Munro double-checked that the street below his large shop was empty. Nobody suspected him but you could never be too careful. Once satisfied, he turned and looked around at his lieutenants. Most of those in his network of informants did not know each other and it was far safer that way. Each one of his lieutenants – mostly men but also one clever woman, Jen – had little groups and they spread out across the city like tentacles, funnelling information back to him. Before he had sent that information to Regan, but now the Duchess had taken over that role. As long as the money kept coming, he did not worry about who was paying him.

This, however, was something different.

"We have new orders," Munro said. "We need to spread rumors on the streets, rather than report them. A word here and there, pick your targets and get them to gossip and this will take on a life of its own. Food is going to get scarce in the city. We want the streets to echo with the story that Fallon's men are getting the best of it, and the Kottermani prisoners are eating well, while the people of Berry must go hungry. Spread it carefully, so that they hear it from every direction and each time it is repeated, people believe it even more."

His lieutenants nodded sagely. Once people were hearing it from several different directions, the lie would take on a life of its own and Fallon could never stop it.

"Find some of your most trusted men and get them into this new army Fallon is building. We need to find out not just what they are doing but also need to be able to spread rumors through the ranks," Munro told them. "The most important one is that this is a fight between Fallon and the Kottermani Prince, not between Gaelland and Kotterman. We want them to believe that Fallon intends to fight to the last Gaelish man and woman, but if he were gone there would be peace. Meanwhile, in the city, we can spread that rumor as well."

"That one will be harder to spread," someone muttered.

"Aye. The people love Fallon and fear Swane," Jen added.

"Did I say anything about Swane?" Munro demanded. "I don't want a word of Swane to hit the streets. We're not here to build him up. We're here to bring Fallon down. And the more rumors we spread, the more they will doubt him. As soon as they start to get hungry, they will begin to question him. We just have to give them the right answers to those questions. Now go to it. By this time next moon, the people will be begging for someone to come and save them. Fallon will learn that he should have stayed in his filthy village."

His lieutenants scattered, leaving from both the front and back of the building, some waiting behind so they were not all leaving together. In the silence that followed, Munro sat and thought. There was one more task that he had been given, the hardest of the lot, which was the reason why he had not mentioned it to them. He had to break into the castle, get into Prince Swane's old rooms and find a book hidden behind a secret panel, then somehow get that across the Spine to the Duchess. This order came from Dina directly and none but the two of them could know about it. It was a task that set the hairs on the back of his neck bristling, but the money she was offering was staggering and there were other men he could call on, outside the usual network, who might be able to help him. Of course they would have to die afterwards but that was the least of his concerns.

*

When Fallon signaled, men swept around the sides of the Guild of Bankers. It was a magnificent building, one that made the Moneylenders' Guildhouse look like a hovel.

Once he was sure the place was surrounded, he waved to Brendan and the big smith strode up the doors, a squad of crossbowmen right behind him and a company of swordsmen following them. If nothing else, Fallon expected they would be needed to carry away the bags of gold inside this building. It stank of money.

But while Brendan was ready to slam his hammer through the beautifully carved doors, there was no need. They were hauled open and a worried-looking man appeared. Small and thin, he was balding but had brushed his remaining hair carefully across to partially hide that. His clothes were neat but hardly rich enough to mark him as a man high in the Guild.

"What is going on?" he cried, his voice deep and rich, sounding ridiculous in such a reed of a man. "We are not open for business today!"

"You are going to be closed for some time," Fallon said grimly. "We are here to see your Guild leaders."

"And do you have an appointment?" the man asked.

"Here it is," Brendan said, brandishing his huge hammer.

The man blanched but he rallied. "But that is exactly the problem. They have vanished and we do not know what has happened. They are not at work, they are not at home – it is a mystery!"

Fallon gritted his teeth. This was exactly what Bridgit had warned might happen. But, then again, it could all be a trick. This could be a delaying tactic for the Guild leaders to hide. Let them try – he had the place surrounded and he would break down every wall if that's what it took.

"Who are you?" he demanded.

The man drew himself up and offered a slight bow. "I am Turlough, the Greeter for the Bankers Guild. I am the man who escorts our honored customers to their appointments."

"Then you can escort us inside and show us everything," Fallon said.

Turlough looked doubtful. "I don't know if I can do that, sirs. I would need permission from the Guild and that would mean finding them."

Fallon grabbed him by the shoulder. "Make an exception. Or you will have an appointment with Brendan's hammer."

Turlough took one look at the ominous bloodstains on the head and handle of the hammer and shuddered.

"This way, please," he said faintly.

Fallon strode confidently into the beautiful lobby of the Guildhouse. Like the Moneylenders, it was designed to impress but it took it a step further. The Kottermani hangings alone would have kept his village fed for a year, he judged.

There was little activity inside, however. A handful of scribes stood or sat around, talking worriedly among themselves and there was no sign of anyone important.

"Where are they all?"

Turlough shrugged. "I told you. They did not appear yesterday and none of our efforts to find them worked. When they did not arrive today we became far more worried. It is like the time of the witches, when people mysteriously disappeared."

"We killed the men who were doing that," Fallon growled. "And this is nothing like that."

Turlough bowed his head and led them towards a huge wooden staircase.

"Nobody is to leave. And send some squads through downstairs. Make sure every room is searched. If you find where they keep their gold, then put a guard on it and come and find me," Fallon ordered Brendan.

The big smith signaled to half the swordsmen and they fanned out into the building, while the crossbowmen and the rest of the swordsmen followed Fallon upstairs. But the place was deserted. Well, not quite, for there were a handful of servants cleaning already spotless tables and they fled as soon as they saw the armed men. Fallon glanced around. He was still using many of the Baltimore villagers as sergeants, because he knew and trusted them. He waved one over.

"You want us to get them?" a muscular farmer called Craddock asked.

"They can't get anywhere. And unless the Guild leaders have lost twenty summers and changed into women since I last saw them, that wasn't them," Fallon said.

Turlough led them to room after room, all of which had evidence of having been cleaned out – and then cleaned up by servants.

"You see what I mean? There is nobody left. And they took all their records with them, which means we have no idea what to do now," the Greeter said wretchedly.

Fallon cursed. Now that he said it, the fact there was almost no books or scrolls in sight was obvious.

"Right. Where do they keep the money?" If the Guild leaders had fled in a hurry then they would have struggled to get the money out with them. It would simply have weighed too much.

"We do not just hand out sacks of gold to people!" Turlough said, scandalized. "A signed piece of parchment from the Guild is enough to ensure funds are made available."

"Just take me there," Fallon said, giving him a push.

But although Turlough revealed a small room with walls of thick stone and a door of iron, there was nothing inside. Not even a single coin was left.

"How much is normally kept here?" Fallon demanded.

The Greeter shrugged. "I do not take part in that. I just show them up to the offices and then return downstairs. Besides, our clients are from the highest rank. They would not be seen carrying bags of coin around."

Fallon swore and signaled to Craddock. "Tear this place apart. They have to have left something!"

"And if we can't find anything?"

"Then it's on to the next Guild and we do the same again. But maybe Gallagher and Devlin are having more luck with the ones they are searching."

*

He dragged Turlough out of the Bankers Guildhouse two turns of the hourglass later, sweating lightly and swearing loudly. Even the most violent search of the place had failed to turn up anything useful. He had little faith that he would find anything more useful at the homes of the Guild leaders but he had to finish the job, at least. He owed Cavan, after all.

Like all the richest families in the city, the heads of the Bankers were down by the water. Turlough was not overly happy about being dragged away, nor about the mess they had left in the Guildhouse but Brendan just had to heft his hammer suggestively and the Greeter went along with whatever they wanted. This was not a part of town Fallon was familiar with, for it was near the water but away from the harbor, with its noise and smells, and his recruits had not needed to train within it.

His recruits were getting plenty of stares from the people in this part of town, rather than cheers, which was a little worrying. He knew Aidan's supporters would have come from this area but surely they did not remember their dead king that fondly?

Then he found Devlin and his men emerging from the wreckage of a rich house and it began to make sense.

"Everything was cleaned out in the Guildhouses. All we found was a handful of clerks and cleaners, who only turned up for work because they didn't know different," the farmer said sourly. "So we thought we'd check their homes. All empty and everything gone. They must have known we were coming."

Fallon spat in disgust. Looking back on it, he should have rounded up the Guilds on the morning after the battle, before they could do anything. But his men had been exhausted and the streets were filled with wounded men crying for help.

"See if you can find anything," he ordered Craddock. "Maybe they left something behind."

He rubbed his face as Craddock sent men to kick in doors but had little time to brood, as a delegation of self-important citizens hurried towards him.

"Want me to get rid of them?" Brendan offered.

Fallon waved him down and fixed a smile on his face.

"What is going on here?" their self-appointed leader, a large woman with a florid face, demanded.

"The leaders of the city's Guilds have fled Berry, taking all their documents and money with them," Fallon replied. "We are searching for reasons why."

"The Guilds are gone?" the blood drained from her face.

"It will make no difference to the city," he assured her.

"That's what you think," she declared, to much head-nodding from the ones behind her.

Fallon restrained his urge to take out his frustration on these idiots.

"You will see that things will get much better without them," he said. "Now, we shall finish our business here soon and leave you in peace."

"Well, do you have to do it so violently?" she asked. "It looks as though you are looting the place!"

"These people are in league with our enemies!"

"Your enemies, perhaps, Fallon," she said tartly, turning away and hurrying off before he could say anything more.

"Should we follow them?" Brendan asked.

"Leave them," Fallon said dismissively. "We have bigger problems than a rich woman with a loud voice. Probably thinks we're making a mess on her nice clean street. She's the sort of rich bastard who would scream out for guards to protect her, but then make them come to her back door so her respectable neighbors wouldn't see them on her doorstep."

The smith chuckled but Fallon kept an eye on the retreating citizens. He was tempted to get Rosaleen out here and question a few of them, see what they knew about the Guild leaders but once he went down that road, then he would be organizing informants and dragging people away to be executed. It wasn't supposed to be like that. He was supposed to be freeing the people from an evil king, not putting fresh chains around them.

"What about me?" Turlough asked.

"Well, there's no longer any money to pay for you and the other servants. So you might as well come and work for me," Fallon replied.

"Ah, you need someone to speak to the people for you?" Turlough asked excitedly, his voice throbbing with pleasure.

"No, you can learn how to use a sword," Fallon said flatly.

Turlough staggered back a pace. "Sir, I saw the battle of Berry! I would not last ten heartbeats in that!"

"Well, I don't have any other work for you. And you're not going to last the winter if all the skills you have is talking nicely," Fallon said. "Come on. We're getting nowhere here."

*

Bridgit could see that the raids on the Guilds had been a failure long before Fallon made it back to the castle, just from the way the men were marching. She was so tempted to say that she had told Fallon so. But she bit her tongue as Fallon returned empty-handed.

"Were all of the Guilds gone?" she asked.

"Well, not all. A few of the minor Guilds are still here but they have little money and influence. Ones like the Engravers and the like. Anyone who dealt with anything we want, like money or magic or food, is gone."

She had suspected as much and saw instantly there was a bigger problem looming. The Guilds employed thousands of people across the city. Berry was going to come to a grinding halt and, worse, there would be many hungry people soon. And winter was looming.

"Then hardly anybody's going to have money to buy food soon. We need to get ahead of this. We have to seize whatever food we can find and store it safely, share it out to the people so none go hungry. We don't know how much more we can get into the city so let's act now, before the situation gets any worse," she said briskly. "We did that on the ship as we sailed home and it was all that kept us alive."

"Surely it's not that bad?"

"No, it's worse. Not now, but in a moon's time the city will be in chaos unless we act. We have secure warehouses and armed guards. Once we have the food supplies under our control, not in the hands of merchants and Guilds, we can make sure everyone gets a fair share. But we have to go now. Word will already be spreading through the merchants of what you have tried to do to the Guilds. If we leave it any longer, they will be disappearing out of the city and hiding food away, then selling it for ridiculous profits while poor people starve. We have enough food to last us through the winter. But not if they hide it away."

He nodded and waved to his officers, bringing everyone in close. As well as his friends there was the black-bearded Bran, the bald-headed Gannon and the youthful Casey.

"Gall, Dev, you come with me and we shall sweep through the docks. Brendan, go through the slaughter yards. Bran, Gannon, your men go through the markets. We need armed guards on all warehouses, and scribes to start making tallies of everything. Nothing goes out until we know how much we have. Anyone complains, they can come and see me. And send word to the harbor and to all gates. No wagons are to leave this city until we have searched them.

Nobody takes any food or flocks out. The Guilds think this city will collapse without them. We have to prove them wrong."

Bridgit breathed a sigh of relief. Then sucked it in again when she saw a bedraggled bunch of men walking in the middle of Fallon's soldiers.

"Why have you brought back a pack of cleaners and clerks? I didn't think the castle looked that bad," she asked.

"They were all that was left at the Guilds. They no longer have anyone paying them, so I'll swear them into the army."

"And you will be able to turn this bunch of cleaners and scribes into an army strong enough to first defeat Swane and then the Kottermanis?" she asked, unable to keep the disbelief out of her voice.

"If we must. I will do whatever I have to, to keep you and the baby safe," he said, enfolding her in his arms. "In a couple of moons I created an army good enough to defeat Kemal. Given twice that much time, we'll be able to make an army to defeat whoever his father sends."

She held him back and kept her fears to herself. The men he had rounded up were a far cry from his battle-hardened recruits. Still, at least they had some time to get it right. The Kottermanis would not be a threat until spring and Swane could not get his men across the Spine in this weather.

CHAPTER 8

"The biggest problem is getting across the Spine, of course," Dina said, smoothing the map carefully with her hand. She found it useful to stand up and lean across the table, always making sure she was opposite Swane, to give him the full benefit of her low-cut dresses. It was like an elaborate dance, with her leading and Swane following blindly.

"Tell us something we do not know," Ryan said testily.

As she had spun her web around Swane, the silver-haired adviser had become ever more hostile towards her, as he saw his own place being supplanted.

"Shall we talk of all the problems I have solved by coming here?" she asked gently, smiling warmly at Swane. "Already my men sow dissension in Fallon's ranks and turn the city against him. The Guild of Magic has shown us that the earlier messages you received from the nobles around Berry are lies. Fallon does not have garrisons in every town, waiting to fall upon us. And the Bankers have brought men rushing to your banner."

"Rushing to earn coin, not serve their true King," Ryan said sourly.

"But as long as they restore Swane to his rightful place on the throne, who cares what their motivation is?" she countered.

She had used the Guild of Magic to spread the word that anyone who wanted to fight would receive a gold piece and a pardon for any crimes committed. Every thief, outlaw and desperate man in towns and villages up and down the east coast had rushed to take advantage. They were not trained, they were armed only with crude weapons, but they all looked ready to kill. And that was the main thing.

"So, to the Spine. We need to open up one of the passes and then we need to have shelter waiting for us on the other side so the men can recover. The first thing we must do is gather enough food to take not just us but the magicians we shall need across the Spine. It would not do to lose some of them along the way and be trapped. We need to order the eastern counties to send food here. The only thing that matters is that we make it across the Spine. Once we have taken Berry, we can send food back across to the people here, if needed."

"We can take food from the traitors in Berry for those who helped us here," Swane declared.

"Well, the next question is when we should go. It is a delicate balancing act. The longer we wait, the more men we can attract to our banner, the more food we can amass, the more we can turn the people against Fallon and the more surprised he will be when we arrive in the west. But, if we give him more time, he will train more men. Yet if we go while he is still weak, we will arrive with fewer men and less food and find the people are behind Fallon."

"We go sooner rather than later," Ryan said immediately. "The men you are bringing in are useful but the real weapon is the one we gave the King – our guards and their horses. Fallon does not have anything like that."

Dina inclined her head. It was time to cut Ryan down a little more. "Then the final question is where we should meet him."

"Well, Berry, obviously," Ryan said with a snort.

"Yet he and his men have spent more than a moon training to fight in Berry and have just defeated the Kottermanis there. He also has a castle to retreat to, if we manage to surprise him, while our cavalry will be of little use in the tight streets."

"Why didn't you think of that?" Swane demanded of Ryan.

Dina watched as Ryan spread his hands helplessly and bowed his head. It was easy enough to keep the smile on the inside, she had long practiced keeping her true feelings from her face or she would never have been able to stay married to Kinnard for so long.

"So where do you think we should meet Fallon?" Ryan asked, unable to keep the bitterness completely from his voice.

"Lake Caragh," she said triumphantly, stabbing her finger onto the map, the site of a long-ago triumph over a peasant rebellion.

"Why?" Swane asked.

"I know Fallon. He will be unable to resist it," she said, permitting herself a small smile at the thought of finally bringing that bastard down. "Where the King's men destroyed the rebels. He will ache to change that history and will eagerly march into our trap there. No doubt he will think to use the marshland around there to destroy our cavalry but this is winter. The land will be frozen solid. Even the edges of the lake will be ice and the ground will be hard and flat, perfect for our cavalry. It will be a fitting end to his arrogance and we can turn to the people and tell them it was decreed by history. Remind them that the first battle there led to many years of peace and they will fall over themselves to forget about Fallon."

She paused and looked hard at Swane. "The final decision is yours, sire," she said.

"I like it," Swane said after a short pause. "I like it a lot. Except for the fact the people will forget about Fallon. I intend that they should remember his death forever. It shall be so terrible that none will dare to cross me ever again."

"You are wise indeed, sire," Ryan said, bowing his head again.

"Meinster, you need to make a tally of the men we have now, and Ryan you need to see how much food we have. As soon as we have enough to last a journey to Lake Caragh, we shall leave, to bring the throne back to its rightful King."

"To victory, sire," she said.

"I will drink to that!" Swane declared.

Dina immediately poured out two measures of wine, one for Swane and then one for her.

"Duchess, where is mine?" Meinster asked.

"You do not have time for wine. You have to follow your King's orders and get everything ready for the march," she told him. "You and Ryan both."

They both turned to Swane, mute appeal on their faces but, to her pleasure, he waved them away.

"Go and do my bidding," he ordered.

"To your return to your throne and a glorious rule," she toasted him, not bothering to wait until the other two were out of the room.

He drank and then looked at her over the rim of his goblet. "I never realized you knew so much, and could be so useful to me," he admitted.

She stood and leaned over him. "You have no idea," she purred.

CHAPTER 9

Asil screamed while Orhan vomited.

Feray did not make a move towards cleaning it up, beyond shuffling the boy backwards from the spreading pool. Because getting up and fetching water and cloths was impossible in the ship's crazy motion and calling for someone to help was pointless because nobody could hear them.

For two days now the ship had been hammered by the storm. At first it had seemed bad enough, with the ship pitched violently backwards and forwards as it slammed into waves. It would pick up speed going down a wave and then run into the next one with a shuddering crash that seemed to bring it to a stop and made everything shake. The wind threatened to pluck the masts right from the spine of the ship, while rain thrashed at every exposed surface, making it sound as though they were inside a huge drum.

Half the fine glasses in their cabin had been reduced to shards by the first night and sleep was impossible. Yet Feray had clung to the hope that dawn would bring relief from these huge seas and howling winds.

It only brought a new terror.

The waves seemed to be coming from all directions now, corkscrewing the ship through the water. They were now struggling to get up some of the waves, the ship tilting sharply to the skies and then after bursting through the crest, pointing downwards and picking up speed as if they were destined to plunge to the sea floor without stopping. If that was not bad enough, they were also being hit by waves from the side. First they would lean to the left, far enough over that they could see the foaming waves through the side windows of their cabin, then they swung all the way back over. All the while, the waves shook the ship, like a dog would shake a rat to death.

The combined motion was too much for the boys' stomachs and the resultant smell was enough to make Feray want to vomit. But, luckily, she had not eaten anything and there was nothing to bring up, beyond the sour taste of fear.

Clothes, toys, possessions and objects flew or rolled around the cabin, breaking themselves or other things.

The two body slaves, who usually helped the boys dress, wailed with fear from their adjoining tiny cabin. She ignored them. If she had the energy, she might have offered them a scrap of comfort. But she did not have the strength to even do that.

They had no idea of the passage of time and nothing with which to mark it. The sand had not been pouring straight through the hourglass due to the crazy motion of the ship and then, sometime during the night, the hourglass had been smashed anyway. The sand was now a fine coat across the cabin floor. They did not know when dawn was, and the sky certainly did not change and they had no idea when they should be praying. Not that it mattered, because they were praying all the time.

To Feray's fevered brain, it seemed as though this was now the whole world. Memories of warm afternoons and gentle breezes had been washed away by this tempest of storm and sea.

Each time when she told herself that, surely, this was the worst, it seemed to find a new torture to inflict on them.

The cabin stank of vomit and fear and, suddenly, she had enough. She could not bear to die in here, dragged down to the bottom of the sea.

"Come! We are going up on deck!" she shouted at the boys.

They turned terrified eyes on her, looking even more scared than when Fallon had held them at knifepoint.

"If we are going to die here, we shall go out staring the storm in the face and not waiting for it to claim us!"

They did not seem convinced but she clambered and slithered across the floor to where their clothes hung in a cupboard. Half of them were now on the floor and the rest hung on grimly, their wooden hangers often threatening to come off the rails and be hurled around the cabin. She grabbed three cloaks and three belts and scrabbled back to her boys, where she dressed them in their warmest cloaks, oiled leather on the outside, warm fur inside, then used the belts to fasten them to her.

"What is the third one for?" Asil shouted.

"To hang on to the ship. Now come, gather your courage. Do not show anyone that you feel fear, for you are Princes of Kotterman and the heirs to the Elephant Throne."

She was not sure they would understand but it was still important. For herself, she was terrified, but making the decision to go out into the storm made it easier. She would face death on her own terms and if Aroaril willed it, they would all go to meet him together. She remembered fleeing from the Fearpriests under Aidan's castle and having to cross a floor covered with the bodies of rotting children. Nothing could be worse than that and she used that to give her strength.

With Asil and Orhan hanging on to her, she lunged for the door as the ship leaned that way and the three of them thudded into the wood. Panting, she hauled the door open as the ship rocked back and then they were in the dark passageway. Usually this was lit by lanterns, or at least by sunlight streaming in from above. But there was no light here and the three of them staggered down, bouncing from wall to wall as the ship surged. Orhan slipped as the ship tried to climb up a wave but the belt stopped him going too far and Feray hauled him up and they kept going. The closer they came to the hatchway, the more they could hear the wind howling, while the hatch itself was almost closed, just the occasional snatch of rain coming in showed where the corner was not quite fastened.

Feray made sure they both had their hoods up and then hauled her sons up the ladder and shoved open the hatch with her shoulder when she got to the top. Instantly the full force of the wind and rain hit them, battering them and almost driving them back down the ladder. It flipped the hoods of their cloaks down in a heartbeat.

The force of the rain on her head was almost painful, rushing into her eyes and drumming incessantly on her head. She lifted Asil out onto the deck, making sure his hands were clutching the rim of the hatch opening, then climbed out herself and dragged Orhan out.

The three of them lay on the deck, Feray to get her breath back, the boys obviously because standing up was impossible without her. Out here, the cold sucked the breath from their lungs and had their teeth chattering, despite the warm cloaks she had put around them. Pulling up the hood of the cloaks was impossible in the wind while, out here, the motion of the ship was even more extreme.

Holding tight to her son's hands, Feray got to her knees and began to crawl across the deck to where the occasional flash of lightning revealed a huddle of figures around the ship's wheel on the aft deck.

The rain tried to drive them into the deck, while the violent motion of the ship alternately helped and hindered their progress. Waves rushed across the deck, coming ever closer to them. One enormous one sent a torrent of water across their boots and tumbled Asil and Orhan over. The belts did their job, pulling both boys up as soon as they were knocked over and she hauled them up, slithered through the last of the white water and made the stairs up to the aft deck.

Talking was pointless, for the wind snatched words away before they could be even formed but she hung onto the rails grimly while the boys hung onto her for their lives. Slowly they clambered up, making the deck above their cabin, where a giant figure rushed over to help.

"What are you doing out here?" Gokmen roared, his enormous voice barely able to compete with the wind.

"We will not die in there! We will face the storm!" Feray screamed back at him, her lips almost pressing against his ear.

It was impossible to see his face but he said no more, merely helping her fasten the belts to the ship's rail, so they could stare out into the storm and watch the waves advancing on them, towering above the bow and crunching over the top, forcing the ship to fight to bring its nose up each time.

Feray's fingers were almost numb with the cold but she fastened them tightly about her sons' shoulders. Now she was here, it was tempting to remember how warm and dry it had been in the cabin below but she could not stand to be back there. It was harder to fight the thought she should not have risked this voyage, that she should have instead tried to find somewhere safe to stay the winter in Gaelland. But she told herself that was foolishness. Gaelland was either controlled by Fallon, who would imprison her with Kemal to protect himself from the Kottermanis, or run by Swane, who would sacrifice her to Zorva. Either way, they would die. If not on an altar to Zorva then when Kemal's brothers took Gaelland for the Emperor. No, this was the only way any of them could survive. Although making it to dawn seemed like it would be a miracle.

Each time they reared up over a wave or crashed back down into a trough, she felt her stomach being sucked up towards her throat, and the faint cries of her sons, which just reached her ears before being whipped away by the wind, said that they felt the same.

"Do what you will! We shall never give in!" she screamed into the wind, knowing it was but a gesture, for nobody could hear them.

Then they reared up over another enormous wave, which broke across the bow and sent saltwater coursing down the length of the ship. And Feray saw a strange light ahead.

For a few moments her tired and battered brain wondered if the last wave had actually sunk them and she was seeing Aroaril himself in the afterlife. She clutched her sons' hands and thanked Aroaril that they would at least all be together there. But surely in Aroaril's realm it would not still be pouring with rain?

Then the ship went over the next wave, still huge but far smaller than the rest, and she saw it clearer. It was the sun, breaking over the horizon.

Her first thought was they were sailing due east and obviously in the wrong direction, then that was swamped with relief, a wave of it as huge as any the ship had battled.

"The sun! Look!" She let go of Asil's hand and pointed.

Even as she did so, the wind and rain began to die back, the wind reducing to gusts, the rain to something they could recognize.

Even the motion of the ship changed, riding easier on the sea. As they went over each wave, the ship stopped pitching around so violently.

She turned her face upwards, to let the now-gentle rain wash the salt off her face and lips.

"Ana, are we alive?" Asil asked.

The wind relaxed, to something that was barely stirring their hair and the ship slowed down, the scrap of sail that remained on its mast barely enough to keep it moving now the storm was gone.

"Yes, we are," she said with a smile, feeling as though her salt- and wind-battered face would crack.

Now they were rocking gently on what was still a choppy sea but a millpond compared to what they had gone through. From the lower decks, battered and sick-looking sailors dragged themselves into the sunlight to see what was happening. Behind them, she could hear Gokmen and Gemici and the sailors on the tiller, quietly marvelling that they were still alive.

Overhead, the sun broke through the last of the clouds and bathed Feray and her boys with its rays.

There was a shout from below and the sailors, who had been staring at the clearing sea and sky with bewilderment, turned to look at her. Next moment they had fallen to their knees, bowing their heads to her.

"You did it, Highness," Gokmen said, his usually powerful voice reduced to a hoarse rumble. "You were the one who broke the storm."

Feray was about to explain that was impossible but thought better of it. After all, having these men think she and her sons were blessed by Aroaril could not hurt.

"I doubted what we were doing, but Aroaril has shown us that we are doing His work in helping you," Gemici added, coming to stand by her side.

"Three cheers for the Princess Feray!" Gokmen cried.

This time the sailors needed no prompting and their celebrations were almost hysterical in their relief.

"Command us, Highness, we are yours," Gemici said.

Feray put her hands on her sons' shoulders and composed her face.

"Then let us get the sails up and this ship turned around. We need to get back to Kotterman as fast as we can," she said.

CHAPTER 10

Fallon had thought his problems had ended with Kemal's defeat. But there was more to do than ever. He had men scouring the city for recruits for his new army, one big enough to defeat a Kottermani invasion. But that had to be put aside while he secured enough food to last the city through the winter, before the merchants sold it to Swane or smuggled it out and they were left with nothing. Of course, the merchants were outraged. And with every warehouse that he confiscated, replacing the merchants' private guards with his own battle-hardened men, the fury grew.

"You cannot just take our goods! That is stealing!" went the common refrain.

Fallon was proud of the way he refused to lose his temper at them. He reckoned Cavan would be proud of the way he was handling it. Although that thought always brought a pang. It would be so much easier if Cavan could give the orders and he could just carry them out. "You will be paid for them in the spring," he promised, wishing he had managed to seize the gold that the various Guilds had hoarded. If he could but give these merchants a few coins, they would be happier. But he needed every remaining coin he could get, to arm the new army he was building. The Kottermanis had thoughtfully provided them with plenty of weapons, shields and armor but much of it was damaged or unsuitable and he had every blacksmith he could find working to fix it or convert it, or repair the many swords and spears his own men had lost in the battle, to say nothing of damaged crossbow bolts. All of this was skilled work and these men needed paying if they were to work at the necessary speed.

A few of the merchants took this news philosophically but most raged on, forcing Fallon to give them a taste of reality.

"There is nobody else to complain to. The nobles are gone and I would not listen to them even if they were here," he told them. "And the people need the food you have here."

Either his words or the expression on his face convinced almost all of them. But there were a couple who signaled to their guards to defend their property.

That did not go anywhere. The merchant saw a pack of young boys led by a peasant trying to take his goods but the dozen or so guards at each warehouse instead saw hard-faced soldiers, led by a grim warrior and stepped away.

Fallon was partly disappointed that none of them were tempted to fight but mainly relieved. Because it meant he could swear them into his new army. He certainly could not leave them in the city to cause trouble. By themselves they were nothing much but, as his fights with the Guild Bashers had shown, if enough joined together then he could have a problem.

Most of them were not happy about learning they were about to become soldiers. They were invited to go and see Brendan. Then they took one look at the big smith – and his bloody hammer – and decided they would love to fight for Berry.

Fallon enjoyed that. He knew Nola had asked Brendan to put aside the hammer, but it was seemingly part of him now and even his love for his wife and daughters had not persuaded him to put down the weapon. Fallon was grateful the smith had kept the hammer, for it was fearsome and had a reputation that made his own men braver while striking fear into others' hearts.

He went through the warehouse district methodically, concentrating the food supplies in a group of warehouses, to make them easier to guard and also easier for the food to be distributed. Once he was sure it was safe and no merchants or their guards were going to make trouble, he let Bridgit and some of the other women come in, to make a proper count of the food.

Brendan, Devlin and more than a hundred of his best men were staying there to make sure there would be no trouble. Kerrin had also turned up, crossbow at the ready, although he kept trying to hide from Bridgit, much to the amusement of Fallon's men.

"Are you going to stay with mam or come with me?" he asked his son.

Kerrin rolled his eyes. "Count sacks of flour or show your new army how to use a crossbow? What do you think?"

"Well, the sacks of flour have it then," Fallon said with a wink.

As he marched through the city he felt happier about the day's work. True, they had not seized the Guilds' money, but they had secured the city's food and picked up perhaps two hundred new recruits at the same time, which would be a valuable addition to his new army.

Gallagher and Bran joined him, the fisherman and black-bearded guardsman reporting how they had taken control of the slaughterhouse district, as well as the market areas.

"We'll have it all by nightfall," Gallagher said.

"That will only be half the job though. The merchants will have plenty more hidden away throughout the city, ready to sell when things get colder," Fallon predicted. "Tomorrow I want you out with squads and comb through the city. We have to get as much as we can if we are going to make it fair for all. We have to reckon that what we have now must last us for a good five moons, until the first new crops start to come in."

"We're not going to be popular," Gallagher warned. "Have you noticed something different?"

Fallon looked his friend up and down. "I don't know. A new tunic?" he hazarded.

"No!" the fisherman snorted. "Nobody is out cheering us."

Fallon looked around the streets. A few children were running alongside, waving, while now and again someone would give a bit of a cheer or clap their hands. But the rest simply went about their business.

"A few days ago we couldn't walk a mile without a mob forming to applaud us. Soon they'll be shouting at us, sure as eggs."

"They've just got bored with cheering," Fallon said with a shake of the head. "They still appreciate what we have done. And when they realize that we are making sure everyone gets enough to eat this winter, they will cheer us."

"And what about this new army?" Bran pointed at the mob of former warehouse guards ambling along, the threat of armed soldiers behind them the only thing keeping them from running off. "Might be better to only take those that want to fight for us."

"We need them all and it'll be better to have them where we can keep an eye on them," Fallon replied.

The black-bearded officer said nothing but his silence spoke volumes.

Fallon left it there. These men might look like a rabble now but eventually, when they were split up and surrounded by his original recruits, they would add some backbone to his army. All of them were big and tough, used to wielding fist, knife and shillelagh. Surely it would not take much to turn them into soldiers. And when the other choice was bowing to Zorva and sacrificing children, they would fight. Anyone would fight.

*

"They're no good in a fight," Casey said.

Fallon looked over the ruins of the makeshift shieldwall and sighed. His former recruits, who had fought through night and day and rain and blood in Berry's streets, were shouting instructions at the mass of new men, but they might as well have been trying to get cows to juggle. He watched Brasso, the hero of the battle of Berry, demonstrating to sullen men how to use a shield and shook his head at the sight.

"It's different," the youthful Casey said with world-weary experience. "That first group was young, excited and proud to protect their country. These are men from Berry who saw and heard the battle. They know what they face. And they are older, fatter and lazier."

"They can't all be flabby cowards!" Fallon growled.

"And they're not. Half of them will be good and most of the others will stand in line. But there's enough troublemakers in there to affect the others."

Fallon rubbed his jaw. Just one man running at the wrong moment could doom them all. Time and again during the battle his recruits had turned and fought. If a handful had kept running, then the rest would not have stood and Kemal would have won that night.

"They don't listen like the others, Dad," Kerrin said, adding his voice to the argument. "They say a boy can't teach them anything."

"Split them up into small groups. Any that cause trouble get put in a special group. I'll work with them and if they can't be trusted, then we'll just send them back to their homes. We can't risk taking men into battle we don't trust."

Casey looked happier but Kerrin was still gloomy.

"There's not enough crossbows for them to practice with, either," he complained. "You lost too many of them in the battle."

"That was Gallagher's fault," Fallon said with a wink at his friend. "But they take too long to make. We are better off having the smiths work on spears and swords that are easily fixed."

"We're going to need them. Nobody is any good with the Kottermani bows."

Fallon grimaced. They had seized hundreds of these bows and he had hoped his men could learn how to use them over winter, for there were thousands of arrows on the Kottermani ships. Except they couldn't hit anything. Men could part-draw them and still aim them reasonably well but those were only good at distances of about twenty yards. If they tried to draw them back fully then they struck problems. Only the strongest men could get the string back far enough and then the arrows were flying in all directions. Barely one in ten hit the target.

"Add it to the list of things we need to talk over," he said with a sigh.

*

The idea had been for them all to sit around a table and work out the problems facing the city. Fallon had particularly liked it because it meant it was not just him making the decisions. Try as he might, he could not get out of his mind King Aidan's dying words, that his choices would doom the country. If it was not just him making these decisions, then surely that was safer?

Except, although everyone had problems, few had any solutions.

"We shall have a good idea of how much food is in the city within the next two days. But how much are we going to give people? Do they get a daily ration or a weekly one? And how do we stop people coming back for a second ration, or sending their children to beg for more?" Riona asked.

"And does everyone get equal shares? Or do you get more if you have more children?" Nola added.

"Do you pay for them? There's some who have money aplenty. Others who would pay if they could but they no longer have work with the Guilds or the merchants," Devlin said.

"Then there's the recruits. They have to eat extra because we are making them do more work," Gallagher said.

"Don't forget the Kottermanis. They need feeding as well. We cannot just let them starve," Devlin pointed out.

Fallon groaned. "Let's start with the easiest one. We have to get the Kottermanis out of the city. They can work farms and boats to earn their food. It is the least they can do after what they put our people through."

"But don't you think they might cause trouble? They are soldiers and we are putting them with farmers and townsfolk," Bridgit said.

"Well, we can't keep them here. They are living in shelters outside the walls for now but the nights are getting colder and we shall have the first snows within a moon. Already we wake to frost. We might as well chop their heads off as make them sleep outside in that," Fallon said.

"Then we need a quiet village where they aren't going to cause trouble. And we can't throw out Gaelish families for them. That means we should send them to Baltimore," she said.

"What? I don't want filthy Kottermanis in my home!" Riona growled.

"Firstly, you're not living there now. Nobody is. Which makes it perfect, as the closest village, Killarney, is also gone. They will be by themselves but can fish and hunt through winter. And when the weather warms up, we can get them to clean up Baltimore and then work farms across the country. Padraig and the few wizards we have left can keep an eye on them," Bridgit said.

Fallon did not have a better idea. Nobody was happy about giving up their old village to Kottermani soldiers but where else were they going to go? He looked around the table and nobody else had anything to say, so he nodded agreement.

"What about the Kottermani bows?" Devlin asked. "Are we going to keep trying them?"

"Perhaps we might get good at them with more practice," Gallagher suggested hopefully.

"And maybe not. Look, why not use slingers instead?" Bridgit asked. "Most of the country folk will know what to do with them and we won't have to worry about smiths coming up with arrows. A dozen men could collect enough stones off the beach in a day to last for three battles."

"I like that idea," Devlin enthused. "Takes me back to when I was a boy."

"What, you mean last moon?" Brendan said.

"Of course slingshot will be useless against Brendan. Hitting him on the head would be a waste of time," Devlin fired back.

While Fallon was happy to see the pair of them back to insulting each other, he was conscious there were many other things that needed discussing as well.

"How much money have we got left?" he asked.

That brought all laughter to an end.

"We'll need to count it. We haven't been keeping much of a tally because we just asked the Guilds to supply some when we needed it," Gallagher said finally. "We'll get an idea by tomorrow and try and see how long we can make it last."

"Well, we can give some people promises, as well as half-payments for a bit. And when we start rationing out the food we'll get people to pay what they have. They won't like it but it's going to be a long winter and there will be no more money until the spring taxes arrive, or we can find the Guilds," Fallon said.

Nobody looked like they were laughing as Fallon could see them all contemplating a hard winter. Normally, back in Baltimore, they would have laid in huge stocks of firewood as well as smoked fish, salted lamb and bacon, while the cellars would be full of potatoes. But this was the city and everything had to be brought in through the gates.

"Should we make sure we have all the supplies of peat and firewood as well? We don't want people stealing anything not tied down so they can burn it to keep warm," Nola said.

"If it comes to it, we can always pull apart the Kottermani ships," Riona suggested.

"No, we need those to sail north in the spring, so we can find and crush Swane. He will have the Guilds with him, and all the gold and silver. After all, the mines are on his side of the Spine," Fallon said.

"Well, we need to get through this winter before we start thinking about spring," Bridgit said mildly.

"I'd rather strip out the Guildhouses and use what's in there. Come to think of it, we should do just that and hand it out to the needy," Fallon said, warming to the idea.

"Aroaril, we're going to need a lot of men to do all that," Gallagher said. "We've got to keep watch on the streets, on the food, collect the firewood and peat stores and guard those – and then train the new army as well."

"The training will have to wait for a while. As long as Casey has a score or so of men he can get the new recruits fit and we can worry about them using weapons later. We have to make the city safe first," Fallon said strongly.

"But how do we divide up the food?" Bridgit asked.

"Everyone will have to register. We'll get all the scribes that the Guilds left behind and use them. Name, address and how many children. And then we can set it up from there," Fallon said heavily.

"That is going to be quite the list," Bridgit said. "And it is going to be an even bigger task on the day to make sure it does not turn into a riot."

"I know," Fallon said heavily. "But what other choice do we have, if we want to be fair?"

"It's going to be like the biggest flock of angry sheep you ever saw," Riona said.

"We could maybe use ink," Devlin said. "When I want to go through the flock we put a splash of dye on them to make sure we don't do them all twice."

"Perfect! Then we could maybe shear them as well afterwards," Brendan said.

"No, that's a good idea," Bridgit said. "Mark the hand of each adult as they come up and then we'll know them again."

"Gall, when you go back through the Guildhouses tomorrow, make sure you find as much ink as you can," Fallon said, then stretched. "There's probably more things we need to think about but surely that will do for today."

Once everyone had been given their tasks for the morning, they split up, heading back to their rooms.

"Fallon, I'm worried about Brendan. Nola is scared. He's not the man she knew. It's not a nice feeling, knowing he is only too ready to kill people now. She makes him leave his hammer outside their room."

"He'll be fine," Fallon said, brushing a stray hair away from her face.

"At least Riona is happier because it seems Devlin is back to his old self again. And Rosaleen and Gallagher look more than happy."

"I am happy that you are not just back but stronger than before," he said. "You even look different."

"Maybe that's because I'm pregnant."

He grinned. "That is part of it but only part. I was watching you in there. The old Bridgit would never have been so strong. You were in charge of that meeting as much as I was."

"And quite right too! Aroaril knows what you will get up to without me. You certainly made a mess of things before."

"Now that was not my fault," he protested, then subsided when he saw she was just joking. Or at least mostly joking.

"It's going to be hard work," she said, looking far more serious. "I know some of what will follow. We nearly starved to death on that ship and I saw people at their best and worst. I threw three men overboard for stealing food – and yet saw other people jump over the side of their own free will, hoping that their death would mean their children survived."

"It's not quite the same as that," he said gently, hearing the pain in her voice.

"But I fear it will be. That was just a small selection of people and most of them were good country folk, used to working together as a community. We are in Gaelland's biggest city now and most of these people don't like their neighbors. Then there's the rich ones who lived off the King and nobles and don't like that they are gone. We are going to have to be careful with them, for they will be looking for a chance to stab us in the back and help Swane."

He put his arm around her shoulders. "The people love us," he said. "They have been cheering us every day."

"I know. But we have to be ready for it to stop."

Fallon heard an echo of what Gallagher had been predicting but he could not bring himself to believe that. These people had been chanting his name, for Aroaril's sake! At least he had that in common with Cavan …

"It will be fine. You will see. They will understand."

CHAPTER 11

"It's time to see if everything is ready, sire," Dina said, tossing her hair at Swane.

For the last few days she had been conducting an elaborate dance with him, teasing and tantalizing, always leaving just when his lust seemed about to consume him. She had played a similar game with both her husband Kinnard and the foolish young officer Keverne, who she had used to kill Kinnard. It was a technique she had perfected on the streets of Lunster. She had been born with nothing but her looks and her wits and she had used them to claw her way higher, until the King's cousin had married her – and now the heir to the throne was following her around with his tongue out, like a dog in heat. For a woman with ambition and a total lack of conscience, the streets of Lunster were a playground. Guilds and nobles alike were there to be used and learned from. She knew, from a very young age, the world was a simple place. Anything that helped her was good, everything else was bad. It had taken her this far and, with a little luck, would see her not just sit on the throne of Gaelland but rule an empire. Not bad for the daughter of a whore and an unknown sailor.

"Are we about to march?" Swane asked.

"Nearly. Ryan and Meinster are in charge of preparations."

"So finally I shall have my kingdom back!" Swane said, his face flushing.

"It will be a hard road to Berry, sire. Even with the help of Finbar and the other magicians," she warned gently. Magic might be able to hold open the passes but it was not going to keep men warm at night, nor feed them. That was another reason to seduce Swane. His tent was going to be bigger and warmer than anyone else's and she would rather share that than shiver in something less comfortable.

"All must be prepared to suffer for their King," he declared.

"And they will. Whatever is needed to get you back on your throne and Fallon dragged down to die in agony," she said, the thought sending a fierce pulse of pleasure through her. That righteous bastard had thrown her away like a rotten potato, forcing her to change her plans to be the country's next Queen. She would show him. That was the thought that would bring her passion when she was in Swane's bed. And being that much closer to him would make it easier to learn his secrets. He wanted power to change the world. She wanted that also.

"What are you thinking, Duchess?" Swane asked and she realized she had been silent for too long.

"Forgive me, sire, I was thinking if you would be offended if I did this." She reached across and kissed him, forcing her tongue into his open mouth.

He stiffened, before most of him relaxed, and she knew she had him.

CHAPTER 12

Bridgit suggested they show the city that, even though there was no king or nobles, things could go on like before and, in fact, could be much better. So town criers were sent around the city to announce the following day was Petition Day, when any could bring a grievance forward.

The queue was halfway across the square by dawn and Bran was sent out with guards and scribes, to tell any later arrivals that they would not be heard that day and to come back on the morrow, then give them a scrap of parchment with a number on it, so they would not miss out again.

Meanwhile the throne was taken away and dumped in a back room, replaced by a simple table and seven chairs for the new Ruling Council.

Fallon had hoped they might be able to break up Aidan's throne and use it for money but, while it looked imposing, it had proved to be simply gold leaf painted over wood. And not even good wood.

"Like Aidan himself. Looked pretty but inside it was rotten," Devlin said, giving it a huge shove and nearly making the arm fall off while they were waiting in the meeting room.

"Talking of that, do we really have to wear this stuff?" Brendan complained, pulling at the stiff collar of his tunic, the one made for him on his first day in Berry, when they had been presented to King Aidan.

"Well, you can't wear your old smith's apron. Nobody will take you seriously then," Nola said briskly, adjusting the way the tunic sat on her husband.

"I'll show them the hammer and then they'll stop laughing," Brendan rumbled.

Fallon looked at Nola's stricken face and groaned inside.

"I didn't mean that," Brendan said awkwardly but nobody believed him.

"Well, at least the ladies are looking stunning," Fallon said hastily.

Riona laughed. "I never thought to see myself wearing this!" She twirled around to show off her dress. It was not of a Kottermani cut, nor was it the Kottermani silk, but it was the best spun wool, clinging in all the right places and disguising the rest.

"You always look beautiful, no matter what you're wearing," Devlin said.

"Aroaril, that's the sort of shite I expected to hear from you, Fallon," Bridgit said, walking in and holding her long skirts up from the floor.

"Well, I never had the chance to say it. You were taking so long," Fallon grumbled lightly, then grinned. "Although it was worth the wait. You look like a princess."

"Oh please," Bridgit snorted. "The Queen's mother, maybe!"

"No, that dressmaker has done an amazing job, although it is you who makes the dress look truly good," he said, stepping forwards and taking her in his arms.

"Oh please. The poor girl is feeling queasy enough as it is without your blarney," Riona said.

"Besides, by the time you manage to work out how to take the damned thing off, the passion's gone and everyone's fallen asleep," Nola added with a chuckle.

"Munro was a good dressmaker," Bridgit said. "Where did you find him?"

"Apparently all the nobles used him. So I reckoned if those greedy bastards used him, then he had to be the best," Devlin said.

"Really? I didn't know Munro worked with them. I'm not so happy about having him in the castle with us then," Bridgit said.

"What? He's a dressmaker, nothing more. They use only the best, that's all. Besides, if he was part of some noble's plot, he would have left the city," Devlin sniffed.

"Well, still watch him. I want men to escort him everywhere when he is in the castle," Fallon said.

"More to the point, how are we paying him?" Bridgit asked.

"These three dresses are free. Now the nobles are gone he wants to be known as the man who dresses the Ruling Council. So take care of them, because we can't afford to buy any more from him."

"If we have perhaps finished discussing clothing choices, perhaps we could get this underway. As it is we'll be hearing cases until dusk," Gallagher said pointedly.

So Brendan was sent in to announce them and they followed him, walking in to a packed throne room and taking their places at the table, Fallon in the center, Bridgit to his right, with Brendan and Nola on her side, then Riona to Fallon's left, followed by Devlin and Gallagher.

Fallon had seen the throne room filled before, many times, but the crowds then had not been dressed like this. Now they were almost all in ordinary clothes. Even those who obviously had money were not displaying it as ostentatiously. Jewels no longer sparkled on fingers or hung from ears or other places. There were still guards as well, although they weren't in surcoats. Fallon had not liked the idea of too many guards but there was always the possibility one of Swane's men was in this crowd and he would not risk his friends, let alone Bridgit.

"The first session of Gaelland's Ruling Council is now in order! Come forward and be heard!" Brendan roared into the throne room, thumping the handle of his hammer on the floor both to call for silence and remind everyone that Aidan might be dead but there was still punishment on offer.

"Let us begin!" Fallon called.

The first case could have come straight from Cavan's days. A poor family accusing a rich landlord of building extra stories on the homes around them, so close that, when it rained, the water seethed from his roofs into their home. In Aidan's time, of course, Fallon knew that the case would have been decided instantly.

A tidy sum of money paid in exchange for the decision and move on to the next case.

But it was different now.

"We must see the permits to build these extra levels," Fallon ordered.

The smirking landlord, whose face looked familiar to Fallon, handed over a scroll to Bran, who in turn placed it on the table. Fallon picked it up absently, glancing instead at the landlord. He looked suspiciously like one of the crowd who had confronted them at the home of the Bankers' Guild leader.

"Are you going to read it or just pretend?" Bridgit whispered and Fallon unrolled the scroll to see it was a simple approval to add extra rooms, stamped with the King's Seal.

"As you can see, everything is in order," the landlord said smugly.

"Not quite," Fallon said. "There is no address here."

The landlord's smile faltered a little. "But that does not matter! The King's chamberlain told me I could use it anywhere I liked!"

Fallon rolled the scroll back up. "Do you have that in writing?"

"No, but—"

"You are ordered to pull down the top stories on all your houses around the Ciaran house. You have a quarter moon to do it or you will forfeit all those homes and we shall do it for you," Fallon said.

The landlord's face went white. "But you can't do that! This is an outrage!"

Fallon tossed the scroll back to Casey. The youthful officer caught it deftly. "And a fine of ten silver pieces is imposed. You must pay it before you will be allowed to leave. Half will go to the city treasury, half to the Ciaran family."

"You can't do that!"

"The fine is now fifteen silver pieces. Do you have anything else to say?"

The landlord opened and closed his mouth like a fish but nothing came out and he finally shook his head.

Fallon slapped the table with his hand. "Next case!"

There was a tentative cheer from at least half of the room as the landlord staggered out and the Ciarans – a father, mother and five children – bobbed their heads excitedly, bowing their thanks.

Behind them, scribes hurriedly recorded the judgment and Gallagher stamped them with the new seal of the Ruling Council, which Fallon was particularly proud of. A shillelagh and hammer were crossed, with a fish above and a sheep below, signifying all four of them, as well as the main symbols of Gaelland.

"You are having fun," Bridgit accused him quietly.

"By Aroaril, yes I am!" Fallon said with a grin.

He was not sure of all of the law, particularly about property, but he remembered much of what Cavan had told him when they had discussed the cases while Aidan ignored the laws and chased the bribes. Of course, there was also common sense and he was quick to seek Bridgit's thoughts, as well as the advice of the others. Nola, in particular, knew all about the laws of getting money out of customers, having done that for years in the face of men and women who knew Brendan would never resort to violence to get paid.

They were particularly harsh on merchants who had tried to cheat with their scales or delivered faulty goods or rotten food. The cheers from those who had come more in hope than expectation grew with each ruling against the rich and powerful, while the other half of the room was getting angry and indignant.

"Next case!" Fallon called but nobody stepped forwards, although dozens still waited around the sides of the throne room.

"And where is the next case?" he called.

Finally a young man in finely cut tunic and trousers stepped out, a thick woollen coat around his shoulders.

"This is not a fair hearing," he announced loudly. "I shall not plead my case when I already know you will never rule in my favor. So I am leaving and I would advise anyone who does not have six snotty-nosed brats or more than two silver coins to rub together to leave also."

He turned around flamboyantly but Fallon signaled to Bran and a pair of soldiers barred his way, while four more sealed off the doors.

"Anyone who wants to leave can go when I have finished talking. But you will go knowing that we shall immediately rule in favor of whoever you are in dispute with. And we shall send soldiers to your home to enforce our judgment," Fallon shouted.

He paused to let that sink in, then signaled again to Casey. The soldiers stepped aside, leaving the way open.

The young man looked around defiantly. "Come to my home. Drag me out and steal all my money, if you will. But that makes you the criminal, not me. I shall not have any part of this biased court."

He strode out and when he was allowed to go, a score more of the rich and powerful joined him, hurrying away.

"This does not look good," Bridgit warned. "We should get them back and at least hear their stories."

"They know they are guilty, that is why they go. And we can't drag them back at swordpoint for judgment," Fallon hissed.

"And going to their homes is better?"

"Of course. We can double the penalty!"

As he had expected, all of the cases where half of the petitioners had walked out were simple enough. Rich picking on poor, as they had always done. Names were taken and Brendan given the task of tracking them down the next day.

Although the sun was sinking fast and a glance along the table told Fallon his friends were struggling to concentrate, he insisted on hearing the last case, a boundary dispute between merchants in the marketplace. Both had papers claiming the site and nobody had any suggestions so he ordered it divided in half, leaving neither of them happy.

"Thank Aroaril that is over," Brendan said with feeling as the last two stormed out and Bran had the doors shut behind them, the sound echoing around the now-empty throne room.

Fallon leaned back and rubbed his hands together. "The message will be all round the city by tomorrow. There is a new ruling council in Berry and they will be fair to all," he declared.

"Although that message will not be too well received in some parts of the city," Devlin pointed out with a yawn.

"Let them tremble. It might make them stop stamping down on everyone else," Fallon said.

"Well, I am sure we are going to see even more people next time. Everyone who has nursed a grievance but never dreamed of getting a judgment will be first in line when next we hold a Petition Day," Bridgit said.

"And I reckon we made at least two hundred and fifty silver pieces for the treasury. Even King Aidan would have been quite happy with that," Gallagher added.

"But let's not hold these too often, my collar is trying to choke me," Brendan announced. "Meanwhile my stomach thinks the collar has actually cut my throat."

"You think you have a problem," Riona said, putting her hands in the small of her back. 'I can't wait to get out of this dress."

"I never thought you'd ask!" Devlin said, which had them laughing all the way out of the throne room.

CHAPTER 13

"Today you need to inspect the men, sire," Dina said, brushing hair away from Swane's brow. "Time to get up. I have ordered bacon and eggs brought here and your favorite cloak has been cleaned, ready for you to wear."

She watched with satisfaction as he moved to obey her. He was now hers. Completely. Zorva might have his soul but she had his body and mind. He was in thrall to her while thinking he was the one in charge. It had been quite a feat and she was delighted with how he followed her commands, while thinking they were his own. It had come at a price but one she was used to paying.

As he turned to face her, she quickly composed her face into an expression of loving adoration. Well, she was pretty sure that was what it looked like. She had spent half a turn of an hourglass practicing it in a mirror. It was a delicate act, being around Swane. He had to be tantalized and teased, but not too much could be revealed. Only by regular applications of Kottermani powders and lip stains could the tracery of fine lines around her face be hidden. Her own room was cool and empty, having been used only to dress and change for the last few days. But, like her old house in Lunster and her townhouse in Berry, she had a collection of mirrors set up so she could view her face from every angle. Nothing could be left uncovered, everything had to look perfect.

Swane stuffed his face but she did not. As the summers crept by, it became more and more important to watch what she ate.

Men like Meinster or her old husband Kinnard could fill themselves with rich food until their bellies swelled and their jowls swung low and as long as their purses were fat with coin they were attractive. But it was different for her. The moment she let things go, they would turn from her. So she wrapped herself in corsets, went hungry at banquets and used up pots of expensive powders.

Instead she fussed over Swane, making sure he ate well and dressed quickly. Soon, orders from her would be considered orders from Swane himself. Meinster had already accepted it. Ryan was a different matter. He was the voice Swane was used to listening to. Yet that was being washed away in a tide of Swane's passion. Until now, Swane had thought his pleasure could only be taken. She had shown him something different – in fact many different things – and he now could not bear to be without her. Just how she had planned it. And today would seal the deal and finish off Ryan. Again, just as she planned.

"Come, sire, you need to make sure your officers have done their job."

"But of course they have," he said. "I left it in the hands of Ryan and Meinster."

"Yes, but sire, you have to be sure. Remember, I have seen Fallon's men in action. They are not simple peasants armed with pitchforks. They have been training hard and not only have great discipline but are all well-armed, thanks to your father's misplaced trust in Fallon as a general of his army. Worse, you saw how Fallon fights. He can be despised but he must not be underestimated."

Swane's face darkened at that. "You are right. We must be ready. Let us inspect them."

She led him outside. This was not just to humiliate Ryan and Meinster and create distrust between them and Swane. She had seen this army training from her window and they were useless compared to Fallon's men.

The mercenaries they had scraped up would always be a rabble but she had higher hopes for the guardsmen they had assembled. Yet, without a strong leader like Captain Kelty, they lacked discipline and would be easy meat for Fallon.

Getting them had been easy enough. Using Finbar and the other wizards, every noble and their little band of guards had been transported to Meinster, using a magical gateway opened within an oak tree. She had asked Finbar how it worked and he explained that oak not only had far stronger magical properties than any other tree but "knew" where the next one was, so they could pollinate each other. Using that, he could "jump" from one to the next, holding the gateway open, like so many doors in his mind, then physically take that step, to arrive dozens, even hundreds of miles away. She had at first hoped that would be a far easier way of travelling across the Spine and imagined armies appearing where Fallon least expected them, but Finbar showed her the cost in energy to the wizard was terrible. Each time it drove one of the Guild's most senior wizards to their knees and she had reluctantly concluded it could not be done for everyone. A small party could be sent over, however, to prepare a camp and food for when the main army got across the mountains and that was enough.

Meanwhile, it meant while they had more than a thousand guards, each noble had brought their own officer, all jealous of each other. They were less like her husband's old Captain Hagen and much more like his greedy, foolish Lieutenant Keverne, who had been easy to manipulate and seduce into doing her will. There was a place for such men but, when it came to destroying Fallon, she needed more.

A comfortable carriage took them outside the town, to a common area that was normally used for grazing sheep. The animals had been cleared away this morning to leave space for Swane's army. The trip out, with Ryan and Meinster in the carriage, was slightly uncomfortable, for both Ryan and Meinster were eyeing her resentfully, but she let that wash over her. She had been hated with far more passion and by far more dangerous men before.

The guardsmen were waiting, mismatched in dozens of differently colored surcoats, their mail polished and their horses steaming in the cold air.

"Don't they look good, sire?" Ryan said warmly.

"Magnificent!" Swane said excitedly.

"Surely nothing can stand against them," Meinster agreed.

"So what will be the strategy? A charge by the cavalry here and then send in the men we have assembled thanks to the lure of gold?" Dina asked innocently.

"That is the easiest way to achieve victory and was the method used at the original battle of Lake Caragh," Ryan said loftily. "Even if Fallon's men form a shieldwall, our lances will reach over the top."

"Excellent!" Swane rubbed his hands together.

"You should see them charge, sir. Anyone can look good just sitting on a horse," Dina said mildly.

She smiled sweetly at a glowering Ryan as Swane instantly agreed with her and the orders were given.

Almost immediately the perfection of the guardsmen was destroyed. The careful ranks dissolved, men got in each other's way and the lines kept bumping into each other. When they did try and charge, some went into the gallop right away, while others held back, so what went past was not a line but a series of ragged groups. Worse, most were not able to control their lances. Some were still pointing up in the air, a dozen or so dug into the ground and had to be dropped, while a pair of horses were also accidentally stabbed.

"Fallon will destroy them," Dina said flatly, when the last group had trotted past, some of them yelling at each other.

"Ryan, Meinster, this is disgraceful! Were you going to let me take these idiots into battle?" Swane raged. Dina kept her face blank as the pair of them shrank from his anger.

"Of course they were going to keep training on our journey west," Ryan said.

"In the mountains? Surrounded by snow?" Dina inquired and enjoyed watching the pair of them squirm further under Swane's gaze. She let the silence grow and grow, becoming more uncomfortable until Swane finally broke it by turning to her.

"What do we need to do?" he asked.

"Appoint one captain, instead of having a host of them. The others can be his lieutenants. Then have them train for making a charge, again and again. But against Fallon they will not charge first. Instead, we shall send in the rabble we have assembled," she said, making her voice both brisk and confident. There was no trace of purr or coquette now. He could not think of that.

"We will?" Swane said in astonishment.

"Fallon can use up his crossbow bolts on them. And each one he kills saves us coin, because we only pay them after we get to Berry," she said. "Once we have drawn Fallon's teeth, then we send in our real men. We shatter Fallon's army with our charge and the remaining rabble can help chase down his survivors."

She fixed Swane with a confident stare and he gaped at her.

"Perfect," he breathed.

"Send the officers to me and I shall choose the best of them for you. Then I shall set them to training. Half a moon and they shall be ready," she said.

"You do that. And then come and report to me," Swane said, giving Ryan and Meinster a glare. "Now, let us get out of this damned cold."

"Of course, sire. And I know how to warm you up," she said, letting her voice get deeper now.

He held out a slightly shaking hand and she took it.

"Ryan, you and Meinster can find your own way back," he said.

She smiled sweetly at their shocked faces and made sure she swayed ostentatiously as she went up the steps into the carriage in front of Swane. The trip back to the castle was not a long one so she would have to work fast but, all in all, it was a very good morning's work. If the officers she appointed worked just as hard, then Fallon was as good as strung up already.

CHAPTER 14

"What's this?" Devlin asked as Riona and Nola whipped the cloth off the table.

"This is the people's rations, what we are going to give them," Bridgit said.

Fallon walked around the small table, looking carefully at the food. There was a small sack of oats, a slightly larger sack of potatoes, a handful of carrots and parsnips, a chunk of cheese, a little salt and a hunk of bacon.

"This looks quite generous. Do we have so much in the warehouses?" he asked.

Bridgit chuckled. "This is what they will get for a quarter moon! And for the first moon or so they will have beef or lamb as the meat. We shall keep the bacon for later and the dried fish for last. Most people only eat two meals a day anyway and those that don't will learn to soon enough. They can have porridge to break their fast, then meat and vegetables after work. It will keep them full, even if they will be sick of it by the time spring is here. Pregnant women and families with young children will get twice as much cheese. Now, we cannot have people queuing up every day, not only would we never get finished but no work would get done around the city. No, we shall have part of the city come in each day, to get their food for the next quarter-moon. That way we can keep order."

"What about the sick? They might need extra food to recover, once we have healed them," Rosaleen warned.

"And then there's the recruits. They need to eat more meat to stay strong," Devlin added.

"I know all that!" Bridgit said testily. "We have been working on nothing else these past days. The recruits will get twice as much meat, while the sick will get extra vegetables. But they will have to prove they were sick. I know what people will do to get more food."

"Surely people are not going to pretend to be ill?" Devlin cried.

"They will do anything after a moon or two of this," Bridgit said warningly. "By the end of winter they will be starving their children to get more food out of us – anything they can think of and plenty we haven't."

"Well, I don't know about that. But is it enough food? I reckon I could eat that in a day, let alone a week. What if people fill their bellies on the first few days and then go hungry?" Brendan asked.

"Well, they will only do that once," Bridgit said. She felt the familiar churning in her stomach that said she was afraid but she breathed through her nose and reminded herself this was different. This was not the ship sailing back from Adana. There would be plenty of extra food hidden away in larders and cellars inside this city. On the ship, there had been no way to get extra food beyond trying to fish. Here, there were many ways. And they were not alone.

"Will this get us through not just to spring but until the new harvests start to come in?" Fallon asked.

"It should. It won't give us much of a reserve and we will need to begin bringing in fish as soon as the seas calm a little," she admitted. "We could also wait and see which families seem to be keeping the weight on. If they are poor, that will mean they are stealing food, if they are rich that means they are hoarding it and we have to punish them."

"And how do we do that?" Fallon asked.

"Well, it has to be severe, so no others do it. I would suggest the stocks but we can't waste food to throw at them. Perhaps their ration will be cut in half for the next quarter-moon."

"That's not going to make us popular," Fallon observed.

"Keeping them alive through winter will make us popular," she retorted, remembering what had happened with Blaine and Carrick and how she had to tell the families of the wounded men that their loved ones could not be given food or water and had to be left to die. "We have to be strong from the start, or we shall have to be twice as bad afterwards."

"For Aroaril's sake, listen to your wife!" Riona said fiercely. "She has been through this before and has the scars to prove it."

Bridgit unconsciously reached up and scratched the scar on her breastbone, left there by Carrick's knife.

"We will do all you say," Fallon agreed and she could see he had remembered the tale as well. "We had better start soon, for we shall need all our soldiers for the first few days and we have to get the Kottermanis out of here as well."

*

Bridgit felt as though all she had been doing for days was counting barrels of food and sides of bacon and looking through sheaves of parchment. The scribes from the Bankers Guild had been invaluable. Used to adding up long columns of numbers, she could give them the figures and they would come back with answers a few turns of the hourglass later. They had been at a loss without anything to do and she had given them new purpose. She had divided them into two groups, each headed by a woman about her own age. She instinctively liked them both; Glenda was calm and organized while Ann was more inclined to tell hilarious stories about the fools she had worked for at the Guild but both were able to power through the work.

Now she had them working on a way to make people pay at least a little for the food. The richer would pay more, the poor only what they had. It was incredibly complicated but both Glenda and Ann worked hard and complained not at all. Bridgit's head was whirling, however, and to clear it she went looking for Kerrin.

Talking to him was different now and while she loved the fact he was stronger and healthier than she had ever seen or dreamed possible, there was a part of her that wished for her little boy back. It was hard to see him wanting to do things without her. Yes, there were times when all he wanted to do was sit with her, read a book and talk, but now he could only do that for a turn of the hourglass before he became restless and wanted to go and use a crossbow or throw a knife. Maybe now that she had more time she could bring him back to the boy he had been.

She found him in the castle courtyard, near the crossbow range. He was looking innocent enough but splintered targets suggested he had been practicing with the weapon again.

She gave him a hug. "I thought we said you didn't need to do that anymore," she said.

"I haven't been using it," he said.

She just looked at him and he dropped his eyes. "I like using the crossbow," he muttered.

She embraced him again. "You can put that down. I promise you," she said.

"But I have to be ready if anyone comes for you again," he said. "Or if Dad is in danger."

She sighed. Yes, she was glad not to be living in fear anymore. But sometimes she would take imagined fears over real ones, such as invading armies and Fearpriests plotting their deaths.

"How about we go to the kitchen and make some honeycakes. Before all the flour gets used up," she suggested brightly.

He grinned and, for a moment, looked just like the little boy from Baltimore.

"Great," he said. "But first I have to return this crossbow I found."

She ran her fingers through his hair and sniffed back the tears before he saw them. *What have we done to our boy?*

*

Fallon patted Caley absently as he watched his men in action. Many of his original recruits had come from country areas, where they had used slings growing up. The city men had rarely used them, for a sling was a country weapon, perfect for children to knock down birds and knock over hares to add to the pot. Many of them had not used a sling for ten summers or more but it was a skill not easily forgotten and he watched admiringly as they sent stone after stone whizzing into the straw targets, sending puffs of straw into the air with every strike. He had sent a company of men to the nearest beaches at low tide and they had returned with wagonloads of perfectly smooth, egg-sized stones. At anything up to a hundred paces they would be deadly. The men whirled the slings around their heads and then released, the missiles making a whipping sound as they shot through the air.

"Faster than crossbow bolts and, at fifty paces, just as accurate," Devlin said.

"Not quite the same though," Fallon said sadly.

"Well, it's not like we will get sent from the field of battle for breaking rules," Devlin said with a wink.

Fallon grinned. "If only the new men were coming on as well with their sword and spear work."

Devlin grimaced but was saved from replying by Padraig's approach.

"Come up with a way to magically improve the new recruits?" the farmer asked with a wink.

But the old wizard's face did not even break into a smile.

"We have a problem. And we might need to use these men sooner than we thought," he said urgently.

"How do you mean?" Fallon demanded.

"Not here. Let's talk inside the castle," Padraig said, glancing meaningfully upwards.

Fallon and Devlin looked up, to see a handful of birds circling overhead.

"What, are you afraid of being crapped on?" Devlin asked.

Padraig shook his head. "Not here. Inside," he said insistently.

*

Getting everyone inside had been difficult, with Rosaleen particularly hard to find, but eventually they were all together, watching Padraig cover the windows with sacking.

"Can you please tell us what this is about?" Bridgit pleaded.

Padraig sighed. "I am sorry to be so mysterious but we cannot take chances. Today I tried to see what Swane is up to over the Spine but I could not. Finbar and the other wizards that fled Berry have cast a net across it. I cannot get a bird there. That was not unexpected but then I tried closer to home and found I cannot even look at the towns in the west. Now that scares me. Why would they do that unless they are planning something?"

"We did it to them. And, after all, they expect us to attack them," Devlin pointed out.

"In the spring," Padraig said. "Not the middle of winter."

"How much magic would it take to get an army across the Spine in winter?" Fallon asked.

The old wizard whistled. "A fearful amount. You would need the entire Guild working at it and even then you would have to push men and beasts almost to their death, for you are not talking about one piece of magic but a sustained effort for days. And, by the end of it, most of those wizards would be helpless and a few might even die along the way."

"Unless Swane has learned to help them with blood magic," Rosaleen said softly.

Fallon felt a touch of fear but quashed it. "That cannot have happened. I killed his Fearpriest and Swane ran rather than face us. If he had Zorva's power, he would've been back here before now."

"There's only one way to know for sure. We need to get out into the countryside and see what's going on," Bridgit said.

"We can't just leave the city undefended," Fallon said.

"What about your new army? Can we use them?"

"Not yet," he said. "They aren't even half-trained, and we can't even be sure they can be fully trusted. Many of them worked for the Guilds, or the merchants."

"Well then, leave me two companies to look after the food warehouses, as well as Gannon and his Lunstermen to keep us safe. The city is still with us and quiet enough. We'll be fine. Besides, you were going to escort the Kottermanis down to Baltimore anyway."

"But can they be trusted to leave our people alone?" Nola asked.

"We have their prince. We'll tell them if they cause any trouble then we kill him," Fallon said.

"It's settled then. You march out tomorrow and leave us to take care of the city and the food rationing," Bridgit said.

"Are you going to be all right?" Fallon asked, before he could stop himself.

She raised her eyebrows at him. "We managed to escape from Kotterman without you. I think we can handle this."

*

Munro allowed himself a smile of mild satisfaction.

"I now have access to the castle and to three of the women on this self-styled Ruling Council," he said. "Already that has proved fruitful. I have learned they intend to make lists of every person in Berry, to allow food to be rationed out over winter and a fair price paid by each. We have to make the people angry and ungrateful, rather than relieved that they are going to be fed through winter."

His lieutenants nodded, none looking happy.

"We need something to change our fortunes," Jen said. Munro found it ironic she was willing to say what the men were afraid to. "We are not having much luck stirring people to anger. They still see Fallon and his Ruling Council as their saviors."

"The biggest landslide starts with a small pebble," Munro said. "Keep sowing the seeds of discord and we shall reap a grand harvest. Remind people that we are shipping cartloads of food off to feed the Kottermani prisoners, while the Ruling Council enjoyed a feast for their friends where everyone ate until bursting, just like the nobles of old. And I hear there is talk of people being made to pay for their food rations. That will play into our hands. The rich will want more for their money while the poor will resent paying anything."

"Should we also say they are spending people's coins on pretty new dresses?" Jen suggested.

"No," Munro said immediately. "There can be no suspicion on me. Being able to get in and out of the castle is vital. Now leave me. You have work to do."

Chastened, they took their leave to begin their new round of whispering in the streets. Munro did not add that he needed access to the castle because he had to get into Swane's old rooms. That was information they did not need. At the moment he was watched and escorted from the moment he stepped inside the castle to the gates again. But that would change, he knew. He just needed half a turn of the hourglass and Duchess Dina would have what she needed.

*

"This is madness!" Riona cried.

Bridgit would have agreed with her but doubted she could be heard over the din. As she had feared but not mentioned to Fallon, the day of the name-taking for rationing was chaos. Rather than have the entire city turn up at the castle, they had split the city into quarters and town criers had been going around the city for the past two days, announcing what was happening and where to go.

That had led to its own problems, for scores of merchants had taken that as their cue to come and complain about their goods being seized and being handed out. Bridgit had their names and claims taken down and issued them promises of at least part-payment, as the people paid what they could afford for the rations. But the merchants were furious. Winter was their time of greatest profit. The rich would pay huge sums of money for fresh food. Except their supplies had been seized and would be divided equally, not go to those with the biggest purse.

Bridgit had liked the idea of having just one quarter of the city turn up at a time but, while the poor obeyed the instructions and formed an orderly queue with their whole families, the rich turned up late and tried to push in front, or had sent servants to hold their place and claim they had enormous families.

"We need more soldiers," Nola said grimly as they surveyed the seething masses. Armed men tried to keep order as well as stop angry people from attacking the scribes. Gannon and his second, a tough warrior called Jason, were trying to keep control but they could not be everywhere at once.

"Well, we just keep going. There's nothing else we can do. We cannot take anyone away from the warehouses because the moment people think the food is unguarded, we'll have gangs of thieves stripping it out. And I will not go through that again. Get me Gannon."

The bald-headed sergeant hurried over from where he had been bellowing at feuding families.

Even though it was a cold day, with frost on the cobbles that morning, his head was shining with sweat.

"It's almost as if some people out there are deliberately trying to stir up trouble," he said. "They won't listen to reason."

"It's time to get strong with some of these people," Bridgit said. "Get the troublemakers and throw them in a cell. Use the shillelaghs if you have to. We have to get this done."

He did not hesitate but hurried off, bellowing orders to his men.

"Should we be doing that?" Nola asked worriedly. "Hitting people and throwing them in cells?"

"The alternative is worse," Bridgit said. "These people are our children now. Would you let this behavior go unpunished at the dinner table?"

"Not bloody likely! They would get a begorrah clip over the ear!" Nola growled.

"Exactly," Bridgit said with a nod. "And that's what we'll do here."

It took a little time for the new approach to work but it swiftly began to filter through as Gannon's men used shillelaghs on the loudest mouths. The noise dropped as people realized shouting would get them nothing but pain and then a visit to the cells.

"You realize some of them will be lying to us, while others will not understand what we are doing and are staying home," Riona said.

"Of course. It is going to take the best part of a moon to work properly. But we shall find the hungry ones and punish the greedy and it'll all work out," Bridgit said. "It has to. I owe it to the ones we lost on the ship out here."

"You don't owe anybody," Nola said.

"Well, I think differently," Bridgit said firmly, letting her two friends know that conversation was at an end and then opened a new one. "How is Brendan?"

Nola shook her head, seeming to shrink down a little. "He is a changed man," she said sadly. "I try to be understanding but he is not the man I left and lost. That accursed hammer is always with him and violence is just below the surface. I mean, he was always a big man but I was never scared of that strength, never thought he would harm me or the girls. He never got angry. Now he is always angry and there are times when I am scared to be around him. He uses his strength and size to make people do what he wants and I hate that."

Bridgit put her arm around her friend. "He will return to the old Brendan. It just needs some time. You see, he will calm down a little each day. There are things inside some of us that are best left hidden. He called upon the darkest part of himself to help get us back but he is still the old Brendan." She shuddered a little at her own words. They had all changed, and not necessarily for the better. She still found it hard to believe that Fallon had tortured a man and held a knife to a child's face. It was something that lay between them. She had not been able to bring it up. When they fought he usually went off and did something foolish. That was fine when there was nothing at stake but now there was a whole country riding on everything he did.

Nola nodded and wiped away a small tear. "It will be fine, I know it will," she said briskly.

"And one day it will be. We shall steer Gaelland through this and then call for a new Ruling Council. We'll go back to Baltimore and bore our grandchildren stupid with tales of what we did," Bridgit promised.

*

"You didn't have to come with me. You could have stayed back in the castle with the others," Fallon said lightly.

Brendan grimaced.

"What, don't tell me you've got shagger's back and need a rest?" Devlin asked with a grin.

Brendan held up his scarred fist. "I don't know about shagger's back but you'll be eating gruel for a moon through a broken jaw if you don't shut up," he growled.

Devlin chuckled, then caught sight of the expression on the smith's face. "Aroaril, it was just a silly joke! You kept pestering me to make them before and now you're threatening to knock my head off. There's no pleasing some people!"

Fallon nudged his horse over, pushing Devlin out of the way so he was riding next to Brendan.

"What is it? Now that Nola and the girls are back, I didn't think you'd be so eager to really punch Devlin," he asked softly.

Brendan glared at him but Fallon said nothing, just watched his friend and finally the smith cracked. "I was glad to get away," he said finally. "I hate that look that gets in Nola's eyes and the way my girls act around me. It's almost as if they think I might hurt them."

"They know you'd never do that. You'd tear the head off anyone who came near them, but that's all," Fallon said stoutly.

"All I know is what I see and I see fear in their eyes when they look at me. It's like I'm a stranger to them," he said miserably.

"Aroaril knows I need you but, if you have to, throw away that hammer," Fallon said.

Brendan hefted his stained hammer in his scarred hands. "But I don't want to put it down," he said softly. "I've never felt so alive as when we are fighting. Seeing men run away from me and feeling that power run through my arms – I have never known anything like it. I enjoy it when men walk around me, back away from me. They never did that before."

Fallon looked over at Devlin and the farmer grimaced back at him.

"The day will come when you want to put the hammer down," Fallon said. "Just make sure that Nola is still there when it comes. She loves you, man. Aroaril, she wouldn't have stayed with such a useless lump for so long otherwise."

Brendan looked at him sideways and for a moment Fallon also felt a thrill of fear at the fire in the smith's eyes, and then Brendan relaxed.

"Thank you, my friends," he rumbled.

"Well, is anyone going to ask me about how happy I am?" Gallagher asked.

"Don't want to hear it," Devlin said immediately. "And I hope you get shagger's back as well."

Their laughter was interrupted by Casey riding down the column of marching men towards them. "This can't be good," Gallagher said.

Fallon ignored him and waited for the young officer to slow his horse down.

"There's a village up ahead but it's like Baltimore or Killarney all over again. Almost all the people have gone and they say Rexford is gone as well."

"The town?"

"No, sir. The Count. He and his guards left in the middle of the night, just vanished, according to the men we spoke to. People are fleeing in all directions, thinking it is the selkies and the witches come back. The ones that are left don't know what to do. With nobody to give them orders, they are sitting around doing nothing."

Fallon glanced around at his friends. "We'd better see what's happening," he said.

*

But talking to the handful of remaining people at the village of Mallow made nothing seem any clearer. They had tried to send their usual tithe off to the county seat of Rexford but discovered the place was in an uproar, with rumors flying about. The Count was definitely gone but nobody else seemed to know what to do.

"Right. We need to go there and see what is happening," Fallon said. "Casey, escort the Kottermanis south and then get back to us as fast as you can."

The two Kottermani leaders, Nazim and Mahir, were summoned and they listened sourly to Fallon's words.

"You have oats and barley enough for the winter and there will be boats for fishing, as well as birds, hares and squirrels that can be trapped in the woods around. You can use the empty houses for your men to keep warm and build whatever other shelter you need. We shall leave no guards, but our wizard will be watching you always and if you harm anyone, then we shall inflict double the hurt on your Prince Kemal, understand? You can use the sailing boats though if you try to sail away, not only will you die but Prince Kemal will suffer."

Neither spoke good Gaelish and Fallon had no Kottermani so he had to repeat several things before they understood.

"And if we do this, will you free us in the spring?" Nazim asked.

"That is up to your Emperor," Fallon said. "But we do not wish you harm."

Both Kottermanis sniffed at that but Fallon had no time to waste with them. Casey and a score of mounted men went with them, while Fallon turned the rest of the column towards Rexford.

"Do you think the Kottermanis will keep their word and stay out of trouble?" Gallagher asked.

"I hope so. But we have bigger worries," Fallon said. "My guess is that Rexford has fled to join Swane. If all the nobles in the west have done it as well, we could have a real problem."

"Pack of useless guards. We destroyed Kelty and his men and they were better than any scum from Rexford, or Rork or the other places," Brendan snorted.

"But it's going to make Swane more confident and if he gets over here and calls out the fyrd, we're going to face a lot of men, most of whom we don't want to hurt," Fallon said. "So let's get to Rexford and have a look."

"What are we going to find there?" Devlin asked.

"Trouble," Gallagher predicted.

*

As the folk of Mallow had warned, Rexford was in uproar.

With the local noble and his guards gone, some people had taken the opportunity to gain a measure of revenge on his former favorites, while others simply saw the chance to steal things. A small crowd was ransacking the Count's manor house when Fallon showed up but they scattered like rats in torchlight when the soldiers arrived.

By then it was too late of course and Fallon, who had spent his whole career catching thieves, was in no mood for mercy.

"Find me one who looks like they know what's going on, then give the rest a thrashing and send them back home," he ordered. "And Dev, get into the Count's study and see if you can find anything useful."

"You were looking perhaps for a nice chair?" Devlin asked, then caught sight of Fallon's face and hurried off.

Brendan dragged over a weasel of a man and Fallon was about to order him thrown away and given a quick beating when he caught sight of the man's eyes. They were just as cunning as the animal he so resembled.

"Tell me what has happened here. Answer me true and you could get out of here with your skin intact. Try to play me false and you will be limping for a moon."

The man glanced at Brendan, who stared implacably back at him and gave an ingratiating smile.

"What do you want to know?" he asked, his voice coarse.

Despite looking as though he lived in the hedges rather than the town, he confirmed everything that the people of Mallow had heard, and added a little more. He was called Desmond and claimed to have seen the Count and his men ride out of town, to a copse of oak trees about five miles away. Then they had simply disappeared, not coming out again. Once that information spread through the town, everyone started thinking about themselves and settling old scores.

"It will be a hard winter and the Count took as much of his winter stores as his men could carry with him," Desmond explained. "Folk need to survive somehow."

Once he was sure Desmond had nothing further to add, he had Brendan send him on his way with a huge boot up the backside and went in to the wreckage of the Count's home to see what was left.

"Dev, tell me you found something," he invited.

"The Count had a nice fire before he left. Looks like a whole bunch of letters and suchlike. There wasn't a scrap of parchment left whole in the place," the farmer reported, no trace of a jest now. "He probably left some food behind in his winter storerooms but these thieving rats have cleaned it out. There's nothing left."

Fallon rubbed his face.

"Right. We'll clean up the town and round up the food and take it to the church. We'll leave ten men to keep an eye on it and move on. We have to see if the rest of the country is like this."

*

They tidied up Rexford, using speed and numbers to cow the townsfolk. Stolen food, much of it still in casks and sacks bearing the crest of Rexford, was uncovered and stacked in the church and he had the thieves do all the work, all under the lash of his men.

The three priests in the town were all young, the result of Rosaleen taking over the church. Most of the older priests, the ones who had grown rich under old Archbishop Kynan and by supporting the corrupt nobles, had been moved on – or had left of their own accord, unable to stomach doing what they were supposed to.

Fallon left them ten men, all he dared spare, but the priests also summoned a score of townsfolk: steady, sensible men who had not joined in the rioting but kept their families safe. Fallon hoped it would be enough. The place seemed quiet enough when they rode out, but then it had probably been quiet when the Count fled, as well.

He needed Bridgit and her scribes to come in and ration the remaining food out but at least the priests could be trusted until then.

His men marched swiftly through the frozen countryside, the way they had with Duchess Dina, what seemed like a lifetime ago. Unlike last time, they had to find shelter each night because of the freezing cold. The days were little warmer, the weak sun unable to warm anything up. And that was when the sun shone at all. Often they marched under thick cloud and drizzling rain and, once, through flurries of snow. And they found cold comfort in Eastmeath, Rork, Kenkilly and the other towns. Just like Rexford, the nobles had fled with their guards and the place was in chaos. Fallon restored order as best he could but it was obvious that many of these towns were going to run short of food before the winter was out. That was bad enough but Fallon knew worse was to come.

*

"What now?" Gallagher asked, as they marched out of Kenkilly. "You look as though you have the weight of the world on your shoulders. Come on, man, you've been bloody mysterious these past few days, wandering around with a face like a thundercloud. Tell us what you're thinking."

Fallon glanced around at his friends, saw their expressions and sighed. "I fear Padraig is right. Swane is planning to use magic to get over the Spine and attack us."

"But would he be so mad? Surely those guards are just to protect him from our attack in the spring?" Devlin said.

"He's a mad bastard, the son of a madder bastard and infected by Zorva. He will come for us, I feel it," Fallon said. "He will come for me."

"What do we do?" Brendan rumbled.

Fallon scratched his head, forcing himself not to think of Aidan's dying words: that his choices would doom them all. He had to make a decision now, because waiting any longer could be fatal.

"Gall, ride back to Berry and warn the others. We need to find more men from somewhere because we're going to be stretched damn thin. We have to keep an eye on Berry while we take our best soldiers and march them towards the Spine. Swane might be able to get over there but his men will suffer. They will need to rest and eat before marching on Berry. We have to find out where Swane is putting his camp up, then take all his supplies and make him follow us to a place where we can destroy him."

"And where's that?" Devlin asked.

"I haven't decided yet," Fallon said, although he was lying. He just did not want to say it. Lake Caragh had loomed large in his thoughts since he first feared Swane was coming over the Spine for him. In truth, he had fought there a hundred times with Kerrin, endless battles on the floor of their Baltimore home. Things had been so much simpler then and he remembered those nights with a sharp pang. In winter it would be a very different beast. The marshes that he would like to use to trick and trap the horsemen that Swane was surely bringing would be frozen solid. But the lake itself would also be freezing over, which could be used ... he gulped. This was not a game and they could not just set up the figures again afterwards.

CHAPTER 15

Dina held Swane's arm proprietorially as she steered him out onto the common once more to see the results of the training.

She only had to make suggestions to Meinster now and he rushed to obey. Ryan was less malleable but he had been pushed to the side. There was only room for one voice in Swane's life and she was it. That was vital, for once he was back on the throne he would be besieged by younger versions of herself, looking for their chance to be Queen. And he would also be looking for an heir, which she had little chance of providing. If it came to it, he could always suffer a tragic accident, leaving her on the throne. Then she could get on with the serious business of living in luxury while others did the work.

After all, she would have earned it, the things she had to do to bewitch him.

"What are you thinking?" Swane asked, then gave her a little leer. "Is it the same as me?"

She winked at him without thinking. "Well, let's see." She whispered something in his ear and watched him flush. "But that is for later," she said, patting his hand. "Now we have to make sure we are ready to take back your throne."

Ryan and Meinster waited for them with ill-disguised impatience. With them was the man she had appointed as the captain of the guards. She had spoken carefully with all of them, looking for someone with the right mix of brutality, obedience and cunning. She had known it was too much to expect someone with the abilities of Fallon hiding among them but she had been pleasantly surprised by her eventual choice, the former captain of Londegal's guards. Kane was tall, lean and scarred and, importantly, he was well aware of his former master's conversion to Zorva. The last thing she wanted was someone getting an attack of conscience at a crucial time in a battle. She had been concerned he might not be able to enforce his authority on some of the other captains from bigger counties, for Londegal had barely eighty guards to bring to Swane's army, but Kane had brought the others into line swiftly. That was good to know and it was especially handy that he owed his position and newfound wealth to her. She had made that abundantly clear to him, because you never knew when you might have to call in a favor. Having his first loyalty to her rather than Swane could be vital later.

She nodded a greeting to him but she made sure she was standing between her rivals and Swane.

"You may begin, Captain," she told Kane.

He raised his arm and a pair of men a few paces away nodded and waved flags at the far side of the common. Instantly lines of horsemen appeared, at first trotting, then moving smoothly into a canter and then the long lances came down in a perfect line and they spurred to the gallop, shoulder to shoulder, their steel lance tips almost completely in line.

"Much better," Swane said happily.

But it was not finished yet, for two more lines followed the first, each of them in perfect order.

"And our foot soldiers?" Dina asked.

Kane bowed his head and raised his other arm. More flags were flashed and then a horde of men poured across the common, howling and roaring their challenges. Dina could not get a proper count for they were in no ranks, just a solid mass, but it looked impressive indeed. It must be a cold winter to draw so many from across eastern Gaelland. She instinctively liked these men, motivated solely by money and not caring what they had to do to get it.

Few had proper weapons and many had clubs or shillelaghs, while pitchforks and wood axes seemed to be a popular choice as well. They stopped about fifty paces away and brandished these weapons before splitting apart to let one final group of cavalry race through the center of them, to Swane's applause. She joined in but her mind was on other things. It did not really matter whether this mob was trained or not. Their real job was to soak up Fallon's crossbow bolts so the cavalry could destroy Fallon's men.

"I think we are finally ready now, sire, after you and I made those changes," she said happily. "We should leave tomorrow."

"So soon?" Meinster asked.

Dina gestured to the thick clouds overhead. "Heavy snow could come at any time. We shall get over the Spine no matter what but we might as well make it easier for ourselves."

As she knew he would, Swane instantly agreed with her. "Make the arrangements," he ordered.

"But, sire, we were going to send a company on ahead to set up camp on the other side of the Spine," Ryan objected.

"It will take us at least five days to cross the Spine. That is more than enough time to have the camp ready for us when we arrive," Dina said disdainfully.

"See to it, Ryan," Swane ordered. "Send someone reliable over there to do it."

"Can we trust such an important task to just anyone?" she asked. "It could mean the difference between success and failure. We need someone trustworthy to oversee it."

"As always, you are right," Swane agreed. "Ryan, you shall go ahead to make sure all is ready."

"But sire!" Ryan protested.

Dina knew that was to no avail. Swane was like his father and, once he had pronounced judgment, nothing could get him to change it. She had him all to herself now, just as she planned.

*

Ryan watched his Prince walk away, arm-in-arm with that witch and cursed long and loud, all the words he never used when others were in hearing.

"She has possessed him," Ryan said fiercely. "She is inside his head and he can hear nothing else."

"Well, she has helped get us ready. Without her, we would only have a handful of men and no gold to pay our foot soldiers, nor magic to get us across the Spine," Meinster said reasonably.

"Don't be an idiot," Ryan growled. "She does not do this for Swane but for herself."

"We just have to be patient. He will tire of her and discard her. Zorva knows she is old enough to be his mother!" Meinster said with a snort. "We can take our revenge then."

Ryan shook his head. "She is inside his mind. I know Swane better than anyone. Zorva knows I damn near raised him like a son. I was the one to rescue him from Fallon and get him out of the city and up here. I have put up with things that would turn your stomach and I will burn in the pits before I let her come in and take the rewards that are owed to me."

"What can we do?" Meinster asked.

"I will go ahead and prepare this camp. And I will also prepare a surprise for her. She will get across the Spine but she will get no further. I will see her dead in that camp. Swane will return to us for advice and, when he regains his throne, we shall be raised above all others."

CHAPTER 16

"I see land!" Asil cried excitedly.

For a moment Feray doubted it, but then the dark line on the horizon did not waver or change and she embraced both her sons. "We have done it!" she cried.

Surviving the terrible storm had been a mixture of luck and good sailors but, once they were past that nightmare, the rest of the voyage had gone much easier. They had to battle two other storms, neither of them even half as bad as the monstrous one and both over within a few turns of the hourglass. She had been almost contemptuous of the second one, ordering Gemici to keep more sails up so they could make better time.

The sailors had treated her as something sent to save them from Aroaril and they had fallen in love with her two boys, showing them how to climb the ropes and sit up high, to see where they were going. Men competed to carve them little presents and bowed low whenever Feray walked past. Water and food had been running low but the cook kept serving up special treats for Asil and Orhan.

Even Gemici was moved to declare that he had never seen a happier crew. Once clear of the storms, it had been a swift run back to Adana but, now that they could see land, Feray found herself wondering what she would need to say to convince the Emperor Yonetici to give her an army, so she could sail back to Gaelland and rescue Kemal. She had little to do with the Emperor. He had been present at their wedding and she had seen him a few times since, usually when it was something to do with their sons – his grandsons. He had told her an Emperor could never have too many sons, so two was a good start. That was about it. Everything else had been talking to Kemal.

"Can we tell everyone?" Asil asked, again breaking into her thoughts.

"Yes, we shall," she smiled, pushing all worries aside.

Carefully the three of them slipped through the hole in the center of the watch platform and used the rope ladder there to get down to the mainmast, where more ropes led back down to the deck. The boys went down them like a pair of monkeys thanks to all the practice they had had, but she was more careful and was several steps behind them when they reached the deck.

"What news, my brave Princes?" a sailor asked.

"Adana is in sight. We shall be there soon and you shall all be well rewarded," Asil said seriously and the sailors in earshot immediately cheered.

Feray smiled in satisfaction. Learning to lead men was one of the most important tasks for Asil. Once his father took the Elephant Throne, he would be Crown Prince. And, while Orhan would not be seeking ways to overthrow his brother, like Kemal's siblings, there were always challenges for a prince of Kotterman.

"Come, we must go and dress. It must not look like we have had a hard time," she told her sons.

For the past quarter moon they had been wearing old cotton clothes, stained with salt and faded by sun, as they raced around the ship. But now it was time to bring out the silks and remind the people of Adana who was returning from Gaelland.

She had become used to tying her hair back with a simple piece of cloth and letting her arms and legs go bare, so it felt strange to again sit down and wait for her body slave to pin her hair up elaborately and help her into a beautiful dress.

Asil and Orhan squirmed as they were helped into tunics with high silk collars. Even though they were of the finest cut and material, they were still confining after the light cotton they had been wearing.

"Discomfort means nothing to us," she told her sons. "Do not show any sign of it."

When she was finally happy, they returned to the deck to find Adana looming large. Gemici had piled the sails on and the ship had eaten up the distance, but now, as Feray stepped up to the afterdeck, to where an old sail gave some shade from the warm sun, he was bringing them in.

"Are we not still some miles from the harbor?" she asked.

"Indeed we are, Highness," he said. "But I wanted to hear your orders first."

"My orders? Why would they have changed?" she asked warily.

By way of answer, he pointed at the huge flags that flew from every building. Her mouth went dry as she realized what that meant. The Emperor Yonetici was in Adana.

CHAPTER 17

Kemal peered out of his window, trying to see what was happening in the city below. But he was too far away and the angle was all wrong and he sat back, defeated. Not knowing what was happening was more than frustrating. As Crown Prince of Kotterman, he was used to daily briefings telling him what was happening all over the Empire. Even here he had Abbas to tell him the latest news brought from the Empire by fast ship. But, in his cell, there was nothing. He found himself even beginning to look forward to Bridgit's irregular visits.

"What news?" he asked, when he heard her footsteps, the question out before he could stop himself.

"The city is calm," she replied. "People are grateful to be given food for the winter."

"All of them?"

She smiled. "No, there are many in the rich quarter who are offering us ever-larger sums of money for more food. They are not used to having their wishes ignored and they still think that they can do whatever they want as long as they have a bag of gold. We are showing them that things have changed since King Aidan's days."

"You need to listen to them," Kemal said.

"Why should I listen to the rich? There are far more poor and they love what we are doing."

"But the rich have louder voices. They are accustomed to using their money and influence to change things they do not like.

The poor just put up with it. The poor might love you but they will not fight to save you, while the rich will scheme to bring you down."

He stopped himself from saying any more only with an effort of will. Helping Bridgit and, through her, Fallon, was not a wise move. And he could not let his hatred of them slip. It was the only thing that would keep him strong.

"I thank you for your advice," she said carefully. "But I come here today not to talk about the city but instead ask for a favor."

Kemal burst out laughing before he could stop himself. "What can I offer from in here? And why should I help you?" he asked incredulously.

"Because we have a common enemy. The King's son Swane. As you know he has given himself to Zorva and he tried to sacrifice both your wife and sons to his foul God. He has lured much of the Guild of Magic to him and we think he is planning to attack Berry soon. We need to have more men to be sure of victory, yet we need to keep hundreds here to safeguard both the food and the city. You still have more than a thousand warriors here, which we are feeding and keeping safe at my old home of Baltimore. Naturally they see us as enemies, but Swane wants to drag this world down to the pits of Zorva. If you were to speak to your men, tell them to fight alongside us to defeat this evil, you would be doing both our countries a service."

Kemal looked hard at Bridgit. She had changed from the defiant slave he had first met. The worry lines on her face had smoothed away, replaced by a look of determination. She was not to be underestimated, so he shook his head before she even finished speaking.

"I will not order my men to fight and die for you," he said scornfully. "You are wasting your time and your breath."

She looked at him for a long time, then nodded. "So I can see. Farewell."

Bridgit stood and began to turn and he jumped to his feet. "Wait!" he cried. "Will we talk more?"

"Perhaps," she said. "If we are still alive. But if Swane comes next to see you, to drag you off to the altar, I hope your foolish hatred makes you happy."

Kemal glowered at her back as she left. Help Fallon? Was she mad? He could never help the man. And yet, this felt like a mistake. He clenched his fists. Forget Fallon. He had been given a better idea by Bridgit. His men were alive, and at Baltimore. If Fallon and Bridgit were short of men then he had a chance. He went again to his window and looked out. The stones of this castle were rough and did not fit together properly. There were many little handholds. If he was brave enough, he could try and climb. Not all the way down, because that was too far, but maybe across, or even up, to an unguarded room. Of course, at night, the stones would be slippery with frost and the wind would freeze his hands swiftly. A fall to the cobbles below was the likely end to such a risky idea but the more he thought about it, the more it appealed. Sitting here in a cell, waiting to be rescued, was a death sentence. His younger brother, Durzu, would become the next Crown Prince, which would also mean death for Asil and Orhan. Feray would either be killed or forced to marry Durzu, which was worse. Yet if he escaped from here, freed his men and got back into Berry to surprise Fallon, then he had a chance. If his father arrived here in the spring to find him ruling as if nothing had gone wrong, then Durzu would be forced to bow his head and keep his ambitions to himself. Or at least until their father was dead, at which point Kemal planned to have his brother killed.

Best of all, he could return to Feray's arms as a man again, not some impotent weakling. All he had to do was risk his life in the freezing night on a mad climb.

Put it like that, it sounded tempting.

*

"Any luck?" Nola asked.

Bridgit shook her head tiredly. "He laughed in my face."

"It was a big risk," Riona said sympathetically.

"But we still have to find the men from somewhere," Bridgit sighed. "Fallon is going to need everyone we can find, yet we have to make sure there is no trouble in the city."

"Things are quiet now," Gallagher offered. He had brought the news back earlier in the day, riding into what seemed to be a peaceful city.

"It's quiet now because we have patrols on the streets both day and night, guards on the food warehouses and anyone who creates trouble finds themselves in the stocks for a night and paying a big fine to get their next food ration. When you have to behave or go hungry, it is amazing how quiet people get. But, if we take away almost all the soldiers here, people will begin to look at the warehouses hungrily. And, if they get into just one of them, we shall see Berry dissolve into chaos," Bridgit said. She rolled her shoulders, as if stretching them for battle. "Yet we cannot risk losing a battle with Swane. Aroaril knows what Swane has planned but we can be sure Dina has told them all about us and the way we were training in the streets."

"If we tell people what they face," Riona began, "surely they will understand and—"

"Most will. But there's a few that will see this as a perfect opportunity, either to take back what they see as theirs or steal what they can't have, hoping to sell it later," Bridgit said crisply.

"What about Fallon's new army, the men he hopes will defeat the Kottermanis?" Nola asked. "I know they haven't won our trust yet but surely they will fight against Zorva?"

"We can't risk it," Gallagher said instantly. "We daren't use them. Most would fight but we don't really know them yet. Even one man running at the wrong moment could lose us the battle."

That silenced the table but gave Bridgit an idea. "What about the wounded. Rosaleen, where are they?"

"Well, a few went home, but most are still here, so we can keep an eye on them and make sure they are recovering," Rosaleen replied. "Why?"

Bridgit did not reply immediately. There had been hundreds of wounded after the battle of Berry. Thanks to the work of Rosaleen and other priests, most of them – even those who had suffered a mortal wound – had recovered enough to join their comrades again. But, for some, who had lost hands, arms, feet, legs or eyes, there was not quite the same recovery. They were healthy enough and their lives had been saved but even Rosaleen could not regrow a lost arm, nor give back an eye. The dwindling treasury had been raided to make sure they were rewarded for their sacrifice and some had taken that money and traveled back home, if they lived nearby. But, for those who lived in eastern Gaelland or who were too crippled to work on a farm or fishing boat, they had stayed in Berry, where they could be sure of both a roof over their head and care if they asked for it.

"Those men have surely suffered enough. We cannot ask them to fight again," Nola said.

"No," Bridgit agreed. "But we can give them a crossbow and ask them to stand guard on a warehouse. Rosaleen, you know them best. Would they do that for us?"

"Of course they would," Gallagher said. "They will jump at the chance."

"Well, maybe not the ones with no legs," Padraig said, with a wink.

Rosaleen sighed but said nothing to Padraig. "That might be another fifty men. Is that going to be enough?"

"It is a start," Bridgit said. "Even fifty men could make the difference between victory and defeat for Fallon."

"We can't let them die!' Riona said fiercely. "Why don't we take over guard duties? Like you fooled the Kottermanis. We can wear helmets and carry spears. At night and from a distance, nobody will tell the difference."

"Aye," Nola agreed. "Thanks to the Kottermanis, we have more than enough old weapons and armor. From a distance, it will look like we are men. People see what they expect to see, not what is really there. If we have four men on the actual gates, but six women on the ramparts above, people won't think twice about it. Same way on the castle itself. We can all take turns."

"It works as long as nobody actually has to do anything. I don't doubt our courage but we're not trained. And then you're asking women who have worked all day to then stand guard at night," Bridgit said doubtfully.

"We went through worse on the way home," Riona said.

"And it would mean more men for the battle," Gallagher said enthusiastically. "All we need to do is trust in Aroaril and He will keep us safe."

Bridgit saw eyes roll around the table but stopped herself from joining them. "I'm not convinced," she said carefully.

"How about we vote?" Nola asked.

Bridgit looked around the table and saw everyone else putting their hands up. She was tempted to over-rule them but they had made such a show of the Ruling Council being equal. This was not a proper meeting, given that Fallon, Devlin and Brendan were somewhere in central Gaelland, but she could not crush her friends. Besides, it could work, with a little luck.

"We do it. But it will mean much more work for us," she warned.

"Well then, we can also cut some of the pointless duties. If we have guards on the gate and walls, why do we need them inside the castle itself? And Kemal isn't going anywhere. That's two more guards we don't have to provide," Riona said.

"There are no pointless duties," Bridgit said. "We have to keep our families safe."

But the tide of the meeting was running against her and another vote saw Riona and Nola crossing out a dozen guard duties in and around the castle.

"It will be fine. As long as the guards on the wall and gate are vigilant, there is nothing to worry about," Riona said briskly.

"And it means I can take Gannon, two hundred men, as well as Padraig, and every other wizard I can find, Rosaleen and at least a dozen other priests," Gallagher said. "This could be the difference in the battle. After all, if we don't defeat Swane then it doesn't matter how many guards we have here."

Bridgit was not convinced but bit back her objections.

"We shall defeat Swane. We shall take our best and brightest priests," Rosaleen announced.

"Finbar took the best of his Guild but he has left me all the women wizards. It seems our Royal Wizard wasn't too keen on women rising up the ranks of his Guild. Maybe he thought you needed a staff to be a wizard," Padraig said with a wink.

"Can you be serious, Father?" Bridgit asked firmly.

Padraig shrugged. "I don't know. I could try, I suppose."

Gallagher coughed. "And what of Fallon's other news? The towns left by the nobles?"

Bridgit shook her head. "They will have to wait. If we defeat Swane we can worry about them then, because we will have all the time we need. But all that matters is to destroy Swane and his evil."

"If only he hadn't escaped from the castle when Aidan was captured," Gallagher sighed.

"We cannot live in the past. Regretting mistakes does us no good," Bridgit said, and smiled at her friends. "As one who did that every day for a score of summers, I can say that with authority. What is Fallon's plan?"

"I am not sure," Gallagher admitted. "First he wants to find Swane's camp and then use that to lead Swane back towards Lake Caragh. But after that, I do not know."

"Lake Caragh. Why is it always Lake Caragh?" Bridgit muttered.

"Well, it is right in the way between the Spine and Berry," Gallagher said. "It is almost as if Aroaril planned it this way."

"Anyway, I am sure Fallon knows best," Bridgit said briskly. "But he needs our help. Get ready to march." She held her father back when he made to join the others.

"Help Fallon. Let him know I am here to talk, if he needs," she whispered.

"He will be fine," Padraig said. "He led us through battles in Berry."

She hesitated for just a heartbeat. If she could not trust her father, who could she trust? "He heard Aidan say something with his dying breath. He thinks he will make the wrong choice and doom us all. That is why he has embraced the idea of a Ruling Council so enthusiastically."

Padraig reached out and drew her into an embrace. "I'll do whatever is needed to get him back alive," he promised. "Aroaril knows I haven't been the best of fathers. But I can give you this."

"I want you back as well," she said.

"You can't always get what you want. But I'll see you get what you need."

CHAPTER 18

"Many of the guards on the walls of the city and the castle are women. They are being careful but I noticed them changing shifts and they revealed their faces. We can spread the word and throw the city into chaos. They will be forced to pull their real guards out of the food warehouses and then we can strike there," Jen said.

"Not yet," Munro said carefully. He trusted all of his lieutenants. He had to, for all their lives depended on it. This news was fascinating but he could not spread it around the city yet. He had a darker purpose in mind. He was yet to be trusted enough to walk around the castle unescorted, but he needed to get into Swane's old room quickly. The last message he had received from Meinster castle had said Swane was marching. He needed to secure what was inside that room before the new king arrived triumphant in Berry if he was to get Dina's bonus.

"We need to lull them further," he said. "Say nothing about this to anyone for a few more days. Then we shall act."

His lieutenant bowed her head, accepting without question, and hurried away.

Munro waited until he was sure she was gone – old habits died hard – before opening a cupboard. Inside was a set of dark clothing and a grappling hook on the end of a coil of soft rope. The King's castle in Berry faced onto a wide square but, at the sides and back, the homes of the rich were much closer, separated from the wall only by a road and a narrow, grassy rise. The castle walls were as tall as a house and always patrolled by guards. But he believed in his ability to get past a couple of women. Tonight would be the best time to do so, in case the story about the women pretending to be guards slipped out some other way.

*

Kemal tested the window in his bedroom and felt it move in its opening. Perfect. A night's work was all it had taken to dislodge the slivers of wood that held the wooden framework and scraped horn panel inside the stonework. He could pull it out in a few moments, giving him enough room to climb out. It was horribly risky but he was determined to go through with it. Waiting to die here was not an option. From his eyrie, he had seen many of the men march away and how women were now guarding the walls. He had barely seen a guard in the last couple of days, though women had been bringing him food twice a day. There seemed to be nobody in the tower, so all he had to do was get past the barred door and he'd be free. He could not go through the door, so he would have to go around it. Best of all, the weather had cleared up. The swirls of snow would have made such a climb suicide but the clear sky of washed blue gave him more hope. It would be freezing outside but he would not be out there for long – either way. Anyway, his mind was made up. He had to go tonight.

*

Munro watched the sentries march their beat for the best part of a turn of the hourglass. They were spending longer and longer talking to each other as they met in the middle of the wall, where a solitary brazier offered a little warmth. It was understandable, because walking a cold sentry's beat was unpleasant at the best of times but the light from the brazier would hurt their night vision and the talk would distract them. So when they next met up at the brazier, holding out frozen hands for a little warmth, he made his move. He raced silently across the cobbles in soft leather boots and up the grassy slope. He pressed against the wall then sent the grappling hook up with a practiced flick of his wrist. The iron hooks had been carefully bound with silk, so they only made a soft noise as they went across the wooden sentry walkway and bit into the supports beneath it. He tested the rope and then hauled himself up, running up the wall with the ease of long practice. He paused at the top and glanced along, panting a little, to see the two women chatting away. He turned the other way and darted down the walkway and the stairs to the kitchen garden below. In his belt he had lockpicks, and he had no doubt he could get into the entrance inside the kitchen garden. From there it would be child's play to get into Swane's room. Getting out would be more difficult but he had help for that. A pair of throwing knives on his belt and a long dagger in the small of his back.

*

Kemal feigned sleep as his tray of food was taken away. He had noticed the amount and quality had diminished in the last few days. They were obviously running short of food in the city. That was inconvenient now but would become more of a problem as winter went on. For now, he had eaten all he could, to give him as much energy as possible for the climb. Once he was sure he was alone, he warmed a small portion of hoarded lamb fat over his candle flame, mixed it with soot from the fireplace and painted his face and the backs of his hands. Then he used a pair of chairs to block out as much of the fire's light from the room as possible, so he was not shadowed against the window when he went out.

He pulled the wooden window frame out and laid it on the bed, supressing a shiver as the freezing wind knifed through the gap. Before he could have any more doubts, he stood on his bed and leaned out, reaching up to find gaps between the crude stonework that he could use as handholds. The cold stone was icy against his warm fingers but he crushed the beginnings of panic and wriggled his buttocks out onto the windowsill, then reached up further so he could pull himself out of the window, keeping his boots on the sill.

For a moment he nearly gave up and wriggled back inside but then he remembered his brother Durzu's arrogant face and immediately reached up for a new handhold to his left. The first foot was the hardest but he slid his soft boot across and wedged the toe into a gap between two large stones, then followed it with his right hand and right foot, until he was clinging to the castle tower like some strange vine. Luckily the stones sloped upwards a little here, narrowing the tower as it grew taller, creating little gaps and handholds everywhere. Already his arms were trembling so he began to clamber up, ignoring the way his body was protesting both at the cold and at the work his muscles were being asked to do. The foot that Fallon had smashed with a hammer was complaining the loudest but he used that memory to summon a warming anger that propelled him upwards. He moved as he had been taught by the Empire's finest climbers, clinging only with his toes and fingers and trying not to stay still for a moment. That speed helped but the darkness was harder, for he was working more by feel than sight now. He reached out his left hand – and a corner of stone crumbled away as he placed his weight on it. For a moment he swung in the air and had to fight back a scream as his stomach surged into his mouth and his heart pounded like a possessed drummer. Then he swung up with numb fingers and found a new hold, a much stronger one this time and pushed up – finding he had reached the windowsill.

He hauled himself up until he could use his shoulder to thump the horn panel that sufficed for a window in this Aroaril-forsaken country. Unlike glass, the scraped horn panel did not shatter with a loud noise, just cracked and fell inwards. He was beyond caring if anyone heard him so slithered forwards, scraping skin off his back on the remnants of the horn panel as he slipped to the floor in the darkened room.

Instantly he stuck his cold and shaking fingers under his armpits, trying to warm them up as he eased through the dark room. It was both empty and much smaller than his cell, just one floor below, but he did not waste time inspecting it. He found the far wall and shuffled along it until he came across the door. Whispering a swift prayer, he lifted the handle and it opened. He breathed a silent prayer of relief he had not broken into a locked room. The tower was silent as a grave and nearly as dark, the only light spilling up the stairs from his makeshift cell below. He set off down the stairs, clenching and unclenching his fingers to get some feeling back into them. He was shivering and grabbed a blanket that sat on the empty guard's chair, wrapping it around his shoulders. He was cold but, inside, he felt thrilled, as though he was walking on air. He had done it! He had escaped! Yes, he was still inside the castle and very much a prisoner, but he had shown these bastards that he was a true man. He only wished Feray was here to share the moment with him.

He knew the rough layout of the castle, having been advised by both Abbas and hearing the stories from Feray of how she had almost died in here. The most important thing was to act as if he belonged. He pulled the blanket over him like a cloak and walked down the stairs as if he was a bored guard heading off to bed.

The front gate was obviously impossible as a way out, because it would be guarded, but there had to be some rope in storerooms lower down and, once over the wall, he really would be free. All that remained was to head south, find his men, free them and return here. That was a series of almost impossible problems but, after his freezing climb, they all seemed easy enough.

*

Munro slipped his lockpicks back into his pocket with a smile. He had opened the kitchen garden door after a few moments of fiddling, although the lock on Swane's door had proved much harder. Still, it had been simple for him and now he shut it behind him, waiting until he was sure the latch was closed before taking out his tinderbox. A prized Kottermani piece, its toothed wheel could strike sparks from a flint and he used it now to create a small fire in the metal box. By its light he took down a torch from the wall and lit it, blowing out the tinderbox and heading further into Swane's rooms.

Munro had no idea where the Prince had hidden the objects Dina needed, but he worked patiently around the bedroom, tapping on walls until he discovered a hollow panel. Placing the torch in a bracket on the wall, he found a heavy brass Kottermani statue and used it to smash open the panel with three blows. He tossed the ruined statue aside, heedless of the once-prized piece, and cleared away some scraps of timber to reveal a carved wooden box and a thick book, bound in a strange material.

The writing on the front was in a strange tongue, one which he did not recognize, although he spoke both Gaelish and Kottermani. The wrapping also made his skin crawl. It was leathery and yet not leather and he had the horrible suspicion it was human skin. As for the box, there was something inside it, judging by the weight, while it reeked of some sort of musky oil, although the scent could not entirely mask the faint smell of corruption about it. He always liked to know everything but, on this occasion, he kept the box shut and instead slipped it and the book into a soft leather bag over his shoulder.

He retraced his steps. The castle was slumbering, not a guard inside. He made it all the way to the door to the kitchen garden with ease and was just bracing himself for the final steps when a powerful arm grabbed him around the neck.

"Make a noise and you die," a voice hissed in his ear.

For a moment Munro was frozen, then his brain began working again.

"You are Kottermani," he said, his voice just above a whisper. "Am I talking to Prince Kemal?"

The arm tightened. Munro itched to draw a knife but controlled that impulse.

"Careful what you say," his attacker warned.

"Let me go and I shall help us both escape this castle. Or you can try and kill me, in which case the noise I will make will bring guards down on us both. Your choice," Munro said, taking a chance. The next few heartbeats would define his life and he slipped his hand around the hilt of one of the throwing knives.

*

Kemal nearly let go of the man at those words. He had made it down here easily enough, for the castle was quiet as a mouse. He had seen one other person, fifty yards away at the end of a corridor, and given them a lazy wave, which had been returned. But he had not been able to find an unlocked storeroom with rope and had been trying to think of another way out when he'd heard footsteps. He had followed the figure, dressed differently than a guard, until getting close enough to make his move. But this was not what he expected.

"Who are you?" Kemal demanded.

"An enemy of Fallon," the man said softly. "My name is Munro. My employers wanted me to retrieve an object of value from the castle, belonging to the King. I have done so. Now, do we both get out of here or will we find ourselves sharing a cell together?"

Kemal did not trust this Munro. The man was obviously a thief and an expert one at that. He hated thieves but did not have another way out, so let go and stepped back.

"How do we escape?" he asked.

Munro bowed his head. "You need to be quiet, follow in my footsteps and do exactly what I say."

"Agreed. And what happens when we get out of here?"

"We go our own ways."

Kemal nodded. "Then lead on."

Munro smiled briefly, then opened the door carefully. A look around and then he was off, Kemal racing to keep up. The thief was deceptive, seeming to move slowly, but covering ground rapidly.

They darted across the garden until they were safely in the darkness beneath the wall.

"What will you do when you get out of here?" Munro whispered, as they hid beneath the shadow of the walkway.

"And what's that to you?" Kemal challenged.

Munro said nothing, merely shrugging a little and pointing upwards. Kemal heard the footsteps of a guard and kept quiet until the footsteps reached the end and turned back. The tension drew out and twice Kemal wanted to peer upward, only for Munro to jerk him back underneath.

If this had been a normal day, Kemal would have had the man flogged for such impertinence but this was nothing like a normal day.

Finally, snatches of conversation drifted down to them and Munro signaled to go ahead. They crept up onto the dark walkway and the thief produced a rope and grappling hook, which he set carefully underneath, around the wooden supports, then tossed the rope over the wall. He let Kemal go down first.

Kemal's fingers burned with protest as he put them under more stress. But, compared with the freezing, rough stones of the tower, the soft rope was ridiculously easy. He shimmied down it, feeling the strain in his shoulders, and then pressed himself back against the wall until Munro joined him. The thief picked up the end of the rope, which had a small weight tied to it, stepped back and hurled it over the wall into the darkness. It sailed out of sight and the thief smiled.

"With a little luck it will fall down to the ground behind and won't be discovered until well into the morning. But, in case it's still stretched across the walkway, why don't you follow me?"

Kemal raced down the grassy slope, across the road and into the comforting night, then Munro grasped his arm and pulled him into shadow.

"Perhaps we could do each other one last favor. Tell me where you are going and I shall tell you how to get there," Munro invited.

"Why should I share anything with a thief?" Kemal asked. "And why should you want to know?"

"Because you are alone in a city that hates you. And because all knowledge is money."

"How could you help me?" Kemal challenged.

"Because I know this city and its people," Munro said. "And you are quite safe – the last thing I want is to alert any guards. What I took from the castle tonight is enough to see me hung by Fallon and his Ruling Council."

Kemal hesitated. Still, any enemy of Fallon had to be a friend of his. And he still had to get out of this city. He took a breath. He just had to trust his luck.

"I need to head south," he said.

Munro produced a small copper token, the size of a coin.

"Go down this street to the very end, to the home of a merchant. His sign outside is a hay cart. Wake him, give him this token and he will get you out of the city. I take it you will be looking for your men?"

Kemal said nothing so Munro just smiled.

"I hear they are at the village of Baltimore."

Kemal nodded his thanks. He took the token and turned away, marvelling at his luck. He had half-expected this night to be his last, finding himself smashed and bleeding at the foot of the tower. Now he had a real chance to snatch back this country.

Then something hit him across the back of the head and everything went black.

CHAPTER 19

Fallon looked across Lake Caragh, seeing his men digging slowly in the thick snow.

"Work the men harder. It will also keep them warm," he announced.

By the time they had reached the lake, the area was covered with snow. And, in the three days since, that had been added to. The middle of the large lake was only thin ice but the edges were frozen solid. They needed to prepare the ground for when Swane arrived but that was proving a real problem.

"We don't have enough of the right tools and the men have frozen hands after just one turn of the hourglass out on the lake's edge," Devlin warned.

"They have to do what they can. We can't waste this time. Gallagher and the others will be back soon and then we can go hunting for Swane's supplies. But, when we find them, we'll have to come running back here with Swane on our tail. We must be ready," Fallon said. "Believe me, the men might complain now but they will be glad of it later."

Nobody looked happy about that but there wasn't much to smile about. The weather was brutally cold. There were two villages on Lake Caragh, Dunclady and Strabane. Dunclady was on the eastern side of the lake and vulnerable to Swane, so Fallon had emptied it, sending the protesting villagers across to Strabane, which had outraged both communities, for they were bitter rivals for fishing and pasture. But he also needed the huts to give shelter to his men, while he had been forced to take extra clothing and food from both. In exchange, he had to promise that payment from Berry would arrive soon. Of course, if they lost, Swane would not honor the promises he had handed out but that would probably be the least of the villagers' worries in that case.

Fallon shivered, not just from the cold. While the others were around he could pretend to be confident but, at times like this, when he was alone, the doubts came back.

Was fighting here arrogance? Was he leading these men to death and destruction? Without them, there was no hope of Bridgit and the others holding on to Berry. He found himself swinging from confidence to fear. He could defeat men, but what magic could his enemy muster?

Caley chuffed at him and he patted the dog's head. She placed her paw on his knee and he could not help smiling.

"What would I do without you?" he asked her.

"Fallon!" Devlin called and he looked up to see the farmer racing over. "Gallagher and the others have caught up!"

Fallon hurried over, Caley at his heels, to see far more men than he had expected. He quartered the long line by eye and counted them swiftly. More than two hundred! Bridgit must have stripped the city! He felt sick at the thought. What if he won and returned to find Berry in flames?

"Looks like you've been busy," Gallagher said cheerfully as he rode up.

"Where did you get these men from? How many are left with Bridgit?" Fallon demanded.

"Well, I am pleased to see you as well," Gallagher said wryly. "Have a little faith in us, my friend."

"There's no time for that," Fallon said irritably. "I have no time to listen to you babble about Aroaril. Has Berry been stripped?"

Gallagher kicked his feet of the stirrups and dropped to the frozen ground.

"First, given we are about to take on the forces of Zorva, ignoring Aroaril might just destroy us all—"

"Just answer my question!" Fallon snarled. "Ever since you fell into Rosaleen's bed you've been spouting about Aroaril. We've put up with it because we want to see you happy but this is not the time to rely on divine intervention!"

Gallagher poked him in the chest with a broad finger. "Leaving aside that there is probably no better time, I meant have a little trust in *us*!" he growled. "Do you think we would leave the families unprotected?"

Fallon subsided, but only a little. "Then where did all the soldiers come from?"

Gallagher crossed his arms. "We rounded up all the wounded men from the battle. They don't need two legs to sit guard or two hands to loose a crossbow. And the women are dressing up as guards to walk along the city and castle walls, where they will look like warriors but nobody will see them."

Fallon thought about that for a moment, then grudgingly nodded. "Sorry," he said.

"And for insulting Aroaril as well as me? I thought you might be happy I rediscovered my faith. I seem to remember you praying long and hard for Aroaril to protect both Kerrin and Bridgit."

Fallon saw the anger in his friend's face and sighed. "Aye," he admitted. "I'm just on edge. One mistake here will kill us all."

Padraig and Rosaleen rode up to hear his last comment.

"That's why we're here, son. To stop you from being an idiot," the old wizard said happily. "I love it how I am now the wise one that everyone admires."

"That might be going a little far," Fallon said.

"There you go!" Padraig said approvingly. "Once you can joke, things are bound to get easier."

Fallon rubbed his face. Despite his words, he did feel better. As well as two companies of battle-hardened veterans, there were plenty of people wearing either the robes of Aroaril or of magic. "Right. Well, now that you are here, we need to find Swane's camp and get ready to give him a proper welcome once he's finished fighting his way over the Spine."

"He won't have much in the way of magic left after that," Padraig said confidently.

"I pray not," Fallon murmured to himself.

*

Dina shivered as she looked up at the tall peaks of the Spine, the mountains that split Gaelland into two unequal parts. She had never walked across them before and hoped to never do so again. Finbar had been supremely confident this could be done but she had never imagined it would be so hard or that the damned mountains would go on for so long. Already three of the wizards had collapsed, their hearts giving out under the strain. The snow had to be melted to open the road wide enough for supply wagons and horses to get through, then kept clear, while the men and beasts had to be prevented from freezing to death each night. It had been cold in Meinster but nothing could prepare for the mountains. It took a ridiculous amount of effort just to keep the fires going through the night. Although they had plenty of supply wagons with them, they were rapidly emptying them, particularly the ones filled with firewood, for there was nothing to be found in the pass. Then there was the need for fodder for the horses. If the horses were going to be able to charge across a frozen field and slaughter Fallon's traitors, they had to be strong. The wagons that carried food for the men were emptying even faster. The wizards were devouring food every turn of the hourglass, while hot stew was the only thing that was keeping many of the men marching. The mercenaries, who had set off cheerfully enough in the hope of a pardon, gold and the chance of plunder, were a miserable rabble, their morale falling the higher the pass rose. Several had already been left behind to die.

It was not easy for her either, although she was sleeping in Swane's tent, protected from the elements and with plenty of firewood. But there was no thought of bringing out the filmy dresses that Swane enjoyed so much. She was swathed in as much fur as she could find. With Meinster and Ryan already on the other side of the mountains, setting up camp, there was no challenge to her authority anyway. She hoped those two had everything ready, because while they were making good progress, there would be precious little supplies left when they finally got out of this damned pass.

She looked back down the line of tired men slogging forwards and shivered again. Her future relied on Finbar and his wizards now and then Ryan and Meinster. She hated relying on other people. They always let her down. And destroying Fallon was too important to be left to chance.

CHAPTER 20

"Ryan, counsellor to Prince Swane and Earl Meinster, seventeenth of that line, you are guilty of crimes against the people of Gaelland and against Aroaril. Have you got anything to say before you die?" Fallon invited formally. The pair of them were tied to tree trunks, so tight that they had no chance of moving.

Taking Swane's camp had been ridiculously easy. With Finbar and the other traitor wizards obviously concentrating on getting Swane across the Spine, Padraig had been able to find the camp, which was set up by a thick wood beside the main road, using his winged, feathered scouts. Then it had been a simple matter of surrounding the camp and killing the handful of sentries before capturing and disarming the company of men who had been snoring away in the many crude shelters they had been making, obviously in preparation for a large army's arrival.

Devlin and Brendan were going through the supplies Ryan had stockpiled, planning to take as much as possible and then destroy the rest. But the guards Ryan had brought were a problem. They could not be let go, and Fallon was reluctant to just kill them. Ryan and Meinster, on the other hand, were another matter. A much easier one.

"Don't kill us, we can help you," Ryan said urgently.

Fallon chuckled. "And why should I want help from such as you?"

"Because I know the Prince's plans and I know what Duchess Dina is doing to help him."

Fallon laughed. "And why should I believe you?"

"Because I hate the Duchess!" Ryan cried. "I would gladly see her dead and if you had not attacked us, we would have killed her. Let us go and we shall deliver her to you."

Fallon laughed. They must think him an idiot! "You will not be released, but you will tell me everything you know," he said.

"Will you promise us our lives at least?" Meinster begged.

"I will promise you nothing but an eternity of agony if you do not start talking." Fallon strode right up to the bound pair. He knew if they had been able, they would have leaned back, but the cold bark was holding them in place.

"King Aidan liked to burn witches alive. Apparently that was the best way to rid us of Zorva-worshippers. Having destroyed plenty of them, I know they can die in other ways. But, if the heart has been taken, then fire is the only way," Fallon spat at them. "Perhaps we should use fire to make sure." He whirled to face Meinster. "Did you hear how your father died?"

The answer was written all over the young Earl's face but he dared not speak.

"I broke his arms and legs and burned him under braziers of coal. Now that was a horrible death. But it will seem like a merciful one compared to what I give you, unless you start talking!"

Urine steamed in the freezing air as Meinster wet himself, while Ryan went limp in his bonds.

"I might let one live, if they speak first," Fallon invited.

Instantly they both began to shout, spilling out all they knew. Fallon waved to a pair of scribes, who began taking hurried notes as the pair competed to talk.

"Come and get me when they are finished," Fallon told Brendan, as the two tied men gabbled out Swane and Dina's plan to trap him at Lake Caragh.

Fallon left them to it and went to inspect the food and firewood they had taken.

"There's too much for the wagons we have," Devlin said.

"Get the men to eat their fill and carry all the food they can and see what is left then. I would rather it sit in our lads' bellies than in a fire."

"And the guards we captured? Maybe we could use them as human packhorses, get them to carry supplies for us," Gallagher suggested.

Fallon looked over at the miserable-looking group of men sitting in the snow, surrounded by a company of crossbowmen. "Then we will need to guard them at the other end, and we need every man we have."

"Then what do we do?" Devlin asked. "Do we break their hands so they can't fight?"

Fallon shook his head. "No. We shall let them go."

He could feel his friends staring at him. "But strip the bastards first. By the time Swane gets here, they will be half-dead and he'll never be able to use them. The ones that live will be a burden on Swane."

"But most of them will die without clothes and a fire out here," Rosaleen said hotly.

Fallon was spared from answering when Brendan hurried over.

"They spilled their guts, the pair of them. It seems Dina has used the Guilds' money to hire every outlaw and lowlife in the east. For a pardon and promise of gold, they have scraped together a couple of thousand madmen who they plan to send at us until we use up all our crossbow bolts, at which point they will send in the cavalry," the smith explained. "But that's not the worst. Seems Dina is now the lover of Swane and dreams of being his Queen."

"There's a couple made for each other," Fallon spat.

"There was a few other things but nothing important. The scribes are making lists of the Guilds helping them and the wizards as well," Brendan added.

"So which one do we let go?" Rosaleen asked.

"Neither of those two. We are going to let go the other guards."

"Fallon, we cannot send men out into this without clothes," Rosaleen said.

"What else are we going to do? They will be trying to kill us and our families if we meet them on the battlefield. Would you rather we killed them now, or crippled them? There is no good way this ends for them. This way we leave it up to them."

"Still!" Gallagher groaned.

"They shouldn't have come trying to kill us," Fallon said. "But I will let them have a fire. Get all the spare firewood and stack it around Ryan and Meinster. They can stay warm by huddling around those two as they burn."

He glared at them as they stared at him in horror.

"This is a battle between good and evil," he growled. "We have to win."

"As long as we remember which side we are supposed to be on," Rosaleen said stiffly.

"We are not going to beat Swane by playing nice. He killed our friends and wanted to sacrifice Kerrin to his foul god. I will not let him get another chance. And I do not do this because I want to. We have to enrage Swane and make him follow us, so we can lead him into the trap we have spent so much time preparing. Now, if nobody else is going to help me, I will do what must be done."

"This is wrong," Gallagher said. "And you know it."

"I will do whatever it takes to win," Fallon retorted, feeling their eyes on him as he strode off, only Brendan by his side.

CHAPTER 21

Dina had actually begun to fear they would never make it out of the pass alive. As more and more wizards grew so exhausted they could not work any magic, it became harder for the others to protect the small army of men and horses.

The skies had been leaden all day, spitting snow down at them in increasingly heavy flurries and they had struggled to make ten miles. The camp for that night had been terrifying, because there was nothing to keep the fires going but the men themselves. Even though she was in Swane's tent, Dina could not sleep and sat by the flickering brazier, three fur cloaks pulled around her in an attempt to keep warm. It was hard to imagine getting warm again, let alone beating Fallon.

But they survived the night and the clouds melted away the next morning, leaving the sky blue and sparkling. A score of men had frozen to death and twice as many were nursing frostbitten fingers and toes. But the clear skies showed that they were almost out of the pass and the whole column cheered up, pressing forwards with new vigor, driven on by Captain Kane. Dina congratulated herself for choosing him to lead the army.

"We shall eat and rest in the shelters that Ryan and Meinster have prepared for us. Two days should be enough to put smiles back on faces, and then we shall march for Lake Caragh and bring Fallon to battle, where we shall destroy him," Swane announced.

Dina nodded agreement but she would have been happy just to get warm again.

The thought of spending another night in the pass was enough to spur them all on and they hurried out of the Spine as the sun began to set, shining in their eyes.

"Looks like Ryan has set a fire ready for us," Swane said, peering ahead at the thin column of smoke that rose out of the trees.

"Then let us get there before nightfall. We can push men and horses hard, knowing they can recover there," Dina agreed.

Many of the mercenaries were exhausted but the lure of shelters and fires and food inspired one last effort. Even so, night was falling, with long shadows leaning back towards their eyes when they arrived at the campsite.

"It smells like roast pork," Swane said, sniffing appreciatively.

"Strange. I thought they only brought beef," Dina said.

Then strange figures began to emerge out of the shelters, stumbling and even crawling towards them.

"Kane! Get some guards here!" Dina cried, as the pitiful, naked creatures held out their hands.

"My lady, these are some of my men," the guard captain said, swinging down from his horse. "The ones sent through to prepare for us."

"Where is Ryan? Where is Meinster?" Swane demanded.

Most of the shivering, naked men were unable to respond but a couple pointed.

Dina looked around, expecting to see the pair walk out of the trees with an explanation for this, but there was nothing. The next moment Swane cried out and she followed his quivering hand to see the remains of two trees, each reduced to blackened, misshapen stumps.

"Don't tell me—" she began, and then thought of how much she had been looking forward to roast pork and had to swallow down bile.

She followed Swane over to see two charred husks that could have once been men, lying in the remains of the fires.

"Fallon will pay for this! He will burn as they have!" Swane raged.

Dina nodded agreement, although her mind was elsewhere. This left her unchallenged as Swane's adviser, but also meant she had a real problem. The young Prince was like his father in that he hated to change his mind. But following Fallon was foolish. They needed to make Fallon fall into their trap, not the other way around. How was she going to steer him away from this when he was so obviously furious – and the men and horses were almost out of food?

*

They set off the next morning, with Swane still vowing revenge. They had burned the wooden shelters to stay warm and eaten the last of the food.

"We shall take it from anywhere we can find it now," Swane said. "But meanwhile we chase Fallon until we can destroy him."

Dina was sure of one thing. They could not do that. It was what Fallon wanted and, while she hated the man passionately, she had a grudging respect for him as a warrior and leader.

"We need to think again about what we are doing, sire. Fallon did this deliberately, knowing what Ryan meant to you," she said gently. "But we will not avenge him by falling into Fallon's trap."

"What trap? He has stolen our supplies and run away! First he killed my father, now he has killed Ryan. He was the only one who cared for me, when even my own mother and brother turned away from me."

"The only one until now," Dina said gently, stroking Swane's face. She was tempted to say that Ryan had outlived his usefulness but felt that Swane was not ready to hear it yet. A few gentle hints might help but they would take time. And she was not sure how much of that they had. She trailed her fingertips down his neck, thinking that might divert him.

But Swane knocked her hand away.

"We do not have time!" he snarled. "We have to catch Fallon. He might be planning a trap but if we can catch him on the road, he will either have to face us or flee, leaving behind our food."

Dina smiled and nodded, although she was cursing furiously inside. It was much harder to seduce him while swathed in heavy furs. All she could do was go along with him.

"Get Finbar to send out birds as scouts. We shall see where he has gone."

Dina sighed. "Finbar and the rest of his wizards are exhausted. It will be days before they can help us and they need food."

"Then get them some!"

Dina turned away to keep him from seeing the anger on her face. There were other people to do these jobs. She needed considerable time with a mirror and Kottermani powders to help her deal with this harsh light and maintain her hold on Swane.

"Captain Kane!" she called. "We need raiding parties!"

*

"They are following us," Padraig reported, stroking the head of the crow he had sent back to look. "But their wizards are being carried in their wagons and it looks like they are on their last legs."

"Good. I want riders heading out in all directions to warn any farmer or village around here to get out. They are desperate and Aroaril knows what they will do for food and warmth," Fallon ordered.

"They would not be like this if you had not burned up Swane's friends," Rosaleen warned. "I fear we have condemned some of these farmers to a horrible death as a result."

Fallon spat into the filthy snow at the side of the road. "Would you rather we left them food and let them take the country and kill us all? As it is we've added nearly a day to our route because we're leaving them a trail across fields rather than following the road and having them walk right into a village."

"We know there are no easy answers," Gallagher said soothingly.

"Good. Then get those riders out there and, if we have to, drag these people out of their homes. Until we can lure Swane into our trap and destroy the bastard, he can still do this land untold harm."

*

131

Bridgit covered her face with her hands to try and hide her feelings. Finding Kemal gone had been bad enough but a thorough search of the castle had also turned up something else. Someone had broken into Swane's old rooms and emptied out some hidden storage area. What Swane had there was anyone's guess, but she was sure it was nothing good.

The guards on the rear wall, a pair of mothers from Baltimore, were ashen-faced, although she merely excused them from guard duty for a quarter-moon, putting them on double kitchen duties instead. There were no more servants in the castle. They could not afford to pay them.

"Double the guards on the city gates. Search everything, I don't care how long it takes," she ordered. "Then tonight we double the guards on every wall and have patrols going around the castle."

"Should we not punish those two a bit more?" Nola asked. "They let someone get in here without even noticing."

Bridgit shook her head tiredly. "They are not real guards. They are mothers, exhausted after a day working to keep this castle going, who talked by a warm brazier instead of walking their post in the cold. It is not their fault; it is ours for putting them in that position. Besides, if they had been better guards, they would probably be dead now and I would be explaining to tearful children why their mothers were killed."

"What do we do? Kemal was our insurance against the Kottermanis," Riona asked. "Who could have guessed that he'd climb out of his room? He must have a set like a prize bull to try it in this weather."

Bridgit had to stop herself from shouting that she'd warned them of this. *This is what comes of trying to be too nice,* she told herself bitterly.

"We have to get him back, somehow," she said aloud. "Kemal will either try to link up with his men at Baltimore or help Swane at Lake Caragh. Either way, Fallon has to know what happened, because, without Kemal, we are helpless against a Kottermani invasion."

CHAPTER 22

Dina swallowed the last of the soup and shuddered at the taste. If this was the best they had to eat that night – and Swane would tolerate no less – what were the mercenaries eating? Each day they had raiding columns ranging out to either side, searching for villages, hamlets, even farms, anywhere that could yield food. Fallon had obviously tried to clean the countryside, taking away people and food from their path, while his wide trail, the mark of wagons, horses and men through the snow, veered from the road and cut across country to avoid populated areas. Still, every day Swane's guards were able to find things. A couple of cattle, or some breeding sheep and a pig or two. The farmers who had owned them were put to the sword, although not before their women were raped. Dina had suggested this reward to Swane, as it made sure there was never any shortage of volunteers for these raiding parties.

But, while the raiders never returned empty-handed, they only returned with just enough to keep them going. The wizards were perpetually exhausted, using their limited powers to keep the army warm through the freezing nights, then being carried in wagons through the day until they could be revived a little with a broth at night. The men simply melted snow and then threw in everything they could find to eat, sacks of oats, winter stores of vegetables and every piece of animal they had brought back. But it was never enough. Dina could feel a chill about this army, which had nothing to do with the weather. She could feel they were dancing to Fallon's tune and she had to change that before it was too late.

The guards were confident enough, thanks to their bloody raids, although a score of horses had gone lame and had been added to the pot. They all wanted revenge for the company that Fallon had stripped and left in the cold. Dina had ordered the survivors to stay behind – they were probably dead by now – but it was easy to blame Fallon and give the guards another reason to be brutal on their food raids.

But the mercenaries were another story. Every day, a handful more dropped by the side of the road, unable to keep going. Many had poor shoes to begin with and the days of marching had reduced those to scraps. Men shuffled along with bits of sacking over their feet, wearing whatever could be stolen – old tunics and even dresses covering their faces from the wind and snow.

"We shall catch him soon," Swane announced, sucking the last strip of meat off a pork rib.

"And what then, sire? He is obviously planning to make a stand at a place of his choosing," she said gently.

"Which looks like it will be Lake Caragh! He thinks we are walking into his trap and really he is falling into ours!"

She hid her frustration. "Sire, would it not be better to turn aside and find a small town, where we can recover? Our wizards are a powerful weapon, but they are almost useless at the moment. We should force Fallon to come at us."

Swane shook his head fiercely. "I have spoken and my word is law," he announced. "You shall see I am right, when we reach the lake tomorrow and then feast upon Fallon's supplies after we have slaughtered his men!"

Dina bowed her head and ground her teeth. She had thought Ryan's death would have been the final seal on her dominance over Swane but the weather had loosened it.

*

Fallon looked over Lake Caragh with a mixture of fear and relief. Swane's men had chased after him with all the recklessness he had hoped, but rather more speed than he would have liked. His own men and horses were tired, and he could also see smoke on the horizon that said Swane had discovered yet another farmer and snuffed out another few lives.

The news of Prince Kemal's escape was also hanging heavily over him. Bridgit had not held back, warning it was probably agents of Swane's that had him. That was a bitter blow. Kemal had been their shield against the Kottermanis returning in the spring. The only bright spot was that Kemal was trapped in Gaelland. There was no sailing out in this weather. True, there were days when the sea calmed down but they were rare indeed. Usually it threw itself against the coast with a rare fury and anyone hoping to make it to Kotterman was doomed from the moment they stepped on board. All he had to do was destroy Swane and then hunt down Kemal before spring. Then he would chain that bastard to a wall. Aroaril curse the idea of treating him with respect.

"About time we made it back here. Sleeping in the snow leaves me cold these days," Devlin announced, breaking Fallon's dark thoughts.

Fallon bit back a sharp comment about Devlin making everything into a joke. Perhaps it was just the farmer's way with dealing with the tension. Aroaril knew he was feeling it. That was one of the reasons he had burned Ryan and Meinster. He needed an outlet for the fear inside of him. It would not be so bad if it was only his life at stake, but there were so many lives resting on his shoulders: his friends, the families and, eventually, everyone in Gaelland. For Swane and Dina would be ruthless if they won. The punishment would be endless.

"How are the men faring?" Fallon asked, driving his mind away from that dark road.

"Rosaleen and the priests are being kept busy each night healing feet and hands. But if we are struggling, imagine what the Zorva-worshippers are going through," Gallagher replied.

Fallon nodded. That was what he had been counting on, but until he saw Swane's army he would not believe it.

"Ride ahead and get Gannon and Bran to show us the path through the defenses," he ordered. "The last thing we want is for us to blunder into them."

Gannon, Bran and four companies had been left behind – as well as the inhabitants of the two villages that lived on either bank of Lake Caragh – to keep preparing the ground while they marched out to lure Swane in. He hoped they had finished, for Swane had to be close behind, judging by the smoke that accompanied Swane's approach.

Gallagher rode around in a wide circle but returned in a much straighter line with Bran and Gannon.

"We are all ready," the black-bearded officer said, his face in a wide smile.

"And we have hot food ready for the men," the bald-headed Gannon added.

Fallon nodded. Gannon had not let him down yet but he was still uneasy about the big Lunsterman, a fact not helped by Gannon's protective loyalty to Bridgit.

"Then lead us in and then close the line in the defenses," he ordered.

*

A few turns of the hourglass later, after he had a chance to inspect the work, and eat a bowl of hot stew, Fallon was feeling much happier. His plan was complete and all was ready for Swane's arrival. He would form up with the lake on his right, protecting his flank. Swane could either come straight at him or swing around and try to attack his open left flank. He was prepared for either eventuality, after the men had taken the natural features of Lake Caragh and altered them subtly but significantly. The Gaelish weather had also helped, covering all evidence of what they had been doing in an ankle-thick carpet of snow.

"Swane won't know what will hit him," Brendan gloated.

"As long as he doesn't get an inkling of what we have waiting," Fallon said sharply. "Padraig, can your people keep him blinded?"

Padraig waved his hand airily. "Easy," he said. "They have been barely able to send a bird after us."

Fallon wanted to say more but knew he would just sound nervous. The people they had picked up along the way to save them from Swane's path of destruction had been sent back to the village of Strabane, on the "safe" side of the lake. They had abandoned the other village of Dunclady.

Swane could sleep in the village but he would find nothing else to help him. All was ready and all they had to do was wait and worry.

"Bring the men together. I will speak to them, and Rosaleen needs to as well. They have to know that Aroaril walks with them and they are fighting to stop their children from being sacrificed," he said.

"Most of them don't have children," Gallagher said.

"Although there may be a few unborn ones swelling bellies back in Berry," Devlin chuckled.

"Bring them in," Fallon said harshly. *I might be able to ease their fears, but who can stop me from worrying ...?*

*

The massed ranks made an impressive sight and Fallon knew they would be taking strength from that. He certainly was.

"My brothers, we fought the best warriors in the world in Berry and defeated them! No other nation has ever defeated the Kottermanis before – you are the first!" he called out, knowing Padraig's powers would make sure his voice was reaching every ear. He guessed other nations had beaten the Kottermanis in battle before, even if they had eventually lost their war, but he was not going to bother with that. He paused for a few heartbeats, seeing the veterans of that fight remember the stinking, bloody horror of the tight streets. He swallowed. Despite the cold, he was sweating and his stomach felt like it was trying to escape his body. He forced it back down and pasted a smile on his face.

"What you face tomorrow will be nothing like that! When we took Aidan's castle we did it without losing a man. We will be fighting men even more helpless that that. What you go through in training is far worse than what you will see tomorrow. Swane will send a rabble against us and they will be slaughtered like pigs in our defenses, before they even reach us. You will make this country free and safe and you will be honored as heroes forevermore! In years to come, when men talk of Lake Caragh, they will not speak of the King who turned on his people, but of you – the heroes who saved this country! You will live forever!"

With a little prompting, they roared their approval and Fallon nodded to Rosaleen.

"Pray with me!" she called, her voice high and clear. Instantly the men dropped to one knee, heedless of the snow.

"Aroaril, walk with us when we stand against the forces of Zorva tomorrow. Darkness threatens all your friends and families. But if you stand strong, you will turn it back. That is Aroaril's promise to you. Ask him to be with you, now and forever. He will be guarding your back while you fight and you cannot lose."

She paused and Fallon offered up his own, desperate silent prayer that he did not lead them all to doom.

"It is done!" Rosaleen announced. "He is with us!"

This time the cheer was even louder and the men rose to their feet. Now Fallon could see smiles on faces everywhere.

"Eat well. Sleep well. Tomorrow, stand strong and we shall celebrate a victory over evil!"

With a final cheer, the men streamed away to where meat was sizzling on spits.

"Fine words," Padraig said. "I think we are ready for tomorrow. That will put a little steel into spines."

"As long as it keeps Swane's steel out of their bellies, I will be happy," Fallon said. He knew he would not sleep that night. Fear sat heavily on his shoulders and he would have gratefully exchanged his life for the knowledge that his men would not only win the battle but live.

CHAPTER 23

The ship sailed into Adana, exciting plenty of activity on the harbor wall.

Usually the harbor wall was sparsely guarded but, with the Emperor in the city, it was very different. The giant bows were all manned and swung around to cover the ship as it approached, while a pair of smaller ships, each packed with uniformed guards, swung in from either side to escort them to a berth on the docks.

Feray had ordered Kemal's personal banner to be hung from the mainmast, and the escort ships kept their distance as a result, but she knew that word would be racing around the city. The Crown Prince was supposed to be in Gaelland, preparing the new province for the Emperor's visit in the spring, not racing back through storm and sea. She could only guess what was being said but knew it would not be good. Kemal's younger brother Durzu would be plotting furiously.

She took a deep breath. This was going to be tricky. She had hoped a message stamped with Kemal's seal would be enough to release the army that had been assembled in Adana. But Yonetici himself was another matter. She would have to mix truth with half-truths and perhaps stir in a lie or two if she was going to outwit Durzu's ambition.

They swung into the berth, to see a company of guards drawn up at the end of the jetty.

"Come," she told her sons. "We have faced the worst storm and survived. Now we shall face this. Show no fear and speak loudly if the Emperor asks you a question."

She led them down towards where a set of steps was being dragged into place by a gang of slaves, only for Gokmen, Gemici and a host of sailors to block the family's path.

"Highness, we would be your honor guard, if you would let us," Gokmen said loudly.

She looked at the faces of the sailors, at the mixture of weapons they carried and smiled.

"I thank you all for your kind offer but, as you can see, the Emperor has already provided an honor guard. You men have done more than your duty in getting us home and I shall be sure to tell the Emperor that. Rest now, relax and I shall be back to personally hand you the rewards you have earned."

She nodded her head and they stepped aside. She knew, as did they, judging from the expressions on many faces, that they had offered to fight and die for her, if necessary. But she could not ask that of them. They had brought her this far, she must finish the journey herself.

She stepped off the ship and walked carefully down to the jetty, then checked to make sure her sons also made it safely. When she turned, the sailors lining the ship's rail saluted her, as one. She smiled and nodded carefully, keeping a tight control on her emotions. It took a few moments but she took her sons' hands and then turned to see a man step out of the ranks of the honor guard.

"My dear Feray, what a pleasure to see you. But where is my honored brother?" Durzu asked.

Her heart did not sink – it plummeted – but she let none of that show.

"My dear Durzu, a pleasure to see you also. My husband, your elder brother, is back in Gaelland. He sent me with an urgent message for his father, the divine Emperor Yonetici," she said formally.

Durzu's smile lit up. "Then let me escort you to my father," he said.

She looked at him carefully. He appeared to be a slightly younger version of Kemal, except without the beard, unless you looked into his eyes. They had the cold glitter of the crocodile.

"Lead on," she said smoothly.

He bowed a little and the guard formed up around her as she walked down the jetty, head held high. It felt like the bars of a cage.

CHAPTER 24

Dina sighed with pleasure at being inside after so many days on the road. True, even the finest home in this dung heap of a village was a dump, but it was shelter from the wind and snow, and the fire burning fiercely in the hearth filled the place with warmth. There was even a bed, even if it was probably full of fleas. They had little food, horsemeat soup was the best the guards and mercenaries could expect, while she and Swane at least had the last of a roasted pig. The horses were in beast sheds, eating the last of the fodder.

At her suggestion, the officers had been summoned to get their orders for the morning, although she had snapped at a pair of them for not closing the door quickly enough and letting in a cold breeze. Men slowly dripped as snow melted off their clothes and she wished she had thought to hold the meeting elsewhere. The already dirty floor was now covered in mud and muck and the stench of men who had been riding horses for the last half-moon was filling the room, overpowering the fragrance she had sprayed around.

"Our scouts report Fallon has taken up position here, using the lake to guard his flank," Captain Kane announced, drawing a rough sketch on the wooden table with water. "We can either go straight at him or try to circle around to strike his flank and rear. But surely he will have dug trenches or similar to defend himself."

"How much will the snow slow down your horsemen?" Dina interrupted, before anyone else could.

"Not much," the officer said, after a moment's thought. "It is no more than ankle deep. The horses are tired after such a long journey, but they will be able to muster up one charge."

"And that is all we shall need," Swane said proudly.

"As long as we know where, sire," Dina said, before Swane could start trying to inspire them with one of his speeches. Now was not the time. "If we charge in the wrong place, then we might waste our effort. What is the word from Finbar and his wizards? How can they help us tomorrow? Can they discern where to attack?"

The officers parted to reveal the thin form of the Royal Wizard. Dina was shocked to see how bad Finbar looked. The flesh had melted off his frame and he appeared to have aged twenty summers since they had set off from Meinster.

"We can do little," he warned. "Keeping this army alive through this weather has drained us all. Many of my brothers have scarcely got the strength to lift a soup spoon. We shall rest tonight and might be able to help tomorrow, but it would be best if you planned to use other methods."

Dina nodded, so it looked as though she had been expecting that answer all along.

"Perhaps we should not attack at all tomorrow. Fallon has had time to prepare this. We don't want to fight on ground of his choosing. We could leave the mercenaries behind to slow Fallon down and the rest of us could ride around and go for Berry. It has to be lightly defended if he marched here with all his men. If we take Berry, then we have their families and they will surrender."

"We don't have any food left," one of the captains warned. Dina recognized him as the former captain of Meinster's guards, Dearin, a man furious that Kane had been given the command he wanted. "The horses will not make it in this weather. They have traveled all the way from Meinster and over the Spine and done well but they will fall like spring plants in the frost soon. We could find Fallon catching us from behind and we would then have to fight him on foot."

Dina smiled stiffly. It was true but she did not want to hear such defeatism. The idea of racing Fallon to Berry was surely better than attacking him on his own ground.

"Captain Kane, can we make it to Berry ahead of Fallon?" she asked.

Kane hesitated for a moment. "We could, my lady, but it is a risk. We don't know how much more the men and horses can take, or if the weather will turn. If it holds, we can make it. But one big storm could end us. And then if they bar the gates to us, we shall have to fight our way into the city with Fallon on our tails."

All eyes turned to Swane.

"I am here to fight, not run," he declared. "We have Fallon at our mercy and we are still strong. We shall destroy him and then march into Berry triumphant. Here is where we shall fight and win."

Dina marked the triumphant sneer on the face of Captain Dearin and resolved to wipe it off.

"Then the mercenaries have to mark Fallon's defenses, draw any sting in the tail he has, before we strike," she said briskly.

The various officers muttered their approval, although Kane frowned.

"But, my lady, the mercenaries are hard to control. We planned to just point them at Fallon and let them go," he said.

Dina smiled. "Captain, how many horses have we lost so far?"

"About three score, my lady."

"Then we have that many guardsmen who can lead them in, to mark where the defenses are and, while the mercenaries are being slaughtered by Fallon, to come back and report. To make sure all goes well, we shall need a few of our officers to supervise, for the mercenaries need to attack everywhere, to give us a perfect picture of what Fallon plans."

She locked eyes with Kane and understanding flashed between them. Those officers would be lucky to return with their lives, knowing Fallon's skill with a crossbow. It would be best if they were the ones who had shown the most loyalty to Swane. Dearin would be the obvious choice, as well as his cronies.

"But, my lady, if they are to attack everywhere, the mercenaries will be spread out. Fallon's men will massacre them," Dearin said.

Dina shrugged. "They are only here to open the way for our cavalry. Every one that dies is one less we have to feed and pay." *Just like you*, she added silently.

The officers mumbled approval and she leaned back on the uncomfortable chair, one of only two in the room.

Swane stood up from the other.

"You have your orders. We shall destroy Fallon and, once I am returned to Berry, those who have been loyal to me shall enjoy rewards that they only dreamed of! Tell your men that they will feast tomorrow night and then we shall walk into Berry to be showered with gold, land and women!"

The men erupted into cheers and Dina watched them file out with relief. At least they were taking most of the smell with them. Once they were gone, she planned to let the place warm up and then change. It was time to remind Swane of her powers. She was about to turn a dazzling smile on him and invite him to help her change when someone thumped on the door.

"What?" She turned with barely disguised anger.

"My lady, there is a man here to see you. He says his name is Munro. And he brings a prisoner," Kane announced.

*

Fallon looked around at his friends and raised a cup of water.

"To us! For tomorrow we will have united Gaelland and saved a people!" he told them.

They raised their cups solemnly and drank.

"Did you want us to make a note of that, so when it's time to write the histories, it makes you sound like someone serious, rather than a fool?" Devlin suggested.

Fallon smiled and sat down, as the others laughed. "Sorry, I forgot I wasn't trying to inspire a bunch of farm boys," he said. "Even if Casey still looks like one!"

There was plenty of laughter at that, with the black-bearded Bran ruffling his younger counterpart's fair hair.

"Well, that part is done. They are all talking about how Aroaril is with them. And they particularly like the idea that tomorrow will be easy compared to the battle of Berry," Gallagher said.

"Well, I bloody hope so. I don't want another one of those," Bran said with feeling. "There were about three times when I thought I was going to die."

"Only three? You lucky bastard, you had it easy!" Devlin snorted.

Fallon cleared his throat. "I am afraid of making a mistake and losing it for us tomorrow. I nearly lost Berry and it was only Bridgit that saved us. You will tell me if I am making a mistake, won't you?"

"Whist, man!" Brendan exclaimed. "You are the man we all follow. And tomorrow night we shall get drunk and tell each other what heroes we are."

"That's going to be difficult, given there isn't so much as a drop of beer in the camp," Padraig observed. "And I should know, because I've been looking for the whole afternoon!"

Fallon laughed along with the others but he could not shake the tension. His stomach was in knots and although he was tired, his mind was jumping from one thought to another. He thought he had planned for everything but what if there was something he had missed?

"We are with you," Casey said softly, the first time he had spoken.

Fallon glanced up at the young recruit, who he had eased through landing at Killarney, and smiled at the serious expression on the young officer's face.

"You can all call me an idiot after tomorrow for having foolish fears," he said.

"Why wait? Let's call you an idiot now!" Devlin called.

Fallon slapped his hand on the table. "I shall give you a serious toast now. That tomorrow is our last battle and we shall go home and hold our wives and children and know the future will be better. Once Swane is destroyed, all we have to do is find Kemal and exchange him for a deal with the Kottermanis."

They raised their cups and he drank with them. If Kemal was with Swane, there was no escape for him tomorrow. And no escape for the bastard ever again.

"How did Prince Kemal come to be here?" Swane demanded.

Dina would have liked to control this conversation but this was the only question that really mattered.

Munro bowed his head. "Sire, I am Munro, head of your father's secret informers. Can I say what a pleasure it is to serve you. Working for your father was more than a duty, it was an honor. When he was killed, I did not know what to do. When the Duchess contacted me and said I would be working to return you to the throne, I jumped at the chance."

Dina glanced over to see Swane preening visibly and wondered where Munro was going with this.

"I broke into your father's castle to see if I could find out how much food was in the city, so I could stir up Berry against Fallon and his Ruling Council. Before I could discover that, I came across the Prince. He had escaped from his cell but could not get out of the castle. I got him out and brought him here, because I knew you would much rather he was with you, rather than in Fallon's control."

Dina breathed a silent sigh of relief. Munro's lie meant he was not going to reveal his real mission to retrieve Swane's package. But had he got it? Or had he found Kemal first?

Swane gestured and guards escorted the tied and gagged Prince Kemal forwards.

"You have done well, Munro," Swane said fervently. "We have the Prince of Kotterman to use as a bargaining tool or, if necessary, a sacrifice to the great God Zorva. Take him away, keep him safe."

Behind his gag, Kemal was making noises, but Dina ignored that. She thought Kemal would have more use alive than dead, though that could be discussed later.

Munro bowed deeply.

"What of Fallon? Do you not have men in his camp? Do you know what he plans tomorrow?" Dina asked sharply.

Munro spread his hands. "Alas, my lady, most of the men I had managed to get into Fallon's army were thrown out. The remaining ones have all been left behind at Berry."

She nodded. It was what she had expected but it was still worth the question. She wanted to know Fallon's plans. She had outsmarted him in Lunster by knowing what he was doing and desperately wanted to do so again.

"You may return to Berry," Swane said. "You will be a busy man when I make my triumphant entry, because I will need to know every last person who cheered for Fallon and called for my father's death in that square. They will all die to avenge my father and for Zorva's glory."

Munro bowed and backed away but Dina hurriedly followed him.

"Watch the Prince like a hawk. If he escapes from you, then your agony will last for days and you will pray for death," she told the guards sternly.

As they saluted and stiffened to attention, she took a step to her left, standing next to Munro.

"Did you get it?" she murmured.

"Yes, my lady," he replied, his lips not even moving.

She smiled to herself, even as she glowered at the guards who dragged Kemal away. Once they were out, she barred the door and hurried back to Swane.

"Did you say something more to Munro?" he asked suspiciously.

"Only to tell him to ensure we were not disturbed. I have been too long without you and cannot wait anymore," she said, slipping open her fur cloak to show him she was wearing a Kottermani outfit that was so filmy it could not even be described as a dress.

He made a strangled noise and she ran her fingers through his hair, pressing his face to her breasts. She needed to make him fall asleep, so she could go and see what Munro had brought.

"What are you thinking?" he asked thickly.

"That tomorrow you will truly be the King, sire," she lied, helping him pull off his tunic.

*

Kemal cursed at the guards but they ignored his gagged mumblings, instead dragging him into a small shed next to the farmhouse. It truly was as if he was an animal. The two guards started a fire and covered him with an old sack but that barely kept out the wind, which whistled underneath the rotting door. He tried to get warm. It was icy in the shed but that little audience had told him some truly chilling things. He had met Munro going out of the castle, not coming in, which said he had already found whatever it was he was looking for. Far worse was the thought he might end up sacrificed to Zorva. He had escaped from Fallon but had found something even worse. Now he had to try and escape from here. But that was near-impossible, with his hands tied and guards watching his every move. He looked around frantically. There had to be a way out. And he had to find it.

CHAPTER 25

Fallon finally gave up trying to sleep and went out to walk among the men as dawn lightened a gray sky. The clouds looked ominous and he shivered. There was a very good reason why people did not fight in a Gaelish winter. Only Swane was mad enough to try it. Caley looked at him reproachfully as she struggled to walk through the snow but he merely ruffled her head. "You were the one who wanted to come along," he told her.

He would have liked to see some blue sky but that was wishful thinking on a Gaelish winter's day. Instead it looked like there would be more snow. He drew his cloak around himself and held back a shiver. The bloody rain had been bad enough in the battle of Berry. Still, at least snow would help to further hide what he had been doing. He crunched through the snow to where Casey and a handful of men were looking towards the village of Dunclady and the smoke that was rising from the village chimneys. Fallon nodded greetings to the men, recognizing one as Brasso, the young guard who had raised the alarm at the harbor.

"Looks like they aren't going to let us sleep in," Casey said, pointing to where a mass of men was slowly forming up outside the village.

Fallon nodded. Padraig's birds had seen the two distinct parts of Swane's army and he wondered, for the fifteenth time, which way they would attack first. If he was in Swane's shoes he would send the infantry at the front and the cavalry at the side, at the same time, but Ryan had sworn that the mercenaries were there merely to use up his crossbow ammunition. They might well do that but they would not use up the slingstones.

"Get everyone up. And get some hot food into them. Aroaril knows we are going to need it," he said.

*

Dina had not liked the look of the two objects Munro had found in Swane's room. The book had been bad enough, clad in human skin and obviously containing foul rituals of Zorva in some strange tongue, but the box had been worse. She had forced it open to find a shrivelled, blackened heart inside. She did not know whose it was or what it was for and she did not particularly want to know. She liked the idea of power, but Zorva's Fearpriests were all men and she did not trust them. Killing others was far better than being killed yourself and she would do what she always did – whatever was needed to survive. These objects would be hidden until she decided it was necessary. Or *if*. If they could take the throne and she could become Queen without resorting to the Dark God, then she would be quite happy. Still, it was nice to have it if they needed it.

The two objects went deep into her bags, amid the powders, potions and stains that were the tools of her trade. They seemed to fit among there and Swane certainly wouldn't go looking in there. She had made that clear. There were some things that needed to stay a mystery between a couple and just what she needed to do to look presentable was one of those.

Not that there was going to be time for any of that today. There was nothing but a thin stew for breakfast for all of them, even Swane, and merely the hope of real food that night, taken from Fallon's men.

"Sire, the mercenaries are cold and hungry. It is going to be hard work getting them to attack," Captain Kane warned.

"What?" Swane shoved the last of his stew away in disgust. "Take ten and hang them from a tree. That should make the others more eager."

Kane nodded but Dina could see the doubt on his face.

151

"Sire, how about we offer them double their money," she suggested.

"What? Can we afford that?" he grunted.

"Well, it will make them attack all the harder. And, with any luck, Fallon will kill twice as many."

Swane chuckled, then nodded. "Do it, Kane. And get the guards formed up as well. I'm cold and hungry. I want to be eating Fallon's supplies at luncheon, not for dinner."

Dina reflected that Swane had eaten more and slept in warmer conditions than any other man that night but everything was relative to a royal. As she had predicted, the mercenaries were delighted with the news they were getting twice as much money and their sullenness was gone in a moment.

Eight officers who Kane had nominated as being more loyal to Swane than himself had been selected to lead them forwards in two groups, while another three-score disgruntled guards whose horses had gone lame were scattered among them. With their shields, swords and surcoats, they stood out amid the rough cloth, makeshift cloaks and crude weapons that the rest of the mercenaries had. But, if they did get among Fallon's men, Dina had no doubt the mercenaries would do some damage. For a moment she entertained the fleeting thought they would win the day on their own but a glance towards the tight, ordered ranks of Fallon's army said that was foolish. Still, as long as they used up the crossbow bolts, that was good enough.

"Forward!" Swane drew his sword and waved it vaguely in Fallon's direction.

The mercenaries sent up a ragged howl and shuffled off in two groups.

"We shall follow behind, to see what happens," Swane said eagerly.

"Kane, we need some guards here too," Dina said instantly. After all, not only would Fallon be trying to kill them if he got the chance, but some of the retreating mercenaries might think of taking their money early.

*

"Where did they get this mob from?" Devlin asked as the mercenaries shambled towards them, splitting into two uneven parts.

"Every outlaw and chancer in the east," Gallagher said. "All fighting for gold."

"Well, we'll be paying them in a different coin," Devlin said, tossing a slingshot up into the air and looking around with a grin on his face. "Do you get it?"

"Many more jokes today and you're going to get it," Brendan rumbled, flexing his fist.

"They want to know where we are weakest," Fallon interrupted. "Get the crossbowmen to pick off the leaders. The slingers need to take the rest of them apart. They can't run in this snow, so we'll have more than enough time to send them packing. But we can't let them get close enough to see what we have prepared for his cavalry."

"How do we tell the leaders in that?" Gallagher pointed at the formless waves struggling towards them.

Fallon pointed. "Pick out the ones with swords and shields and surcoats."

Gallagher peered into the gloom. "Good point."

"Move everyone up," Fallon ordered.

"But won't that be dangerous? And difficult for everyone to keep their feet?" Bran asked.

"Yes, it will. One man to help each crossbowman or slinger. But we can't let them find out what we have done. If just one of those bastards sees it and gets away, they might not attack."

"And that's a bad thing?" Devlin asked.

"It is if they ride around us and go for Berry and our families," Fallon said grimly. "We want to finish it here."

"Right, let's move everyone up," Brendan said fiercely.

*

Fallon drew back the string of his crossbow and grunted with the effort. All the weapons had been heavily greased but the cold air had stiffened the horn-bow arms and made the strings fragile. He was not sure how many shots he would get out of it, so every one had to count.

"Stop wriggling around," Devlin complained, his blunt, powerful fingers holding Fallon's belt at the back.

"Easier said than done," Fallon replied, bringing the bow up and placing his feet carefully in the snow, seeking a firm stance. He glanced to his left and right, seeing the rest of the crossbow company follow his lead. As soon as he loosed, they would also release. He raised the bow to his shoulder and felt it wobbling in his hands. His heart was pounding and the shouts of the approaching mercenaries was putting him off. All he could think of was how he could lead everyone to their doom here.

"Do you want me to shout and yell, like we used to?" Devlin asked softly.

Fallon lowered his bow and smiled. He was overwhelmed by the memory of that simpler time. He had once hated those days, when his biggest concerns were farmers who had drunk too much or if Kerrin would get a cough. How he longed for them back.

"Thanks for the offer but I don't think the rest of them will understand. They'll think you've got a hedgehog stuck down the front of your trews," he said.

"Don't knock it until you've tried it. They keep you nice and warm!" Devlin said. "And you know how hedgehogs like to gobble a fat slug …"

Fallon laughed aloud. He raised his bow again and this time it was rock steady as he lined it up on a tall man in the surcoat of Meinster, who was slipping and sliding as he led the mercenaries forwards. Fallon let out a breath and, in the moment before inhaling, loosed.

A heartbeat later the rest of the crossbowmen released also.

Fallon's target staggered backwards, as the quarrel struck home, and then fell over backwards, while other men in bright surcoats also disappeared, plucked away by the strike of the crossbows. Fallon hauled on his crossbow string as Devlin held him steady and saw the mercenaries' advance speed up as the men instinctively wanted to suffer as few crossbow shots as possible.

"Get the slingers up!" Fallon roared as he slipped another quarrel into the groove and sighted on another brightly surcoated man. The mercenaries were still more than a hundred paces away and only able to muster a fast walk on the snow, and he reckoned to loose at least three times more before they reached him. But this time, as he loosed, his target slipped, and the quarrel whipped over the top of him to smash into the face of a cloaked mercenary behind him and send him crashing to the ground.

The mercenaries slid and shuffled forwards faster, the crossbows picking off men in ones and twos, rather than bringing whole files down, and Fallon could see the remaining guardsmen were encouraging them onwards, while keeping themselves carefully hidden by a rank or two. Fallon smiled mirthlessly. Time to unmask more of his surprise.

"Slingers loose!" he bellowed.

Instantly he heard a new sound in the cold air. The snap of the crossbows and the faint screams of the wounded mercenaries was overshadowed by a whipping and whistling as the scores of slingers whirled their slings around their heads then released the cords, sending egg-sized stones flashing out across the snow to crash into the mercenaries.

Now they began to go down in swathes. The slingers had grown up trying to hit a bird on the wing or a running hare and the huge mass of mercenaries was unmissable. The sound as stones thumped into bodies, smashing skulls, ribs and other bones, began to echo across the lake. Any hit knocked a man down, for the long slings propelled the stones at a fearsome pace. The screams were constant and now the remaining guardsmen were being unmasked as lines of mercenaries were mown down.

Fallon sent a bolt through the chest of another, seeing the man stagger forwards and collapse face-first into the snow.

"Keep going!" Fallon shouted.

Each slinger had a sack of stones at their feet and they were sending them out as fast as they could get the long slings up to speed. It was a slaughter. The mercenaries tried to run forwards but they were slow and clumsy in the snow and they had no protection from the stones. The guardsmen raised their shields and the clang of stone on shield echoed across the lake – until the crossbowmen picked off those with shields.

Fallon saw one guardsman stagger backwards, driven by the impact of a stone and crossbow bolt striking his shield. Fallon lowered his own weapon, striking the man in the leg. The guardsman went down on his knees instantly, his shield dropping. A stone vanished into his eyesocket, jerking him backwards onto the snow, where he writhed briefly before going rigid. Mercenaries tried to pick up shields and rush forwards but there were not enough shields and they were taken down, one by one. If they had tried to form a tight line then maybe that could have got them closer, Fallon judged, but none showed that ability. Then they discovered the pits that Fallon's men had dug, not deep because the ground was too hard but calf-height, covered with a few sticks and plenty of snow. At the bottom was a sharpened stake or two and the agonized howls from those caught by them were payment for the hard work each had cost.

The mercenaries finally stopped about fifty paces away, survivors hunched over against the incoming rain of stones, unable to get closer but seemingly unwilling to turn and run.

Fallon tapped Devlin on the arm and, with the farmer's help, stepped slowly back until he could see what was happening on his open flank. This side was secure.

For a moment his heart jumped as he saw mercenaries not twenty paces away from his lines – but they were stuck in the pits, not rushing forwards. He sighted on one guardsman further down the line trying to use a shield to get closer and put a quarrel into his chest because nobody was protecting his side. A little further around, a thick group of mercenaries was rushing closer but, just as Fallon prepared to hurry down there, they hit the next line of his defenses, a narrow but deep trench, a pace wide and calf-deep. Men went down screaming with broken ankles, while others dithered, making themselves easy targets for the slingers.

"Is this the best Swane has got?" Gallagher asked, watching the slingers fell the mercenaries like weeds with a hoe.

"He thinks we will run out of crossbow bolts," Padraig said.

"And we might. But we have another wagonload of the stones," Fallon said. "Get a few squads to bring up more."

"I don't think we will need them," Brendan said, gesturing with his hammer.

Fallon saw that the mercenaries were now edging backwards, because there was no pressure from the ones at the back to press forwards. The slingers were relentless, stones bouncing off skulls and back and chests. The crack of bones was easy to hear, even above the howls and cries of the wounded. Wounded mercenaries crawled and writhed on the ground, trying to drag their shattered legs and arms out of reach of the deadly stones and succeeding only in bringing down more of their comrades. They were taking too much punishment for trained soldiers, let alone men fighting only for silver. A trickle of men running away became a flood and then they were all going, even the injured ones getting to their feet and staggering back, broken limbs hanging loosely.

"Send them on their way!" Fallon called and a final volley reached out to pluck down the slower ones and send the rest into panicked flight.

"Let's see what Swane thinks about that," Devlin said with satisfaction.

*

"The cowards!" Swane spat. "How could they?"

Dina said nothing. There was nothing to add. Instead of using volleys of crossbow bolts, like she had expected, Fallon had unleashed a storm of slingstones. The mercenaries were flooding back, hundreds limping and crawling, like some hideous, wounded beast.

"I will not pay those bastards a copper coin for that pitiful display! Kane, ride them down!" Swane snarled.

"Sire?" Kane asked, startled.

"Wipe them out. Set the cavalry onto them. If they won't kill Fallon for me then they are no use. Let our men blood their swords on easy prey before they hunt something better."

Kane glanced towards Dina and she nodded quickly.

"Into lines! Prepare to charge! Swords only!" Kane bellowed.

*

"What's this?" Padraig asked.

Fallon turned back to see Swane's cavalry spur their mounts into movement, shaking themselves out into two long lines.

"They want to charge us already?" Brendan asked incredulously.

"Pull back twenty paces! Prepare slings and aim at the horses!" Fallon shouted, heart pounding again.

"Wait – I don't think they're interested in us yet," Rosaleen said, her voice sounding strangled.

Fallon and the others stared, open-mouthed, as the cavalry spurred into a gallop and crashed home into the ragged ranks of the mercenaries. Swords rose and fell and blood steamed in the freezing air as men were hacked down, the butcher noises of metal in flesh carrying all the way to where Fallon stood.

Mercenaries reeled in all directions as the cavalry dealt terrible blows to heads and shoulders. The smarter men rolled themselves into balls and tried to cover their heads, to protect themselves from swords and hooves but most just ran.

There was no way men could outrun horses, especially in snow, and they were cut down without mercy. Some of the guards swung their swords in huge strokes, striking at backs, but Fallon saw some of those victims stand up and run off in another direction, their heavy winter clothes and packs cut but their skin intact. Other guards aimed only at necks and many heads were sent flying, the bodies sometimes taking an extra stride before collapsing into puddles of bloody slush. Some rode almost past the running men and then cut back into faces and chests. None of those men got up again.

"Come and try it on someone who can fight back!" Devlin roared and many of the other men began shouting something similar.

Fallon smiled wryly. They had been trying to slaughter those mercenaries only a short while ago – the evidence was still flopping and thrashing out on the blood-spattered snow – but seeing them cut down mercilessly by Swane's cavalry had horrified them.

"Hold where we are. Make sure everyone has more than enough stones. This battle is only half over," he said.

*

"Magnificent," Swane said admiringly, as his cavalry slowly trotted back to position. The men's swords, arms and even their horses were splashed with blood, while the field looked like some demented butcher had run amok. Pieces of men and splashes of blood turned the snow red, while the bodies added a brown cloth layer. In fact it was hard to see a patch of white out there.

Dina saw the heaving chests of the horses but kept her angry comments to herself.

"Sire, we shall need to let them rest before we commit them to an attack. And I think we need to get Finbar to see if he can tell where Fallon's defenses are and if there is a weak spot. Because those mercenaries did nothing," she said calmly.

"Yes, we shall do that," he agreed.

Dina waited impatiently as the Royal Wizard was fetched. Finbar looked, if anything, even worse than he had the previous night. He clutched his cloak around him and coughed hoarsely every time he tried to talk.

"Sire, I shall do what I can but I cannot promise anything," he wheezed. "My life hangs in the balance."

"A life you swore to me. If you fall, know you do so in a great cause," Swane said pompously. "Begin."

*

Fallon exchanged jokes and smiles with his men. Not one of them had been killed defeating the mercenaries and the only casualties were half a dozen men who had slipped and fallen, breaking wrists or arms. These men had been helped to the back, where the priests were waiting. The paltry losses had raised everyone's spirits. Half of Swane's army was gone, ridden into destruction or crying pitifully as they froze out on the snow, unable to go forward and too scared to go back.

"As soon as he tries something else, we shall destroy the rest of them. The horses can't run with broken legs, so aim low with the stones," he said, time and again.

He was wondering what else Swane would do when Devlin tapped his shoulder.

"Looks like some real bad weather on the way," he said, pointing over towards where a dark cloud had appeared over the woods to the south and was speeding towards them.

Fallon had been expecting snow all day but when he saw where Devlin was pointing he snapped his fingers. "That's not a normal cloud. Too small and fast moving. Get Padraig. Now!"

The old wizard waddled over, surrounded by a determined-looking group of young helpers.

"They're birds. They're trying to use magic to see what we have done," Padraig said briskly. "We'll take care of them." He turned to his group of wizards. "Work fast. Kick them out of the birds' minds like scooping an oyster from its shell. They will be using their power to hold the group together. Break it apart."

Fallon watched the young wizards nod nervously and loaded his crossbow out of habit. He did not like this sort of fighting, where he could do nothing and just had to trust in others. But Padraig gave him a wink and he swallowed his worried words.

Nothing happened for several long heartbeats, then the cloud began to splinter, little parts flying off in all directions as it grew smaller by the moment.

"Keep it up! They won't get close enough to see anything!" Padraig encouraged his troops.

Fallon began to relax as the cloud shrunk rapidly – then heard shouts from his front lines and started running, his heart racing again.

He skidded to a halt, slipping a little in the snow, to see his men laughing and pointing. For a moment he could not see what they were looking at and his mind jumped to feverish conclusions. Had they somehow been affected by magic that had rendered them helpless? Then he saw small shapes out on the snow, picking their way around the pits, as well as where the ankle-breaker trench had been dug. He blinked and looked again to see rabbits nosing around.

"Maybe the noise woke them up," Casey chuckled as he looked at them. "Or maybe they want some tips in digging!"

Fallon brought his crossbow up. "Or maybe they are possessed and are looking at our defenses while we laugh at them. Kill them!" He loosed, bowling over one of the rabbits and turning it into scraps of fur and flesh. "What are you waiting for? Get them! And get Padraig over here!"

They stared at him dully until he raged at them and then the stones whistled out once more, thumping into the ground and sending up sprays of snow. The rabbits were slower moving than usual, seemingly more intent on what they were doing than evading their sudden attack and dozens were killed. But others hunched down, making them hard to hit.

Padraig and the other wizards took an age to arrive and Fallon was snarling in frustration as he loosed and missed a fast-running rabbit.

"Birds are all gone," the wizard puffed.

"Well, these little bastards aren't!" Fallon growled.

"They soon will be," Padraig said calmly.

Right away, the rabbits stopped exploring and either ran or vanished back into their deep winter burrows.

A last few stones whumped into the soft snow and then they were gone.

"Watch for anything strange. If you see a bird or creature doing anything unusual, kill it," Fallon shouted.

"Do you think they saw what we've done?" Casey asked worriedly.

"Some of it," Fallon said. "But hopefully not everything."

"Trust in Aroaril and all will be well," Gallagher said complacently.

Fallon reloaded his crossbow. "I'll put my trust in this for now," he said.

*

Finbar and the other wizards had all collapsed into the snow and Dina waved for help. She had to know what they had discovered.

"Get some food and water into them," Dina snapped.

Soldiers jumped up to obey her. Finbar was the only wizard able to stand, but he was unable to feed himself. There was little food but the soldiers managed to get some soup into him, then move to the other wizards.

"Some of them are dead, my lady," a guard called.

"Well, don't waste time on them. Feed Finbar until he can talk and then bring him over," she ordered.

She glanced over to where Swane sat stiffly, staring at Fallon's defiant army. She sighed. Pointing out that she had been right was not going to help. These idiot men had wrecked everything and it was up to her to put it right. There was no choice, for Fallon was not going to show any mercy to them.

"Hurry!" she urged, then cursed as Finbar choked on the soup they were feeding him.

The wizards had begun well enough but as soon as Fallon's people began fighting back, they started collapsing, most going down without a sound, some uttering a strange shriek as they fell. Finbar had been the last. He struggled to swallow the soup but it seemed to revive him and he was able to walk over to Dina with a little support.

"They have dug pits all around their position, as well as some sort of thin trench. But there is something else. They were struggling for balance. I think they have built a final trench just in front of their position."

"How big? How deep?" Swane demanded.

"I could not get my creatures close enough to see. But it surely cannot be too bad. The ground is frozen," Finbar said tiredly.

"You have done well," Dina said hastily, as she saw Swane's eyebrows knit together in anger. "Rest now."

"I think I shall," Finbar said, then toppled over once more.

"Take him away," Swane said irritably. "So what do we do now? Attack?"

"I believe the wizard, sire," Kane said quickly. "If they have dug a trench, then it cannot be wide and deep. If we tell the men to jump into Fallon's lines, they will get over it. Most will, anyway. Fallon might have destroyed the mercenaries but he doesn't have many men. They don't even have two thousand. Once we get inside their lines, one of our cavalrymen is worth ten of theirs anyway. Look at what riders can do to running men."

"Yes, I can see that," Swane said bloodthirstily, gazing at the remains of the mercenaries.

Dina sighed. It was time to inject some sense into these men.

"But we forget the slingers that Fallon has found," she said. "Our men will charge across a field littered with dead bodies and pits, get across one trench and then try to get across a second? By the time they have done all that, with crossbowmen and slingers picking them off, they will be a rabble. It sounds like it could be a disaster. If we lose these men, then we have nothing. We have stripped the east of anything useful and summoned every guard of every noble in this land. Maybe it would be better to slip away, skirt around Fallon and make a run for Berry—"

"And how would we fare without the wizards?" Swane asked, pointing at the pile of exhausted and dead men.

"It is a risk. But less of one than sending our men into Fallon's trap," she insisted. "Sire, I beg you—"

"Captain, can your men crack Fallon's line?" Swane interrupted.

Dina groaned to herself. A question that had but one answer.

"Of course, sire!" Kane replied.

"Good. Then off you go."

Dina looked away, feeling sick. This was a ridiculous gamble and she could see it ending but one way. Then she caught sight of something out to the west and new hope flared.

"Sire!" she cried. "Victory is on its way for us!"

*

"I wish they would bloody hurry up and attack. I'm cold and hungry. I could do with some of those rabbits right now," Brendan grumbled.

"Maybe they are too scared to attack," Devlin suggested.

"Or too cold." Gallagher pointed to where thick clouds were rolling in. "Look, Aroaril is sending help for us to defeat them."

Fallon glared at his friend. How could a snowstorm help anyone? At first the snow was light flurries, but then it got worse and Swane's men were lost from view. The wind was not particularly strong but it had the unnerving effect of making the snow swirl and ghost around, until they could barely see fifty yards in any direction.

"Be sure to thank Aroaril for me. This is really helping us," he told Gallagher sarcastically, then stamped away before the fisherman could reply. "Padraig! Can you do anything about this snow? We need to see what they are doing and where they are attacking," he shouted, his words vanishing into the wind.

The old wizard, with snow coating his head, shook it. "Shifting this would take more power than every wizard in this land combined," he shouted back. "And forget about using a bird – nothing can fly in this."

Fallon would have spat in disgust but feared it would turn into a ball of ice before it hit the ground. "What about the men? Can you keep them warm?"

Padraig blew on his own hands. "I'll be doing the best I can, but you've got a lot of men and I don't have many wizards with me."

Fallon stamped his feet and waved to his friends. "Keep walking. Keep the men moving. If they stand still they will be too cold to fight. Keep swapping companies over and for Aroaril's sake get some fires going and get some sort of soup cooking for them. If I were Swane I would attack now. All the advantage passes to him. We can't see him so we just have to hope we can hear him."

But, even as he said it, he suspected that was impossible. With the snow falling, the air felt deadened and sound was not traveling. If he were Swane, he would have dismounted men lead the cavalry through the pits and then mount up and charge before their presence could be detected. He was tempted to send a few men out into the snow to give them early warning but feared that would be their death sentence. With all the snow on the ground, they could not hope to outrun cavalry.

"Get a score of slingers loosing stones off to see if they can hit anything," he ordered.

He loaded his crossbow and brushed the snow off the horn tips with frozen fingers. Even gripping a sword was going to be difficult if they stayed out here too much longer.

With Padraig at his shoulder he prowled around the lines. Every ten paces or so a slinger was out the front, periodically releasing a stone into the whiteness, while Gallagher, Devlin and Brendan were exchanging companies up and down the line, making men move to keep warm. Those who were standing in the lines were stamping feet and rubbing hands in a vain attempt to stave off the encroaching cold. Snow accumulated on heads and shoulders and even on spear tips. Wizards were moving among them, heating up armor until snow melted off it and steam rose into the air where new flakes touched it.

"Can you see anything?" Fallon asked, time and again. His lips were feeling numb and he kept his right hand inside a fold of his cloak, working his fingers to try and keep some feeling in them.

He strained to hear something – anything – but the snow stung his eyes and all he could hear was the shuffling and coughing of his men around him.

"What was that?" someone called and he raced down the line to the shout, slipping and nearly falling twice on the snow and ice. He was glad of the warmth forced into him but it also made the blood pound in his ears and he struggled to hear anything. Whatever it was, it was faint.

"Send a couple of stones out there," he ordered the nearest slingers.

They began to whirl their cords around, building up speed – and then the first of Swane's horsemen exploded out of the gloom, swords raised high.

"Loose!" Fallon roared, jerking his crossbow up to his shoulder and triggering the weapon in one motion. He just had time to notice that the horses' hooves were bound with some sort of cloth, muffling their noise further, then watched his bolt slam into a man's chest and flip him out of the saddle backwards.

A handful of crossbowmen and the two slingers released but it was a paltry volley and only a pair of horses went over. The other slingers tried to get their weapons up to speed but there was scarcely enough time and Fallon saw instantly there was no stopping this charge.

"Back! Back!" he cried, his voice magically boosted by Padraig and thundering over the lines of men.

Instantly men turned and shuffled backwards but they were slowed by the cold and the uneven ground. A dozen slipped over instantly and brought down others.

"Move!" Fallon's voice was magically huge and he hustled men backwards. "Back!"

He glanced over his shoulder and saw Swane's cavalry racing ever closer. They were spurring their horses to greater effort, seeing Fallon's lines seemingly disintegrate and run in front of them. He had no doubt the memory of how they had slaughtered the mercenaries was in their mind and their tight line became ragged as men raced to be the first to strike Fallon's lines.

"Hedgehog! Form the line!" Fallon roared.

They had practiced this so many times in the streets of Berry but now they were on snow and most of them were half-frozen and this was ragged. The spears reached out but there were gaps all over the place. A handful of fallen men, covered in snow, were also trying to push their way into the lines past the spears. It was a recipe for disaster and Swane's horsemen roared in triumph. They jumped their horses, soaring over where they guessed the ankle-breaker trench was. A handful misjudged it and went over, horses screaming as their legs snapped in an instant, but the rest made it and drew back their swords for the first stroke.

Fallon smiled.

In the next moment the horses went in all directions as they slipped on ice, their hooves not helped by the bulky cloth coverings the riders had lashed to them.

Fallon's men had carefully spread snow and vegetation over the edge of the lake, to make it seem as though the bank was in a different place. The ankle-breaker trench had been dug on the very edge of the actual bank. Their position had been on the lake itself, which had made it hard to stand but that was a small price to pay for the protection it provided now.

Horses skidded out of control and crashed into each other as the ice beneath gave them no purchase. Some of the ones on the edge of the charge, thinking they were riding along the river bank, were actually on even thinner ice and a couple went through, into the freezing water. All along the lines, riders were hurled to the ground, while those behind tried to stop their charge but slid helplessly into the fallen. Men and horses screamed as bones snapped and were crushed by the impact.

"Get them!" Fallon roared, his voice magically reaching every ear.

His men raced forwards, driving spears into the few horses still standing and stabbing down at riders struggling to recover from a heavy fall.

Brendan led the way, his hammer swinging down to snap the leg of a horse with a gruesome crack, then reversing it to crush the skull of the rider as the horse toppled over.

Now Fallon's men slithered as well, but they dug spears in to help themselves up and slammed the heavy iron heads into flesh.

Blood steamed in the air and the snow was turned pink in an instant.

"Kill them all!" Brendan howled. A helpless rider held up his hands, his leg trapped beneath his terrified mount, but the hammer came down to turn his ribs into matchsticks.

Fallon blocked a sword blow from a staggering man, slid his foot behind the cavalryman's leg and punched him in the chest with his pommel. The man went back over and Fallon stabbed down once, feeling the tip of his sword grate into the ice beneath the man's neck. He jerked the blade free and swept it in a wide arc, shaking hot blood off.

"Get the next line! Finish them!" he shouted.

The first two lines had been turned into chaos but the third line arrived now, able to see what had been done to their comrades and using their lances to stab and thrust at Fallon's soldiers.

"Take it to them! Get inside the lances!" Fallon roared as he saw a dozen of his men pierced.

He clambered over a twitching horse and ducked a lance thrust. He smashed his sword into the horse's mouth and, when it reared in pain, blood dripping from its teeth, thrust the sword deep into the rider's thigh, ripping open the big vein there.

"Bring them down!"

The cold was making more men than usual reluctant to fight. It was easy enough to stay on the lakeside, within the wreckage of Swane's charge and stab at helpless men there but that was not going to destroy the last third of Swane's cavalry. Fallon waved to his men, beckoning them forwards. They had to finish off Swane's men now, not give them a chance to withdraw and salvage something from this.

"Close! Get close!" Fallon roared. He ducked under a lance thrust, grabbed the cavalryman's leg and tipped him out of the saddle. The man hit the ground hard and Fallon slipped past the wild-eyed horse to stab his blade into the man's groin, raising an unearthly scream. "Don't let one get away!"

But Swane's horsemen had recognized Fallon, by his actions and his bellowed orders, and now they rushed to kill him. All of a sudden he found three men lunging lances at him and he had to defend himself frantically, dodging thrusts and parrying with his sword. But the footing was treacherous and he went down, his left foot slipping away. He rolled desperately as a lancehead plunged into the snow where he had been a moment before, but he hit a body, unable to roll further, and then realized he was trapped. He glared up at the guard who drew back his lance for a killing thrust – only for Casey to get there first, ramming his spear into the rider's guts and driving him howling to the snow. Another guard lunged for Casey, and Fallon reached out and grabbed the young officer's leg, jerking him off his feet so the point missed his head. Now they were both on the ground and more of Swane's guardsmen were looming.

Fallon groped for his sword but then a howling mass of his men surged past and tore into the guardsmen, long spears battling lances. The horsemen could not evade because their horses were struggling for footing, while the men could still duck and weave and they hauled the guardsmen down.

"Here you go, sir." Someone held out a hand and Fallon took it gratefully and got back up, helping Casey in turn.

"Just in time," he said, recognizing the helping hand as belonging to Brasso, the man who had saved them all by raising the alarm when Kemal attacked.

Brasso grinned. "Some of the men were hanging back but when they saw you go down, there was no stopping them," he said. "We can't lose our captain."

Fallon dredged up a smile for him and patted Casey on the shoulder. "And thanks to you, I am still here," he said.

"I still owe you a greater debt, sir," Casey said breathlessly.

"Today you won't need to repay it. Today we end it," Fallon said and plunged into the fighting.

This was the chance to release all the fear and worry and anger that had tormented him for so long now. Swane had done his worst but it wasn't good enough and Aidan's prophecy was undone. All he had to do was destroy this confused rabble and Gaelland was safe. He let the fear of his narrow escape and his fury propel him into the chaos. Shapes loomed up and then disappeared into the snow and there was no way to really see what was going on, only a need to kill what was in front of him. A cavalryman jumped up from where he had fallen off his horse and Fallon drove his sword into the man's mouth, mangling teeth and lips before it punched out the back of the head. He had to put his foot on the dying man's shoulder to rip the steel free, sending a bloody tongue flying lazily up through the air. Another man turned to run but skidded on the ice and Fallon hacked into the back of the man's neck, almost but not quite severing the head.

Brendan waded in, his hammer taking down horse legs with one brutal blow, while recruits then shoved spears into screaming men and horses alike.

The air steamed, rising from fighting men, pouring from open mouths and open wounds, snow melting as it settled on the fighting and dying.

Devlin was there at Fallon's shoulder, and together they hunted men on horseback. As Fallon knocked away a lance with his sword, Devlin ducked under a horse's belly to come up behind the cavalryman and cut his throat.

The recruits were flooding forwards, mobbing the fallen cavalry and engulfing those trying to get clear. It was a frenzy of men, slipping and sliding as they hacked and punched and stabbed and bit at each other.

Some of Swane's men were trying to get clear and Fallon looked around desperately, before seeing Padraig waving through the shifting snow.

Instantly the horses began to rear, throwing their riders, tossing and kicking out until they were free of even the best riders, while Gallagher had some of the men get out their slings again to pick off any cavalry trying to escape. At less than twenty paces away, the stones were even more deadly and the more confident slingers even sent theirs whistling in between fighters to strike cavalrymen.

One rider levelled his lance at Fallon and tried to spur his stumbling horse into some semblance of a gallop, only for a slingstone to strike him in the cheek. His face distorted as bones shattered and he collapsed into the snow, lance falling from his hand. Fallon took two paces forwards and grabbed it, sinking the butt into the ground and levelling it at another rider. The heavy head punched into the horse's chest and the horse screamed and collapsed, crushing its rider as it rolled away.

Wounded horses shrieked in every direction, the noise even more distressing than the cries of dying men.

A bellowing cavalryman swung at Fallon's head but he ducked under the lance, then shoved the man, where he slipped on the ice and went over, easy prey for hungry men with thirsty spears. A howling recruit stabbed down so furiously that his spearhead sank into the ice and pinned the dying man there. Another guardsman lunged and Fallon literally slipped sideways, then came up against a dead man and used him as footing to smash his sword around in a massive blow. It struck the side of the cavalryman's head and took it off, leaving an almost headless corpse standing there, one jawbone still attached to the ragged stump of neck.

Fallon looked around but there were no more cavalry near him. Dozens were streaming away into the falling snow, dropping swords and melting into the cold murk, although the slingers were still picking them off. He leaned on his sword, digging the tip into the ice to keep him upright, fighting for breath after the furious exertion, clouds of steam pouring off him.

He let out a cry of triumph, a wordless release of everything that had been bottled up these past moons and heard it echoed by his men. Devlin patted him on the shoulder, wiping blood from his face and Fallon searched around for a clean patch of snow – something to cool his dry mouth – but could not see any.

The last few cavalry were begging for surrender, dropping swords and holding out their empty hands.

"What do we do with them, sir?" Bran asked, the bearded officer looking as if he had bathed in horse's blood.

Fallon glanced at the cluster of surrendering men.

"Herd them out onto the ice and leave them there. We need to get our own horses and every man who is fit to hold a sword," he said raggedly.

"But I thought that was all of them?" Bran asked, looking over his shoulder into the swirling snow.

"It is. But we haven't got Swane, nor that bitch of a Duchess. We can't rest until we have them. I won't be happy until I see them both dangling from the end of a rope."

*

"Can you see anything?" Swane asked angrily.

Dina did not reply. It was pointless. They had ridden carefully after the final line of cavalry and could hear the sounds of battle not far ahead but could see nothing through the swirling clouds of snow. It was frustrating to wait here, unable to tell what was happening, and doubly frustrating to hear Swane worrying. His father would never have let his guard down like that, she reflected, but perhaps that was all to the good. After all, it made Swane easier to manipulate and, eventually, replace.

The screams and shouts and the ringing of steel on steel echoed eerily through the shifting clouds of snow. Worst of all was the crying of the horses. Sometimes they caught a glimpse of figures but then the snow swirled and it vanished as quickly as it had come. Dina concentrated on staying warm. Her fur cloak was thick with snow and her toes and fingers were fast losing feeling. She edged her horse away from the body of a mercenary who lay nearby. A stone was embedded in his forehead, and snow had settled over his eyes and open mouth, giving him an eerie appearance. At least he hadn't started to smell but it was disquieting to look at. She eased her horse forward until he was out of her sight and had almost drifted into a doze, lulled by the sapping cold, when a roar jerked her awake.

"What was that?" Swane gasped.

It went on and on, a dreadful, triumphant howl, and Dina shivered violently.

"Is that our men?" she asked, unable to stop herself. Obviously none could answer her and she turned to where Kane sat with a score of guards, all that had not charged into the snow. "Send three men to see what is happening."

But then shapes began to emerge from the gloom, men in bright surcoats slipping and sliding and running, looking back over their shoulders and crying with fear. At first there were a few, then dozens of them, going in all directions, heedless of the falling snow, of the waiting Swane and Dina, of everything but the need to get away.

"Where are they going? What are they doing?" Swane demanded angrily. "Stop them!"

Kane spurred his horse forwards and caught one of them, a tall man in a tattered blue surcoat of Rork.

"What happened? Tell your King!" he demanded, hauling the man in front of them.

The man gasped for breath. "We thought we had them but they were standing on the ice, not on the ground. Our horses fell and they tore us apart. We're all dead and now they're coming for the rest of us!" he panted. "We must run!"

"No!" Swane cried. Kicking his horse into motion, he fumbled his sword out and lashed down, the blade tearing out the Rorkman's eyes as Kane hurriedly let go of the man's shoulder. "How dare you lie to your King!"

The man fell to his knees, weeping blood, and Swane slashed down again and again, until the Rorkman finally collapsed, kicking weakly.

"No!" Swane shouted, his eyes wild. "I cannot have lost!"

Dina looked over his shoulder, to where more of their army was disappearing into the drifts of snow. A couple of figures were limping away from the battlefield still, struggling men holding themselves upright against the pain of their wounds but nothing else. There was still the eerie screaming of wounded horses but no more ringing of clashing weapons, which was even more alarming than the earlier scream of triumph. The Rorkman had obviously been speaking the truth.

"This is not true! I shall ride forwards and kill Fallon myself! Without him, his pack of traitorous dogs will surrender!" Swane declaimed, holding his bloody sword aloft.

Dina nudged her horse forwards until she was by his side, then her hand flicked out and slapped him across the face.

Stunned, he dropped his sword and turned to face her.

"How dare—" he began.

"Listen to me now or we are all dead," she said, her voice colder than the air. "Our men have been killed and Fallon will be coming for us soon. We must get away or we shall end up like your father. Murdered in front of a mocking crowd."

"Run? We can't run!"

Dina was saved from replying by a shout from the battlefield. "Find Swane!" someone roared. It was the unmistakable voice of Fallon.

"Come," she said, a little more gently. "He will not find us in this snow. We can still get away."

Swane looked like a whipped dog. His mouth hung open and his lip trembled. "But how will I get my throne back now?" he whimpered.

She gestured to Kane and the guards began to move, their faces almost whiter than the snow. 'We shall bring along Finbar and any other of the wizards who still live. And we have Prince Kemal as well."

"What good is any of that going to do? I might as well die here," Swane cried, snatching his arm free of her grip.

For a moment she thought about killing him. But she quashed the temptation. The nobles would not follow her. She needed him as a puppet for the throne and, more importantly, he was the one who knew how to use Zorva's power. She took a deep breath. "And I have the book from your room, the one left by Brother Nahuatl."

Swane's face changed instantly, transformed by a terrible lust, and he followed her swiftly into the shifting mists of snow.

CHAPTER 26

"It's no good," Devlin shouted in Fallon's ear. "We can't see anything and the wind's getting worse. Night has almost fallen and we have to get these men out of this snow before we lose them. The sweat from the battle will turn into ice and then they'll die."

Fallon swore furiously, his curses lost in the swirling snow. They had searched for the best part of two turns of the hourglass and found no trace of Swane or Dina. They had rounded up a few score wounded guardsmen but that was it. The snow had wiped out any hint of a trail. It was a bitter disappointment at the end of a triumph. There was always the chance that Swane and Dina would freeze to death in this weather and that was a thought to warm the heart. But until he saw the bodies and cut off Swane's head, Gaelland was not entirely safe.

"Right, let's get everyone into the village of Dunclady. At least they can cook a hot meal and stay out of this weather. When it blows itself out we'll look again for them."

But that was easier said than done. While their losses had been light compared to the battle of Berry, there were plenty of wounded and they had to be carried into the deserted village, which was littered with the mess left by Swane's army.

As for Swane's wounded guardsmen and mercenaries, as well as the ones who had run off into the snow, Fallon could not spare any men to take care of them. Nor, truthfully, did he worry much about them. They had wanted to kill his family and his men and if they froze to death out there then so be it. He had not forgotten the columns of smoke that marked where farmers and their families had died during Swane's advance.

He pasted a smile over his black mood as he visited his own wounded, resting in the deserted homes. Raging fires kept the cold at bay and stew bubbled over those fires. Barely two score of men had been killed in the battle and, while more than a hundred had been wounded, only a handful would not recover and take their places in the ranks again. They cheered him until he left them and joined his friends in a smaller house.

"Now this is more like it," Brendan said. "A neat little house, a raging fire, hot stew and a bed for the night. Almost like home."

"Well, if you go looking for Nola during the night, make sure you don't come near my blanket," Devlin told him with a grin.

Brendan's face darkened and Padraig hastily stepped in. "This is not a night to be out in the cold. I'd wager not a one of Swane's men out in this storm will last till morning. And we'll probably find Swane, frozen stiff, in a day or two."

"Brendan's frozen stiff, which is why I don't want to sleep next to him tonight," Devlin added.

"That's enough," Fallon said warningly, as Brendan scowled into his bowl of stew.

"Come on!" Devlin protested. "We should be celebrating! For Aroaril's sake, we beat Swane and united the country. It's all ours now and we can make it secure by spring, ready to turn back the Kottermanis. Our troubles are over!"

Fallon snorted. "Not exactly over," he said. "We have to find Swane and Dina, and we have to find Kemal, alive."

"We just need to trust in Aroaril," Gallagher said complacently. "Thanks to Him, we have our families back, and we have turned back both Kemal's attack and Swane's. Tomorrow we shall find them and all will be complete." He put a hand on Fallon's shoulder. "It is clear that you are destined to rule Gaelland. Our long journey has led us to this point. Happiness is within our grasp. We just have to have a little faith and all will be well."

There was the usual awkward silence that followed Gallagher's pronouncements about Aroaril. Fallon had noticed how Rosaleen was even looking uncomfortable with some of her husband's words, not that she was saying anything in public. And if she was saying anything in private, it was not doing any good. Still, Fallon did like the sound of Gallagher's last words. They were close to complete victory, for surely Swane and Dina could not escape the snow. He could go back to Berry and start remaking the country, just the way Prince Cavan imagined it, so it could be a place where Kerrin and the new baby could grow up free, and safe. Maybe Gallagher was right. Maybe he was blessed by Aroaril. God knows he had surely earned it. He became aware of the silence and thought it best to break it.

"I thank you all for your help. I could not have done this without you," he said.

"Well, here's to finding something to properly toast us with soon," Padraig added, raising his water.

"Show me Swane's body tomorrow and I will buy you whatever you like." Fallon grinned. The King's words had proved to be nothing but the last gasp of evil from a sick man. Everything would work out.

*

Kemal thought the previous night spent locked in a beast shed, with only old sacking for blankets, had been bad enough. But it seemed like paradise compared to tonight. He had been unceremoniously dragged out of the shed and hurled into the back of a wagon. At first he thought he had been thrown in with a bunch of dead bodies but he swiftly realized they were instead sleeping, although some of them looked close to death.

The wind was howling and the snow was settling on all of them but, with these strangely dressed men obviously uncomplaining, he wriggled down into the middle of them, using his feet and teeth to draw their cloaks over the top of him to both give some shelter and use their fading body heat to warm himself. He could not hear what the riders were saying but, from their demeanor and lack of numbers, it seemed obvious that they had been defeated by Fallon. They were worried about what would happen if Fallon found them.

And that was something that also worried Kemal. With Swane running for his life, having a Crown Prince of Kotterman as a hostage was seemingly a luxury not worth having. Talk of sacrifice to Zorva seemed like it was back on the agenda.

But nothing happened while they escorted the wagon into the growing gloom. He assumed they must have a destination in mind but, as night fell and they were no closer to stopping, he wondered what was happening. After all, there was almost no chance of seeing anything in the remaining light and surely, if they kept going, they would all freeze to death out here.

*

Dina hated every moment of the ride but she had been through far worse things in her youth and, when the alternative was being executed by Fallon, it was easy to keep going. They had tried to retrace their old trail, the one they had left from the Spine down to Lake Caragh but, swiftly, it vanished under a layer of snow. There were abandoned farmhouses along this way somewhere and all she could do was hope they found one.

It seemed a fool's hope in this weather but she had no other.

As she rode, she was thinking furiously, partly to stave off the cold that threatened to destroy them all but also because Swane was going to take even more careful handling. Helping him discover how to use the Dark God's power might save them but what would it mean for her? Once he had all the power, then he would not need her. There was no way she would let herself be discarded or, worse, end up sacrificed to Zorva. Not after what she had already done to win him over. No, she was going to have to be his high priestess. As far as she knew, Zorva didn't have priestesses, but she was sure she could persuade any man, even a god.

But first they had to survive this night.

There was no sign of any shelter and the chance of seeing a house in this weather was remote anyway. They could ride past one just twenty yards away and they would not notice it. Just when she was beginning to fear they would die out here, shapes loomed out of the gloom and a small copse of fir trees appeared. The bedraggled party made for them and, once under the evergreen canopy, things seemed a little calmer and warmer.

"Find Finbar. See if he can do anything," Dina shouted into Kane's ear. The officer nodded, the snow on his helmet cascading off as he did so.

The exhausted wizard was found among his half-dead companions and, although he protested at first, he was able to get the trees' branches to knit together, forming a crude shelter and wind break for them. Tired guards swept away the snow, creating a fire pit. With his last gasp of energy, Finbar sparked alight soggy fallen pine needles, giving them a chance to build a fire.

The few scraps of food they had scrounged from Swane's supplies were thrown into a pot with handfuls of snow and topped up with generous amounts of horse blood from the tired mounts. Dina took a cupful of this strange mixture and almost choked at the foul taste but it was warm and she could feel her body waking up as nourishment eased through her. Guards hacked off branches and soon they had a fire raging, filling the little magic-made clearing with warmth. Gusts of snow still penetrated but she looked around and decided they would survive. She took another cup of the horse blood soup over to where Swane sat hunched against a wheel of the wagon.

"You need to drink, sire," she said, pressing it into his cold hands.

"What is the point? Everything is lost. That bastard Fallon has won. We might survive the night but they will find us in the morning. There is no way we can escape. It has all ended."

She sat down next to him. "No, sire," she said. She unwrapped the book Munro had taken from Swane's room. She stroked the cover. "Look, it is just beginning."

CHAPTER 27

Feray was so proud of her sons. They showed their uncle nothing as the little group walked through the streets. It seemed that time in Gaelland, when they had been Fallon's prisoners, had proved useful. Naturally she would not give Durzu the satisfaction of knowing how worried she was. It would not be safe to sail for Gaelland for at least three more moons, so for the Emperor to be here already, disrupting the Empire by moving the court all the way to Adana, showed how much he wanted Gaelland. Yonetici desperately needed to have the scrolls record he was the first Emperor to add a new province to the Empire in living memory. They had passed workers creating huge new statues honoring this achievement, before it had even happened. Feray feared this obsession would make her mission nearly impossible.

They were taken to one of Aroaril's churches, the biggest one in the city. Its huge dome was truly beautiful, while from its tall spires the clergy called the faithful to prayer three times a day.

No more. Its clergy had been moved out, the congregations shifted to other churches and instead it was ringed with guards and surrounded by petitioners from all over the Empire, come here to beg for trading rights and favors, or to protest decisions made by the local governors. In between those two groups scurried an army of scribes, the real lifeblood that kept the Empire's heart beating. Another army of messengers waited by their horses, being replaced by fresh arrivals as fast as they were sent out. She knew this was a chain that went right around the Empire; messages could be sent like lightning across the disparate countries that made up the Kotterman Empire, handed on from one messenger station to the next. Was this how word had reached the Emperor's ears so swiftly?

She put such thoughts aside as all made way for Durzu's guards. Even the most desperate petitioner knew Durzu's symbol and his reputation for ruthlessness.

The huge church doors were open, although guarded. Again, they were waved through without Durzu's men breaking step. Feray would have expected the same thing to happen for Kemal, except there would be less fear on everyone's faces as they bowed.

Once inside the church she had to keep back a gasp of surprise. She had been here many times, for there was no finer place for the Crown Prince to worship. But the inside had changed completely. Where worshippers had once sat on long benches, now desks filled the open space in all directions.

Durzu led them through the middle, scattering clerks and courtiers like frightened pigeons until finally they reached a barrier even he could not cross with impunity.

The Emperor had been installed on a large golden throne where the altar to Aroaril had once stood. Even in her agitated state, Feray found time to wonder if that was a sign of some kind.

The commander of the Emperor's guard blocked their way and stared at Durzu with none of the fear everyone else had showed. Like the rest of the guards, he was not a large man, but they were all trained from birth in fighting and none dared cross them. His cold black eyes swept over the party. Like all of his kind, he had had his tongue torn out, so he could never speak of anything he saw inside the Emperor's chambers. But beside him was one of the Emperor's many officials.

"Princess Feray, Princes Asil, Orhan and Durzu. The Emperor Yonetici welcomes you but you know the protocol. You are required to leave all weapons and guards here."

Durzu snapped his fingers and his guards peeled away, leaving just the four of them. He unbuckled his belt and handed it, with its attached dagger, into thin air. A servant raced forwards and caught it before it hit the ground.

The guard stepped aside.

Feray smiled down at her sons then lifted her chin and walked up the few steps towards the throne. The Emperor was speaking with a gaggle of officials but waved them away. He turned his attention on them and Feray sank to her knees, snapping her fingers for Asil and Orhan to join her. At her side, Durzu bowed deeply before dropping to one knee.

"Rise," Emperor Yonetici said loudly.

She looked at her sons' grandfather and husband's father and saw a little of both of them in there. But where Kemal was thin, Yonetici was fat, his features hidden behind pouchy layers of good food and wine, the sharp lines of his face blurred by high living and the passage of time. It was in the eyes that she saw the greatest difference. This man held the lives of uncounted thousands in his hands. He but had to raise his voice and not just families but whole towns would die and that knowledge shone out of his face.

"Exalted One. We have returned to you with news from Gaelland," she said respectfully.

"Where is my son, the Crown Prince?" the Emperor demanded. "Why does he not come here to report to me in person?"

Feray took a deep breath. Time to start lying and hope she could get away with it. Luckily she had been given plenty of time to come up with a good story. Some of it was even true.

"Exalted One, my husband, your son Prince Kemal, has been forced to stay in Gaelland to keep control of the new province. The King of Gaelland has turned to worshipping the Dark God in an attempt to defeat you. He is dead, as is his son and many of his supporters, but it took fierce fighting to stop them. They had even brought in a Fearpriest from a strange country far, far across the seas to make their evil plan succeed."

She paused for the gasps of horror to stop. The courtiers, who were not supposed to be listening but of course were all agog, had been unable to restrain themselves.

"They intended to sacrifice us all to Zorva and then use that power to take over the entire Empire. King Aidan wanted to rule the world in the Dark God's name and have every one of us bowing down to him while the sacrificial altars ran red with blood and the hearts of our children were burned in fiery pits."

This time there were actual cries of horror and indignation from among the courtiers. The Emperor did not say anything but he leaned forwards a little on his padded throne and she took that to be a good sign.

"But this plot was destroyed and King Aidan killed, while his Fearpriest was also destroyed and the nest of worshippers executed." She did not mention that it was Fallon who had done that, instead hoping the courtiers would leap to the wrong conclusion.

"Aroaril praise Prince Kemal!" someone shouted and then the rest of them took up the cry.

She used that time to bow her head, as if in respect, although it was more in relief.

"Prince Kemal controls about half of the country now, ruling those Gaelish who are as horrified by their King's evil as we are. But one of the King's sons escaped and is trying to build up his forces. With the danger ever-present, my husband sent us back to bring back more men in the spring, so we can stamp out these Zorva-worshippers and make Gaelland secure for you to inspect, Exalted One," she said, finishing with a flourish and touching her forehead to the ground.

Immediately there was applause from the courtiers and she straightened up, feeling much more confident.

The Emperor, however, seemed unmoved.

"A fascinating tale," he said flatly. "However, it does not explain why we heard reports of a slave revolt and mass escape from Adana, as well as answer why my son let his family risk the storms of the northern seas to return here, when he knew I would be arriving in Gaelland with an army in the spring anyway."

Feray bowed her head briefly, before holding it high and speaking clearly, her voice calm and steady. Any hint of nerves now would be fatal but, after what she had gone through in that storm, even facing the wrath of the Emperor seemed like nothing.

"The first was a ruse. Prince Kemal had discovered King Aidan's plot and knew that he was being watched by magical means.

By helping the Gaelish slaves to escape, which was one of Aidan's demands, he was able to return to Gaelland with an army and surprise the capital of Berry," she said strongly. "As for myself and our sons, he knew the Zorva-worshippers saw us as the key to unlocking enough power to take over the Empire. He could have sent anyone to warn you but we were chosen to both protect us and to persuade you that the danger was very real and Gaelland is not yet safe for you to claim. It will be, for Prince Kemal will make it so, but he feared you landing in the wrong part of Gaelland and falling into the hands of the Zorva-worshippers."

"So the slave escape was a ruse?" the Emperor asked again, seemingly ignoring the rest of her story.

"Of course, Exalted One. Why else would he order ships to sail away and guards to leave their posts?"

"And the men who died?"

"A necessary sacrifice to prevent a greater evil."

The Emperor rested his chin on his hand, the extra flesh spilling over his chunky fingers. He fixed her with a stare and said nothing.

She made sure her back was straight and met his gaze evenly. He would not find any chinks in her armor.

"It sounds suspicious, Father," Durzu said, breaking the silence. "We know that Kemal crossed the seas himself, why did he not send a warning then?"

Feray saw the danger instantly. She had built a beautiful house of half-truths and lies and while it had been crafted with care, it would not take much to bring it down. She rounded on Durzu.

"He was being watched, as I told you. And because I and our sons had been captured by the Gaelish," she said defiantly.

"Oh, so he put his own family before the Empire?" Durzu said, pouncing on the bait she dragged in front of him.

"He risked his life for the Empire and fought in the front line to bring down King Aidan," she fired back, secretly delighted that this was now the focus of the argument. "He risks his life now, holding a new province with just a small army, while we risked our lives to deliver the warning."

She looked around the circle of courtiers, every one of them a powerful man who controlled lands, trade routes and money flows.

They believed her but they were hesitating, for none wanted to risk crossing Durzu unless it was with the Emperor's support.

Then they all fell to their knees as the Emperor rose with a grunt and stalked down towards her.

She lowered her head a heartbeat before Durzu and sensed the Emperor stop just in front of her. He reached down a hand and helped her to her feet, looking in her eyes.

"Tell me," he said. "Did the Gaelish really have you?"

She met his stare easily. "I was tied to a bloodstained altar to the foul God Zorva and a Fearpriest stood over me with a knife, ready to kill me and my sons," she replied.

The Emperor inclined his head slightly. "What metal was the knife made of?" he asked.

She paused for a moment, taken back to that smoky chamber when she had been sure she would die, until Fallon had gone mad and freed them all.

"It was not metal," she said, remembering with a shudder. "It was a strange black rock, sharp enough to cut our ropes with one blow."

Yonetici's hand came up and landed on her shoulder. For a moment she was terrified she had made a mistake and the guards were going to drag them out of there, then he smiled slightly. It was probably meant to be sympathetic but it looked like a crocodile showing its teeth.

"Princess Feray has seen a Fearpriest and lived to tell the tale," he rumbled. "She is a worthy wife for my son, the Crown Prince. This is disturbing news and we must decide whether we should purge Gaelland with fire, to make sure the taint of evil is completely gone."

"Exalted One, not all the Gaelish are evil. Many hated their King and cheered his death. They would welcome you," she said, knowing she was pushing her luck but also determined to make the most of this.

The Emperor returned to the throne before speaking. "Then what do you suggest?" he asked.

"Exalted One, I merely follow the orders of my husband," she said, bowing her head a little to help hide that lie. "Send a score of ships filled with our best soldiers and within two moons you will have the province you always dreamed of, happy to be part of the Empire and ready to honor you."

"And you would lead this force?" Durzu asked, a sneer hovering beneath his words.

"Prince Kemal would lead them but, if you are concerned, you could take the reinforcements across the seas, before putting yourself under your brother's command," she invited.

Durzu's confidence cracked a little. "That would not be necessary," he said hastily.

No, it would not, because if you were ever at Kemal's mercy, he could get rid of you and your scheming, blame it on the Zorva-worshippers, and nobody would ever know the truth.

The Emperor snapped his fingers and a pair of scribes emerged from behind his throne, scrolls of papyrus at the ready.

"Prepare fifty ships and fill them with our best men. When we are dealing with Zorva-worship, we shall not take any chances. With the men Kemal has already, that should be more than enough. I shall follow myself, two moons after you, with another fifty ships, if I have not heard from you," he instructed.

Feray pressed her forehead onto the step in a gesture of respect that was also one of massive relief.

"All praise the Emperor Yonetici! His wisdom has saved us all!" she cried.

Not to let a chance like that go past, the courtiers echoed her words. She looked up to see the Emperor nod to dismiss her and, as she turned, she saw Durzu's bitter disappointment and anger and hid her smile. She had achieved everything she wanted and more. Once the storms were gone, Kemal was as good as rescued. They could then have the country on its knees, ready for the Emperor's arrival. It could not have worked better.

CHAPTER 28

The light thrown off the fire was almost impossible to read by but it did not really matter, because they could not understand the words anyway.

"What do you remember Brother Nahuatl saying? Did he have a catechism, like the priests and priestesses of Aroaril do?" Dina asked as they turned pages with half-frozen fingers.

"He usually spoke in his own language," Swane said sulkily.

"Relax," she soothed. "Think. Let your mind go back. Was there anything he said about Zorva?"

Swane closed his eyes but she could see the frustration on his face, even in the dim firelight. "I can't remember!"

She restrained her frustration. How did men truly think they were the rulers of Gaelland when they possessed such little intelligence? She produced the box that Munro had also stolen. With numb fingers she opened it, revealing the blackened, shriveled heart. Luckily her nose was so cold she could not smell the tang of decay.

"My brother's heart," Swane said, his voice betraying the first excitement she had heard since producing these dark items.

"Hold it," she urged.

With trembling fingers, he scooped it out of the box.

"What would Nahuatl do with it?" she urged. "Close your eyes and pretend to be him."

Swane did as he was bid, raising it above his head. "I dedicate this heart and soul to you, O Zorva," he intoned, then jerked his eyes open excitedly. "That's it!"

"Keep going," she urged. They had been sharing a bed for almost a moon now but, despite all they had done, this seemed strangely far more intimate.

Swane closed his eyes again. "Flesh of my flesh, blood of my blood, the source of all power," he said, then cast it into the fire. The shrivelled heart burst into flames instantly, something that should have been impossible. She felt a blast of heat that, again, made no earthly sense.

Swane's smile changed from relief to something darker and he shivered a little, something she could see had nothing to do with the cold.

"Give me the book," he said eagerly.

She opened it for him and he hissed in anger, a noise that made the hairs stand up on the back of her neck.

"I still don't know what to do! I sacrificed many serving girls in Meinster but I could not unlock the power," he groaned. "It is so close and yet so far away!"

"Think again," she urged. "Did Nahuatl use gestures? Did he have a special knife?"

Swane stared at her and then laughed. "That's it! I have been using a metal knife and Zorva hates that!"

Dina jumped to her feet. "Kane! Make your King a wooden spike."

"Wood?" Swane asked disdainfully.

"For now," she said. "Until you have the power."

He nodded. His eyes shone with a strange light. "Yes, Zorva will listen to me and the more blood I give him, the more power I will get. I shall make a knife of pure bone that can carve open men's hearts. Get the Kottermani Prince. We shall sacrifice him now and then I can get us out of this storm, then take us back and destroy Fallon!"

Dina liked the idea of getting out of the storm but rather less the thought of taking on Fallon again. Not with a handful of men and against a horde of priests of Aroaril. She reminded herself that as Swane's consort her word was unquestioned but as a mere Duchess she could not command the nobles waiting back in Meinster's castle. She just had to step carefully and use her skills to guide Swane down the right path.

*

Kemal had never known cold like this. He floated in and out of consciousness, wondering if he could ever be warm again. The snow was no longer falling on them and they were out of the worst of the wind but he was too far away from the fire to get much heat.

There was something going on over by the wagon but he was too hungry, tired and cold to take notice. Until a quartet of guards dragged him from the back of a pile of unconscious wizards and into the firelight. For a moment he luxuriated in the warmth, and then they pinned him down on his back in the snow, using a knife to tear open the sacking he was wearing, as well as the filthy tunic he had underneath. He struggled but the cold and lack of food had sapped his energy and the four men held him down easily.

"What are you doing, Swane?" he snarled.

The young Prince stood over him, a book clutched in one hand, a sharpened chunk of wood in the other, the Duchess Dina at his shoulder. Kemal did not show it but he did not like the expression on their faces.

"Rejoice, Prince of Kotterman. You shall be the instrument of Fallon's destruction, as you wished. Your heart and soul will go to Zorva and I shall use that power to grind Fallon into dust."

Kemal felt a tremor of fear at the thought but, after what Fallon had done to him, he was not going to back down in front of this bastard.

"Kill me and you kill yourself," he shouted. "Sacrifice me to Zorva and my father will not rest until you and every trace of Gaelland is gone. You think you have seen a large army? He can send two hundred ships, every one packed with veteran soldiers, and then three moons later have another two hundred ready. They will turn Gaelland into a wasteland."

"I shall defeat them," Swane boasted.

Kemal forced a scornful laugh. "You won't be able to sacrifice people fast enough. They will drown Gaelland in fire and eventually there will be only you left, and then they will burn you. You will unite the entire Empire against you. Every country that wants to leave the Empire and fears my father will clamor to be part of an army that stamps out the worship of Zorva by a Fearpriest-King. You will have woken a sleeping giant and it will grind your filthy dreams into dust."

"You don't know the power of Zorva," Swane fired back, but Kemal could see the beginnings of doubt in his eyes.

"I won't see it but I shall know about it, when your soul arrives for Zorva to torment for all time because you failed him," Kemal taunted. "The Empire is bigger than you could ever imagine and I am the key to it. By killing me, you seal your own doom."

"I have Zorva with me. And the Great God will not let me fail."

"Like he saved your Fearpriest, when Fallon gutted him and left him to die?" Kemal sneered.

Swane paused and Kemal enjoyed watching the doubt on his face. Then Dina grabbed the Prince's arm.

"Sire, he is right. We cannot take on the Empire in a straight fight. They would not rest until we were destroyed and, even if we won, we would have inherited a smoking ruin. Both Gaelland and Kotterman will fall. It is far better to destroy the Empire from within and then take it over. Kemal is the key, and we can use him to unlock unlimited wealth and power."

Kemal saw Swane stare at her and he glared at the pair of them.

"What if we were to take him back to Kotterman and say we rescued him from Fallon and wanted to return him to his father? That would get us inside, right to the Emperor, and then we could strike. We could take over the Empire."

Kemal was very aware that she was arguing to save his life but he could not keep quiet at this.

"My father would never convert to Zorva. He would rather die!" he growled.

"Probably true," Dina agreed, then turned back to Swane. "But there will be another son, or relative, or noble, who wants the throne more than anything. If we can get there, we can find them and use them. Through them we shall take control and then, when we are ready, we shall become the true rulers."

"But won't they have even more priests there?" Swane asked.

"Not like ours. They can't use magic. They are no more danger to us than a nest of ants and can be stamped on with as little effort."

Kemal fought to keep his face impassive. Durzu would certainly jump at the chance to rule Kotterman, no matter what he had to do. The fact he would be a dupe would not worry him, for he would always think he could outwit the Gaelish. Then Kemal thought more about it and could see a chance for himself. The Duchess and Swane did not know the Empire, nor did they know his father. If he could but get back to Kotterman, he could turn the tables on these evil bastards. He tried to make it look like he was worried but that he was trying to hide it.

It must have worked, for Dina pointed at him.

"Look at his face. He knows I am right but he fights it," she said triumphantly. "Why just use this power to take Gaelland and fight Kotterman, when we can use it to take them both?"

Swane grinned wolfishly and Kemal contorted his face into something looking like anguish.

"How do we get there?" Swane asked. "And how do we survive this night without Zorva granting me power?"

"Well, we have plenty of useless wizards here, doing nothing to help us."

"An excellent idea," he agreed. "Take care of Kemal. But drag over a couple of the wizards and we shall see how Zorva likes the taste of their blood."

Kemal was hauled away and propped against a fir tree, a wizard's ill-fitting robe draped over him. He closed his eyes but nothing could shut his ears against the noises coming from the clearing. He sent up endless prayers that he could turn the tables on them and that their plan would be their doom. But the stench of blood and evil filling the little clearing washed away his hope. He almost wished he was burning in Zorva's pits rather than freezing here, with the evil laughter of those twisted bastards ringing in his ears. But their day of reckoning would come.

CHAPTER 29

Fallon swept the map off the table onto the floor and then tipped the table over for good measure.

"Maybe they are still lost, buried out in a snow drift somewhere," Gallagher suggested. "You just need to have faith."

Fallon did not bother replying.

The snow had finally stopped the next morning, leaving drifts waist-high in places across the frozen marshland. They had searched the surrounding area carefully but had been unable to find Swane and Dina. Padraig had sent birds in all directions but even they had turned up nothing. All they had found were the bodies of Swane's army. All those who had run off after the battle had frozen to death. It was unpleasant but at least it solved the problem of what to do with the survivors.

"We have to have them. Until we know they are dead, we are not safe. And then there is Kemal. Without him, how do we stop the Kottermanis?" Fallon snarled.

"They can't get out of Gaelland. We can send out messages across the country and catch them later. But we can't stay out here," Padraig said calmly. "The cold will start to kill the men and we have other problems we need to solve back in Berry. The country is yours now. It needs food, it needs law and order and it can't get either of those things if we are slogging around Lake Caragh."

Fallon knew the wizard was right but it was still a bitter draught to swallow. Victory had been sweet but losing Swane again had tainted it.

"Right. Break camp. We head for Berry," he said.

*

Fallon waved at Bridgit and Kerrin, rushing forwards to embrace them while Caley gamboled around them, barking to join in, while the crowds cheered the returning men.

He picked Bridgit up and whirled her around.

"Put me down you great fool! You'll hurt yourself!" she cried, but there was a big smile on her face as she said it.

Fallon eased her down and laughed, only a little breathlessly.

"Enjoy this while it lasts, because we have a mountain of problems," she said softly.

"I know. But let's at least enjoy today. At least I have returned with more food for the winter," he said. "As long as everyone is happy to eat horse."

Bridgit pulled a face. "I don't think anyone is happy to eat horse," she said.

"Well, the wagons are full of them. Hundreds broke their legs in the battle and had to be killed, or froze in the night. We'll have to thaw them out but they'll all go in the pot."

"And what about the rest of the country? Didn't Swane strip the east of food for his army? And isn't the west in an uproar as well without the nobles? And what are we going to do without Kemal?"

"Tomorrow," he said firmly. "The least we can do for these lads is roast a few horses and have a party!"

"You and I have very different ideas of what is a party," she said with a shake of her head. "We have so much to do."

"Did you need me, Dad? Did you keep yourself safe?" his son demanded.

"I wish you could have been with me but you were needed here, to keep an eye on your mam. You know she gets into trouble without me," Fallon said with a wink, picking up his son.

"That's right, only the other way around," she said.

Fallon tousled his son's hair and put him down. "We just need to kick over a few rocks and find where Swane, Dina and Kemal are hiding," he declared. "Then we can make Prince Cavan's dream of a better Gaelland come true."

Bridgit stepped closer to him. "So I take it you're not still having those dreams where you have destroyed Gaelland with your choices?" she whispered.

"Not since the battle," Fallon said, running his hands down her back. "Since then I've been having very different dreams."

"That's enough of your blarney," she said, with a smile. Fallon released Bridgit reluctantly. "I'll start my hunt for Swane tomorrow. At least Berry is safe now."

*

Munro looked down the street outside his shop. He had been followed for the last two days but he had easily spotted the watchers' clumsy efforts. They had seemingly given up today but he was still wary. "This changes nothing," he said.

He had made it back to Berry long before Fallon and his men. He had heard news of the battle won by Fallon but nothing of Swane and Dina. He had ordered his men to keep working and gathering information, because he knew someone would want it, at some time, and pay handsomely for it. Then had come a message from Dina, brought to him by a magicked bird. They had escaped the destruction of their army and were traveling south, to Lunster. There the Duchess had friends and they would sail for Kotterman, where they planned to return with a Kottermani army under their control, then unite the two countries into one Empire, ruled by them.

It was ambitious but she promised him untold wealth if he undermined what Fallon was doing and prepared for their return.

"Winter is biting," Munro said. "And hunger will be biting deeper. They will have to send huge amounts of food to the east of the country, if there is not to be a huge famine there. We shall whisper that they are selling it and making themselves rich, while keeping the best for themselves."

"They brought in a herd of horses, as well as hundreds of dead ones loaded into carts. And they had all the supplies they captured from King Swane as well. That much food, as well as that fresh meat, will go a long way to feeding the city," one of Munro's lieutenants muttered.

"Not if most of it has to be sent out again. And that is perfect. Everyone has seen how much food arrived in the city. They will think they are getting more. But when they get nothing, or even less, then the disquiet will grow. When the bellies rumble, then the people grumble. All we have to do is help that along," Munro said. "Repeat a lie often enough and people start to think it is the truth. So get out there."

CHAPTER 30

"Fallon, you need to wake up," Bridgit shook his shoulder until his eyes opened. She had not wanted to wake him, because he'd looked tired, despite the brave face he was putting on things. But there was so much to talk to him about before he rushed off to begin hunting for Swane.

He sat up, rubbing his eyes, and she handed him a warm tisane. He normally didn't like those but she had packed it full of honey because she needed him wide awake.

He drained it and she saw his eyes widen.

"What is it?" he asked.

"I know you liked the idea of this Ruling Council, because it meant everything was not resting on your shoulders. I thought it was a good idea as well but we made some bad decisions. We let Prince Kemal escape. We have to be better now. We don't just have Berry to worry about, we have the whole country. You already said the western towns are falling apart without anyone to tell them what to do. And, if I know Swane, the east will have been left in a mess. It could be even worse there."

"So what are you saying?"

"I think we need to take a stronger role. Nola is consumed with worry about Brendan, because he can't shut down the anger inside him, while Riona is happy to laugh along with Devlin rather than look at the serious side of things. And as for Gallagher—"

"I know. They are all struggling," Fallon said. "And you are right. I need to lead them more."

She hesitated. "Don't you mean *we* need to lead them?"

"You need to rest and take care of the baby. We can't risk that," he declared.

"I'm sure I can handle sitting and talking," she said testily.

He pulled on a shirt. "We both know it is more than that. Long days of work and worry. I can't let you go through that. Don't fret, now that Swane is defeated, Aidan's words won't come true. I can do this."

She was not convinced but he was like a man on a mission, rushing around, getting ready to leave.

"Fallon, sit down and talk for a moment," she said.

He shook his head. "No time now. Talk later," he said as he hurried out the door.

CHAPTER 31

Fallon tapped the map of Gaelland that was stretched out on the table before them.

"We'll start at Meinster and work from there. If Swane and Dina aren't there then we keep going, until we find them. Padraig and his wizards will open up gateways for us to travel through and then bring us back."

"We need to send not just soldiers but priests and food to every major town. Then we can spread the word that anyone who is running out of food can go to one of the big towns and at least they will not starve," Rosaleen said.

"And the villages?" Nola asked.

"We leave them for now. There's just too many. Besides, there will be many villages that don't even know what has happened," Bridgit said. "Some of them probably still think Aidan is King but it's probably better that way. They are used to getting through the winter without anyone helping them anyway."

"None of that matters until we have Swane," Fallon said gruffly.

"It all matters," Bridgit said crisply. "We can't let the country slip into chaos, like Rexford."

"How bad was that really?" Riona asked.

"Well, the manor was stripped and the people almost rioted. Those who had lorded it over the others were lynched and there were scores of fires as people took revenge for years of misrule.

197

Pretty much like every party night in Baltimore," Devlin said, looking around the table with a grin.

"We have to win them over. They have to trust us," Bridgit continued, ignoring him.

"If we come bearing food, they have to like us," Gallagher said. "And we bring them news that Aroaril is stronger than Zorva, and has won the battle."

There was a short pause.

"How do we get the food to them? We can't get carts through an oak tree gateway, only what can be carried," Padraig warned. "And we can't hold open a gateway for too long. Even with a wizard at either side, it is exhausting."

"Horses," Nola said promptly. "They can carry it through and then become the food as well."

"Wait," Fallon said. "Obviously any horse killed in the battle might as well go into the pot but the ones we captured are warhorses, the only ones we have. We might need them."

"We will need people alive enough to ride them more," Nola said tartly. "And won't they just sit around all winter, eating their way through fodder that we don't have?"

"It doesn't matter. We shall still need them. The Kottermanis are still out there and a few hundred cavalry could be all the difference. No, we have to keep as many as possible."

"Well, should we not put it to a vote? There are seven of us for a reason, after all," Nola said reasonably.

"But I am the leader of the army and it is my decision to keep the horses for that. We captured some cart horses as well, those can go through if need be."

"But there's two score of cart horses but hundreds of warhorses," Nola protested.

"My decision is made," Fallon said. "If we still had Prince Kemal, maybe we wouldn't need to worry about cavalry but you decided it wasn't important to guard him."

Bridgit winced at the expressions on her friends' faces and composed herself as both Nola and Riona looked at her appealingly. Her first instinct was to keep the people alive, not the horses, but Fallon was right in that they could need a cavalry force against the Kottermanis. And she had just spoken to Fallon about taking a stronger stand in the Ruling Council. It hurt to go against her friends but she had to back her husband, even if she was not sure he was right.

"I think Fallon is right. We keep the warhorses back for now. And we can always use them later, if things get truly bad, or they begin to sicken," she said.

Fallon slapped the table. "Once we get Swane and Kemal back we can think again. They can't escape Gaelland in this weather." He pointed out the window, to where a fine snow was falling. "We just need to kick over enough stones until we find them."

*

"I never thought I would be glad to see the back of that place," Swane said, as Lunster slipped over the horizon.

"I never wanted to see it again and I was delighted to leave it the first time, let alone this time," Dina countered, drawing her cloak closer around her as the raw wind pushed icy fingers underneath.

"Are you sure this was the best ship we could find? It would barely be allowed in the docks at Berry," Swane sniffed, looking up at the rough sail as it pushed against the creaking mast.

Dina grimaced. She had known that her underworld contact was gone, captured by Fallon's men, but she had thought it would be much easier to find some of her former servants and use their knowledge. Yet much had changed since she had been away and it had proved almost impossible to find anyone she knew. Rather than bribe their way onto some proud trading vessel, they had to scour the harbor for something suitable. That was not easy, as most traders stopped sailing through the winter and had hauled their ships out of the water to work on the hull and refit everything that had broken during the sailing season.

The only thing that looked remotely suitable and nearly seaworthy was still a poor choice, a coastal trader that had seen better days. But, between Swane's powers from Zorva and the assorted powers of the remaining wizards, who had recovered on the journey south, they were confident they could get across the sea safely. Rather than bother with bribing the captain, they merely grabbed his family and gave him a choice – help them or see his wife and children sacrificed to Zorva. In a short time they saw the ship refloated, filled with food and enough of a crew rounded up by Kane and his handful of guards to enable them to sail in darkness with the rising tide, slipping out of the quiet harbor without anyone asking questions.

Yet the ship was hardly comfortable, while the wailing of the crew's families imprisoned in the hold, hardly made for a peaceful trip.

"Should we not just begin to sacrifice them now?" Swane grumbled, fondling the bone knife he had made from a wizard's leg to replace the crude wooden one he had first used.

"We need the sailors," Dina cautioned, delighted that he was still seeking her advice. That had been her greatest fear, he would think himself invulnerable with Zorva's power and then she would be at his mercy and in danger of ending up on the sacrifice table herself. "If we start killing their families then they could do something foolish. Better to save them for when we might need them, if Finbar cannot keep us safe."

Swane nodded, although she could see he was not happy.

"I will remember this," he said viciously. "And when I rule the Empire, I shall live a life of luxury such as nobody can even imagine."

Dina nodded thoughtfully, although she reflected that she could imagine a pretty luxurious life. That was, after all, the only reason she was doing this. That and revenge on Fallon, of course.

"The Empire will welcome us into its heart, not knowing that we are the poison that will destroy it from the inside out," she said.

"I cannot wait to get there," Swane said fervently. "If only to get off this stinking tub."

CHAPTER 32

Feray smiled broadly and fought to keep a tear from her eye as the sailors bowed as one, before cheering her name to the heavens. With the Emperor's approval, she was letting these brave men go home, after delivering them their promised reward. Each man received a bag of gold, equal to five years of normal pay and more money than almost all of them had ever seen before.

"You have been honored by the Emperor himself and he knows your bravery in risking the seas to deliver warning of the Zorva-worshippers. In the spring, I shall call on you to come back with me, as we go to reinforce my husband's men and to drive out the scourge of evil from the Empire's newest province!" she told them loudly. "Tell your friends and family of how Gaelland is now part of the Empire and you helped make it that way, and how my husband rules it in the Emperor's name. But do not mention anything about the Zorva worship. The Emperor will be most displeased with any who spread fear that way!"

Some of them looked somewhat bewildered, although the quicker-witted among them quickly whispered the explanation.

"Fine sailors, but they look a bit foolish," Durzu remarked from behind her shoulder.

She did not bother to turn around. He had insisted on accompanying her and she had not been able to refuse. It was a curious case as to who had more power. If Kemal was here there would be no debate, while if she had no children then he would clearly have the power but she wielded the power of her sons, the offspring of the Crown Prince. That put her as Durzu's equal, although he would not take orders from her. He had been expecting she would give a speech to the sailors, so speak she had. If he had not been there then she would have spoken to them quietly, emphasizing that they could not say anything at all. She hoped that message had got across in the way she had spoken to them but it was impossible to know.

"The fact they got us here through terrible storms reveals their quality," she said stiffly.

The sailors now lined up and servants deposited bags of money into their hands. Each one bowed their head to her and she smiled at them, particularly the ones who knelt to bless her.

Durzu took a step closer, until she was forced to turn her head to look at him. He was half a head taller than she was and loomed over her deliberately.

"My father might have swallowed it but I do not believe your story," he said softly. "My brother has made a mess of things and you are trying to get him out of it. You will fail and your punishment will be terrible, while your children will not survive. But you can save them. All you have to do is tell me the truth and I shall see you protected."

She laughed scornfully in his face. "I do not need protecting," she said.

"But you will," he said, his lips compressing into a thin line. "The only way for your children to live is to abandon Kemal to this filthy province and move into my household. As my wife, I will protect you and your sons. But, as the wife of a disgraced Crown Prince, their lives will be measured in days."

Feray felt her hands clenching into fists. "My husband will deal with you, when I tell him of this treachery," she snarled. "And if you were not surrounded by guards I would deal with you myself!"

Durzu shook his head. "This is a one-time offer," he said. "I will not be able to protect you once the truth comes out."

"The truth is already out," she lied back fiercely. "And I would not trust you even if you had not already shown your treachery. You had better pray for mercy when Kemal catches up with you."

His guards took a step forward as her voice rose, while Gokmen and Gemici both strode over to stand with her.

"Are you all right, Highness?" Gemici asked. "Is there anything we can do?"

Durzu smiled thinly and offered her a slight bow. "Farewell, dear sister. We shall talk again, under different circumstances," he said, then turned on his heel and strode away.

"What was that about, Highness?" Gokmen asked.

Feray locked eyes with them both. "Go home and find your families. But, for Aroaril's sake, make sure none of these sailors says anything. The wrong word in the wrong ear could end us all. Prince Kemal's brother longs to replace him and will seize on any chance. I spoke to the Emperor and he believed my story about Kemal staying in Gaelland to fight the Zorva-worshippers. If we can just keep the men quiet until we sail, then we can put everything right."

"They understood. But I'll talk to them, just the same," Gokmen agreed.

She smiled. "Thank you both. My husband will be most grateful. Aroaril willing, we can come through this."

CHAPTER 33

Fallon leaned up against the tree. "So how does this work again?" he asked nervously.

"There's magical woodland spirits that open a door in the tree if you know the secret knock," Devlin suggested.

"How about we be serious?" Fallon suggested.

"It's quite simple," Padraig said airily.

"Really? I seem to remember not too long ago you couldn't find your own arse with both hands and a map," Devlin said skeptically.

"Well, I could make an exception for you, Devlin, and leave you lost somewhere between here and Meinster, trapped forevermore inside a tree," Padraig said.

"How about we concentrate on everyone getting there safely and in one piece," Fallon said.

Padraig sniffed. "We have long known that oak trees, being the longest-lived in Gaelland, are especially in tune with magic. And they seem to know where other nearby oak trees are, so they can pollinate each other."

"What?" Brendan asked.

"So they can have a good tree shag. You know these oak trees, they like to get a woody," Devlin said with a leer.

"One more jest out of you, Devlin my lad, and I'll make sure you end up coming out of two different trees," Padraig said sharply.

Devlin held up his hands in mock surrender but Padraig still gave him a long stare before continuing.

"We use that magical affinity and the knowledge to jump from tree to tree, fixing the location of each in our mind, keeping them in the right order. Then, when we have reached our destination, we use the magic to turn the oak wood into something more insubstantial, so that it effectively opens up a doorway that we can step through, holding it open with an oaken staff from the first tree. Now, it is most important that you do not let go of the staff, for then you can become lost in the journey forever. Understand?"

"Not really. I think I preferred Devlin's stories about magical spirits and a secret knock," Brendan rumbled.

"Well, no matter how it works, let's get going. We don't have much daylight," Fallon said and signalled to the waiting men.

"Right. Meinster it is. Now, getting back is a little trickier. I shall open a gateway each day at noon and push an oaken staff through. Knock three times on the staff if you want to come back and I shall bring you through. But be quick, because opening a gateway is bloody hard work."

"Come on, let's get it over and done with," Fallon grunted.
"Wait here until I signal it is safe."

Following Padraig's instructions, he grabbed the staff, took a deep breath and stepped into what his eyes told him was a solid tree. But instead it felt like he was pushing against a gentle breeze as he closed his eyes and walked forwards, going hand over hand along the staff until he came to the end. He opened one eye, worried at what he might see, only to find himself in a completely unfamiliar park, surrounded by tall buildings. He let go of the staff, knocking it twice with his shillelagh. Almost instantly, men began to pour through, some of them with their eyes closed, others with wide eyes. He counted a hundred of them and then tapped the staff three more times. Instantly it withdrew back into the tree. Then he pressed on the trunk experimentally, only for it to feel and sound solid once more.

"Right, let's see what we can find," he said. "And hope to Aroaril it is Swane."

*

Bridgit looked down at the map and rubbed her temples. Fallon was right in one way. Ruling a country was not just about sitting and listening and talking. She had a throbbing headache and none of what she was looking at was doing anything to make it easier. Winning the rest of the country had created a huge problem. Between Fallon's march through the west and the supplies he captured from Swane, Berry had plenty of food for the winter. But nowhere else did. So she had to work out rations for them and how much she could spare and still keep Berry going.

"Bridgit, we have another delegation of merchants," Nola said, interrupting her thoughts.

"Are you sure it's not just the same one coming back time after time?" Bridgit asked.

"I wish it were. But it appears they are taking it in turns, to put more pressure on us," Nola sighed.

Bridgit snorted. "I could just about recite my speech to them in my sleep by now. I suppose I shall have to do it again."

"Any word from Fallon?" Nola asked hopefully.

"I wish! Nothing yet." Bridgit paused and looked at her friend. "How is Brendan? Anything changed there, after the battle?"

Her friend shook her head, and then the tears began to spill down her face. Bridgit leapt up, forgetting about the endless scrolls filled with lists of food and towns and people and embraced Nola.

"I am sorry, what is it?" she asked.

"He is worse after the battle, not better. His sleep is tormented by dreams and I am afraid to wake him, for fear of what he might do. He is even quicker to anger than before. It is like he has been taken over by another man."

Bridgit patted Nola's back and murmured soothing words, although she had no idea what could be done, other than wait and hope. Under all the violence, the old Brendan had to be lurking. Surely, with time, he would come back? But when? After all, they were all losing their patience and snapping at each other.

Then the door opened and she turned to see Riona bustle in. "Bridge, the merchants are waiting," Riona said, jerking her thumb over her shoulder. "We need you out there. Nobody can calm them down like you can."

"Go, I am fine," Nola said, her streaming eyes giving lie to her words.

Bridgit sighed. She treated the merchants like the crying children she had dealt with in Kotterman. It seemed to work.

"All right. I just hope Fallon finds Swane soon. And the money the Guilds took," she said.

*

Fallon slammed his hand on the table.

"Where is Swane?" he snarled, looking around the grand hall of Meinster castle.

The assembled men looked terrified, but none answered.

Fallon had found Meinster slumbering in blissful ignorance, still thinking Swane was marching triumphantly on Berry and they were about to be restored to power. Nobles, senior priests of Aroaril and Guildsmen alike were wandering around or relaxing in Meinster's castle, gorging themselves on hoarded supplies and indulging themselves with painted mistresses while people shivered and starved outside. It had been like old times' sake for Fallon, spotting the former cronies of King Aidan. But while he captured them easily, there was no Swane, Dina or Kemal. There was barely even any money.

"Prince Swane left to march on Berry and we have not seen him since," the head of the Bankers Guild said plaintively.

Fallon smiled. It was not a nice smile and he could tell that by the way the room recoiled from him. He stared at them in loathing. Plump old men, made fat by the suffering of others and willing to embrace the Dark God and human sacrifice if it meant they could keep worshipping their real god: money.

"You know that Swane was sacrificing children to Zorva?" he asked conversationally.

"We heard ... stories. But we never witnessed it, nor did we take part in anything like that," the Banker declared, perspiring lightly.

"How about you, Archbishop Kynan?" Fallon asked. "Did you not take some oath to serve Aroaril and protect this country against the Dark God? I seem to remember you lecturing my village about the love of gold being the lure which Zorva uses to hook foolish hearts and minds. Obviously you knew what you were talking about."

"I do not answer to the likes of you," Kynan said fiercely.

"Yet you will answer to Aroaril. And right soon," Fallon told him. The Archbishop shrank back, pulling his rich robes around him, while the assorted bishops with him quaked in their seats.

Fallon glanced over at where the nobles glowered at him. "What say you, Lagway and Maeyo? Are you innocent? And you, Rork? Do you remember what I said I would do if I caught you working with Swane?"

The younger noble actually started shaking and Fallon felt his control slipping. "I promised that people would stop talking about what I did to King Aidan and instead start talking about what I did to you," he snarled. "Unless you bastards start talking, *right now*, I will make that come true."

The room was silent, except for Rork's harsh breathing.

Fallon turned to his men. "Get me rope, and bring the rest of them," he ordered and his men jumped to obey.

The nobles and Guildsmen were hustled up onto the castle wall. It was nearly as impressive as Berry's castle, not that it had ever been attacked. Below, quite a crowd had gathered. The sudden appearance of armed men in one of the city's parks had excited plenty of attention and they had naturally followed Fallon to the castle, where others had joined them to see what was going on.

"Please, I did nothing!" Rork babbled as he was dragged to an embrasure between two wide merlons. The long rope was tied securely about the thick base of the merlon and then around his neck.

"Sir, it's a long rope. Do you want it cut?" a young soldier asked.

Fallon shook his head. "No, that will be perfect," he said and pushed Rork up onto the low stone embrasure, where the noble had to clutch onto a merlon to keep his balance.

"Now, start giving me answers or he will be executed. And then I'll keep going until someone finally talks," Fallon told them.

For a long moment nobody said anything, then Archbishop Kynan pushed his way to the front. "You cannot do this. You have no right. He is a noble of this land and you are nothing!" he said angrily.

Fallon whipped out his shillelagh and jabbed the tip into Kynan's face, smashing his nose and sending him reeling backwards.

"Anyone else?" he asked disdainfully. "Feel like telling me where Swane is?"

When only shocked silence was his reply, he slipped his shillelagh away and drew his dagger, stepping up behind Rork on the deep embrasure stone.

"This noble allied himself to Zorva and sought to sacrifice all your children to the Dark God!" he roared down at the crowd. "This is the punishment for his evil!"

"No, please, I did nothing!" Rork begged, then he screamed as Fallon sank his dagger into his side and then ripped it across, spilling his guts open.

As the noble tried to both hold in his intestines and hold onto the wall, Fallon kicked him off the embrasure.

The screaming Rork, his guts unraveling and dropping with him, fell for what seemed like an age, until the rope finally came to an end and the resultant jerk snapped his neck with a loud crack, silencing his cries. Fallon glanced down to see Rork's body dangling almost to the ground, his intestines a series of coils around his legs, slipping the rest of the way.

The crowd had drawn back in horror and now stood in silence, staring up at the group of figures on the wall. Fallon nodded in satisfaction. The story would grow with the telling and hopefully people would speak of how he had hanged Rork with a rope made from his own guts.

He turned back to the assorted Guildsmen and nobles. The closest of them took half a step back.

"So who is next? Or do you want to talk?" he asked.

"We don't know! We never even saw Prince Kemal! Swane and Dina left to march on you and we have not seen nor heard of them since then!" the Banker gabbled as hands reached for him.

Fallon held up his dagger, dripping with Rork's blood and the Banker looked as though he might faint. "I swear on my life!" he pleaded, urine staining the front of his rich robe.

"You don't want to swear to Aroaril?" Fallon asked dangerously. "How about if we go into church?"

The Banker's eyes flickered left and right, looking for a way out. "Swane made us pledge ourselves to him and Zorva," he mumbled. "We had no choice!"

"You always have a choice. But you chose to help him butcher children to the Dark God if he got back on the throne."

The Banker said nothing. But Fallon could see the truth on his face, on all their faces. What was a few peasant children to them? After all, they had sacrificed hundreds of them over the years, letting them die from starvation or neglect, all in the name of profits. Fallon was sick of them.

"So none of you know anything?" he asked.

"That's right!" the Banker nodded desperately, the others joining him, all but Kynan, who still held his bleeding nose.

Fallon looked into his beady eyes and then up at the rest of them. "I believe you," he said finally. "But what use are you to me now?"

"We can do so much more for you. We worked together before, when the Duchess ruled Berry. We can do so again. Let us help you rule Gaelland—"

Fallon had drawn his sword and now slammed it down onto the Banker's head, smashing open his skull and spattering brains across the stone battlement.

"I do not want, nor need any of you," he told the shocked men. "You have been a cancer in Gaelland for too many years. Today, we cut it out. Get more rope. We shall hang them all."

They wailed and pleaded as they were dragged away. Fallon was unmoved, although he turned when someone grabbed his arm.

"Fallon, you cannot do this!" Gallagher exclaimed.

"They are scum and deserve to die. We thought that often enough, when we served Prince Cavan," Fallon retorted.

Gallagher shook his head. "Think of your soul. This is not a good deed."

"We have to do it," Fallon said coldly. "Let go of me."

Gallagher shook his head but then Brendan grabbed the fisherman's arm and pulled his hand clear. "They are lucky to die like this. If I had my way I would beat in their brains," the smith rumbled.

Gallagher wrenched his arm free. "You don't see it, do you?" he said sadly. "We are becoming like them. Aroaril would not be pleased—"

Fallon gave him a shove. "If you don't want to help, then go and search the castle," he said roughly. "We have work to do."

He could feel his friend's gaze on his back but he did not turn around.

*

When the last of them was dangling from the castle walls, he left two squads of his men with Gallagher, searching through the castle for anything useful to bring out and give away to the ordinary people, and took the rest of the men into the town.

He had not expected wild cheering but thought people would have been happy to see them, for they had freed Meinster from the greedy bastards now swinging gently on the castle walls. But people rushed inside, slamming and barring doors against them.

Fallon stalked through the streets, getting angrier as he went. He needed to find some reliable men, honest men, that he could trust to look after the town but he had no idea where to start. In the western towns, and indeed most of the eastern as well, the priests were the first port of call. But here, the churches were empty of priests and instead the crowds of people praying for deliverance screamed when they saw him appear and raced out of other doors.

He finally called a halt. "Time for a new approach, lads," he said. "If we can't find the good people of Meinster, we can at least make sure the bad ones don't rule the place once we are gone. We'll round up all those who have profited from Meinster and Swane."

So his men kicked in doors of the biggest houses, dragging out crying and begging men away from their families or discovering young women living alone, surrounded by luxury that would have astounded half of Berry. Most Fallon recognized as the mistresses that he had thrown out of the castle only a few turns of the hourglass ago. His men dragged out the furniture, the clothes and the food into the main square, to go with what was being carried out of the castle. The mistresses were indifferent to the news their noble lovers had been hung from the castle walls but driven frantic by the thought of losing all they had been given. Fallon was unmoved by their pleas, although he had to order some of his men not to let them secrete a few choice items away, for the young soldiers were not immune to the begging of beautiful young women. But Fallon looked at them and saw younger versions of Dina and had no sympathy.

As for the men they found in the richest houses, he ordered them questioned and found they were merchants, men who had grown fat and rich at the expense of others. Well, today it was time to pay the price.

"Drag their furniture, food and clothes into the main square and everyone else can take what they will," he ordered. "The men can join their masters on the walls."

Men and women begged and pleaded, or raged and protested, but he ignored all of them. The merchants' families wailed and wept as their husbands died, one by one, on the wall but he fancied the town would be far better without them. If he had left them there, they would have taken the place of the nobles within a quarter moon and the ordinary people would have been no better off. At least, this way, the town would have a chance.

When taking the piles of food, furniture and clothing to the main square had been finished, he had two of his men help him up onto a table. The doors were all barred to him but he knew people were listening and watching out of half-opened windows, wondering what he would do next.

"People of Meinster! Swane is dead!" he shouted at the top of his voice. He didn't know if that was true but they needed to hear it. "Earl Meinster is dead, as is every other accursed noble and Guildsman who has robbed you for all these years and secretly worshipped the Dark God. You are now free and your children are safe from their blood sacrifice. Come, take what you need to survive the winter. We shall return, with more food and priests, real priests of Aroaril, to help you rebuild. No more will you have to pay huge taxes, nor will you worry about being thrown out of your home or off your land. You will have a say in running this town and ruling this country. Rejoice, for the darkness has been lifted!"

His last words echoed around the empty streets but nobody came out. He jumped down and signalled to his men.

"Come on, lads. We shall go back to the castle and see what they do now. They won't come out while we are around," he ordered.

He didn't like the lack of response but, he reflected, Meinster had not been plagued by attacks of false witches and fake selkies, like the rest of the country. These people had not known anything but the iron fist of Earl Meinster. They would thank him later, he decided.

*

The huge pile of goods they had placed in the main square all disappeared overnight but the town seemed to be empty and still again the next morning.

"Let's get out here, lads. It was too obvious for Swane to come back here. He's probably hiding in another town," Fallon ordered.

None of his men were sad to go, because the big town was eerie, with nobody moving around. In fact, Fallon was uncomfortably reminded of some of his dreams, when he was looking over a destroyed Gaelland.

"What about the bodies?" Gallagher asked, the first words they had exchanged all day.

"Leave them there," Fallon said immediately. "They will remind the people of what was done and keep them out of the castle as well. I'd rather we didn't return to find we missed one noble's relative and they had set themselves up like a king in there."

Gallagher did not look happy but Fallon turned away from him. They marched through the dead streets towards the park where they had emerged the day before. Fallon could feel the hairs on the back of his neck itching as hidden eyes stared at them. He was looking over his shoulder when he saw a stone arc out of the sky towards him. He skipped aside and it bounced off the cobbles.

"Watch out! Shields up!" he roared.

The men reacted instantly and just in time, as half a dozen other small rocks bounced off shields.

"Shall we go and get them, sir?" one of his young sergeants called.

Fallon was tempted but there were only a few rocks and there were plenty of people in the town who did have good cause to hate him and his men – the mistresses of the nobles and the families of the merchants, for a start.

"Leave them. But quick march away," he said.

It felt like a retreat, when he should have been cheered every step of the way. *They will grow to understand what we have done here and when we return, they will be grateful,* he told himself.

CHAPTER 34

The journey was one endless nightmare for Kemal.

It was bad enough at the start, even though the boat skipped through the water thanks to magic. Certainly the food left plenty to be desired. A cauldron of oatmeal was kept bubbling through the day and chunks of rancid meat and dried vegetables were thrown in there. Swimming in grease and tasting foul, it was nonetheless the only thing to be eaten on board.

Kemal and the sailors were getting two bowlfuls a day, morning and night, to keep them going. The families were getting only one.

Swane, Dina, their guards and wizards, however, were dining on fish and even seabirds that they were bringing in to roast and devour. Although he was treated as a valuable prisoner, he received none of that food, although he begged and threatened.

He thought that was unpleasant but he forgot about eating when the storms came, black clouds filling the horizon and lightning flashing. Kemal was at first afraid they would all die in it. But, as soon as the storm was sighted, a family was brought up from the hold and, along with their sailor husband and father, sacrificed to Zorva. Then Kemal began to pray the storms would kill them all.

He had been barely aware of what Swane and Dina had been doing to the wizards during the snowstorm near Lake Caragh. The cold and the reaction to his own escape had left him fading in and out of consciousness. There was no such escape this time.

He heard and saw everything on that small ship. The first time he watched a screaming child have its heart ripped out he tried to attack them, only to be restrained by guards. The second time, they locked him in the hold with the women and children and he watched the children weep as all heard the death cries of friends above, while blood dripped through the planking into the dampness of the hold below. He heard the sailors above crying out in fear as Swane promised this would be the fate for any who did not obey his orders. He cursed Swane and Dina and their guards, swearing that he would see them pay for their crimes if it was the last thing he did, but his words were ignored.

A mother grabbed his arm, making him jump.

"Save us, please," she whispered, her eyes huge in the dim hold. She had two sons, both young, one tucked under each arm.

He found himself imagining Asil and Orhan there. He had been horrified to learn Aidan wanted to sacrifice his family but that had been lost in the tidal wave of hatred he had felt for Fallon. Now that anger seemed misdirected. If he had not been so determined to gain revenge, he could have made a deal with Fallon, turned Gaelland into a Kottermani province and wiped out Swane's evil. Instead, all he could do was reflect bitterly on the mistakes he had made. If they had the power to move storms, then maybe they had the power to seize control of the Empire. He shuddered at the thought of such sacrifices going on in every town across the Kotterman Empire.

He searched quickly through the hold. He needed a weapon and he could do what Fallon had done, release his anger in an orgy of violence on these evil murderers. In the corner was a broken oar. It was not much but Fallon had apparently had little else.

"Be ready to act when I do," he told the families. "Unless we take this ship back, they will kill us one by one. Better to take some of them with us."

Swane wanted him for his evil plot. Well, if he could not destroy Swane then he could ruin his plans by fighting and dying. And at least it would be a clean end. The women and children looked terrified rather than ready to fight but he had no time to inspire them further. The foul rites were over above, because they could hear the splash as bodies were hurled over the side, then the hold cover was thrown open and a pair of guards jumped down.

"Now!" Kemal roared and sprang at them.

The first guard went down as he crashed the oar shaft over his head and Kemal grabbed for the man's sword, only for his limbs to freeze. He struggled to move but he was locked in place. His mind sent commands but his arms and legs would not obey them.

Instead he was hauled out on deck. The feeling returned to his arms and legs but the guards held him helpless now.

"You fool. Did you really think your cheap heroics would succeed against the power of Zorva?" Swane asked him pleasantly.

"I didn't care. I just wanted to end your evil," Kemal told him.

"I think the Prince needs to be punished," Swane announced loudly.

"Kill me then, you filthy bastard," Kemal spat.

Swane smiled. "You are worth too much to us. No, I think you need to work for your passage. We are down a couple of sailors now, so you can work the ship."

"I will never do that. I don't care what you do to me," Kemal snarled.

Swane clicked his fingers and guards dragged over a handful of women and children.

"Let me make a bargain with you. Every day you do not work, we sacrifice one to Zorva in your name. Starting with today. How about that one?"

A guard dragged out a screaming child, a lad of no more than ten summers. His mother was going crazy, his father begging, while the families below were also crying and screaming.

Kemal was horribly reminded of the night when Fallon had done something similar to him. He had sworn to never give in again. He told himself these people meant nothing to him, that they would probably all die anyway. But while giving in to Fallon haunted him still, he knew letting a child die for his pride would never leave him.

"Stop," he said raggedly.

"What? I couldn't hear that," Swane said, with a half-smile.

"Stop," Kemal said louder, hating himself but hating Swane even more. "I will do what you wish. Leave the child."

Swane smiled widely and snapped his fingers. The crying families were hustled below and a bucket of seawater and a thick cleaning stone were placed in front of Kemal.

"You can start by scrubbing the bloodstains out of the deck," Swane told him.

Kemal's arms were released and he picked up the thick stone. He had seen his own men use them to scrub the decks clean, had even ordered them to go back and do it again when they had missed a spot but he had never dreamed he would do this. He was tempted to use it to smash Swane's foul head open but the guards held swords near the children, so instead he placed it on the wooden deck and began scrubbing it backwards and forwards. He could rub away the blood on the deck but he felt as if he could never rub away his hate.

*

Kemal was in agony. He thought he had been toughened by years of working with weapons but nothing had prepared him for manual labor. Every muscle ached while his hands were on fire, palms and fingers torn open by blisters. He was dumped back into the hold, in a world of pain, but gentle hands helped him, offering him extra food, binding his hands and rubbing cramping muscles in his back and shoulders. He could not even hold a spoon to force down the greasy oatmeal so someone carefully fed him, spooning the mush into his mouth. He finished the bowl and found himself weeping with gratitude.

"Thank you," he whispered, looking up at the face of the woman whose son had so nearly been sacrificed. "You are kind."

She looked away. "If you cannot work, then my son might die," she said softly.

That woke him up a little and he wanted to refuse her help – except he could not. His legs spasmed with cramps and she rubbed them, soothing the muscles until he drifted to sleep.

The second day was, if possible, even worse, but he used his hatred of Swane to push himself on, while the women and children took turns helping him and each day after that got a little easier as his body adjusted. He found himself developing a new respect for these people, the same people he had thought were far beneath him. They had dignity and humor and an unshakable spirit that not even this nightmare could break. They did everything to protect their children and keep their minds off the horrible fate that hung over them and he had to admire that.

As he got stronger, he began to plot again. Time was running out. White water foamed at the bows day and night, while the worst of the waves seemed to slip past. He had sailed between Adana and Gaelland five times now but this trip was passing far faster than any other. Forget about half a moon, it would be little more than a quarter moon before they saw land. He had to be prepared to act fast once they reached land. They had to have some plan to keep him quiet, for just a few words in Kottermani would be enough for the guards to swoop on Swane and end his foul plans.

"Land ho!" the lookout cried from the top of the mast and Kemal joined the rush to the rail as best he could, although he had a rope around his ankle that prevented him even throwing himself overboard to thwart their plans.

One glance was all it took. Adana was less than a day away. His big advantage was knowing the port, while Swane and the others would be ignorant. As soon as they passed inside the harbor wall, he could call out to the guards there, long before Swane and Dina would be worried about him escaping. That way the families would be safe and he took a few moments to imagine their gratitude at the way he had saved them.

"Prince Kemal. Almost home," Dina said conversationally.

Kemal glared at her.

"You make a fine servant. If only your people could see you now," she said mockingly.

Kemal looked down at his ragged clothes and swollen hands and smiled back. "And how are you going to explain this to my father?" he asked.

She patted him on the shoulder. "A good question," she said.

Kemal opened his mouth to answer but then everything went black.

*

"Is he asleep?" Dina asked, as they surrounded the fallen Prince.

Kane leaned down and slapped Kemal's face, then lifted up one of his eyelids.

"Nothing. The magic has worked, my lady," he said.

"Of course it did," Dina said dismissively. All was proceeding as she planned.

"Are we sure about this?" Swane asked softly, turning his body so the others could not hear what he was saying.

"How do you mean?"

"We are about to risk everything. If this goes wrong then we shall all be killed. Maybe we would have been better taking Gaelland and then trying to deal with them."

"And if all goes right, we shall rule the world! We have nothing to lose and everything to gain. These Kottermanis sit in their golden palaces thinking they are better than the rest of us. They will not see what is coming. With a little magic and plenty of convincing lies we can take their Empire. Is that not worth a little risk?"

Swane looked a little happier and she smiled at him, thinking that she was far better suited to rule than he was. But she needed the fool for a while longer.

"Finbar, when you are ready," she ordered.

The wizard, who still looked drawn and haggard, moved to obey. Even regular meals had not restored him to his usual condition and it was obvious that what he had gone through at Lake Caragh affected him still. That was why they had been forced to call on Zorva to save the ship from storms, rather than use ordinary magic, as planned.

The wizard passed his hands over the comatose Prince Kemal and his body stiffened in response. Then Finbar lifted up Kemal's tunic, took out a thin knife and dug it into Kemal's side. He tossed it overboard and then closed his eyes. Sweat broke out on his face and he gasped for breath as the wound he created healed over, but not entirely, looking for all the world like an old injury that had been inflicted half a moon ago.

"It will appear as if he is in a coma, and nothing any of the Kottermani physicians can do will restore him, until I release him," Finbar said wearily. "We shall tell them he was struck by a poisoned quarrel and they shall waste their efforts trying to save him from that."

"Excellent. We shall need only a few days," Dina said. "I will pick our target and then we just have to convince them. And I can be most convincing."

CHAPTER 35

"You killed them all?" Bridgit gasped.

Fallon shrugged. "Well, I wasn't about to leave them behind to cause trouble for us. Half of them only got out of Aidan's filthy chamber where he wanted me to offer Kerrin's heart to Zorva because they are cowards and ran rather than face me. It was justice, just delayed."

Bridgit had to resist the temptation to bury her face in her hands. "But to execute them all at once, and the way you did! Tell me it's not true you actually hung the Count of Rork with a rope made of his own guts?"

Fallon grinned. "No. But that's the tale people are telling then?"

She hit his arm. "Be serious! That's being whispered around the streets, and not the real story, that the nobles were made to pay for their crimes. We should have brought them back here, where judgment could be passed, and then they would have been taken out to their old counties and executed there, so the people could see their tormentors punished."

"Dead is dead. And don't forget how many of these scum have escaped us, one way or another. We couldn't take the risk," he argued.

"It's not about that. We are turning this country upside down and we have to be careful that we don't destroy it. People fear change anyway and we are taking away everything that is familiar to them. What we are removing was no good but until we replace it with something better, they are scared and rightly so."

"And you know what everyone in Gaelland is thinking?" he asked skeptically.

She grabbed his hand, wanting him to listen, *really* listen to her. "Yes, because I was one of them. Remember? I was terrified of change. I didn't want to leave my home, let alone my village. I didn't know or like the Duke of Lunster but when he disappeared I knew something bad was on the way and I hated the thought of something new and different."

"That was not the same," he said, his voice becoming gentler.

"But it is! That is being repeated in homes right across Gaelland. People are asking who the new ruler is and they are hearing stories of Fallon, who gutted King Aidan in front of a crowd, who hanged the old Archbishop and all the nobles, one of them with a noose made of his own guts. Then he went through the town and kicked people out of their homes and hung them too, if they argued with him."

"Now that was not how it happened!" he protested.

"I know that," she said, tugging on his hand. "But they don't know you like I do. We may have killed the nobles but there are still plenty of their supporters out there, people who made a good living from the King and his cronies. Yes, they are few in number but they are all loud and they are telling anyone who will listen that you are more dangerous than Aidan."

"What? I am the one who stopped that bastard from killing children!" Fallon cried.

"Listen to me!" she snapped. "They will see that and understand it. But we have to be more careful. We have to show that we listen and care, the way we did when people petitioned us. We have to travel around the country and do the same in every town, so they can see we bring justice and fairness to Gaelland."

He relaxed and pulled her into an embrace. "You are right. It is a good idea. But I cannot be sorry about killing those bastards in Meinster. I saw their faces leering at me under this very castle, when they wanted me to kill Kerrin."

She held him tight. "You are a good man. I know it, we just have to show the country that."

"Then we will." He stopped and looked at her sideways. "Are you doing too much? You are looking tired."

She forced a smile. "I am tired. But I would rather be busy than worrying about the baby. Running around and working hard seems to suit me, so I don't want to stop." She did not have to add the rest of it. He knew as well as she did how the last few pregnancies had gone, the early hope descending into fears, worries and finally blood and tears. This time was different – she was different – but she could feel the old fears lurking at the back of her mind, ready to attack if she let her guard down.

He ran his hand over her stomach. "You have to take it easier. I don't want you to do as much. Take the day off, maybe get some new dresses made," he said gently.

She hesitated. She had noticed how her clothes were becoming tighter around her middle, even accounting for the weight she had lost on that voyage back from Adana, yet getting new clothes would not only be a bad look in a city literally tightening its belt every day but would also be a challenge to the bad luck that had robbed her of every pregnancy but Kerrin. She did not know if she was ready for that.

"I can't take the day off. There is too much to do," she said.

"I won't allow it," he said firmly. "I could not forgive myself if something happened to you. Rest, spend time with Kerrin. Get more dresses made so you look good when we travel around the country. I will look after everything else."

"You can't do that," she protested.

"I can and I will," he retorted. "And that is the end of it."

She forced a smile. "Then I shall do so. And what will you be doing?"

"The same," he said grimly. "Hunting Swane and Dina."

*

"How many dresses do you need, my lady?" Munro asked respectfully.

"I think at least six," Bridgit said, after careful consideration. She had been unsure about Munro because of his connections to the nobility but having him watched and even followed for a few days had revealed nothing suspicious. It seemed he was nothing more than a dressmaker. "We shall be traveling quickly, and lightly, but we need to look respectable. People must take us seriously and they will only do that if we look the part."

"Traveling, my lady? In this weather? Where?" Munro asked, gesturing towards the horn panel that shook a little in the window opening as winter winds rattled around the castle.

"Everywhere," Bridgit said with a slight smile. "We go to spread the good news around Gaelland, that the evil King is dead and a new Ruling Council will bring justice to all, and that everyone can have a say in who is on that Council. And please, Munro, don't call me a 'Lady'. Call me by my name, Bridgit."

"I give respect where it is due, my lady," Munro said with a slight bow. "I call you that because you are that. Now, the dresses will be easy enough but when do you need them by? When do you leave?"

"As soon as possible. A couple of days, perhaps," Bridgit said. "But all six do not have to be ready by then. We shall travel by magic, so we can return and pick up others."

"Would you like the dress colors to reflect the traditional colors of each county, my lady? To show you pay them respect?"

She thought for a moment. "That might be a good idea," she conceded. "We are replacing the nobles but people still associate themselves with their county and its flag."

"Excellent. So where are you visiting first, so I can make dresses to match?"

She hesitated for a moment but if she was going to have dresses resembling the counties, he had to know which ones. "Meinster, Lagway and Maeyo," she said.

"Excellent. I am sure you will make a good impression, my lady."

She turned to look closely at him. "Munro, you must be a man who hears many things as you travel around the city and speak to your many clients, many of them rich and important people."

He gave her a strange look and she suddenly felt uneasy. "I mean no disrespect," she said. "I am not asking you to betray confidences you might have overheard."

"Thank goodness for that, my lady!" Munro said, with a shaky laugh and she joined him.

"No, I just wondered what the word on the street was about the King being replaced by our Ruling Council?"

Munro shook his head sadly. "Alas, my lady, I would have no idea. I pay no attention to idle gossip. All I care about is making people happy."

She looked at him for a moment before nodding. She was tempted to ask him more questions but she had so many other things that needed to be done, she could not waste more time here. She was barely sleeping as it was. "Of course. Forget I asked. Now, about the dresses?"

Munro bowed again. "I shall work as fast as possible, my lady. I shall have at least a few ready in two days' time, and the rest a day later."

*

Munro gazed out over the city, ignoring the houses below but instead trying to gauge the weather. It was blustery and gray but no more than an average Gaelish day. Crucially, it did not look like snow was on the way. He turned to the small wooden boxes he had lined up along one wall of the top story of his house. It smelled in here, the sharp tang of bird guano, but he only came here a couple of times a day and used a thick, lined trapdoor so that the smell, and the birds, stayed up here.

Bridgit had given him valuable information and he would have really liked some magicked birds to spread the word around. He had a couple left for the longer trips but, just to be on the safe side, he would send regular ones as well, pigeons trained to return to their homes. He had men in each county seat around the country, keeping an ear out for what each noble had been doing, and he was used to getting regular reports from them. He occasionally sent back instructions and this was one of those times.

He wrote a series of identical messages in his neat handwriting, making it as small as possible, then used a pinch of sand to dry the ink before rolling each tiny scroll up and placing it in a series of oilskin pouches, ready for fastening to the birds' legs. He would send out two birds for each town, and a third magicked bird to the first three towns Fallon and Bridgit would be visiting. The message was simple: stir the town up against them. The Ruling Council wanted to make the common people think that killing the King and his nobles was good for them and ordinary citizens would now get justice. Well, when they called for petitioners, it would be Munro's people and not the commoners who came forward.

He watched the birds flap away and turned to another scroll, one that Duchess Dina had given him on the night she left Berry. It was addressed to Keverne, the Lunster guard she had seduced and tricked into killing her husband. Keverne had bungled the job and now languished in a cell under the castle, along with the other guards who had disposed of the Duke of Lunster. Munro's instructions were simple: get the scroll and a set of lockpicks to Keverne and let him do the rest. It had taken a great deal of control for Munro not to break the seal and open the scroll to read what was inside, because not knowing something was like a thorn in his foot that stung all the time.

He had put this scroll aside because it had been too dangerous before and more important that he get Swane's hidden package out. But perhaps it was now time to deliver it. If the Ruling Council returned intact from the ambush he planned, they would discover death inside their own castle.

CHAPTER 36

"You look lovely," Fallon said.

"I know your hair is receding but I didn't realize your eyesight was going as well," Bridgit said.

"No, I am serious!" he protested.

"No, you are full of blarney, as you always have been," she said with a smile. "But thank you anyway."

"Can we get this over with?" Padraig asked. "It might seem simple but this is devilishly hard magic and I'd rather get it over and done with."

Bridgit nodded and took her place in the line. Padraig and two other wizards stood ready to open a gateway for this company of men, as well as the Ruling Council. Fallon had wanted to bring more but Padraig had drawn the line, saying keeping a gateway open for any longer was impossible. Just in case there was any trouble on the other side, a score of soldiers would be going first, with orders to make the area secure, then the rest would follow.

Bridgit had never traveled this way before and, although she knew Padraig and the other wizards had been sending people in all directions for days, she was still nervous. What if the magic did not recognize the baby and it remained behind when she traveled through? She almost stepped out of the line at that thought but Fallon gripped her hand and smiled and she took a deep breath. *It's just a fear. One of many you have faced down and defeated. As you will defeat this one.*

Then the line moved forwards, not slowly, as men almost running through the tree, and she did not have time to worry, just to follow them. She emerged in a strange park.

"It's quick but I don't know if I will ever get used to it," she admitted.

"At least there is nobody around," Fallon said. "Form up! Straight to the main square!"

Meinster was quiet, doors and windows shut, and the few people they saw on the street scuttled off to safety as soon as they spotted armed men.

"The people must still be afraid," Fallon observed.

Bridgit caught sight of the bodies swaying gently in the wind from ropes fastened to the castle battlements. "I can't think why," she said crisply. "Get some men to cut those down. And send more around the town shouting out that we shall be hearing petitions. Anyone who has a case, or who needs something, should come to the main square."

Fallon turned and she caught his arm. "And they are to say that nobody will be harmed," she ordered. "Not one person will be hurt this day."

"What if we find Swane here?" Fallon protested.

She held up a finger. "Don't be foolish. Not one person. Understand me? We have to show these people that we are here to help them, not harm them. We are different from Meinster and Aidan and all the others."

Fallon looked exasperated but she fixed him with her favorite stare and he nodded with bad grace.

"Not one person hurt. I swear it," he said reluctantly.

"Good. Now get working. It's freezing out here."

Some of the castle furniture had been returned to the main square, showing signs of being left out in the open. With the bodies cut down, tables moved to create somewhere they could all sit down – even if there were no chairs and they had to make do with heavy chests and the like – and a series of fires burning around the square, she was feeling much better.

"Let's see who comes forward. We just need one. After all, I can feel a hundred eyes on me now," she commented.

Yet, despite the soldiers shouting out that all were welcome to bring their grievances forward and have them heard, nobody appeared.

"Maybe we need to come back tomorrow," Riona suggested.

Bridgit was about to agree when she heard a door open and a young man strode across the cobbles towards them. Soldiers stepped aside for him and he avoided the fires to approach the table.

"Greetings," Fallon said, although she could hear him forcing warmth into his voice. "Who are you and what petition do you bring?"

"My name is Cleary and I demand justice for a wrong done to me," the young man said in a clear, loud voice.

"Then tell us of this wrong and we shall see if it can be put right," Fallon said, with far more enthusiasm.

"Three days ago, a man came to our town, sent his men to break into my house and throw me and my sisters onto the street, then he had them drag out all our furniture and he hung my father, an innocent merchant who had done nothing to break any Gaelish law all his life. My mother died yesterday of a fever she caught while waiting through two freezing nights for my father's body to be returned, and our furniture replaced. You now sit on some of our items and the man who murdered my father sits with you. I demand judgment on him." He put his hands behind his back and stood with a strange expression of satisfaction on his face.

Bridgit hung onto Fallon's arm but it took all of her strength to restrain him. "Be calm. Remember, all are watching," she hissed urgently.

She could see Fallon's face was pale, while there was a terrible tension in the square as the soldiers grasped what had been said. The wrong word or action and things could get bloody.

"For Aroaril's sake, leave it to me," she told him.

For a moment she thought he was going to jump to his feet anyway, then he nodded jerkily and she turned her attention back to their accuser.

"Tell me," she said, her voice cutting through the square, "how did you father make his money? Was he a supporter of Earl Meinster? Did he sell goods to the Earl?"

Cleary's face showed a mixture of surprise at not being arrested and, strangely, of disappointment. That made Bridgit even more suspicious of what was going on here.

"My father was a law-abiding man. He sold goods to anyone, including the lawful lord of this county," he said. "And for that he was murdered!"

"Did you know Earl Meinster worshipped the Dark God? And that your money was bought with the blood of innocents?" Bridgit shouted. "Did your father reveal that Earl Meinster insisted his trusted circle also had to convert? Have you lost a sibling lately?"

Clancy's self-satisfied look faltered.

"So you will give me no justice? You will let a murderer walk free?" he cried.

Bridgit slapped the table. "We need you to take an oath before Aroaril, before we can give you judgment," she said.

Clancy hesitated, then he threw up his hands. "I should have known better than to expect justice from the likes of you! We would have had more justice from the old King!"

"Only if you paid for it!" Bridgit shouted.

Clancy looked furious and then stormed away.

"Laugh," Bridgit said to the others. "Laugh at him."

It took a few heartbeats for them to begin, and it was a strangled sound at first, but it swiftly spread and by the time Clancy got out of the square, it was echoing with laughter.

"Send ten men to follow him. I want to know where he goes," Fallon instructed.

Bridgit leaned back, then remembered her makeshift chair had no back and pulled herself upright. "Right. Hopefully we can get some real ones now," she said.

A handful of people began to appear but, rather than complaints, they were a litany of demands. A succession of young women wanted the money that had been promised them by nobles or bishops or, sometimes, both. Other people wanted money that was owed them by the late Earl for food or drink or services.

"We do not have money to hand out," Fallon told them, time and again. Bridgit nudging him in the ribs every time he looked like he was going to leap into action.

"That is the first duty of a ruler, to pay their debts," one young woman declared, wrapped in a heavy fur cloak that would have cost as much as a small house. "How am I to survive the winter?"

"I am sure you will keep warm somehow," Bridgit said sardonically. "One way or another."

"And you complain about me not being nice!" Fallon muttered as the woman flounced away.

"Are there no normal people in Meinster? It's as if there has been some town discussion to make us look bad," Bridgit muttered.

"That's ridiculous. They had no idea we were coming," Fallon said.

"Or did they? That Clancy didn't just offer himself up for punishment," Bridgit said darkly. "I reckon he had friends waiting to rescue him if we did anything."

"Maybe we should go looking for them."

Bridgit blew on her frozen hands. "No," she decided. "It will only cause more trouble. We need to get out of here. The Earl of Meinster was clever enough to have created a class of people beholden to him. They may not mourn him but they mourn his money. We are doing nothing here except freezing our backsides off. I can barely feel mine."

"I'll feel it for you, if you like," he said with a wink.

"Well, at least you can still make a jest," she said. "At least you haven't been slaughtering so many at all the other towns you've been searching."

"But we haven't found Swane, either. Not even a word of him. He must be hiding somewhere quiet."

"You will find him," she said.

"We'd better. Or places like this will be the least of our problems."

CHAPTER 37

Dina prepared herself with extra care as their ship was escorted into Adana's harbor by a pair of large ships bristling with Kottermani warriors, with enough bows trained on them to turn them all into hedgehogs if the wrong order was given. If that was not enough, huge crossbows up on the harbor wall had followed their progress, the spear-like missiles looking as though they could tear the hull out of their ship. Of course, they had enough magic to turn them into splinters and the harbor into a death pit, but it was far better to let the Kottermanis think they had all the power. For now.

She put the finishing touches on her face as they tied up the ship, then walked out on deck to see a large company of soldiers, all of them again carrying bows, surround the ship on three sides. An impressively dressed officer stepped out of the ranks, a pair of shield bearers on either side, ready to protect him if necessary. He shouted something at them but they had no idea what he was saying.

"Does anyone speak Gaelish?" Dina called, standing at the bow and keeping her empty hands in plain view. She was wearing the best dress she had and it fitted her like a second skin. She had gone hungry on the trip across from Gaelland to make sure it flattered in all the right places.

"Who are you and why do you come to Adana?" the officer demanded, his Gaelish thickly accented but understandable.

"I am the Duchess Dina of Lunster and with me is King Swane, the rightful ruler of Gaelland. We have rescued Prince Kemal and

233

seek to return him to his father, the Emperor of Kotterman," she called, making sure her words were clear and well-spaced.

The soldiers did not move, proving they did not speak Gaelish, but the effect on the officer was dramatic.

"You have Prince Kemal? Where is he? Show him now!" he demanded, the agitation showing in both his voice and face.

Dina spread her hands wider. "Alas, he is sick and cannot wake. He was injured and, we believe, poisoned. We have kept him alive but hope you might have doctors who can help."

She watched the officer carefully and saw a variety of emotions flick across his face. Worry replaced shock, then a different expression wiped that out before a mask fell into place. She liked the glimpse he had given her – it looked a lot like raw ambition. "Please, we need to see the Emperor," she added. "We have vital news about a rebellion in his new province of Gaelland. Can you escort us to his court?"

The officer looked up at her. "I can do better than that. I can take you to him, for he is here in Adana. But, we have had word that Aidan was King, until he was killed for worshipping Zorva, while his son Swane is steeped in evil. So I think you had better explain, before I let you anywhere near the Emperor. And be convincing."

He snapped an order and bows bent, a hundred arrows pointed at her. Finbar and Swane had promised they could protect her but that was scant comfort at such a moment. Still, she had risked her life on convincing a man so many times that once more was nothing.

She laughed lightly. "History is always written by the victors! That is a story told by cruel rebels, who want to pretend that their murder and pillage is not evil but somehow approved by Aroaril. King Aidan was overthrown by a vicious rebel called Fallon and the Kottermani force led by Prince Kemal was defeated and captured. We managed to save the Prince and brought him here. There is no Zorva-worship going on, it is a simple rebellion. If one of your other provinces rebelled, would they say the Emperor was a fair man or would they paint him as a demon?"

The officer nodded slowly but still looked unsure, so she used her final card. Apparently none of the Kottermani priests could use magic, so it followed that they could bluff their way past their conversion to Zorva.

"Take us to one of your churches. Bring us inside and let us pray to Aroaril if you doubt us," she challenged, saying it as if it were nothing, as if she and Swane had not worried over it all night.

The officer nodded again, but this time decisively. "Follow me. Try to attack and you will die."

"We shall do only what you say. Sir, may I have the honor of your name?"

The officer rattled off a string of orders in Kottermani before turning back to her.

"I am Prince Durzu, brother to Kemal."

Durzu's men brought a litter and Kemal was carefully loaded into it and carried through the city. Kane and his remaining men handed over their weapons, then joined the procession, while a company of Kottermani guards watched the ship and the sailors. Dina had no fear of the sailors betraying them. Not only did none of them speak Kottermani but she had taken special pains to remind them of their fate should they try anything.

Prince Durzu lingered near them and she caught him gazing at her figure-hugging dress several times. Perfect. She tossed her hair at him.

"You must be shocked to see your brother like this. I am sorry we had to meet under these circumstances," she said gently.

His eyes flicked across to Kemal's litter and she saw a sudden hunger in there.

"If anything was to happen to him, who would be the next in line to the throne?" she asked innocently.

Durzu turned back to her. "That would be me," he said.

"Oh, I hope it does not fall to you like this," Dina said, her voice throbbing with sympathy. Durzu looked like a perfect candidate but she would need to keep an eye on him before making a final decision. This was not to be rushed. After all, she had thought Fallon could be used. It wouldn't do to make such a mistake twice.

"What has really happened in Gaelland then?" Durzu asked.

"What have you heard?" she replied swiftly. "I thought nobody else could have made it through those winter storms."

"Prince Kemal's wife Feray returned perhaps a moon ago, bearing strange tales. She insisted that Prince Kemal sat on the throne of Gaelland but needed an army to help secure the country from the evil you were creating."

Dina made herself look shocked, although it was not all acting. "Oh, I fear for the future of both our countries if she is believed. We shall all be in grave danger."

"So the truth is different?"

"Most different," she said heavily, then sighed. "But I say too much. This is for the ears of the Emperor alone. Will Feray be at our audience?"

"I am sure of it," he replied.

"I am looking forward to it," she said, which was only half a lie.

*

"Highness, the Emperor himself requires your presence, and that of your sons."

"Thank you, Ely," Feray said. The girl was not the perfect servant but having her around allowed the boys to keep working on their Gaelish. They were going to need all the mastery of that language if they were going to get Kemal out safely.

The past moon had been both relaxing and frustrating. Their home was more than comfortable but seemed empty without Kemal there. All they could do was wait for the winter storms to blow themselves out in Gaelland. Now and again the Emperor wanted them to attend some meaningless meeting but, other than that, the only other thing of interest was trying to avoid Durzu.

"What is it this time – did they say?" she asked.

Ely did not reply and she turned on the girl. "Well, speak!"

"A party of Gaelish has arrived, Highness," Ely replied softly.

Feray felt fear close its icy grip around her heart. How in Aroaril's name had they made it across the sea? Then she pushed that aside. All that mattered was they were here. If it was to negotiate for Kemal's life, then things were about to get far more complicated. Suddenly boring did not seem so bad.

"Who?" she demanded.

"I do not know, Highness," Ely said softly.

Feray suppressed the urge to shout. "Get the boys dressed, then send a message to Gokmen," she ordered.

She saw the fear in Ely's eyes and shook her head irritably. "It is nothing to do with you, nor your mother or sister. It is about our survival. Now move!"

Ely scuttled off and Feray grabbed a piece of parchment and scratched out a quick message. If all else failed, she would stall for time and then set sail back for Gaelland with just her crew. They would be loyal to her and, while she did not know how she could free Kemal with just a handful of men, it was better than falling into Durzu's clutches. Besides, there was more than a thousand Kottermani soldiers being held captive somewhere. As long as she was free, there was still hope.

She finished the message and looked at herself carefully in the mirror. She just had to keep her head and she might still come out of this. The Emperor was going to be more inclined to believe her than some strange bunch of Gaelish. Just lie and deny and everything could be fine.

Her sons hurried in, dressed formally and she banished all worry to paint a smile on her face.

"Come, we must not keep your buyukbaba, the Emperor, waiting," she said briskly, handing the parchment to Ely at the same time. "Make sure it gets here, and then hurry back here and pack. Warm clothes only, as if we were going to Gaelland," she instructed.

Ely nodded and hurried off, then Feray took her sons' hands. "Be brave," she said to no one in particular.

*

"You may not enter here until you have proved yourselves," Durzu said, halting them all before a magnificent building.

Dina could tell it was a church to Aroaril but nothing like the brooding stone squares that served as places of worship in Gaelland. This had a soaring dome and fine chased stonework all around. It was the sort of place she would like to have as a palace.

After the cold of the pass across the Spine, she was enjoying the heat of Adana and even the smells were more pleasant than most of the stenches that infested Gaelish towns.

A senior priest of Aroaril, presumably their equivalent of an Archbishop, judging by his golden robe, brandished a golden sunburst at them – the symbol of Aroaril.

"You must embrace our holiest symbol and swear your loyalty to Aroaril. And if you fail to do so, God's vengeance will be the least of your worries," Durzu said casually.

Dina glanced around at the massed guards and made herself smile. "Of course. But perhaps your Archbishop could bless it himself, so there can be no doubt how holy it is."

Durzu nodded and had a rapid-fire conversation with the Archbishop, who responded by holding up the sunburst, his voice booming out in what had to be a prayer. He sounded almost like Kynan, the former Archbishop now languishing in Meinster, except for the language barrier.

The Archbishop held the sunburst out towards them and Dina accepted it eagerly, although her hands were itching at the thought of what might happen. She could not suppress a gasp of relief when it did nothing to her and she smiled at Durzu hastily.

"It is surprisingly heavy," she said, then closed her eyes and muttered what would sound like a genuine prayer, although it did not follow anything she had ever said in church before. You never knew, after all. Then on impulse she quickly kissed the sunburst and handed it on to Swane.

She gave both Durzu and the Archbishop a dazzling smile as Swane muttered his own version of a prayer, before it went around the small group of Gaelish. Kane was the last to hold it and he walked forward to hand it back to the Archbishop, who buffed it with his sleeve, as if the Gaelish had dirtied it. They had, but not in the way the old fool thought, she reflected.

The Archbishop and Durzu had a hurried conversation and then Durzu nodded.

"You have proved yourselves. You cannot have worshipped Zorva and also held that relic as well," Durzu said. "Enter, and greet your Emperor."

Again, Dina was the first to cross the threshold, her body braced for something horrible to happen – but nothing did. She smiled and led the way into the cool gloom of the huge church. It was a relief to get out of the sun but not as much of a relief as knowing that Aroaril had no power here and they were safe. She could feel hundreds of eyes on them as they strode through the soaring room and she reveled in it.

Then there was an explosion of sound from one side of the room and she glanced over to see a well-dressed woman stride forwards, shouting in Kottermani.

*

Feray joined the throng of courtiers and nobles and satraps hurrying to obey the Emperor's summons and join him inside the church, but she made sure she lingered behind. She wanted her first sight of the Gaelish to come before anyone else. There were several ways out of the church and she also wanted to be sure she knew where they were.

"Stay close to me. If I say run, follow me instantly. Do not ask questions," she told Asil and Orhan.

They looked shocked and troubled but, after all they had been through, they merely nodded. She squeezed their hands, wishing she could do more to tell them how much she loved them and how proud she was.

She made a point of speaking to a number of clerks to see which ships were provisioned and ready for the long sail back to Gaelland and where they were berthed. The clerks were delighted to receive such attention from a future Empress, but she stopped the conversation instantly and pushed through them when she saw the light-skinned Gaelish walk into the church.

They were led by a woman, and for a moment she was afraid it was Bridgit, with Fallon right behind – but then she saw it was Dina and Swane. She did not know the Duchess well but she could never forget Swane from that horrible time when she had been strapped to an altar and expected to see her sons sacrificed to Zorva.

"Stop them! They are Zorva-worshippers! Protect the Emperor!" she screamed, pointing at the group of Gaelish.

The guards that lined the long path to the altar reacted instantly to the phrase that had been drummed into them from the moment they had taken their oaths. Swords hissed out of scabbards and they instantly blocked the way, advancing on the Gaelish.

"Kill them quick!" Feray bellowed.

She was not even thinking about the need to protect her lies from the Emperor, just to destroy these Zorva-lovers.

"Stop! They are under my protection!" Durzu jumped in front of the Gaelish and the guards instantly checked.

Feray pushed her way through the guards to face Durzu. "Don't be a fool, these Gaelish have used dark magic to get here – there is no other way to get across the ocean. They worship Zorva and will destroy us all," she cried.

Durzu held up his hands as the guards tightened their grips on their swords.

"They have just passed a test set by the Hierarch himself," Durzu snapped. "They have held Aroaril's Crown, our holiest relic. And they stand in Adana's greatest church, all without the slightest discomfort. How can they be Zorva-worshippers?"

"Perhaps their dark powers protect them. Or perhaps because we have turned the church into a throne room, and there is no power here. But I saw them. They have been sacrificing children. Their hands are covered in blood. We have to destroy them now!" Feray insisted.

Durzu shook his head. "Powerful words, wife to my brother," he said. "I might be more inclined to believe them if you had not already lied to us in this very church."

"What do you mean?" she asked indignantly. "These Zorva-worshippers have addled your mind and clouded your eyes!"

"Really? So is that not your husband, my brother, Prince Kemal, lying in that litter, brought here by the Gaelish you say are evil?" Durzu challenged.

The Gaelish parted before her, revealing a dozen slaves who carried a comfortable litter. A familiar face was lying upon it and she gave a wordless cry of shock and horror. She would have rushed forwards but Durzu caught her wrist.

"I think we need to hear from these Gaelish as to why he is here and not, as you said, ruling Gaelland," Durzu said.

Feray could not answer, her eyes and attention were solely on Kemal. "What have you done to him?" she demanded.

"He was struck by a poisoned quarrel and has not woken since," Durzu said maliciously. "Perhaps he never will."

"Get them away from him! And get some physicians down here. Now!" Feray ordered. She could sense that everyone in the converted church was watching them closely, wondering which side to support. She turned to Durzu. "This is a trick," she said urgently. "They are using Kemal to get close to the Emperor—"

"They have no weapons and can do nothing with all the guards around," Durzu said dismissively. "As for the doctors, they must wait until the Emperor gives the order. Or have you learned nothing in all your years at court? A few moments more will mean nothing for Kemal, for he has been like this, without change, since they arrived on the ship."

"You will pay for this," Feray swore, her voice shaking with her anger. She glanced over at the Gaelish, watching her warily and obviously unable to follow what was being said, and glared hatred at them. "He should have been seen by the Emperor's best men the moment he was on Kottermani land. He is my husband and I should have been told immediately!"

"Why? So you can warn your sailor lovers?" Durzu sneered.

Feray lashed out at his face, a backhand blow that was almost too fast to see. Unfortunately, Durzu was just as fast as Kemal and caught her hand.

"Kemal will have you killed for this!" she snarled.

"I think he will have his own problems," Durzu said and pushed her away, snapping his fingers at the same time. "I wonder what my baba will think of the message your slave was taking through the city?"

Feray staggered back, not just from his shove but because she saw a miserable-looking Ely being held by a pair of Durzu's burly guards.

"How dare you touch my servant? I won't wait for Kemal to wake, I shall have your skin for this!" she snarled at Durzu.

"Guards, if you have any love for my husband Prince Kemal, you will strike down those Gaelish now!"

The Emperor's men tensed, while Durzu's men drew their swords.

"Peace!"

The word thundered through the church, the perfect acoustics of the space making it echo around.

Everyone looked to where the Emperor stood on the dais before the altar. "Swords down! Approach me!" he ordered, then sat down abruptly.

"You will pay for what you have done," Feray vowed.

"You will pay first," Durzu fired back.

"And release my servant. Now!"

Durzu smiled mirthlessly. "With pleasure. I already have the message she was carrying."

Feray signaled to Ely and the girl ran to her side.

"I will keep you safe. Do not fear," she whispered. Explaining the scroll was the least of her worries right now but she felt no fear, lost in a white-hot anger.

*

Dina watched with interest and growing pleasure as Durzu defended them from Feray. She could not understand a word they spat at each other but the meaning seemed obvious. Feray wanted them dead but Durzu did not. It looked like a classic power struggle and she could see it going their way. A younger brother, hungry for a taste of power ... it was almost as if Cavan and Swane's struggle was being replayed here.

The more she saw, the more she liked about Durzu. They had planned to let the situation develop naturally but this was too good an opportunity to miss. She eased closer to Finbar as all the shouting went on. The wizard was looking tense, gathering himself to protect them all with a burst of magic and he glanced around wildly as she touched his arm.

"Look for my signal and be ready to bring Kemal back so he can answer questions, but only the questions we want him to answer," she whispered.

Finbar smiled briefly, as if remembering their plan, then nodded.

She stepped away from him as the Emperor intervened, bringing the room back under control. The two sides shuffled apart and the way down to the altar opened up again. She glanced at Swane and saw the fear on his face and almost laughed. This was when she felt most alive!

Durzu led them almost all the way to the steps up to the altar, before falling to one knee. Dina instinctively did the same, as did the other Gaelish. Swane was a little slower but she grabbed his hand and tugged him down just a heartbeat after the others. She inspected the Emperor carefully while appearing to look at the ground. He was a powerful man running to fat, which she liked. He was used to indulging his appetites, which was exactly the sort of man she had exploited many times over the years. She waited for her moment to make her move.

*

Feray seethed as she hurried down the path to the altar, making sure she got there before Durzu and the Gaelish scum.

"Exalted One. These Gaelish are here to trick you. They are followers of Zorva, the ones who tried to kill your grandsons and me. They have Kemal under some sort of spell and we must destroy them now," she said urgently.

The Emperor pointed at Durzu. "What do you say, my son? Why have you brought them to me?"

"My father, may I present King Swane of Gaelland, his consort the Duchess Dina of Lunster, and their servants and guards. They have traveled here, at great personal risk, to return my brother to his father," Durzu said, his voice echoing around the church as the litter bearers approached, laying Kemal down at the foot of the stairs.

The Emperor snapped his fingers and robed men rushed out of the crowd to fall to their knees beside Kemal and begin to examine him.

"Tell me how my son Prince Kemal came to be like this and what you are doing here," the Emperor demanded.

"Exalted One, they did this to him. This is all a trick. They must be killed now," Feray insisted.

Durzu jumped to his feet. "They have passed the test of Kotterman's Hierarch. Do you dare say that I would bring someone before my father who is a risk to his life?"

"They have blood magic! They sacrifice children! Kill them!" Feray cried.

"They tell me that Feray is lying and Gaelland is not ours," Durzu snapped back. "And I have here a message her servant was carrying to the sailors who brought her here, asking them to prepare to sail her back to Gaelland."

"That is a fake! He attacked my servant in the street and now he plots against his brother. He wants Kemal dead and the title for himself!" Feray shouted, looking around the packed nobles.

"Enough!" the Emperor slapped the arm of his throne. "How can we be sure who is telling the truth, or if the truth lies somewhere in between?"

Silence fell across the church. Then a new voice spoke out.

*

"I can help," Dina announced, standing and easing into the space between Feray and Durzu. She bowed deeply and straightened up to see the Emperor's lecherous eyes roaming up and down her body. She smiled broadly. She had bedded more revolting creatures, but not for many years.

"What are you doing?" Durzu stared at her in shock.

Feray was meanwhile saying something in Kottermani, her hands chopping down violently to make her point. Dina guessed it was a request for her head.

"Tell your father that Prince Kemal can solve this riddle. He will speak truth that will make all clear," she said.

"Are you mad?" Durzu asked, his eyes widening.

"Please trust me, and translate for me. I would not do this unless I knew exactly what Kemal was going to say," she said confidently, almost arrogantly. "Remember, we have more to lose than you."

She could see his worry but met it with a serene smile, making it look as if everything was going according to her plans. Which it had been. But now it all depended on Durzu. If he trusted them now, then he was theirs.

Durzu hesitated for what seemed like an age, then he nodded and shouted out something in Kottermani. Dina nodded to Finbar.

*

Feray put all her fear and anger into a plea for the Gaelish to die, to pay the price for what they had done to Kemal, and to her, when Durzu interrupted.

"The Gaelish have offered an answer. Let Prince Kemal solve this," he announced loudly.

She was so shocked she stopped in mid-sentence. "What?"

"My brother knows better than anyone what happened in Gaelland and the truth of whether these Gaelish can be trusted. We need to hear from him."

Feray agreed but could not believe Durzu would suggest such a thing. It had to be a trap. And yet, how could she refuse to hear her husband's words? She was backed into a corner.

"If he can be woken, then of course we need to hear from him," she said.

The Emperor clapped his hands together. "It is decided. Our best physicians will work on my son. Everyone else will be confined to houses in the city and watched by my guards until Prince Kemal is awake. Durzu, take these Gaelish to the house where the other Gaelish escaped and make sure they do not leave. Food and drink is to be brought to them but nothing else, understand?"

"Of course, Father," Durzu said with a florid bow.

'Exalted One, I wish to stay at my husband's side, to help him recover," Feray said, also offering a bow.

For a moment she though the Emperor would refuse, then he nodded. "Agreed. But do nothing to distract my physicians," he said.

She smiled and bowed again but her mind was racing. What were the Gaelish playing at? She offered a heartfelt prayer that Aroaril could watch over Kemal and bring them all out of this safely.

*

"What is your plan? How can you know what my brother will say?" Durzu demanded as he escorted them through the city.

Dina smiled. The relief at having faced the Emperor and not just survived but set their plan in motion had her almost giddy. "Prince Durzu, I thank you for the way you stood up to the madwoman Feray for us. You showed true nobility and it seems to us that you should be the man most ready to take on the burden of the Empire, not your foolish brother."

Durzu grunted. "Your flattery is nothing more than I can hear from a score of others. I have risked much to submit to a ruling by my brother."

"And you will not be disappointed," she said smoothly. "We shall bring Kemal out of his sleep in a natural-looking way but he will be unaware of what is going on around him and will only reply to questions that you put to him. Should Feray question him, it will be as if she speaks in another language."

Durzu's eyebrows rose but his face did not change otherwise.

"He will speak the truth but we shall give you the questions that will make him give answers that will see him disgraced and humiliated. Feray will be imprisoned and you will take his place as Crown Prince," she said.

Now he smiled. "I like the sound of that. But we need to discuss things further. Nobody gets something for nothing, least of all the throne of the Kotterman Empire. What is it you want in return?"

Dina gave him her sweetest smile. "Let us not make promises now, when we have nothing to offer. We shall give you the questions you need to destroy Kemal and then, when you are the new Crown Prince, let us talk again. We can help you but first let us prove ourselves."

She felt Durzu's eyes on her, weighing her up, and she kept her expression light, as if his agreement was not something on which their lives depended.

"Agreed," he said finally. "So, what are the questions I need to ask my brother?"

Dina smiled gently, although inside she was celebrating. Durzu was hooked, although he did not realize it yet. And just wait until he got a taste of blood magic …

CHAPTER 38

"If we have to listen to another bastard complaining that some noble broke a contract with them and they need a bagful of gold as compensation, I am going to get out my shillelagh and show them how a contract really gets broken," Fallon snarled.

Bridgit slumped into a chair and rubbed her eyes. "I know our tour did not go as well as we hoped—"

"Didn't go as well as hoped? It's like the whole bloody country is against us! It's like we robbed their children, rather than freed them from a mad King and his Zorva-worshipping nobles!"

It had been another fruitless trip to eastern Gaelland. It seemed each time they held a Petition Day, it had been swamped by ridiculous complaints from petty merchants and the like, with scarcely an ordinary person in sight.

"We knew it was going to be difficult. Berry was different because the people had a chance to know you, and Aidan told them you were a hero. He had you get rid of the Snatchers and the last of Swane's men and make out that you had saved them. Of course they believe in you. But the rest of the country has never heard of any of us. They are going to be suspicious," Bridgit said soothingly.

"It's more than that," Fallon insisted. "I smell the hand of Swane in this. Somebody is hiding him and he has stirred up what's left of his father's supporters. All those blood-sucking bastards who have lived off the sweat of others, who are terrified we are about to end their cozy little world, are trying to make us look bad."

"Are you sure? The chances are Swane is dead and we shall find his frozen body when spring comes and the snow melts," Devlin said. "After all, the trail has gone cold. *Really* cold!"

"This is not the time for jokes," Fallon said from between gritted teeth.

"Perhaps we need to pray to Aroaril for guidance. He might well reveal where Swane is. Once we subject Swane to the church's justice, the protests will calm down," Gallagher suggested.

"Honestly, we are going to have to kick you off this Ruling Council if you don't stop blabbering on about Aroaril all the time. This is the same God that you said could not be trusted to organize Midwinter drinks for the ale-brewing Guild," Devlin said.

Gallagher thumped the table with his fist. "You mock Aroaril at your peril. I opened my heart to him and my life has changed—"

"Oh for Aroaril's sake, will you two shut up!" Fallon roared, then pointed a finger at Gallagher as the fisherman opened his mouth. "And I know I shouldn't have said that. But we have bigger issues. I think we need to impose our rule on those towns properly."

"And how do we do that? The way you went looking for Swane in Meinster, with ropes and swords?" Nola asked pointedly.

"We have men from all over the country in my army. We go around and discover which ones came from the different towns and then send them back there to keep order. We can also trust them to keep an eye on things," Fallon said.

"What about the training? We have to get ready for the Kottermanis to arrive in the spring. Those men hold the key to preparing our new army," Brendan said.

"And who guards the city? You will leave us very short here in Berry," Riona said. "And you know what happened last time."

"We have to find Swane and stop what he is doing," Fallon growled. "If we have men in every town, they can keep eyes and ears open for word of Swane and Dina. It will be a long winter, someone will talk in exchange for food or gold. And if they have Kemal then we have a weapon to use against the Kottermanis. True, the training will take longer but if we find Kemal we can use him to buy us more time. And then we can throw everything back into getting an army ready. Meanwhile, Berry is safe," Fallon added. "The city is behind us. They are accepting the rations we have given them and, after all, it is winter. People don't want to roam the streets looking for trouble when the frost is trying to freeze their noses off."

"Still, it is a risk. We could send everyone out and still not come across a trace of Swane or Kemal and find ourselves with a mob of half-trained fyrd, not an army, when the Kottermanis arrive," Nola said doubtfully.

"We have to take risks. We need Kemal and I want Swane. Everything else is just talk," Fallon said harshly.

"We need to trust in Aroaril. He will show us the right way," Gallagher said complacently.

"Will you listen to yourself for a moment?" Brendan roared, thumping the table. "Who are you and what have you done with Gallagher?"

"He's shagged all his brains out, that's what the problem is," Devlin observed.

"You will show some respect, or you will be punished," Gallagher warned.

"How? Fiery lightning bolts from your arse? You're not the bogging Archbishop, you're just married to her!" Brendan snarled. "If you can't offer us anything beyond praying, then you need to piss off, Gall."

"Brendan!" Nola exclaimed.

Gallagher scraped his chair back and stood. "I understand your pain, Brendan. But I beg of you, open your heart and—"

"So help me, I will knock your teeth out if you finish that!" Brendan snarled.

Gallagher walked across to him. "I am not afraid of you, Brendan. My faith is my shield," he said calmly.

Fallon jumped up and stopped the fisherman before he could get close.

"Gall, please leave. This is not helping," he said.

"Maybe we need to get everything out in the open," Gallagher argued.

"No, you need to go. Now!" Fallon said forcefully.

For a moment Gallagher looked as if he would argue more, then he turned and walked away, shutting the door behind him.

"That's right. Run away back to church," Brendan rumbled.

"Stop it! Stop it!" Nola cried. "Could you just stop it? That is your friend and you chased him away!"

"He ran away himself. Nothing to do with me. He wasn't fit to be part of this Ruling Council anymore. And others could do well to heed that message."

"And who's that?" Bridgit asked sharply.

"Devlin never says anything serious. He needs to stop the jokes," Brendan said, slapping the table.

"And you threatening to hit everyone all the time is better?" Devlin sneered.

"That's enough!" Fallon cried but they ignored him.

"Do you want me to punch you?" Brendan threatened.

"Stop it!" Bridgit shouted but it was too late.

"That's it! I cannot take it anymore!" Nola cried and raced out of the room, tears streaming down her face.

"What is it?" Brendan asked, then swung around to Devlin. "See what you've done?"

"What he's done? You great lummox, can't you see it's you that has upset her?" Riona cried, hurrying after Nola.

"Where are you going?" Devlin called.

"To look after my friend. Which is more important than listening to this!"

"You need to control your wife," Brendan told Devlin.

"You know what your problem is, Brendan? You can't take a joke anymore," Devlin announced and also stormed off.

Fallon rubbed his forehead. "Do you plan to go anywhere, Brendan?"

"No, I'm staying right here and doing my duty," the smith said, thumping back into his chair.

"Well, we only have three of us left now. We cannot make a decision with just us three," Bridgit said.

"We can if the three of us say that is what we can do," Fallon pointed out. "And let's face it. What useful argument were we getting from the others anyway?" The more he thought about it, the less sense this Ruling Council was making. All they were doing was bickering and yelling at each other. Things were easier when he was making all the decisions. Yes, he had been terrified of Aidan's dying prophecy coming true but that had been proved false, the last spite of an evil man. He didn't really need the others. He would listen to Bridgit, of course, but that was all that was needed.

"They have worked well in the past and they will again," Bridgit said.

"Or will they? I can't see Gallagher waking up any time soon. His head is stuffed full of foolishness and we have to wait for that to drain out," Fallon said. "I say we vote now and then get something to eat. Brendan?"

"Agreed," the smith rumbled.

"This is ridiculous. Fallon, stop and think about it for a moment. We have to get everyone back in and do this properly."

Fallon gestured towards where an hourglass sat on a side table. "Time is trickling away and we have to act."

"How does the old saying go? Marry in haste and repent at leisure. This is not something that should be hurried."

"Well, we married quickly enough and look how well that turned out," he said with a smile.

"Can we just vote? I am hungry and need to go and apologize to Nola," Brendan growled.

Bridgit rubbed her face with her hands.

"Look, we send the men out now. If things start going bad here, we just get them back. Thanks to Padraig, we can move people around the country in the blink of an eye," Fallon said persuasively.

"I agree," Brendan said immediately.

Bridgit groaned, then threw her hands up in the air. "All right. Do it. But don't say I didn't warn you if we have to bring them back again!"

"It will be fine. Nothing to worry about," Fallon assured her.

"That's what makes me afraid," she retorted.

CHAPTER 39

"Prince Kemal is awake."

"Of course he is," Finbar muttered. "I was the one who woke him up."

Dina ignored the wizard and instead gave Durzu a dazzling smile. "Are you ready, my dear Prince?" she purred.

"I know what I have to ask. I don't know if it will work," Durzu replied.

"We have bet our lives on this. Feray will settle for nothing less. But we shall win and you shall get everything you ever wanted," she said, giving him another smile. Manipulating these men was becoming all too easy, she felt, although it was also tiring. She had just spent two turns of the hourglass reassuring Swane and now she had to do it all again to Durzu.

"And if I am announced as the next Crown Prince, what then?"

"Well, how about we prove we can help you before we go any further? We have a saying in our country: don't count your chickens before they hatch."

Durzu stared at her blankly. "What has this to do with chickens?" he asked. "I just need to know what my allies want."

Dina looked at him carefully and decided he was not going to be fobbed off with just a smile this time.

"It is simple. We want what you want," she said. "King Swane is a king without a country. We want your army to destroy the rebels and make Gaelland safe again. Then we can rule in your name, as valuable allies, sending you tribute and slaves."

"And that is all?"

"We want to be honored above other client rulers," she admitted. "But nothing more."

She knew Swane was eager to introduce Durzu to the powers of blood magic but she felt one step at a time was the better approach. Durzu looked at her carefully but she had many years of experience at hiding her thoughts from men and he finally nodded.

"Come then. My father does not like to be kept waiting," he said.

*

Feray was dreaming, being chased by strange creatures through a dark wood, something that made no sense because she had never been in a wood, dark or otherwise, although it seemed very much like ones she had seen from a distance in Gaelland. She had finally fallen asleep sitting beside Kemal's bed. If Kemal's words were to be the final ones in her argument with Durzu, she needed to be the first to hear them. But, despite all the potions the physicians poured down his throat and the poultices they strapped to various parts of his body, he had not stirred. Something touched her hand and she came awake, her heart racing, to discover Kemal had reached out.

"My love! Can you hear me?" she cried, holding his hand tight.

His eyes opened and he stared at the ceiling, saying nothing.

She stood, looking over him, so her face had to be filling his vision.

"My love, what is it? Are you in pain?" she asked softly, hoping the physicians would not hear, for then her chance would be gone.

But although she met his eyes, he looked right through her. He groaned, a deep, rattling sound, and tried to sit up, but fell back to the bed.

"What happened to you?" she persisted.

Again he did not answer her, merely tossed his head from side to side, drawing his legs up at the same time.

Feray was torn between continuing to speak to him in the hope of getting his story before anyone else – as well as telling him what she had told his father – and helping him in his distress.

Then the decision was taken out of her hands when he uttered a long wordless cry. The physicians could not fail to hear that, for they were just outside. Their lives may not depend on healing the Crown Prince but their status as Royal Physicians certainly would.

"Quick! The Prince is waking up!" she cried, just in case they were asked to report to the Emperor.

Two of them came racing into the room a heartbeat later and, although she eased backwards, she kept her hand entwined in Kemal's. The physicians tried to ask him questions, to which they received no reply, although they also listened to his heart and urged him to pass water.

"If he can't say anything, I doubt that is going to tell you anything," Feray said, but they ignored her.

"He is coming out of his deep sleep. We have brought him back from the dead," the older of the two announced. "We must tell the Emperor immediately."

Feray kissed Kemal's hand. "Come back to me, my love. Where does your mind wander?" she asked. But he did not answer.

*

Only the arrival of the Emperor forced her from the bedside. Kemal's eyes were still open and he was moving weakly, although not talking. The Emperor was accompanied by guards and two dozen senior nobles, most of whom had to wait outside.

To hear the physicians, however, it was as if he had made a miraculous return from death's door. She tolerated that but her worry turned to fury when Durzu and some of the Gaelish arrived.

"What in Aroaril's name are they doing here?" Feray thundered.

"I sent for them, because I was told my son was awake and talking," the Emperor said coldly. "We have agreed he shall speak the truth about them. Once I hear what that truth is, I will judge what to do with them."

She bowed her head in apology, although inside she was seething. "They were the ones who did this to him!" she insisted.

"Father, can I at least try and speak to my brother?" Durzu asked humbly.

"What good will that do? We have all seen that he is not capable of speaking," Feray snapped.

"You may try, my son," the Emperor agreed, as if she had not said a word. That hurt but she would not show the bastards a moment's weakness.

Durzu approached Kemal's bed, where the Crown Prince was still. "Brother, who rules in Gaelland?" he asked.

"What sort of a question is that?" Feray protested. Durzu ignored her and she was about to say more when, to her shock, Kemal replied.

"The rebel Fallon rules in Gaelland," he said, clearly and distinctly.

Feray's gasp of horror was lost in the general gasps of surprise at Kemal speaking.

"And your army? What of them?" Durzu asked.

"Forced to surrender. The survivors are being held prisoner," Kemal said.

"This is not right!" Feray shouted, hurrying to Kemal's side. "He is still sick, he does not know what he is saying! His mind is lost!"

"Stay back!" Durzu commanded. "You had your chance. Now my brother is speaking to me. Tell me, Kemal, who am I?"

"You are my brother Durzu," Kemal said instantly.

"See, Father, he knows what he is saying," Durzu said.

"Continue. I would know more," the Emperor said.

"Is Gaelland ready to be part of the Empire?"

"Fallon refuses to bow before us. He will defy us until he is destroyed."

"What did they plan to do with you?"

"They planned to bargain with me, threaten to kill me if we did not leave them alone. I would have been a hostage. Fallon wanted to see the Emperor kneel before him, in order to get the Crown Prince back."

"Monstrous!" someone exclaimed.

Feray was caught between a seething fury and a numb shock. Why was Kemal saying all this? He knew as well as she did what that would mean for them both.

"This is not my husband talking! He is being made to say these things!" she cried.

"Impossible. Nobody is touching him," Durzu said sharply. "You just do not want the truth to come out."

"The truth? You want to hear the truth? What about that your allies sacrifice children to Zorva? Ask him about that!" she snarled.

"This is nonsense. They have passed every test set for them by the Hierarch," Durzu said dismissively.

"My love, have you seen Swane and Aidan worship Zorva? Are they not evil?" she cried, rushing to his side and shaking his shoulder. "Speak!"

"Father, she is forcing a sick man to say what she wants!" Durzu appealed.

"Step away," the Emperor agreed.

Feray looked again into Kemal's eyes but they seemed to slip right through her. She sensed the Emperor was about to order guards to drag her away so she stepped back.

"They have cast some sort of spell on him," she said bitterly and pointed at Swane. "They are using their dark magic to put words into his mouth!"

"That is nonsense. It was the skill of the Emperor's physicians that have revived my brother," Durzu said fiercely. "Does she accuse them of lying to their Emperor and not knowing what they are doing?"

"Exalted One, the Gaelish have not been anywhere near Prince Kemal," the lead physician said immediately. "It is surely our care and skill that has brought him back from the dead."

The Emperor nodded, then beckoned the Hierarch forward. "Can you feel anything? Is dark magic being used?" he asked.

"I can feel nothing," the Hierarch declared.

Feray saw the Emperor's dark eyes turn on her. "Nevertheless, ask my son anyway, Durzu. I would hear it from his mouth."

"I never saw them pray to Zorva," Kemal said, when bidden by his brother.

"Where then, do these rumors come from?" Durzu asked.

"I made a deal with King Aidan to make Gaelland's submission easier. We gave them three of the Emperor's special guards, who stole children from their beds to allow Aidan to pretend there were witches loose in his city. Meanwhile I helped steal people from ships and villages, to make the Gaelish afraid."

Feray closed her eyes as gasps of horror echoed around the chamber and the Emperor's face went pale with fury. She did not know what to say. This was the truth but there was no way Kemal would ever reveal any of this unless some sort of trickery was involved. But she could not see how she could force them to reveal what they were doing. Unless ... she let her shoulders slump and shuffled closer to one of the guards.

"And this worked? The Gaelish are scared and willing to embrace us now?"

"They hate us now and this tactic created Fallon and his men. If we had not stolen his family, none of this would have happened," Kemal intoned flatly.

More sighs and groans came from around the room as Feray took another half-step towards the guard, her eyes on the dagger at his hip.

"And what of the slave revolt that happened here? What is the truth in that?" Durzu asked, unmistakable triumph in his voice now.

"My wife and children were captured by Fallon. He offered to exchange them for his family. I freed the slaves here, sent guards off in different directions and let them escape, even helped them get home."

The gasps and mutters had stopped now and there was a deathly silence, for all could see the Emperor was in a rare fury. Feray, however, was within reach of the guard's dagger now. There was no stopping the flood of truth from Kemal's mouth. The only way to show he was being made to say this was to prove the Gaelish were using magic. A quick grab and throw of the knife and she would force them to use magic to protect themselves. And then their other lies could be proved.

"You let Kottermani guards die and property be destroyed to help these slaves?"

"Yes."

"And when you returned them?"

"I signed a false treaty with Fallon, making him think Gaelland would stay independent. Then I tore it up and attacked. But I was defeated and captured."

Strangled gasps from around the room were drowned out by the Emperor's snarl of fury. Now was her last chance.

She took half a step forwards, snatched the dagger out of the scabbard and then looked up, whipping her hand forwards to send it whistling at Swane's chest.

Cries of alarm echoed in her ears but she only had eyes for Swane. The only way for him to save himself was to use magic to force the blade away from him. She savored snatching triumph from the jaws of defeat as she was sure he had to prove he had dark magic.

Her heart jumped into her mouth as she realized he was not moving, and was not doing anything to save himself, either. For a horrible moment she thought she had killed him, and forfeited her own life at the same time – and then Dina shoved Swane out of the way. The dagger did not thump home into his breast but instead sliced across his arm before clattering into the wall.

"Treachery!" Durzu howled as the room erupted.

Feray felt guards grab her arms, while the physicians rushed to Swane's side.

"Bring her before me!" the Emperor thundered. "By Aroaril, I will have silence here!"

The room went whisper-quiet and Feray did not fight as she was dragged in front of the Emperor. She had gambled and lost and she could not see another way out of this. But the Emperor did not even look at her.

"King Swane, are you badly hurt?" he asked instead.

"It is but a scratch, Exalted One," Swane said, sitting up as physicians fussed over him, Durzu hurriedly translating between them, although Feray could understand both languages.

"What would happen if we returned you to your throne in Gaelland?"

"We would rule in your name, giving you all the tribute and honor you deserve. Once I have my throne back, my people will accept what I say. All the fighting will stop and any Kottermanis being held as prisoners will be handed back, while we shall punish those who defied you," Swane said.

The Emperor nodded. "Then that is what we shall do."

"And what of my brother and his wife and their plotting?" Durzu asked.

The Emperor's eyes lit up with fury as he contemplated Feray. "You and Kemal have lied to me. Repeatedly. You have jeopardized my conquest of Gaelland, wrecked my careful plans and nearly killed one of the few allies we have left. What did you hope to gain by such an act?"

"Exalted One, they are lying to you. They have dark magic and they are using it here. If you trust them, it will mean not just your life but your soul and even the existence of the Empire itself," she said urgently, persuasively.

Her words vanished into thin air, as if she had not even spoken.

"You and your sons shall be held in your home until I have decided what to do with you," the Emperor said heavily.

"Exalted One, do what you want with me. But see my husband restored to full health and hear his words then," she tried one last time. "You cannot trust Durzu. He longs to be Crown Prince but he does not know what to do with the role. He will destroy all you have built."

"I cannot imagine how my son Kemal could undo what he has already done," the Emperor said heavily, seemingly ignoring her other words. "It is clear to me that he is no longer fit to be Crown Prince."

Feray could not see Durzu's face but she could imagine what it must look like.

"We cannot speak of what he has revealed in this room," the Emperor continued. "If I hear one word of this has escaped, then that person shall not only lose both life and lands but their families down to their third generation of relatives shall die. Is that understood?"

Feray was the only one not to speak as they fought with each other to promise their lips would be sealed.

"The people cannot know the mistakes that were made. As far as they are concerned, all is normal. The last thing we want is for some of the more troublesome provinces to take encouragement from this news of the Empire being defied. As for Kemal, we shall return him to Gaelland in the spring and he shall die there, falling in battle to bring Gaelland into the fold of the Empire. All shall mourn his passing but none shall question it."

"Who will you name as the new Crown Prince, Father?" Durzu asked, his voice almost hiding the desperate longing.

The Emperor sighed. "I must consider that. Kemal has shown himself unworthy and has created a host of problems for me to solve. But although I can detect no magic here I can see your hand in this, Durzu. You have made it a personal quest to remove your older brother and assume his position. I fear that the lure of the power it presents may be beyond you. I shall not make the same mistake in appointing the wrong son twice. The next son I appoint as Crown Prince will be the final one. I must consider whether you are the right man, or whether I should choose one of my other sons. You shall know my decision in the next few days."

Feray felt a small flicker of triumph – a feather against the lead weight of despair – that Durzu at least would miss out on the reward he so transparently wanted. She would have loved to see his face at that moment.

"Meanwhile, I want every ship we have ready to sail as soon as the weather improves. Fill them with the finest soldiers the Empire has!"

CHAPTER 40

Munro slipped down the staircase to the castle's lower levels, his soft boots making no sound on the stone. Since the soldiers had been sent out in all directions, there had been fewer guards in the castle. It was time to risk passing Dina's message to Keverne and his men. His trusted lieutenant Jen had bribed a couple of the castle servants and reported that the Ruling Council seemed to be falling into chaos, with fighting between the members. If Munro could kill Fallon or Bridgit, the Ruling Council would fall apart. And, if not, they could also be incited to some rash actions by a failed attack. Either way he would win. Of course he would have to stop coming to the castle, but Jen's servants could still provide him with gossip, at least.

Meanwhile, he was expected upstairs to adjust the fitting for a pair of Bridgit's new dresses and was conscious he did not have much time to deliver his message. The castle cells were almost empty; there were a handful of rich fools who had fallen foul of Fallon, as well as the cell with Keverne and his crew of traitorous guardsmen. Gold had lured them into killing their liege lord and Munro instinctively liked them for that.

A quick glance down the corridor showed him there was no way of getting in and out of the cells without being seen. A pair of young soldiers sat at the far end of the cells, chatting quietly, and they could not fail to miss him. If he tried to sneak in, it would seem suspicious but he had a far better idea.

Walking briskly, he strode down the corridor, palmed the message and waved his arms.

"Excuse me, I seem to be lost!" Munro called, waving his arms even wider and using that to disguise flipping the message and the lockpicks into Keverne's cell. "I am Bridgit's dressmaker and must have taken a wrong turn down a set of stairs. Can you show me where to go?"

The two soldiers stood and hurried towards him as he held his hands together and adopted his meekest pose.

"Can you help me, please?" he asked again. They showed little suspicion and he breathed a sigh of relief when they agreed. With a little luck they would both be killed when Keverne broke out, and with a little more, Fallon would be dead by morning and his reward from Swane assured.

*

Keverne had almost given up hope when the parchment landed in his cell. He hated it when his former comrades from Lunster were on duty, for they never missed an opportunity to spit in his food and threaten all sorts of punishment for him for killing Duke Kinnard of Lunster. Still, at least when they were on duty he was able to find out a little of what was going on, because they never missed an opportunity to tell him that the Duchess had abandoned him. He knew that was a lie – their love was true.

Keverne waited until the soldiers and the strange man who had tossed the scroll into his cell had walked past and then he ripped open the familiar seal and read the words with rising excitement. She loved him still! She kept herself pure for him and waited for the chance to embrace him once again. He felt his eyes mist up as he read how she had been forced to flee because of the monster Fallon and how she had been trying to return to his side. She needed him to be a man and prove he loved her as much as she loved him. All he had to do was break out and cut Fallon's throat and she could return to his side and they could rule the country together. Keverne felt his loins swell as he read how she had never known a man like him and could not wait to embrace him again. Once Fallon was dead, the same man who had brought this message would get him and his men out of the city and reunite them with her. He folded up the parchment and slipped it inside his filthy tunic, next to his heart. It would be safe there, until he saw her next.

"Listen," he told his guardsmen. They had all seen the parchment arrive – the most interesting thing that had happened to them since they were thrown in here – and they were looking more alert than they had been since that day aboard the Duke's ship. "We can get out of here."

*

The lock was stiff but they greased it with bacon fat from their meager dinner. One of Keverne's guardsmen, who boasted he had once been a thief before joining the guard, worked on it until, with a soft click, he turned to them and gave a nod of triumph.

The two young soldiers were gone, replaced by a pair of Lunstermen, two of a handful of Gannon's men who made it their business to torment Keverne. Well, no longer.

Keverne led his men in a silent rush down the corridor and by the time the Lunstermen had realized some of their prisoners were out of their cells, those men had beaten the guards senseless and then cut their throats with their own swords.

Keverne took one of the swords, giving the other to his biggest man, a hulking killer called Driscoll. The others had to make do with breaking the legs off the chairs for weapons.

"Do we let the rest of them out?" Driscoll asked, jerking his thumb at the other prisoners, who were now pressed up against the bars of their own cells.

Keverne hesitated, then shook his head. "They might give us away. Besides, the Duchess' agent may not be able to get them out of here. We don't want to risk our own escape for the likes of them. Come on."

He led them in another rush towards the stairs. As well as Dina's loving words, her man had also slipped him a rough sketch of the castle and the way to Fallon's room. He had been in the castle a few times with the old Duke but although he remembered it roughly, most of his attention then had been on Dina, not on the layout. Still, once he came across the King's old rooms again, he was sure he would find the way from there. And then he would win back the Duchess' hand and, more importantly, the rest of her body.

*

Kerrin could not sleep. He missed his friends Asil and Orhan, although not as much as he missed training with the rest of the recruits. Now that they had been sent off all around Gaelland, it was not the same. He found himself restless and his room was too warm. He had asked his mam time and again not to make the fire so big but she would not lose the habit of a lifetime and he had to go and walk the frigid corridors because he couldn't get comfortable in bed. Out in the corridors, with the wind rattling the horn frames in the windows and sneaking freezing fingers inside, he found himself relaxing. Mam and Dad kept getting themselves into trouble and if he was not around to save them, then what would happen?

Kerrin felt calmer when he was walking amid the castle's eerie noises, the creaking of wooden frames and rattling wind, rather than sitting in his room wondering if there were raiders coming in the night again. Lying in his soft bed, every strange noise seemed to be another midnight attack. But seeing the horn panel shaking in its frame or feeling the floor bounce under his quiet feet showed him it was nothing.

Then he heard something different again: boots on the floor. At first he thought it might be someone returning from guard duty but there were too many footfalls and his sense of calm disappeared, replaced by a pounding heart. Yet he did not run, because it could be nothing and he was a soldier now, not a frightened boy. He told himself that, time and again, although it was hard to believe it. He pressed himself against a wall, beside a tattered tapestry, and listened hard. There was little light in the corridor – some moonlight filtering in through the thick horn panels and that was it. But he could smell the men now and he knew instantly something was wrong, because they stank of the cells. Everyone smelled in winter but these men reeked.

He stayed frozen by the wall. Should he just hide there, let them go by? Then he took a deep breath. This was what he had trained for. Mam and Dad were depending on him. He stepped out into the middle of the corridor.

"Halt! Who goes there?" he demanded in a loud voice.

The men stopped instantly, then one of them cursed. "It's just a boy. Get him!"

They charged forwards and Kerrin brought up his small crossbow. Holding it steady, he loosed at the leading dark shape. A man shouted in pain and collapsed, bringing several others down behind him, and Kerrin turned and ran, fear and adrenalin and excitement driving him faster than he had ever run before.

"Stop him!" someone shouted, while another man was howling in pain.

Footsteps thundered behind him but his mam and dad's door was close by and he flung himself at it, hauling at the handle.

"Awake! Attack!" he roared, as he prepared to vanish into the safety of their room, hearing answering calls and shouts echoing up and down the corridor.

But the handle refused to budge under his hand. His relief and triumph disappeared in a heartbeat. He hauled at it and shook it but nothing happened.

"Got you, you little bastard!" someone snarled and he spun to see a hulking giant, a man nearly as big as Brendan, loom over him. Kerrin brought up his crossbow, preparing to at least ram the tip into the man's eye, but then a hand grabbed his shoulder.

*

Fallon had been enjoying a beautiful dream about Bridgit, but that vanished like the morning mist when he heard Kerrin's shout and then the door began to shake. He remembered, with horror, that he had locked it the night before so they did not get any night-time visitors. He raced across the cold stone floor to flip up the locking bar and haul it open.

The fire in their room had died down to embers but it threw enough light into the corridor to show Kerrin standing his ground as a large man in stinking clothes reached for him. Fallon grabbed Kerrin's tunic at the shoulder and hauled him backwards, tumbling him into the room.

The prisoner snarled and slashed a sword at his head. Fallon ducked and the blade crashed into the door, making it shudder.

"Fallon!" he heard Bridgit shout and he risked a glance over his shoulder to see his shillelagh flying towards him. He took a step back and half-turned to catch it, just as more men filled the doorway. The giant with the sword freed his blade from the door with a screech of tortured wood and drew it back for a thrust. But Fallon was faster, turning back to ram the end of his shillelagh into the man's throat. The man dropped his sword and staggered backwards and Fallon changed his grip and punched out the ends, breaking a nose and then a set of reaching fingers. Then a familiar face pushed his way through, a sword in hand.

"You will die for your treachery, Fallon!" Keverne hissed.

Fallon did not waste time with insults. While Keverne was still sneering at him, he slammed the end of his shillelagh onto the man's foot.

Keverne screeched as his toe broke and his balance went as he staggered sideways. Fallon whipped the other end up, an uppercut blow that smashed into Keverne's jaw and sent the traitor flying to his left, while his teeth went to the right.

The other men hesitated as Fallon hefted his shillelagh and beckoned at them, then a bellow of pure rage announced that Brendan had arrived.

The giant smith waded into them like a sheepdog scattering a pack of lambs. His hammer rose and fell with pitiless ferocity, breaking men apart and crushing ribs and skulls. The last of them tried to run but Fallon rammed his shillelagh into a stomach and then crunched the other end into an ear and they were all down.

"What in the name of Aroaril is going on?" Brendan demanded, his chest heaving and his hammer dripping.

"Exactly what I was going to ask. This is Keverne and his little gang of traitors. They were supposed to be in a nice, cold cell," Fallon said. "We need to find out how the begorrah they ended up here."

"Maybe you should put some clothes on first," Bridgit suggested, wrapping a cloak around herself and tossing him one.

Fallon felt a chill breeze remind him he was not wearing anything and put his shillelagh down to put on the cloak.

"Who raised the alarm?" Brendan asked.

"Kerrin," Bridgit said, her voice betraying a mixture of pride and concern. "I don't know why he was out walking the corridors—"

"But thank Aroaril he was," Fallon interrupted.

"He should not have been. They nearly got him. If anything had happened ..." she said, her voice trailing off, betraying the fear hiding behind the words. "That was not his job. He can't protect us – we need to protect him!"

Fallon stepped across a body to embrace her, only for one of the prisoners to rear up, a chair leg held like a spear. Brendan bellowed but was too far away, while Fallon jumped across to shield Bridgit. He braced himself for the impact of the blow but then a crossbow bolt flickered past and vanished into the man's eye. He stopped dead, the shaft protruding where his left eye should be, then fell face-first onto the floor.

Fallon and Bridgit turned to see Kerrin standing there, two hands holding his little crossbow.

"You were saying?" Brendan muttered.

Fallon saw the shock on Kerrin's face and instantly recognized that the boy was horrified at what he had done. Hitting targets was one thing but to see a man die at your hand was another. He raced to Kerrin's side but Bridgit was even faster and the three of them held each other.

"It's all right. You are safe. You saved us. You did everything right," Fallon told his son softly, urgently.

"How did they get in here? He should not have needed to do this," Bridgit whispered.

Fallon nodded his agreement and kissed them both, hard.

"I'll get some of the lads and sweep through the castle, make sure all is safe," Brendan said awkwardly, reminding Fallon that he hadn't put that cloak on yet.

But such concerns were nothing compared to his trembling son and crying wife. A huge anger was filling him.

"Do that. Some bastard is going to pay for this!"

CHAPTER 41

"Well, you have what you want but it looks as if I will be robbed of my reward," Durzu snarled.

Dina fixed a smile on her face and prepared to go to work. This was the final step to their plan and the most important one. The Emperor might have thought he was being a careful ruler by not naming Durzu as his heir but it was driving the Prince into their arms. He had seethed all the way back to their quarters, only the presence of other people stopping him from blurting out his anger.

"We can make sure you get everything you deserve," she said sweetly.

"How? Do you think you can play with my father's mind the way you twisted my brother's?" he demanded.

"That was fine work, was it not?" Dina agreed. "Finbar showed his mastery of magic there. Kemal thought he was secretly confiding to his wife but instead he was telling his deepest secrets to everyone. He is finished as Crown Prince and his life will be finished when we return to Gaelland."

Durzu jabbed a finger at her face. "And where does that leave me? If my father names one of my brothers, then I am worse off than before, for all will know I was passed over for Crown Prince!"

"Or we could show you how all your dreams come true. You become not just Crown Prince but Emperor, with more power than you dared think possible and nothing and nobody to challenge you," she said seductively. She was looking closely at him and saw the flicker of interest in his eyes. "You saw what we did with Kemal. We can give you all you want," she promised.

The struggle was obvious on his face but the battle was swiftly won. Greed and interest won out.

"How is that possible?" he asked suspiciously.

Dina took a deep breath. This was the final risk. The bait had been taken but she had to be sure the hook was set deep and he would never wriggle free. She was aware of both Swane and Finbar close by. Durzu might have a score of armed guards within touching distance but there was no way they could save their Prince if he said the wrong thing.

"There is a reason we were able to escape Fallon's men and live through a snowstorm that killed many others, a reason why we could cross the seas in the middle of winter, when vicious storms would destroy all other ships and a reason why we could walk into your church and handle your holiest relics with a smile," she said, putting excitement into her voice. "It is the secret we shall use to not just see you named Crown Prince but also Emperor. And then will begin the greatest era the Empire has ever seen. The whole world will fall beneath us and your name will echo down through history as the greatest man alive."

"And what is that?" Durzu asked hoarsely, longing dripping from every word.

"Feray was right," she said casually. "Our power does indeed come from worshipping Zorva."

She saw the dreadful fear in his eyes and was about to raise her hand in the signal that would see Finbar strike – but then the fear drained away, to be replaced by a look she had seen so many times it was as familiar as an old friend. Well, if she had any old friends. Lust shone out of his eyes at the vision she had conjured for him. Then he focused again. "If this is so powerful, why are you here like beggars, pleading for our help?" he accused.

"Because we did not have the power to fight the whole Empire. But you will not need to fight the Empire. You will take it over and Kotterman will accept you as it never would us."

"But they worship Aroaril three times a day and fear Zorva," he said uncertainly.

"They will accept whatever you tell them!" she fired back. "Only your closest advisers ever need know. You merely have to use slaves. As for the people, you tell them what you like. Tell them that the other countries are evil and must be destroyed to bring them to the light. It will be easy for you, for Aroaril has no power here. Your Hierarch could not even feel what we had done."

"But to pledge my soul to Zorva! I will be lost for eternity!"

"Would you rather spend eternity with your brothers, talking about why you did not have the courage to take up your birthright and the throne that should be yours? You will be the greatest Emperor this world has ever seen and then you will be raised high among Zorva's followers afterwards. Or you can spend eternity singing hymns and praying, whimpering about how you had a chance to carve your name in legend but you lacked the courage to do it. What would you rather?"

Again Durzu said nothing, although she could see the struggle going on behind his eyes and she began to fear she had not been persuasive enough and then Swane stepped forward.

"All your life you have been told that your elder brother is better than you," Swane said into the silence. "He is more handsome, more charming, more suited to being Crown Prince. All your life you have been measured against him and been found wanting. As long as you can remember people have been whispering how lucky it was that you were born the younger and will never take the throne. Yet you know you are far better suited than your muddle-headed brother and you would be a far greater ruler."

"Yes ... how did you know?" Durzu whispered.

"I have lived that my whole life," Swane said. "Help me get my throne and I shall help you get yours and we shall work together to make this Empire greater than anything your father or brother could hope to imagine."

Dina hid her smile but turned her head and gave Swane a careful wink. He had been perfect and for the first time she was relieved he was there.

"That is exactly what I feel," Durzu said slowly.

"We were born empires apart, but we are brothers of the heart. And together we can change the world," Swane said.

Durzu reached out a hand and Swane clasped it.

"Tell me what to do," Durzu said.

*

"What has happened, mistress?" Ely asked as the guards slammed the door shut and took up position outside her rooms.

"We have been tricked and betrayed by Durzu," Feray snapped. "Are my sons safe?"

"Yes, mistress."

Feray breathed a sigh of relief but knew it was only temporary. The Emperor might not name Durzu as the Crown Prince but whichever brother was given the honor would be foolish to leave Kemal's sons living, where they could be used as a figurehead by any rebel with a hatred for the Emperor. They might live a few more years than they would if Durzu got the throne but death would follow, as sure as the moon followed the sun. And what sort of life would that be? She had to escape and give her sons a chance to live and maybe even seek revenge. Her first thought was to head further south, to her ancestral lands. Her people would surely welcome her there – but then she remembered the Kottermani garrisons and that message riders would surely spread word of their escape ahead of them. If she did run, then not just Durzu or one of his brothers but the Emperor himself would see her hunted down and killed.

And where did that leave Kemal? He would be taken back to Gaelland and quietly killed, to be mourned by the common people, who would never know he had been murdered. How could she walk away from her love for him? What could she say to her sons?

She took a deep breath. There was only one answer. They would have to escape from here and sail back to Gaelland. Kemal's men had been made captive by the Gaelish. They had to be waiting somewhere, desperate for a chance to regain their honor. And her crew would sail through anything for her.

She rubbed her face. So all she needed to do was break out of this guarded house, find Gokmen and Gemici, round up all the sailors who were being watched by Durzu's men, steal a ship, sail out of Adana, cross a storm-tossed sea, find her husband's captured men, somehow free them and then free Kemal from the hands of his brothers, who were eager to remove him out of their path to the throne. *Could I make it any harder?* she wondered bitterly. But there was no other choice. Those evil Gaelish had done something to Kemal. The whole Empire would fall to Zorva if she did not do anything.

She rubbed her eyes. Kemal had been so obsessed with proving he was still a man that he had set in train the events that had led them into this disaster. It was up to her to clean up his mess. As usual.

"Ely, tell me, how did the Gaelish you were with escape from the city?" she asked.

CHAPTER 42

Durzu raised up the dripping heart and tossed it into the flames. His young mistress had died swiftly, although the whole city would have heard her terrified screams if they had not gagged her first.

Dina watched Durzu's face and saw the ecstasy there as Zorva's power flowed through him. The Prince shook with the intensity of it and opened his eyes wide, panting a little afterwards.

"There is nothing like it!" he gasped. "I never imagined it could be like that. Why does the church of Aroaril never mention anything of it?"

"Because they fear it," Swane said. "They know that the meager rewards Aroaril grudgingly offers can never be like this."

Durzu closed his eyes and a shudder went through him yet again. "I feel it," he said roughly. "I can see myself ruling the world!"

"You must get us in to see the Emperor. We shall do the rest. You will be named as Crown Prince, just before the Emperor falls sick. We shall take both him and Kemal to Gaelland and there we shall sacrifice them to Zorva and begin the rise of a new Empire," Dina promised.

CHAPTER 43

Fallon glared at the pair of young soldiers before him. "And you never thought to tell anyone before this?" he growled.

"He was the dressmaker," one said defensively. "He looked harmless!"

Fallon closed his eyes briefly. Keverne was the only prisoner left alive and, with his jaw shattered in several places, he wasn't doing much talking. But the scroll he was carrying told them everything they needed to know. Dina had reached out and tried to finish them. She had failed and had also revealed she was using King Aidan's old network of informers at the same time. It should have counted as a victory but instead Fallon was just enraged that Kerrin and Bridgit had been placed in danger. The two men who had been on guard were dead, so they could not be punished. These two had come forward to say they had escorted Bridgit's dressmaker out of the cells after he had wandered in, claiming he was lost. The traitor had to be Munro.

"Nobody is harmless," Fallon said, as angry at himself as at these guards. "Anyone wanders into the cells again, you arrest them and send for me. Now get out of here and get some sleep, because you'll be on night duties in the cells until the next full moon."

They saluted and walked out.

"They are so young. You can't expect too much from them," Bridgit said.

Fallon sniffed. "We were saved by Kerrin last night and you say those lads are too young?"

She did not smile. "That was too close. We were all fooled by Munro."

Fallon gritted his teeth at the thought.

"I've sent Devlin and a company of men to his shop. But I doubt he'll be there, unless he's a complete idiot and he's already proven himself to be far from that. Do you think he had a hand in getting Kemal out of here?"

She shrugged. "We will probably never know but it seems likely. There are too many people getting out of supposedly secure rooms in this castle for my liking."

"Aye. We can only use men we trust in the castle from now on," Fallon agreed.

"And I want Kerrin to sleep in our room," Bridgit added.

"What?" Fallon gasped. He had been enjoying the Bridgit who had come back from Kotterman, happy for him to lock the door each night. That would all come to a screeching halt with Kerrin there in the room.

"You said it yourself, we can't trust anyone. And we can't risk him being elsewhere."

"But that will never happen again. And look at how he did last night, he saved us—"

"Fallon, he was out wandering the corridors in the middle of the night, in this freezing weather. I can't risk it. And there is plenty of room for him. He can even have that dratted dog with him."

"But we were enjoying the time we had together," Fallon said, putting extra warmth into his voice. "It was almost like when we were first married."

She looked at him sideways. "Don't give me that blarney. I have known you too long. You can keep your pants on for a few nights at least. Or don't you think your son is worth it?"

Fallon winced at being so neatly trapped. Inside he was swearing furiously but he had no choice but to paste a smile on his face and nod. "Of course. I'll get Brendan to help me drag the bed around later. After we've hunted for the leaders of Swane's men in this city." He stood, seething with anger again. Yet there was also hope. Catch Swane's man and he could find out where Swane was hiding.

*

Munro's house, a three-story home in a busy street, was empty. The ground floor was the dress shop, while only one other room looked like it was lived in. But there were some interesting things left behind, including empty bird cages and many empty rooms.

"So this was how he was talking to Dina and getting his orders," Padraig said, inspecting the cages.

"Magicked birds, or trained?" Fallon asked.

"Probably both. In this weather you would need magicked ones to get anything done."

Fallon looked at the window at the raw sky. It wasn't snowing but he wished it would. The clouds hung heavy and a bitter wind whipped through the streets, biting into any exposed skin. "Anyone find anything else?" he demanded.

But the place had been cleared out.

"It's not even worth talking to the neighbors," Padraig grumbled. "Dress shop on a busy street, people would have been coming and going all the time."

"We talk to them anyway," Fallon said flatly.

But the neighbors had nothing useful to offer and Fallon's mood was made even worse when a crowd began to gather.

"Get rid of them, unless they claim to have known Munro," he said irritably.

But it swiftly became apparent they were not there to admire what Fallon had done to free them.

"We need more food!" someone shouted from the back.

"You get your ration and nothing more. It is fair for everyone," Fallon shouted back.

"Ain't fair!" another took up the cry. "You're sending food out to feed the easterners. Wagons of food that should be in our bellies!"

"Not true!" Fallon bellowed back but he was drowned in a cheer for the man's words.

"And those in the castle are having parties and feasts while we shiver and starve out here!"

"Even the Kottermanis are eating better than us!"

The complaints were coming from all different directions, each one of them getting a small cheer and stirring up the crowd even further.

Fallon beckoned to Devlin and Padraig.

"This is too convenient. We turn up here and next thing you know there is a crowd here spreading lies about us. I reckon it's full of Dina's informers," he said.

"What do you want us to do?" Padraig asked.

"Make my voice louder. I'll talk to them while Devlin spreads a net around this crowd. When I give the signal, we'll get in there and round up the leaders. Rosaleen can get the truth out of them and then we might be able to unravel their little plot."

They nodded and hurried away, letting him turn back to the grumpy crowd. Many were obviously ordinary people but he was sure some of the faces glaring at him were Munro's men. He would have most of them after today, he vowed. And then some bastards would pay.

"This is a hard winter!" he called out. "King Aidan left us with little. But we are doing all we can to help you through it. If you know of rich people still living like kings on hoarded food, tell me who they are and we shall share everything out fairly," he called, his words echoing off the surrounding buildings.

He was not surprised when nobody could volunteer a name. He was sure there were rich bastards who had cellars stuffed full of treats, still sending servants out to claim their rations, but finding them was the trick. He stared around at the crowd, forcing them to either meet his eyes or look away. It was making them quiet down.

"And there's food being sent out to other towns. We feed everyone else and go hungry!" someone cried, and the crowd sparked up again, adding their agreement.

"Do not listen to these lies! There are agents of King Aidan still among us, who seek to destroy all we are building here. We are making sure all is fair for you!" Fallon shouted, keeping an eye on where Devlin was. The farmer looked to be in the right position, so he raised his hands.

"We shall catch these traitors and show you that they lie. And we shall get them now!" he cried, dropping his hands.

Instantly, Devlin and a score of men plunged into the crowd, searching for the big talkers. Fallon hefted his shillelagh and went in himself, a pair of soldiers at his shoulder.

But then it all dissolved into chaos.

"Save yourselves! Run!" someone bellowed and the crowd, raised from birth on how brutally King Aidan's soldiers crushed dissent, instantly scattered. Screaming women and shouting men ran in all directions, while children howled and wailed. A man swung a punch at Fallon and he swayed back and cracked the man briskly across the head with his shillelagh and he went down like a sack of potatoes.

"Don't let him get away," he ordered a pair of his men and searched for anyone else who looked suspicious.

But the crowd was fleeing in all directions and his men were struggling to find anyone who looked like an organizer. People were covering their heads and racing away, rather than trying to fight back and while half a dozen men had been rounded up, the rest were gone.

As Fallon inspected the haul, he suspected that the men he wanted had got away, sprinting off at the first chance, and now he had merely a collection of the unlucky and stupid. But he was not about to take a chance.

"Take them back to the castle and have Rosaleen and Gallagher talk to them. If we have got one, then send a runner to find me," he told Devlin.

"And where are you going?" the farmer asked.

"They were saying the rich had hoarded food. I plan to find out if that's true or not," Fallon said grimly.

*

But three turns of the hourglass later, he had merely found more trouble. As he had done in Meinster, he went straight for the biggest

279

houses, suspecting that anyone living there would be used to living richly and would be trying to either find extra food or hold onto it.

It seemed that they also had the money to pay for really good hiding places, because he had found no great stores of luxuries. There were a few things squirreled away that he took back to the warehouses, in the face of furious complaint from the owners, but it was small beer. In fact he would have been delighted to find a little beer, because all the shouting was giving him a headache.

"I bought this three moons ago! You have no right to take it!" one plump man screamed in his face.

Next moment the merchant shut his mouth, because Fallon's shillelagh was an inch away from his nose.

"I can do what I like," Fallon told him coldly. "But if you want to keep doing anything, I reckon you need to shut up. Now."

That gave him a little satisfaction, seeing the fat man deflate so rapidly, but his relief was swiftly washed away in a new tide of complaints. A growing crowd seemed to follow them around, shouting out complaints and then scattering when he turned his men loose. Another dozen men were grabbed but, like the others, Fallon doubted any of them were useful. The smart ones who were behind this were at the back and close to boltholes. Only the fools were being grabbed.

"That's enough for today," he finally told his men, after another fruitless attempt to catch their tormentors. "Back to the castle for some peace and quiet."

*

"Have you taken leave of your senses?" Bridgit roared.

Fallon rubbed his forehead. "I might do, if you yell at me anymore," he grumbled.

She shook her head despairingly. His tale of what he had been up to that day had left her horrified, both at the knowledge there were people out there working to undermine them and that Fallon had played into their hands.

"Have you forgotten we planned another Petition Day tomorrow?" she asked, more softly this time.

He groaned. "That was tomorrow?"

"Aye. And I think we both know what is going to happen. It will be just like the ones in Meinster and Lagway and the other places."

He sighed. "Well, should we postpone it?"

"No!" she cried. "We've got to hold faith with the people. We will have to sit there and listen to their whining and smile in reply." She shuddered at the thought but there was no way around it.

"Can we even hold a Petition Day? The Ruling Council has all but dissolved. It's just you and I really," he pointed out.

Bridgit closed her eyes. Nola was still deeply upset over what had happened the last time they spoke together. Yet it was not as easy as ordering Brendan to throw away his hammer. When Keverne and his traitors had been outside their door, she had been delighted to see Brendan scattering them in all directions with his monstrous hammer. People were scared of him and he was worth a company of men in that respect. More, perhaps, the way things were going. Men and women who would happily jeer and shout at a line of armed men all shut up in the face of Brendan and his hammer. There was something dangerous about him, a sense that he did not care who he hurt and it quietened trouble like nothing else.

Of course, that was the very quality that repelled and scared Nola and their daughters. Bridgit wanted to see her friends happy but, as a member of the Ruling Council, she could see that Brendan could be the difference between getting through this winter and watching Gaelland dissolve into chaos.

Then there was Gallagher, who was offended by what had been said, as well as Riona and Devlin, who had not been talking to anyone for the last few days, except when they had to. And there was Fallon, who was becoming more and more inclined to do what he wanted, without talking to anyone else. That had worked fine back in Baltimore, when all he had to do was keep order in the village. Here was a different matter. She saw so many ways in which she would do things differently – and better – but there was the new baby to think of, not to mention Kerrin. And she did not know what a confrontation would do to Fallon. He had always listened to her but this was far bigger and so different to anything they had done before. Their relationship had defined both of their lives in many ways and she did not want to change that. She would rather see Gaelland fall. Or at least that was what she told herself. With everything on the line, she was beginning to wonder ...

"They have to be there. We shall summon them and make excuses if we have to," she said.

*

Fallon was delighted to see Brendan walk in, although his smile faded when Nola was not with him.

"Is she coming down? Spending too much time to get ready?" he asked, trying to put a cheerful face on things.

"I don't know. She's not talking to me now," the smith said flatly.

Fallon thought of asking more but the smith's face discouraged further conversation.

Riona and Devlin were the next to arrive, but they sat away from everyone, pointedly ignoring them.

"We can expect to get some angry people from yesterday," he said to them, by way of greeting.

"Don't worry. We know it's not a laughing matter," Riona told him.

He sighed and turned to see Gallagher arrive.

"Did you and Rosaleen get anything from those men we captured yesterday? Any of them working for Munro?" he asked eagerly.

"We could find nothing," Gallagher said.

"Well, we might find some today. Is she ready to check out anyone suspicious?"

Gallagher shook his head. "You have made it quite clear that the Ruling Council has nothing to do with Aroaril. She will stay clear, as will I."

"What? But we need her help!" Fallon growled.

"But you only want it on your terms," Gallagher said. "The church is not at your beck and call. Just as Aroaril does not make rulings on civil matters, the Council cannot order the church around. If you want the Archbishop's help, then you must go through the proper channels."

"Oh for Aroaril's sake!" Fallon snarled, then held up his hands. "Right. What do you want? Something in writing?"

"That would be best," Gallagher said stiffly.

Fallon slowly unclenched his fist. "You know, we are all on the same side," he grumbled.

"Perhaps you should have thought of that before ordering me off the Council," Gallagher suggested.

Fallon glared at his friend. "What has happened to you? This is not the way the old Gallagher would talk to me."

"The old Gallagher had not seen the truth," Gallagher responded. "I have seen the light and it guides my life now. If you let it guide yours, then you too will find peace."

"I could use a bit of bloody peace now," Fallon muttered, as he hunted out some parchment and hurriedly scrawled a request for the Archbishop to attend Petition Day. "Now, will you please hurry?"

"It does not matter how fast I go. It is all happening according to Aroaril's plan," Gallagher said placidly, strolling out the door.

Fallon restrained himself from hurling the ink pot at him only with great difficulty. His fingers were around it when Bridgit walked in.

"Any sign of Nola?" he asked hopefully.

"She is in no state to make decisions," Bridgit said. "It will just be us five."

"Oh good," Fallon said. "I cannot wait."

*

As they had suspected, the line for Petition Day was nowhere near as calm and orderly as the previous one, which had been such a success. Instead, angry men, upset women and confused children filled the square.

Even the icy wind that rattled around the square failed to cool things down.

"Keep your temper, just listen and promise to consider their case, whatever it is, and then inform them of our decision by next Petition Day," Bridgit murmured in his ear. "Yes, the city is behind us, but not if we act like Aidan."

But Fallon found it hard to keep quiet as people declared that their children or elderly parents were starving on these rations and demanded to join the feasts in the castle, where the Ruling Council stuffed themselves. Or that the Kottermani prisoners were growing fat while the Gaelish went hungry, or that the other towns were stuffing their faces while Berry's children went hungry.

Bridgit's firm denials saw people leave calmer, although not happy. Fallon would have preferred to whip the ungrateful bastards out of there. What was going on in this city?

*

Munro watched proceedings from the back of the crowd, his face disguised with a filthy eyepatch, his clothes tattered and grimy. It was a gamble coming here and he expected no mercy if he was seen. But it was worth it. He liked seeing the Ruling Council look diminished and divided. Keverne had failed to kill Fallon or Bridgit and that was a shame but they were fracturing anyway. He especially enjoyed hearing so many of his rumors coming back as truth. His words had taken on a life of their own now. It was also interesting to note how many desperate and hungry people there were in the city. Many of the rich hated Fallon but would not risk their necks to defy him. But while the poor people liked Fallon, they would do anything for silver and food. And, luckily, he had both.

CHAPTER 44

Dina looked idly at Durzu and Swane as they talked together. The two Princes were united in their inadequacy. Each believed they were the best man to rule and that was perfect for her. Their egos just needed flattering and they could be brought under control again. It was tiring but at least they could be relied on not to do something stupid like waffling on about honor. Self-interest was their main motivation and that was easier to work with.

"We are ready to see my father and for me to take the mantle as Emperor," Durzu announced.

Dina sighed. Time to go back to work. "We cannot do that yet," she said patiently. "If the Emperor were to die with his succession still unclear, any number of nobles could step forward."

"But I am the next eldest, so my claim is clear!"

"Yet many were there when your father the Emperor declared he had to be careful with his choice. They will want to advance their own position, so could push for one of your brothers to take the throne. At best, they could tie things up for moons," Dina said. "At worst, we could see your armies marching against each other, rather than helping us get back Gaelland from that scum Fallon."

"How do you know this? You have only been in my country for a short time," Durzu asked suspiciously.

Dina shrugged. "I know men and I know nobles."

Durzu grudgingly nodded. "So what do we do? How do I become Emperor?"

"We have to get your father out of the country and away from ambitious men. Get him to sail for Gaelland as soon as possible, with all four of his sons. Tell him that you should all be given a chance to prove yourselves as the new province is brought into the Empire. The one who performs the best should become the next Emperor. Of course, once we have landed in Gaelland, he can meet with an unfortunate accident. As eldest brother, you will have to take over. Then, when Gaelland is yours, you can return in triumph. What can the nobles say then? The Emperor fell in battle, as did three of his sons, but one remains who led you to glorious victory and is ready to take up the task of the Empire. What can they say then?'

She looked at the pair of them and smiled at the expressions on their faces. Let them do the work and she would enjoy the fruits of their labors. The only decision she had to make was when to get rid of Durzu so Swane could sit on the Emperor's throne. Or she could keep Durzu around, although Swane was the better bet. She was deep inside his head now. She could breathe on his neck, or caress his thigh, and he was her slave. It would take moons of effort to have Durzu in that state, if at all. After all, he did not have the rich history that Swane enjoyed, with lustful feelings towards his mother and his earliest thoughts of sex associated with an older woman. No, Swane it was. They would keep Durzu around for a little longer though – the Kottermanis would not accept Swane as their ruler just yet. A summer or two and the old nobles would be weeded out, replaced by the right sort of men and then it would be time for another change. Of course, if it all went wrong, she was only behind the throne, not on it. Besides, who could resist her?

*

Kemal woke slowly, feeling as though every part of him had been beaten. He looked up at the stone ceiling and wondered where he was. It was dark in here, so it was almost as if he was locked down below again, while Swane and Dina performed their perverted rites.

But there could be no stone on board a ship. He rolled over and blinked, seeing he was in a comfortable bedroom. His heart leapt – he had to be home! But how was that possible? His last memory had been on the ship, getting ready to warn Adana about these evil Gaelish.

He rolled over and winced as pain stabbed through his side. He pulled up his tunic to find a bandage around his lower chest. He pulled it down carefully to reveal a healing wound just below his ribs. How had that happened? He sat up and walked carefully over to the door, feeling light-headed. Had he tried to escape and been struck by the Gaelish? He tugged on the door handle and walked out, almost into the arms of a pair of guards sitting right outside his door.

"High One!" they leapt to their feet.

"Where am I? What has happened?" Kemal demanded. 'Where are the Gaelish?"

He was annoyed to see the men look at each other, rather than jump to obey. Then one of them nodded and raced off.

"Where is he going? What is happening?" Kemal demanded.

"High One, you need to rest. You have been sleeping for a long time," the guard said. "Please, return to your bed and we shall get physicians for you."

Kemal rubbed his face. "I have rested long enough. Now I need some answers. Either talk to me or step aside and I shall find out what is happening and then have you dealt with."

"High One, I cannot let you leave," the guard said stolidly.

"What?" Kemal shouted, then winced because it echoed around his skull. "On whose orders?" he demanded, in a quieter voice.

"The Emperor's," the guard said, his voice betraying his fear.

Kemal felt himself come fully awake. "What is going on?" he hissed.

"I cannot say, High One. But others will come."

Kemal focused on the man's face. "So you will not help me but will stand in the way of your Crown Prince? By Aroaril, I will see you staked out in the sun for this!"

The guard's face paled but he did not move. "I am sorry, High One. But you are no longer Crown Prince. By order of the Emperor."

Kemal staggered backwards and would have fallen if the guard had not jumped forwards and caught him.

"Get my father. Get him and I swear you will be rewarded beyond your wildest dreams," he hissed into the guard's ear.

"I cannot leave my post, High One."

"Lock me in. I will not step away from the bed. But, as Aroaril is my witness, if you do not get my father, then the Empire is lost and it will all be on your head."

*

"Make way for the Emperor!"

Kemal stopped pacing and sighed in relief. The past turn of the hourglass had been excruciating and he had been tempted to break his word and go looking for his father. But he was in no condition to fight his way to his father's side.

The door swung open and his father, the Emperor of Kotterman, strode in the room.

"Father, I cannot say how pleased I am to see you!" Kemal exclaimed. "There has been the most terrible mistake—"

"Indeed there has," the Emperor snapped. "I put my trust in you and it was betrayed! Gaelland is in revolt, your army is destroyed or captured, you helped slaves escape and you allowed yourself to be used as a pawn by our enemies!"

"What? Where did you hear those lies—"

"Silence! You told me and Durzu and the rest of the nobles! I heard it all from your own mouth!"

Kemal felt his heart leap out of his chest. "Father, this was a trick. The Gaelish who came here with me, they are evil, they worship Zorva and they have dark magic. They must have used it on me—"

"Enough!" his father thundered. "The Hierarch himself has decreed them harmless. They are here to help. They want their country back and I want my new province."

"No, this is wrong! Father, they have lied to you. You must believe me—"

His father stepped forwards and slapped him across the face. It was not a powerful blow but it stung.

"Foolish boy. You had your chance and failed. Now you will accompany me to Gaelland with your brothers and we shall retake the province for the Empire. I shall decide which of your brothers shall be Crown Price once we have Gaelland firmly in our hands. With the traitor Fallon dead, we can safely hand over to King Swane."

"Swane is evil! I watched him sacrifice a screaming child!"

But he might as well have been talking to the wall.

"You will die there and all scandal will be forgotten," his father went on remorselessly. "And the throne will pass to a more worthy son."

"Durzu!" Kemal spat. "Is he behind this? Is he a friend of these Gaelish?"

"Try to die like a prince, even if you could not live like one," his father said. "Do not call for me again. You shall be kept below when we sail and your guards shall be told you are to be treated like a common slave."

Kemal stared at his father in mingled shock and horror. "Father, will you not listen to me? I don't care what happens to me but the Gaelish must be stopped! Swane has the blood of children on his hands!"

He looked at his father but the Emperor's eyes seemed curiously blank. Normally they were full of light and life but it was almost as if he were asleep. And his voice, it was all wrong. It was almost as if the Emperor were a puppet ...

"Father, they have got to you! Tell me they did not come to speak to you alone—"

The Emperor turned away and he felt his heart drop out of his chest.

"At least tell me my family is safe!" he cried desperately.

"They will stay here. Durzu has promised to care for them," his father said dully. "Do not call for me again. I shall not listen."

He turned and walked away but Kemal would not, could not, leave it there.

"You are under a spell!" he cried, racing over. Perhaps if he struck his father, or dragged him into church—

But the Emperor's guards were too fast. Four small, lithe men blocked the way. Kemal recognized them instantly. Trained from birth, they were deadly with hands or weapons and obeyed orders without question. He had given the three he possessed to King Aidan and lost them. He could not hope to defeat one, let alone four, but he flung himself at them anyway.

"Father, listen to me—" he cried desperately but it was not use. The Emperor kept walking and the guards moved in. A blow to the stomach and another to his healing side sent him tumbling to the floor and they backed out warily.

He forced himself to his knees in time to see the door slam shut and he heard the bolts being rammed home.

Tears came then, for his wife, his sons, his father and his country. How could he hope to save any of them?

CHAPTER 45

Fallon watched with rising frustration as his new army stumbled through their paces in the snow. Without Kemal, it would come down to hurting the Kottermanis so badly that they would leave Gaelland alone. Despite repeated calls for volunteers, not enough men had come forward. So he had been forced to offer extra food for all those who served. Thousands had responded and he had ordered his men at a score of towns around Gaelland to make the same offer. If they could all train over the winter, by the time the Kottermanis got here, there would be enough men to take them on – led, of course, by his core of trained men.

That was the hope but the reality looked different. Their shield wall left gaps in a dozen places and their hedgehog defense of spears looked about as threatening as a slug – and moved at a similar speed. He had known their progress was slow but this was ridiculous. The Kottermanis would cut them to pieces and he could not even trust them to stand behind his experienced men.

The black-bearded Bran and the baby-faced Casey marched over to him, both looking grim.

"Do you want to tell me what in Aroaril's name is going on?" he hissed at them.

"It's partly the cold but mainly the quality of the men," Bran said with a shrug. "We've previously had men who wanted to fight for their homes and families. Now we have a bunch of men who are doing this because their families will get an extra ration of food."

"Then we have to weed them out! Throw the useless ones away and concentrate on the good ones!"

"We're trying, sir, but it's hard to know where to stop. We only have a few good ones," Bran warned.

Fallon swore furiously. "Right. I'll fire them up and then you will be free to get rid of any who don't make an effort this afternoon," he said. "Padraig, it's time for you to help me."

"I will help you. By not helping you. Don't do this," the old wizard said. "Look at them."

Fallon glanced over to where the new men stood disconsolately. Even their spears seemed to be drooping. "Well, they aren't going to get better by themselves. Do we just leave them be? Maybe pray to Aroaril for them to turn into soldiers by spring?"

"Yelling at them is not going to make them happier," Padraig warned.

"I'm not here to make them happy. If they want extra food they have to earn it. We don't have enough to waste on this bunch of boggers. Now, make me heard by all of them."

Padraig sighed and then nodded.

Instantly Fallon turned to the disgruntled recruits.

"Men of Berry! In a few short moons, a huge army will be landing on our shores. They want to enslave us, take us away from homes and families. We need you to stand with us against them. Your country, your city and your families are depending on you!"

He let his voice ring out across the field and waited for the backs to straighten and for the faces to harden. But only a handful seemed to change. Most looked away or down at the ground. Some were even muttering to each other. He spotted the former Greeter for the Bankers Guild, Turlough, shaking his head sadly at him.

That was the final straw. Fallon began to shout at them, letting out his frustration and anger in a stream of threats and curses. He didn't even know what he was saying, just took his anger and threw it at them. Some wilted under his tongue-lashing, others shouted back, although their words had no hope of being heard against his magically-increased voice. A handful threw down their spears and walked away, his fury pursuing them back towards the city.

He finally petered out, chest heaving, to see a mixture of fearful and sullen faces looking back at him.

"Do what you can with them," he told Bran and Casey in disgust.

He stalked back towards the city, Padraig running to catch up with him.

"Well, that went well. Are you feeling better now?" the old wizard asked.

"Don't you start with me as well," Fallon growled.

"I just did what you asked, did I not?" Padraig countered. "But look where it got you. To be sure, you have a pack of useless bog-shites out there but telling them that will do no good. They need to be told they are heroes and then they might behave like them. You used to be able to do that, you know."

"I used to be able to do a lot of things," Fallon muttered. "How about you do something useful and find Munro for me?"

"I have birds out looking and if they spot him I will know. But trying to find one man in a city? It'd be easier to find a needle in a haystack," Padraig said. "Magic doesn't just work like magic you know."

"Does anything?" Fallon sighed.

CHAPTER 46

"How did your Gaelish friends escape?" Feray asked.

Ely gasped.

"Listen to me, we don't have time for denials and explanations. I don't care what happened before, I only care that we get out of this trap those Gaelish have spun around the Emperor with Durzu's help, curse him! Either we get out or we die, it is as simple as that. So just tell me how they did it."

Ely hesitated but Feray glared at her and the girl began babbling about plans to pull slave chains out of solid rock, then about dancing for guards who had been drugged with sleeping powders. Feray kept a tight hold on her frustration and just listened, finally holding up her hand when Ely said something useful.

"So this Bridgit got out into the city twice to scout around. How?" she snapped.

"We tied sheets together and had teams of children lower and raise her out of the window," Ely explained.

Feray clicked her fingers. "Then we need to do that as well. The guards think us helpless and they are right. But there is help for us, if we can but reach it. I need you to go out into the market and get more of these sleeping powders, then help me turn some of these sheets into a rope."

"But Highness, we don't have enough of us to hold the rope, and what will we do once we are out?"

Feray reached out to grasp Ely's arm. "Help me and we shall free your family. You will no longer be slaves and you can either stay here, enjoying the favor of the Crown Prince and his family, or live in Gaelland, whatever you wish. Or we can stay here and wait for Durzu to sacrifice us to Zorva. It is your choice."

Ely looked her in the eye and she saw a flash of steel in the girl.

"I shall go out now," she promised.

CHAPTER 47

Fallon brooded as he rode down the streets of Berry. A small guard of men, led by one of his faithful Baltimoreans, Craddock, rode behind. His new army was making no progress and he feared they would never be good enough. He needed Kemal back in his power. He had sent town criers out in all directions, offering huge sums of money for word of Munro the dressmaker. In other towns he had even bigger rewards for news of Swane or Dina. If he could get one of them, then Kemal could not be far away.

Hundreds of people had flooded in, so many that he could never have paid them all. But most, perhaps all, were only after the money and now everyone was being kept busy trying to make sense of all the whispers and rumors.

Fallon had wanted to get Rosaleen and her priests to see if there was truth in what the more promising ones said but she had refused to tie the church to what she had called another witch hunt. So Bridgit and her faithful helpers, Glenda and Ann, were organizing all these random claims into something understandable, while Padraig and his wizards were trying to check through the other towns.

The flood had turned to a trickle when no silver had been handed over but, even so, there were more claimed sightings than he had guards to investigate. This was the third one he had checked that day; the previous two had been empty houses, with no trace of anything useful. Only a few moons ago he would have had to push his way through a cheering crowd, hailing the hero who had saved them from the peril of the witches. Now people ignored him, or scuttled out of the way, which at least would stop word of their approach reaching Munro, Fallon reflected bleakly.

"When are you going to give us the food you are hoarding?" someone shouted from an alleyway.

He ignored that. He had bigger fish to fry and had heard that sort of thing all too often.

"This wouldn't be happening if Swane was still here!"

Fallon's head came up at that and he kicked his horse into a run, Craddock and the guards right behind. People scattered while a man sprinted down an alley. This was the first time Fallon had heard someone shout for Swane and there was no way he was letting the man get away with it. Not after what he had seen down in the dungeons.

The alleyway got tighter and tighter, until Fallon felt as though his boots were brushing against the brickwork. His guards were falling behind now, having to sort themselves into single file to follow him. He just managed to get around a tight corner to find his prey had disappeared.

Fallon slowed down, slapping his thigh in frustration as he snarled out a string of curses. He swore so loudly that he almost missed the scrape of leather on brick and looked up just in time to see a pair of men leaping down at him from a window above. Kicking his horse so it sprang forwards, the first man landed just behind him, rather than on top. Fallon ducked and a knife that was meant for his throat hit only thin air as the would-be assassin sprawled across the hindquarters of his horse. As Fallon clawed for a dagger, the second man nearly jumped into the saddle with him.

The man drew back his arm for a thrust and Fallon abandoned his attempt to draw a blade and instead head-butted his attacker, breaking his nose and snapping his head back. He grabbed the man's wrist and bent it back against the joint, so the stunned man dropped the weapon.

Behind him he could sense the other man was ready to strike. With nowhere else to go, he flung himself across and away, using his arm against the nearby wall to stop from falling completely out of the saddle. A moment later, his would-be killer thrust his dagger forward. But Fallon was no longer there, so now his blade sunk into his friend's chest. Fallon pushed himself off the wall, while making a second grab for his dagger. As the assassin tried to pull his knife from his gurgling accomplice, Fallon half-turned in the saddle, slashing out his dagger to rip into the man's throat. The blade caught on gristle and cartilage and then tore through, pumping hot blood over his hand. He turned back to the other man but he had his friend's knife buried in his heart and slid off the horse and to the cobbles below, thrashing weakly.

"Fallon! Are you safe?" Craddock yelled as he caught up with him.

"I'm fine. But that might change when Bridgit hears about this," Fallon said, looking at his dead and dying attackers.

*

Bridgit tried to keep her voice light but it was hard to do. The way her husband was behaving, it was a bloody miracle he had stayed alive long enough to greet her on her return to Gaelland.

"You can't risk falling into their traps. They know what angers you now and they seek to use it against you," she said calmly.

"Am I supposed to just ignore people who say they want Swane back to sacrifice children to Zorva?" he growled, pacing around like a caged animal.

"Yes! Because every time you react, they use it as a weapon against you! It is no longer a simple fight. Swane has lost all chance of seizing the throne back by force but he seeks to poison the people against you. It is his only hope. And, so far, he is doing well!"

"What do you want of me then?"

She sighed. She sympathized with him but there was no room for emotion if they were to steer Berry through this dark winter.

"It is like hunting. You don't ride into the forest, ripping up every bush in the hope of finding a deer. You wait, you watch and you lay a trap. That is what we have to do. We are finding there are patterns in the rumors, areas Munro seems to stay in."

"That's if any of them are true. People are lying to us in the hope of getting money," he grunted.

"Look, you can't act like a village sergeant or even a Duke's captain. You have to be more than that. Riding through the streets is too risky. One crossbow and you are gone and where would Kerrin and I be then? And the baby? Let the others do some of the work."

"Like Devlin? Or Gallagher?" Fallon snorted. "Maybe we should walk away, sail off to Cavan's island and let them all kill each other."

Bridgit bit back her angry words. "You know we cannot do that now. Would you want all those people's deaths on your conscience?"

"Well, you are the one with all the good ideas. Maybe you should be the one ruling the city."

"Maybe I should, if you are going to behave like some sort of spoiled child. Oh, the people don't love me anymore, so I am going to sulk and refuse to think," she snapped back, before she could stop herself.

He stopped his pacing, shock written all over his face. "Do you think *you* should be doing this job?" he asked.

Bridgit knew she could back down, apologize and soothe his anger but she'd had enough of pandering to his moods. Time and again she had tried to calm him and show him a better path and he just went ahead and did what he desired anyway.

"I don't know how to rule, but maybe that makes me better than those who think they do," she retorted. "You can't think with your heart. You have to use your head."

"Oh, and I don't use my head? We cannot surrender the streets to Swane's supporters. I fought and risked my life to save these people, the least they can do is show a little gratitude!"

"You are not thinking like them," she argued. "They cannot sit back and take a wider look at the problems facing Gaelland, because they don't know about them, nor do they care. They don't want to know about people starving in Lagway, or how the Kottermanis are planning to come back to demand the return of their Prince, who we have lost. They only care that their children are hungry and cold. We have to worry about for them. Once they are fed and warm, then they can think about other things but, until then, that is their whole world."

"And you know them all personally," Fallon suggested sarcastically.

"I don't know their names but I know them," she countered. "I was like them, only a few moons ago. So yes, I know them better than you do, because you were always the one worrying about tax quotas elsewhere in the Duchy and whether a bad harvest was going to send a wave of bandits and thieves across the country."

"So you do think you are better than me at ruling!"

"At the moment, yes I am!" she fired back. "You need to stop being foolish and listen to me. Or, better yet, get our friends back together and put the Ruling Council to work again."

Fallon waved his hand dismissively. "They aren't interested and they didn't help much last time."

"Then we try again. And again! There is too much for just one person, or even two."

"Aidan did it."

"And look how that turned out. Put aside your vanity and wanting to be popular. It is like a parent with a spoiled child. You have to give the people rules and discipline. They will complain at first but they will come to love you for it, when they see you have their best interests at heart."

"You don't understand," he growled. "It wasn't like that for Prince Cavan. The people loved him for who he was, not what he did!"

"No, it is you who doesn't understand! You are not a Prince! They might have loved Cavan because he was better than Aidan, but you are not a royal. They owe you nothing."

"They owe me their lives and the lives of their children!"

Bridgit took a deep breath. They were getting into dangerous territory here. This was more of a serious fight than anything they had had before. Little had been at stake then, except their temporary happiness. Now everything was at stake.

She forced a smile onto her face. Fallon was obsessed with finding Munro and hurt by people shouting at him. That sort of thing did not worry her as much. She wondered if that was because she had never sought people's good opinion, while he had become accustomed to the respect and friendship of the village. Yet what had worked in Baltimore could not help them here. She had tried to be liked as a leader in Kotterman, and that had only led to people being killed. Now she was prepared to do whatever it took and let the results speak for themselves. But Fallon still had this idea of being the people's hero. She could see why but, Aroaril, it was making things difficult!

"What is the real problem?" she asked gently.

He bristled for a moment, then threw himself into a chair. "I killed Cavan," he said, his voice stricken. "If only he were alive, all would be different."

"You have to put that behind you," she said.

He looked at her sadly. "But I cannot. It hangs over me all the time. Sometimes I think only sacrificing myself can atone for what I did."

"That is nonsense!" she said but he only shrugged his shoulders. "Come, tell me how the training of our new army is going," she invited, hoping to lighten his mood a little.

But his face darkened instead. "Too slowly," he grunted. "The cold saps everyone, they don't have the enthusiasm of the original recruits and we don't have enough trainers."

"Well, we still have time," she soothed. "The Kottermanis will not dare to sail for at least another moon or two, for fear of running into storms that will destroy their fleet, and then it is another half-moon before they get here. And the storms might even do the job for us anyway."

He snorted. "We need Kemal," he said. "To get him we need Swane, and to get him we need Munro. It's time to start grabbing some of these people who yell at us. Munro has to be behind it. If we get them, we can use Rosaleen to see inside their heads and find the truth."

"She's not going to want to risk that," Bridgit warned. "You know she is terrified of destroying innocent minds."

But Fallon was already leaving their room.

Bridgit sighed and rubbed her eyes. When she had returned to Gaelland, she could not bear to be apart from him for a moment. Now they seemed to fight whenever they spoke. Yet she could not walk away from Berry, not after what had happened on the ship back from Kotterman. She had to find another way of getting through to him. But how?

CHAPTER 48

"We shall sail by the next new moon. Make everything ready," the Emperor intoned.

Dina watched impassively as the lords and nobles looked as though they wanted to protest bitterly but the habit of obedience was too well ingrained, and they merely bowed their heads.

"We shall work day and night to be ready," one promised.

"Do so. Anyone who is not ready will pay for it with their life," the Emperor said flatly. Dina looked on approvingly. Durzu had got them close enough to the Emperor for Finbar to touch him, and through the magic, use that to issue commands. Now the Emperor did whatever they told him. "We must have Gaelland in our hands as soon as possible. Once all is ready, you shall all accompany me on my flagship."

"A great honor, your majesty," one older man said. "But will there be room for all on board?"

"It shall be just you and your families. You will leave all your lieutenants and guards on your own ships. My own guards will take care of everyone else."

The powerful men around the table looked, if possible, even less happy at that, but again they merely bowed their heads.

"I shall receive your reports tomorrow. Do not fail me," the Emperor said and they hurriedly bowed and raced away to begin working.

"Is this wise? All we know about the seas says the storms around Gaelland could destroy our fleet before it has a chance to land a single man," Durzu said worriedly, leaning towards Dina.

Swane pointed towards the Emperor, who sat like a statue at the head of the table, but Dina waved her hand.

"He cannot hear us and, if he did, he could not understand it," she said dismissively. "Of course we would not dare to sail during this time normally but we have the power of Zorva and of magic with us and we can use them both to protect your ships and men. After all, we sailed here, did we not?"

"But at what cost? Don't you need more blood for Zorva's power?" Durzu asked.

"Exactly," she agreed. "And we shall use those nobles and your brothers."

Durzu's face betrayed his shock, then revealed his excitement at the thought.

"Yes. They are the only ones who could challenge you," she said. "Without their guards, they are helpless before us. The Emperor can call for their deaths for treason, disloyalty, or whatever you want it to be. If he is appearing to make the decisions then it does not come back to you and when we are ready to remove him, there will be nobody left to argue. When we return from Gaelland, you can select your own men to the top positions, bind them to you with rewards and threats," Dina continued.

Durzu's face turned thoughtful. "You know much about manipulating men," he said carefully.

She kept her smile warm, and decided that Durzu had to die soon. Swane was a much easier puppet to use.

"I am merely an observer," she said brightly. "The Gaelish court provided ample opportunity to see what men were prepared to do for power. I helped my husband as best I could and then, when he was lost, I tried to help Prince Swane, as I now try to help you. I do not want power for myself, but I am happy to help others achieve their dreams."

She stared deeply into his eyes until he nodded and looked back towards Swane.

"And once we have reached Gaelland. What then? How do we finish this Fallon and take the country? Do we land at Berry and crush him utterly, then wait for the rest of the country to surrender?"

Dina saw Swane glance at her and nodded fractionally to him. They had discussed this many times. It was something they had both dreamed of – how best to exact revenge on Fallon.

"We shall sail into Berry and crush him," Swane said confidently. "It is what your brother tried, but this time not only do we have ten times the soldiers, we also have men undermining Fallon from within. His army will be like a rotten branch, ready to snap."

"You seem very sure of yourself," Durzu said.

Dina leaned forwards slightly. "We are still in contact with the Prince's men in Berry and the other county towns. It will happen as we said. Any who try to stop us will be taken back to Kotterman as slaves and we shall rule in your name, as part of the Empire. You shall be the most powerful man in the world and, when your rule is secured, it will be time to look over the seas for new conquests."

"And your people will really turn on their savior, in exchange for yourself, after they cheered as your father was executed?" Durzu asked doubtfully.

"They are already doing so. They are sheep and easily led."

Durzu looked down at the map of Gaelland and smiled viciously. "Then you shall have your revenge on Fallon."

"But he must be taken alive," Swane said swiftly. "I do not want him dead, not until he is begging for it."

"He and my brother can suffer and die together. The Lord Zorva will enjoy taking their souls, I think," Durzu said with relish.

"He can enjoy Kemal's soul. I want Fallon's soul for my own," Swane whispered.

CHAPTER 49

Fallon inspected the bedraggled crowd of prisoners with satisfaction. His men had rounded up several dozen rumor-mongers and malcontents. The rumors had to be coming from somewhere. Just one of them could lead him to Munro's men and then up the chain, all the way to Swane and Kemal.

"Absolutely not," Rosaleen said crisply.

Fallon's satisfaction disappeared faster than warm air in winter. "I've barely told you what I want!" he protested.

"I know what you want. For me to look through the minds of every fool you have slung into the dungeons and find if any of them are working for Swane. I cannot do it."

"Can't, or won't?" Fallon asked. "If just one of them is Swane's creature, we can use it to find the rest of the nest and stamp them out."

"Both," she said. "I'll turn half of them into drooling idiots. I cannot have that on my conscience. And it will never end. You will want to bring me more every day. I already have more duties than turns in the hourglass each day."

"And what of a Kottermani invasion? Could you have that on your conscience?" he growled.

She folded her arms. "Bring me Munro, or one of his men and I will help you then," she offered.

Fallon shook his head in disgust. "I won't know if I have one of his men without you," he said sourly.

"Nevertheless," she said, her tone implying this topic of conversation was over. "Now, have you thought about allowing Gallagher to return to the Ruling Council?"

"Is he still obsessed with Aroaril?" Fallon asked sourly.

Rosaleen grimaced. "He is. And that is why I want you to help him. I have tried to talk to him but he will not let go of this idea we are all part of Aroaril's plan, that it was destined and he is now being rewarded for his belief. He thinks that if he stops believing so hard then something will happen to me. He needs his friends to help him, for he is as lost now as he was before I met him."

"He's far worse company now though," Fallon muttered.

"He is your friend and I thought you would care about him," Rosaleen said sharply.

Fallon rubbed his face wearily. "Send him along tomorrow," he said. "I'll see what I can do. After all, it's not like I have anything else to worry about."

"Take care of your friends and everything else will come together," Rosaleen said.

"Is that your next sermon?" Fallon asked sarcastically.

"I would have thought, after all you had been through, you would understand the value of having friends you can trust by your side," she said tartly.

Fallon rubbed his temples. It felt like there was a hammer beating in there. He needed to rest, to forget about all these endless problems. When Kerrin started sharing their room the nightmares had returned. Only now they were not of a burning Berry, but a dying Cavan.

"Why can't you do something about Gallagher?" he asked. "He would do anything for you. If you turned him away, forced him to realize what a fool he is being, it would be much quicker and simpler than us trying to convince him."

"I have tried to talk to him. But how can I set him aside? The Archbishop discarding her husband for being too pious? How would that look?"

"Well, how about a ban on the bedchamber? That might bring him around faster," Fallon suggested, with a slight cough.

"First of all, he says everything is Aroaril's plan and so nothing can be changed. Secondly, it is harder to refuse him than you might think."

"I think I could say no," Fallon muttered, but his heart was not in discussing much more of this with the Archbishop. "I guess it is all down to me then."

CHAPTER 50

Fallon smiled as he inspected the careful marks that Bridgit's team had made on the map of the city, the results of sorting through all the tips from the informers. All around him men were pulling on mail coats and tightening belts and straps, getting ready for the raid.

"Brendan, I want you to sweep through this area. Devlin, you take this quarter and Gall, you ride with me," he said. "Grab anyone who looks suspicious and we shall sort them out back here. And if you think you've got Munro, drop everything and get him back here. There's a score of promising places where he could be hiding. Hit them hard and fast and show no mercy."

They strode out, Fallon feeling more confident than he had in almost a moon thanks to the maps pointing out where Munro might be hiding. But there was a new concern. The horses, taken after the battle of Lake Caragh, were getting thin. Fodder was low and the constant work of carrying men in armour was exhausting them.

"We need to give them a rest," Brendan said, stroking the nose of one.

"Maybe you should ride in a cart then, so your fat arse doesn't break their backs," Devlin chuckled.

A few others also laughed but when Brendan turned slowly, the laughs died instantly.

"We have to keep using the horses. They give us an advantage of speed and height," Fallon said. "But after today we shall use less mounted patrols, give them a chance to rest."

The thought of walking the streets from now on dampened them and the icy rain misting the air and finding its way down backs and into boots did not help.

"You do know that most of these sightings are now days old, if not half a moon old. Munro has probably moved on," Padraig said.

"Shouldn't you be somewhere warm, annoying someone else?" Fallon asked sourly.

"But I enjoy irritating you more than anyone else. The others in the castle treat me almost like someone important."

Fallon grunted and turned to where Brendan rode alongside him, hammer over his shoulder.

"Rosaleen has asked us to try and help Gallagher," he said.

Brendan patted his hammer. "You want me to knock some sense into him?"

"Tempting," Fallon admitted. "We need to talk to him, try to get him to realize that all his preaching has gone too far."

"That will go well," Brendan observed sourly. "I don't know what he is doing with Rosaleen anyway. She just wants to interfere all the time. She cornered me the other day, wanted to talk about the sanctity of life and the power of mercy and all that rubbish. Nola probably put her up to it."

Fallon wiped a trickle of rain out of his eye. "What did you tell her?" he asked, lowering his voice.

Brendan snorted. "It's too late for me. I know what I have become. Nola and I sleep in different rooms now."

"Surely she is worth giving up your hammer for," Fallon said.

The big smith sighed gustily. "Aye, she is. But I cannot leave her unprotected again. I know what is coming for us in the spring and my hammer might make the difference between victory and defeat. I know what I can do to the bastard Kottermanis and how the men take heart from that. I swore an oath to keep her safe and I shall keep that, even if it means I lose her along the way."

"Nothing is worth seeing you lose Nola," Fallon said. "Take your family and get away from here. This bloody city is dragging us all down. Find somewhere you can start again."

Brendan laughed harshly. "It is too late for that," he said. "I told you, I know what I am. I enjoy hurting people too much now.

I am not the man she married and she does not want me. Moving somewhere else will not change that."

Fallon fell silent, glancing over at Padraig, who shrugged. "You always lose people in a war. Sometimes you lose yourself," the wizard said softly.

Fallon glanced over at Brendan but the smith had let his head drop forwards and did not look like he wanted to keep talking. He sighed and let his horse ease back a little, until he was riding alongside Gallagher.

Fallon tugged the collar of his cloak higher in a vain attempt to stop the icy trickle of water down his back. And he knew it was going to take all night to get the rust out of his mail. "Rosaleen is worried about you. I am worried about you," he said.

"I don't know why. I have never been better," the fisherman replied calmly.

"Really? You preach more than the old Archbishop, and we all know what a fake he was."

"Are you suggesting my religion is somehow false?" Gallagher demanded.

Fallon sighed. "No. Poor choice of words there. I mean, you spent years hating Aroaril—"

"And now I have been shown the error of my ways. I found Rosaleen and now I have been blessed!"

"Will you listen to yourself?" Fallon interrupted. "Our lives are not ruled by God. We have the power to choose. You need to choose to be yourself again. Because the Kottermanis are coming and I need you."

Gallagher sat up in the saddle. "You have nothing to worry about. I have prayed to Aroaril to protect us from the threat of Kottermani invasion and He has promised me it will never happen."

"Have you gone mad?" Fallon stared at him. "Nothing is going to stop the Kottermanis from coming except swords, spears and steel!"

"Doubt all you want. I know the truth now," Gallagher declared.

"You have gone mad. Wake up before it is too late! Act like that and you'll get yourself killed in battle!" Fallon cried, his voice getting louder all the time.

Gallagher shook his head. "Doubt all you want. I shall be proved right and on that day I shall accept your apology."

He turned his horse around and began going back towards the castle.

"And where are you going?"

"Somewhere I shall be appreciated. Until you let Aroaril into your hearts, you will not make the right choices," Gallagher said over his shoulder.

Fallon thought about going after him. But only for a heartbeat.

"Bran, you will take Gallagher's men," he ordered sharply. "I want to see those cells filled to bursting with Munro's men by the time this day has finished!"

CHAPTER 51

"Maybe you need to take over running the city, Bridgit," Nola said.

Bridgit stopped pouring out the tea, because otherwise she would have spilled it. She took a breath before resuming. She and her friends had discovered the Kottermani delicacy of tea since living in the castle, because it had certainly never been available for ordinary people. All the other luxuries from the castle larders had gone into the warehouses to be shared out – but not this. Mainly because nobody else wanted it. The nobles and some of the richer merchants drank it but the nobles had all deserted the city and she was damned if she was going to share anything with those rich merchant bastards. It was their one treat and they enjoyed the time it gave them in the late afternoon. Of late the enjoyment had been palled by the quality of the conversation. Nola was heartbroken at what had happened to Brendan, while Riona was less helpful and far more irritating than she had been in Kotterman. Still, they were her friends and she would not give up on them.

Bridgit handed out the tea cups, congratulating herself on not spilling any of the precious liquid after Nola's outrageous statement.

"I think she is right, you need to run the Council," Riona said.

This time there was no saving the cup, which hit the floor and shattered, sending tea all over the flagstones.

"I wish you'd wait until they were on the table before you make your jokes," Bridgit grumbled, carefully clearing away the pottery shards and eyeing the lost drink sadly.

"I am not joking," Riona said.

"And I never joke. Especially about something like that," Nola added. "We can all see that the boys are struggling. Gallagher has his head in the clouds, Devlin thinks he can't be serious about anything again, while Brendan—" she paused and took a gulping breath before continuing. "And Fallon doesn't care what he breaks or who he hurts as he chases ghosts around the city. Face it, we three did a far better job of taking care of people in Kotterman than the boys can do now. We would back you and if there was any trouble, we could get Gannon and his men to stand behind you."

"I am not going to fight against Fallon and the others!" Bridgit cried. "Are you mad?"

"Like it or not, we have been fighting with them for the past few meetings. The Ruling Council? Everyone can see it is your way or Fallon's way, with the rest of us supporting one side or the other," Nola said with a shrug.

"We need to work together more, not think how we can divide ourselves," Bridgit insisted.

Riona opened her mouth to speak but shut it swiftly as someone thumped on the door.

"Who is it?" Bridgit called, her heart beating fast, *which is silly really, because I have done nothing wrong,* she told herself.

"It is Jason. My lady, I need your orders," came the reply.

Bridgit looked at her friends suspiciously. Most of the Lunstermen had gone back to their town under Gannon's command, to keep an eye on Dina's former stronghold and also train more men for Fallon's new army. A score had stayed behind under the command of Jason, another Lunster sergeant and Gannon's second.

"What have you done?" she whispered.

They both shrugged, professing innocence. Bridgit sighed and opened the door to reveal the sergeant. He was nowhere near as tall as Gannon but he had a broad, trustworthy face and a solid look of dependability, although his face was now twisted with worry.

"I am sorry to disturb you, my lady," Jason said apologetically, "but we have a problem in the dungeons. The cells we have are already full and now scores more men are turning up, being dragged off the streets. We can't fit them in and it looks like it's turning into a riot, for some of the ones who have been there the longest are threatening to kill anyone else put in their cell. Unless we do something, it will be a bloodbath."

Bridgit sighed again. "I suppose you have sent a runner to Fallon?"

"I have sent two, my lady. Neither have returned. We don't have time for more, because we are struggling to keep things in hand now."

"Right. Lead on," she said immediately. "Come on, ladies. I might need the advice that you tell me is so valuable."

*

The situation was even worse than Jason had said, or perhaps it had just got worse since he left. Men sitting in lines shouted for help, or protested, while guards roared at them and shoved them down if they tried to get up. Meanwhile those already in the cells hammered at the bars and bellowed threats. It stank, a cloying stench of human waste and sweat that brought the gorge up into Bridgit's throat.

"We could bring some of them into the castle," Riona suggested, shouting to be heard over the bedlam.

Bridgit remembered how Keverne had got out and tried to kill them and suppressed a shudder. "No," she said. "That is not an answer. Jason, how long have some of these men been here?"

"A moon or more," the sergeant said.

"Have we got anything useful out of them?'

"Nothing," he admitted.

Bridgit looked at the lines of men. They all looked wet, cold, hungry and frightened. None of them stood out as being in the pay of Swane but then any agent of the deposed Prince would seek to hide their true nature. The ones in the cells looked much the same, except a bit drier and much dirtier.

"It's like looking for a needle in a haystack," she said aloud.

"Almost, my lady. At least there you know there is a needle somewhere. With these men, there's every chance they're all hay and not sharp enough to be a needle."

Bridgit nodded. "Send another runner to find Fallon and tell him we can't take any more until we let some go."

Jason nodded and grabbed one of the harassed-looking guards and shouted orders into his ear.

"But which ones shall we let go?" he asked.

"The ones in the cells. If we haven't been able to get them to talk by now, we aren't going to."

"Unless we persuade them," Jason said.

Bridgit shook her head vehemently. "Then they will say whatever we want them to. Get them out of here."

"Fallon will not be happy," Jason said.

"Let me worry about that. We are half of the Ruling Council and we order you to set these men free," Bridgit said firmly.

The atmosphere in the dungeon changed as each cell was emptied. At first the others were alarmed, then relieved, then demanded to join them. The new captives, however, still slumped on the floor. There were enough of them to easily fill the cells.

"Any word from Fallon?" Bridgit asked Jason, only to receive a shake of the head in reply. She pointed to one of the ragged men sitting on the cold stone floor. "Let me talk to one of them."

The man was hauled across, protesting, until Jason gave him a jab in the ribs. "Talk to the lady and you might get out of here in one piece," the sergeant growled.

Bridgit smiled reassuringly. "What is your name?" she asked.

"Sean," the man replied nervously.

Instantly Bridgit was catapulted back to Kotterman and the brothers Sean and Seamus and what she had done to them to save the others.

"Who paid you to shout that Prince Swane can save Berry and that we are stealing food from you?" she demanded.

Sean shrugged nervously. "I never got no money. The word on the streets is you just have to shout that out and you get a bed in the castle, and food, so your family can share out your rations and the kids don't starve."

"You know you could die in here," she warned.

His expression did not change. "Better than listening to the children crying because they're hungry. I used to work down on

315

the docks but there's no money there now. This is all I can do to help my family."

"You could have volunteered to fight. If you are in the army, you get more food," she said coldly.

Sean sniffed. "I did volunteer. But I got kicked out because I told some of the others what I had seen during the battle here."

Bridgit nodded to Jason and he hustled the man away. She cursed silently. Munro had outsmarted them. He did not need to give orders, he did not even need to be in the city. They were doing his work for him. Desperate men would do anything for their families and Munro was using these men to defeat the Ruling Council. All the spare food had gone to the eastern counties. Feeding so many extra men would leave the rest of the city short, which would cause even more problems. Fallon thought he was getting a problem off the streets but he was only making it worse, she realized. Each man arrested and being kept fed in the castle was inspiring two more to do the same. She turned to her friends.

"Arresting these men not only does nothing to find Swane's men but helps their cause by costing us time, effort and food. We have to let them go."

"What is Fallon going to say?" Riona muttered.

"You need to show that you are in charge," Nola said meaningfully. "This is the time to show your power."

"No, it's just the time to do what needs to be done," Bridgit disagreed.

She stared at the lines of men. They all had the same despairing look on their faces, as if punishment and torture in these cells was not the worst thing that could happen to them. She turned to Jason.

"Let them out. This is ridiculous," she said. "We'd get more useful information out of a wooden door than these men."

"My lady, Fallon has just arrested them," Jason said, a hint of reproof in his voice.

"And I am setting them free! Do it. Now!"

*

Fallon stayed behind in the stables to make sure the men were brushing and feeding the horses. The beasts looked exhausted and he suspected Brendan was right, they would start to lose them if they kept using them through this bitter weather. He would have to only use the fittest for a while, although the little fodder they had left was not going to restore their condition. Still, maybe they had finally snatched up one of Munro's men. Aroaril knew they had dragged enough away. There had been nothing that looked like Munro's base, just a lot of hungry people sheltering in empty houses, but you never knew.

He stretched his aching back. He would have liked to go and rest but the Ruling Council was supposed to meet this evening. Or what was left of it.

As he suspected, Gallagher had not bothered to join them. At least the room was warm, a raging fire going and thick curtains over the windows to shut out wind, which always found some gap in those horn panels to whistle in.

"It doesn't matter," Devlin said. "The Council got twice as smart when he left."

Riona giggled at that and Fallon turned to them irritably. "I don't find anything funny in the way one of my friends is destroying himself."

"When things are darkest, you need to laugh, for it's the only way to lift the spirits," Devlin countered loftily.

"Right," Fallon threw his cloak over a chair and joined the others, trying to ignore that Brendan was sitting at the opposite end of the table from Nola.

"How goes the hunt for Munro?" Bridgit asked.

"We need more men," Brendan said flatly. "Every man and his dog has apparently seen Munro and wants the reward for him. According to this list from the morning, Munro is in a score of places across the city, including working in the kitchens here."

"Really?" Fallon asked sharply.

"Given it's only women from Baltimore working there, I don't think even he would be able to disguise himself for long in there," Brendan said. "But we don't have enough men to look in all these places. And the one we miss could be the one where he's really hiding."

"Then get more men from Casey. Nothing is more important than getting Munro," Fallon said flatly.

"But that will slow down the training. The new men are not like the first batch you trained. They need a trainer each if they are to make any progress," Brendan objected.

"Doesn't matter. I want teams out there hunting for Munro. That is our top priority. Then we can worry about training."

"What do we do with the ones we catch, how do we get them to talk?" Devlin asked.

"We need to ask harder questions," Fallon said.

Bridgit shook her head. 'What you mean is you want to hurt people while you ask those questions."

"We need answers," Fallon argued. "We keep missing Munro but we know he's out there. We need to loosen a few tongues. If we can get them to talk faster then we can get this bastard."

"And by loosen tongues, you mean break fingers and toes. And I suppose you will get Brendan to do your dirty work for you," Nola said stiffly.

Fallon rolled his eyes. "Do I have to remind you that Munro was right inside this castle and got close to all of us? And then he sent Dina's traitorous lover to kill us in the night. He will not rest until we are dead and his master Swane is back on the throne. Do we want that to happen?"

"That is a stupid question," Bridgit said. "The real question is, are we prepared to hurt innocent people to maybe find one man with real knowledge of Munro. If there is one. Anyone foolish enough to be grabbed by our men is hardly likely to be smart enough to be trusted with Munro's hideout."

Fallon rubbed his ears, wondering if he was really hearing correctly. How could they not see things clearly as he did? "Bridge, this bastard tried to kill us. You know how close he came to succeeding, too. Kerrin was inches away from death at his hands!"

"But how does hurting ordinary people change that?" she replied instantly. "Remember, we are supposed to be better than Swane. We have to act like it."

"We are better than Swane! But stopping him will take more than rude words! He's still on the loose somewhere, remember?

318

Finding Munro will blind him and lead us right to him. This will end his threat once and for all. And I am happy to do whatever it takes to make that happen."

He leaned back in his chair, sure they would all agree with him now. How could they not?

"And you would sacrifice Brendan along the way as well? You will destroy him, as well as dozens of families," Nola accused.

"Nola is right. We cannot agree to this," Bridgit nodded.

Fallon turned to Devlin, to appeal to him, but the farmer averted his eyes. Fallon swore at himself. If only he had laughed at the man's jokes! Then he swore at Devlin more.

"Right," he said aloud. "We shall do what we can. But you need to think again."

"We'll let you know when we have," Nola said primly.

"So, what news from around the country?" he said, holding his temper in check.

"Food is getting low everywhere. I think we need to cut the rations to the army," Bridgit said.

"Not going to happen. Those men need that extra food," Fallon said instantly.

"But you said they aren't training properly anyway—"

"The rations stay the same. We can cut it back elsewhere. End of discussion."

"Maybe you're suffering from baby brain, Bridgit," Devlin added with a wink.

"What?" Bridgit gasped.

Devlin smiled. "You know. When women are pregnant they start to lose their mind. It always happens."

"Oh, and what's your excuse then?" Bridgit asked sharply.

"Anyway, what's happening in the rest of the country? Are they also complaining?" Fallon said loudly.

Bridgit sighed. "Much the same as here. We have all towns under our control though. It is only talk. We just have to ignore it. Treat it as a joke."

"Finally!" Devlin said. "Somebody says something sensible in here!"

Fallon ignored him completely. "We have to stop these rumors. We must stamp down on everyone spreading them."

"We might as well try to stop the winter rain," Bridgit said tiredly. "That approach is doing us more harm than good. Fallon, we need to speak about—"

"Maybe we should fight back with some rumors of our own," Devlin interrupted.

Fallon turned to his friend eagerly. "That sounds like an idea. What did you have in mind?"

"How about that Swane is coming back, ready to burn babies to Zorva. That will get people ready to help stop him."

"It could also cause a panic on the streets. What if people head off into the countryside to try and escape? We could see hundreds starving, or freezing, or arriving in towns already stretched to the limit," Bridgit warned.

"You never take my ideas seriously," Devlin said accusingly.

"Because throwing ideas out into the air is not being serious. We have to think about our every action and only act when we have considered everything," she said heatedly. "Or we shall be no better than Aidan and his nobles."

"Are you comparing Dev to one of the nobles?" Riona snapped.

"Enough!" Fallon roared. He was heartily sick of all of this. It wasn't supposed to be this way. For the hundredth time, he wondered what might have happened if Prince Cavan was alive. "This is not helping. Dev, go away and think of some rumors we can spread about Swane without causing a panic, and then we'll look at how we win back the streets. Now, how is the food situation in Berry?"

"It could be better. The stocks are going down faster than we expected, in part because there are too many prisoners in the castle, all demanding to be fed."

"How is that eating up the food? They would be getting it anyway," Fallon pointed out.

"But we don't know who their families are. They are still turning up at the warehouses, to get a full family ration, which they share out or sell, while we feed the father twice a day."

Fallon swore. "Right. What can we do to stop this?" he said.

"I have fixed the problem," Bridgit said.

"Excellent! How?"

"I have let all the prisoners go."

"What? Are you mad?" he thundered. "Was Devlin right and you have baby brain?"

"No! And I would thank you to keep a civil tongue in your head! I had to do it, because the cells were full and then you brought even more back, overcrowding us to the point that something had to give. I would have spoken to you but you were nowhere to be found and, besides, you wouldn't have agreed anyway."

"Then you can go and round up some guards and get them back again," he roared.

"Impossible. And it is a waste of time, money and effort. Some will have run, some gone into hiding and if there was any traitor in their ranks, they hid themselves well. Face it, I had to do it, because you would not."

Fallon slammed his hand on the table. He now expected the others to hinder him, rather than help, but Bridgit? He had always depended on her. "How could you do that?" he snarled. "Those men might have held the key to finding Munro and maybe even Swane and Kemal!"

"By the time we had sorted through all of them, spring would be here. None of them were talking."

"Because you stop us from using the right methods to get them to talk!"

"So we should torture hundreds of innocent men in the hope of finding maybe one guilty? How does that make us better than Aidan? We need to catch Munro and find Swane and Kemal but not like this."

He shoved back his chair and stood. "Right. Well, I had better get back out there and start searching, because if we don't find Munro, all of this is pointless."

"Fallon! Sit down and let us talk about it sensibly—"

But he was already heading out the door. All this talk was achieving nothing. The Kottermanis were coming and he had no way of stopping them. Not unless he caught Munro. Why couldn't anyone else see that?

CHAPTER 52

For the last quarter moon Feray had watched endless caravans of food, water, weapons and armor as well as lines of soldiers snake down to the docks and disappear into the bowels of the fleet of ships waiting there. It was tempting to wish for them to sail into the storm she had somehow survived and sink – except Kemal was on board one of those ships.

But she had not been idle. They had torn up sheets and made a long rope, testing it at night to make sure it reached all the way to the ground – and that it could hold their weight. Ely had also made several trips to the market, slipping out when things were at their busiest, and now they had more than enough sleeping powders.

"The Gaelish acted when it was time for evening prayers, knowing that they had that time before anyone could react," Ely said.

At first thought Feray was scandalized at the idea of doing the same but then the idea grew on her. Yes, she needed all the help she could get to make her crazy plan work but praying to Aroaril at certain times of day had not provided them with the God's power, nor stopped the Gaelish Zorva-worshippers from taking over. Skipping one prayer session, especially in a good cause, was a small price to pay.

She peered out of the window and saw the last of the ships sailing out of the harbor with the afternoon tide, joining the forest of sails that waited beyond the harbor wall. It was an astonishing achievement to have it all ready so quickly but she was not surprised. When the Emperor ordered something, it happened. Or people died.

"We shall go tonight," she said.

"Is it not better to wait for a few days, so that the guards relax even further, without the presence of the Emperor there? And we don't want to sail into the rest of the fleet," Ely suggested nervously.

"Yes, we do. Who knows when they will execute the Emperor and my Kemal?" Feray said. "Besides, they will keep the area where they sail free of storms with their blood magic. We want to enjoy that as well. We go tonight."

Ely smiled, a little. "I never got to escape the last time," she said softly. "I would like to do so now."

"This is only the first step," Feray said. "In some ways it is the easiest. After this we have to find Gokmen and Gemici, then hope our ship is still there. And then we have to somehow free Kemal from the middle of a huge fleet and turn the tables on the evil Gaelish. Go and give those powders to the guards. I'll make sure the boys are ready."

Feray made sure they were dressed in travelling clothes and fastened a small bag on each of their backs.

"Ana, what is going on?" Asil asked.

"We have to go and rescue your baba. Do what I say and say not a word unless I tell you. And you must be prepared to run if I say. Run and don't look back, hide and survive."

"We will never leave you, Ana," Asil declared.

She grabbed him by the shoulder. "No. You have to be stronger than that. You mean everything to me and if I have to sacrifice myself to let you live, then so be it. Find shelter wherever you can and always remember who you are."

"Ana, you're scaring me," Orhan whispered.

She pasted a smile on her face. She had not wanted them to see this side of life until they were much older. But there was no escaping it now. "Good. Because fear will keep us alive. But terror will kill us. Make a noise at the wrong moment and we could all be lost. But I don't intend on dying for many years yet, so stay close to me and do what I say and we shall all laugh about this with your baba in a few moons' time. You are the heirs to the Elephant Throne, so you must live up to that today."

"You can rely on us, Ana," Asil promised, Orhan nodding emphatically.

She reached out and hugged them to her. "You are my world and I will do anything to keep you safe," she whispered. "Some of the things you might hear and see may seem strange but trust me and we shall all get through this."

"My lady, the guards have drunk the powders and prayers will be called any moment," Ely said gently.

"Good. Now, do you have the papers I signed, freeing you, your mother and sister?"

"Yes, my lady. Thank you."

"No, thank you," Feray said. "I will be sorry to see you go but I wish you well. Go far from here and I hope you can make something of a life for yourself. For what it is worth, I am sorry my husband used you as his spy and threatened your family. I only hope taking away your slavery can go some way to make up for that."

Ely nodded her thanks, her eyes shining, and Feray squeezed her shoulder, then beckoned to her sons. "Go with God. And pray for us, for now is the time to go."

*

Feray accepted a cup of water with a nod of thanks. Ely had helped them climb down their makeshift rope to the street, while the comatose guards lolled in the doorway, oblivious to everything. She had made her way to the docks easily enough but finding Gemici's house had been much harder. She had to keep a tight rein on her instinct to order people to help her, instead of asking politely. Luckily the sailor was a well-known man around the docks and she had only taken a few wrong turns before finding his house. But she was conscious that her guards could be found asleep at any moment and then who knew what would happen? Without the Emperor or Durzu, there was no real authority in the city, but she suspected there would still be orders somewhere to have her killed if she caused trouble. Finding Gokmen at Gemici's house was a welcome stroke of luck.

"We have to get back to Gaelland. The Zorva-worshippers have cast a spell over Durzu and the Emperor. Unless we can free Kemal and stop them, we are all dead and the Empire will fall into darkness," she told them.

The two men exchanged glances. "We tried to get a ship ready, just in case, but then the harbor has been so busy with the Emperor's orders ..." Gokmen's voice trailed off. "We have been waiting here, thinking orders would arrive for our death at any moment."

"But we are ready now. Better to go down doing something you love, rather than wait here like a lamb before market day," Gemici agreed. "But how will we free the Prince and stop the Emperor?"

"Leave that to me," Feray said with a confidence she did not feel.

Gokmen stood tall. "I shall defend you with my life," he told her.

"But we need to hurry," Gemici said. "I'll get the crew together, you need to find us some supplies if we are not to starve on the way."

Gokmen grinned. "I'll get them for you. Let me grab a few things." He disappeared into the back of the house and Feray relaxed, a little. There were still so many obstacles in front of her but she could not afford to think of them now. One task at a time.

"Highness," Gemici said softly. "You do know that the only ship left in the harbor is ours? After all she suffered on the trip home, she will not stand up to another storm like the one we survived."

Feray had suspected that might be the case but there was no other choice. "Are you saying you are afraid to do this?" she asked.

The old sailor's weather-beaten face creased further in a smile. "I merely spoke because you might want to leave your sons somewhere safer."

"Nowhere is safe for them. Or for any of us, if the Zorva-worshippers win."

CHAPTER 53

"Are you comfortable, brother?" Durzu asked with mock-kindness.

Kemal looked up wearily, squinting as daylight poured into the small cabin that served as his prison. Durzu had a pair of the Emperor's guards at his shoulder but, even if he was alone, the chain that locked him to the wall meant there was no chance he could exact any revenge on his brother. Yet.

"What do you want? If you plan to gloat, I have better things to do."

Durzu chuckled. "Yes, your new duties. I hear you are quite the worker and can even scrub floors like a servant. Who knew? We just had to find the right motivation. Keep it up and I won't let my allies sacrifice the other servants to Zorva. But surely you would like to take a break and talk?"

Kemal smiled through his hatred. "Actually, there is a louse in my armpit that needs catching."

Durzu laughed. "A thrilling task, to be sure! But surely you want to know your fate? You liked to know everything, I recall."

"How about I tell you your fate, instead?" Kemal offered.

"Oh please. This should be entertaining," Durzu said with a smile.

"Your new allies will use you and then kill you. They will seem to be right behind you, but only so they can better stab you in the back. Do not trust the woman, particularly. She is the real power behind Swane. He is but a puppet."

"Tell me something I don't know," Durzu mocked.

"Kill them now. I would rather see you on the throne than either of them. Do not let these Zorva-worshippers live. They will drown the world in blood."

Durzu cocked his head on one side. "You know, I do believe you are serious." He clapped his hands gently. "Finally, we are able to find something on which we agree. You know, I was going to have you sacrificed tomorrow to ensure a good voyage, but now I think I shall keep you alive a little longer. Besides, I want to see what my allies will do to you when I tell them I have decided to keep you alive."

*

"We have to kill Kemal. As long as he lives, there is a chance things could go wrong," Dina said firmly. "The Emperor's mind is ours but Kemal is a man around which the Kotterman nobility could rally."

Swane nodded enthusiastically. "Besides, he has royal blood. It is a greater sacrifice and Zorva will reward us greatly for offering his soul."

"I want him around until the end. Kill my other two brothers instead. They bore me endlessly, while Kemal is entertaining at least," Durzu said casually.

"This is a mistake. You don't want to leave even the slightest opening for things to go wrong," Dina said. "Believe me, we have been guilty of being merciful. I had Fallon in my power and let him go, thinking he could still be useful to me. And he almost killed us in return."

"Still, this is what I want. And I shall not be denied in this," Durzu warned.

Dina reached under the table to squeeze Swane's thigh. She could hide her anger easily but he had never learned the trick. He did what she wanted almost all the time but she did not want this to be one of those times when flashes of Aidan burst to the surface. On a Kottermani ship, surrounded by the Kottermani army, things would not end well for them. And she needed these Kottermanis as well. Fallon would not die easily. The last thing they needed was to get to Gaelland and then not have enough men to finish the job.

"Then you shall get your wish. Your other brothers have to die anyway," she said casually. "We are only offering advice; you are the one who makes the final decisions."

She did not add: *For now*. But it was a pleasure saying it to herself, anyway.

CHAPTER 54

"We are ready to sail, Highness," Gemici said.

Packing the ship had been a nervous time but she had given the orders and the slave overseers had obeyed without question. Luckily there was nobody left to question them and there had been plenty of extra supplies left on the docks and even more slaves who could be turned into porters.

The sailors, meanwhile, had been delighted to go to work, making sure frayed ropes were replaced and several new sails packed aboard. They saluted whenever Feray or her sons came close and she smiled at the way they were willing to risk their lives for her.

"How seaworthy is she?" Feray asked Gemici. She knew they had to sail anyway but she could not keep the fear entirely buried.

The master mariner grimaced. "I have not had the time to check everything," he admitted. "There has been some work done below decks to strengthen the hull but unless we sent down men with lobster masks to look, we would not know for sure."

Feray nodded as if she had expected that. "That will stay between us," she said softly and Gemici bowed his head.

"My lady, we could use more crewmen," he said. "Not just to sail the ship but to make it appear as if we are just like the rest of the fleet, with many men on board."

"But we can't trust anyone else," Feray said. "Cast off. We need to catch up to the rest of the fleet and try and hide among them. There will be so many ships there that we shall just be one more in the crowd."

Gemici hurried away and Feray strode back to order the last of the slaves off the ship when a disturbance on the dock attracted her attention. It took a few moments to see what was happening, even with the height advantage the ship gave her, and then she grasped the rail in shock to see Ely hurrying down the dock, a group of what looked like Gaelish in tow. Most of them were obviously terrified, many dressed in rags, and the dock guards were instinctively moving to stop them.

"Let them through! They are with me," Feray ordered loudly, her tone leaving no choice but to obey.

The group was ushered on board, and the two standing closest to Ely were obviously her mother and younger sister. But she had no idea as to who the rest of them were.

"Who are they?" she asked the servant girl. She looked different somehow, as if she was now in control.

"They were the crew that Swane brought from Gaelland. They were kept prisoner and forced to watch as he sacrificed some of their children to Zorva. They will do anything to stop Swane and to get back to Gaelland," Ely replied. "They had been locked up with my family, ready to be sold off as slaves, but I told their guards your papers applied to them as well. I shouted at them until they believed me and let these people go. They are sailors and can help us."

Feray was impressed at the girl's quick thinking and waved Gokmen over. "Find space for the families and then get the men ready to serve. Gemici can find duties for them."

The slave master saluted and urged the group of Gaelish away, offering them rough reassurances in his gravelly Gaelish, leaving Ely, her mother and sister with Feray.

"I thought you would use your freedom to find safety, not to risk your lives," Feray said. "You know that we may not even make it to Gaelland and, even if we do, we face even more danger. And how will you be greeted in Gaelland? Will your old Gaelish friends be happy to see you?"

Ely was breathing hard, her face flushed, but she held her head up. "Anything is better than slavery," she said. "Even death. And if we die, we die free. It is worth any risk."

That gave Feray pause for thought. She had not thought deeply about slaves before. You gave them orders and then forgot about it. Kottermani society depended on them but paid no attention to the pain slavery caused. She berated herself for not considering it more carefully. After all, her ancestral home had supplied thousands of slaves for the Empire over the years.

"Find yourself a cabin below and I would be grateful if you kept an eye on Asil and Orhan for me," she said.

Ely's family bowed their heads and hurried past, disappearing below as the sailors threw off the last of the ropes and launched the small rowboats that would tow them out of the harbor and out to the sea.

"Here we go, my lady. A prayer to Aroaril would not go astray, I think," Gokmen said, his face split by a wide grin.

Feray nodded absently but then thought again. Asking for Aroaril's help was all very well but they had done enough of that in the past, with little to show for it. Maybe she needed to offer something in return.

"Help us to stop the Zorva-worshippers and I swear I will end slavery in the Empire. It may not happen right away but I swear on my children's lives that I will see the last chains cast off," she murmured. As soon as she said it, she felt better. That was probably just foolishness but it did not hurt to think they had Aroaril on their side. After all, there were no other allies.

*

"The fleet is on the horizon, my lady," Gemici said. "How far back should we stay?"

Feray shaded her eyes with her hands and looked out to the horizon, where a forest of masts and sails showed clearly. Her crew were veteran sailors who knew how to handle this ship, having sailed it from Gaelland already. They were obviously faster than the fleet because, although they had taken on a full load of food and water, they did not have a hold full of soldiers and their equipment.

"Take us right in there, then pull back on the sails so we match their speed," she decreed.

"And if they challenge us?"

"We shall worry about that then. My guess is they have more than enough to worry about already," she said.

They slowed gradually as they got closer, which gave her more chance to study the pattern of the fleet. Except there was no pattern – they sailed without order, just a mass of ships.

"Whoever is in charge is an idiot. One storm will scatter everyone across the seas. And there is every chance they will run into each other each night," Gemici snorted.

"We should give thanks to them, because they have made our job much easier. The trick will be slipping away from them when we get closer to Gaelland," Feray said.

"If we last that long, it should be easy," Gemici said. And he was not smiling.

CHAPTER 55

Fallon kicked in the door and stepped aside for three of his villagers to race in, crossbows at the ready. He followed them, his own loaded and ready, but it was not needed. The place was empty and, from the dust everywhere and the icy chill in the air, it had been abandoned for a while.

"All right, lads," he said, slipping the quarrel out of his crossbow. "That's the last for today. Back to the castle to dry out and get some hot food."

They walked to the horses and Fallon caught sight of a man lurking at the end of an alley. He was hooded, which was not unusual for everyone was swathed in thick clothes to keep out the bitter chill. But he was different somehow. There was something about his shape that reminded Fallon of Munro. Fallon caught Brendan's eye and gestured that way.

"Listen, lads," he said softly, his voice only just carrying to those nearest. "When I give the order, follow me."

Word spread down the line then Fallon clapped spurs to his horse and charged up the street, followed by the others an instant later, although it was a slow charge because they didn't want the horses to slip on the icy cobbles.

The man vanished around the corner in an instant but Fallon was confident of catching him – until he rounded the corner and saw no running man but instead a cart rattling up the road at a terrific rate, the hooded man at the reins.

"Get him!" he roared, roweling back his spurs.

Yet, try as he might, they struggled to narrow the gap. They should have caught it quickly but the slippery cobbles slowed everything down. The cart turned left and right, the driver leaning from one side to the other to keep it upright. Some of Fallon's men had no such luck. One of the horses slipped, bringing two more down with it in a screaming pile. Fallon only gave them a glance. They could come back for them later.

People flung themselves out of the way as the cart raced by and the horses thundered after it. Their passage was marked with screams and shouts and wails of people falling over and trying to protect their children.

One of Fallon's men tried to avoid a woman and ended up crashing into a market stall, sending pots flying and causing another horse to fall over, where it slid into a group of people.

"Ignore them!" Fallon bellowed as some of his men slowed their horses to help sort out the chaos.

Slowly they closed the distance and the hooded man glanced over his shoulder. With a crack of the whip he turned the cart again, down another street – right into a crowd. The cart ploughed into them, the press of bodies stopping it, but not before men and women were flung in all directions.

The man jumped off the cart as Fallon and Brendan arrived and plunged into the crowd after him. But there were people running in all directions, shouting and screaming and he could not see his prey. Brendan pulled down a struggling man but it proved to be someone completely different. Hurriedly he organized his men to block off the area and go through the people but by the time they did that, scores had disappeared and there was no sign of Munro in those remaining – and then Fallon spotted a hooded cloak on the ground.

"Bastard has got away," Brendan cursed, picking it up. "Now what do we do?"

Fallon looked at the wounded and sighed. "Clean this up," he said. "I'm sure Bridgit will have something to say about this."

The smith grunted. "You are going to have to do something about the women. I reckon they want to run the Ruling Council."

"What? Bridgit would never agree to that!" Fallon scoffed.

"Really? She let everyone go that we spent so long capturing. And she got that Lunsterman Jason to do it for her, one of the men who is loyal to her before you. Do you think that is the mark of someone willing to let you stay in charge or is it someone who has their own plans?"

"Bridgit is with me, not against me," Fallon said.

"That's what I thought about Nola," Brendan said remorselessly. "We have been through too much to lose everything now. Maybe you need to remove the Ruling Council and run things yourself."

Fallon shook his head stubbornly. "It cannot come to that," he said.

*

"What were you thinking?" Bridgit cried. "More than thirty men and women hurt and having to be healed by Rosaleen, to say nothing of four horses killed and hundreds complaining about us!"

"I thought it was Munro!" Fallon said defensively, heading over to the fire. It had taken many turns of the hourglass to sort out the mess in the streets and now he was freezing. "You weren't there. I had no choice."

"Of course you did! You could have sent someone to cut him off, or done something differently, anything but wreck half the city and nearly kill a dozen people!"

He spun around from the fire. "Oh, so it's all right for you to make an instant decision to let our prisoners go but not for me to chase the bastard who tried to kill us?"

"That is different," she said. "I had a choice, either kill innocent men or let them go. Letting those fools go was the easy choice. If you were thinking, you wouldn't make these bad decisions."

He sucked in a deep breath. "So you think you can make better decisions than me? Have you been talking with Nola and the others about taking over the Ruling Council?"

He stared intently at her and was horrified to see the flash of shock on her face.

"You have, haven't you!" he accused.

She hesitated for just a heartbeat and he knew it was true.

"Nola raised it with me. But I never agreed to do anything," she said firmly. "I told them I could never work against you. You know that is true."

Fallon sat down, barely hearing her words. He had turned his back on his ambitions for her, sacrificed his plans to make her happy and now she was second-guessing him all the time and questioning his judgment. This was not the Bridgit he knew and loved. It had to be the baby. People said pregnant women were driven a little mad by bearing a young one.

"The baby is doing something to you," he said sadly.

*

Bridgit rubbed her eyes. Fallon was right about one thing. She felt queasy and hungry both at the same time, while her head was hammering. She kicked herself for letting her guard down for a moment. Still, maybe this was a shock he needed, to make him wake up to what he was doing. He had to think before acting now. Aroaril knew she had to weigh things up these days. Especially as her emotions were all mixed up. One moment she felt on top of the world, the next like crying. She knew it was just the baby changing things for her but it was still hard to keep focused when you felt like screaming one moment, laughing the next.

"Forget about the baby. You sound like a small child," she told her husband. "You need to wake up and realize that everyone is doing the best they can. We all want the same thing. Nobody is trying to replace you, least of all me. Yet you seem to want to be both Lord and Protector of Gaelland."

He stood up. "Tell me honestly. Do you think I am worthy?"

"Well, you are certainly not worthy right now. You are being foolish. Do you truly believe that I would seek to replace you?"

She searched his face and could see a mixture of hurt and anger.

"I don't want to believe it," he said. "But it's like you don't trust me. I know how to protect you. I need to have the freedom to do that. I can save this country, if you just get behind me."

"I thought we worked together," she said quietly.

"And we do. But in this case I know best."

"You know best? I've been cleaning up all the messes you leave behind!"

"You don't understand—"

"That's right, Lord Protector, I don't. I don't understand how you can act like such an idiot!"

"I don't have to listen to this," Fallon growled and stormed towards the door. "I'll be back when you have calmed down and taken your brain back from the baby."

"I have baby brain? Well, you have hay for brains and you'd be better off sleeping in the stables!"

He walked away, his back stiff with outrage, and he did not see the tears falling down her face. She slumped onto the bed. Where was the old Fallon, who could listen and hear the things left unspoken?

CHAPTER 56

The body went over the side with a splash and Dina signalled for Kemal and the other slaves to wash the blood off the deck. They had to be careful. Durzu's other two brothers were dead, the nobles were confined to their cabins, and Durzu had a circle of cronies who had been seduced by a combination of Zorva and promises of gold and land but the days still began and ended with a prayer to Aroaril and there were plenty of Kottermanis who believed they were fighting for Aroaril. It would not do to let them know there was blood sacrifice going on every night. Just to be safe, they were sending one noble a night to Zorva, so that the next day could be smooth sailing. Controlling an area big enough for the fleet was difficult but Swane's powers were growing with each heart he took and dedicated to the Dark God, and so far only one ship had been lost through bad weather, caught by a freak wave that had wrecked its masts and forced it to turn back for Kotterman. Two more had been slightly damaged in night-time collisions but they had not dared to let the fleet spread out any more in case they were lost in storms. Maintaining the fine weather over such a large area was difficult enough as it was. It meant they could not spare any magic to use to speed up the journey but that was acceptable, because every day gave them more opportunity to increase their hold over the Kottermanis. The Emperor and the Hierarch did their bidding, Durzu announced the orders and nobody realized they were part of an army of Zorva.

Dina liked the progress they were making and the news from Gaelland was encouraging. Finbar was sending magicked birds to Munro and passing on her instructions – as well as receiving word that the country was not happy about Fallon's rule. All seemed well, but she was not as happy about Swane. The endless sacrifice was affecting him, changing him, and that was concerning. The surge of power that accompanied each heart offered to Zorva was making him immune to her charms. She had to rack her brain for ever more exotic ways to interest him in the bedchamber. Worse still, he was talking more about his plans for the future and how he wanted to rule the world. Ambition was all very well but she liked obedience more. Perhaps it was time to look again at other options.

*

Kemal helped scrub the last of the blood off the deck and led his gang of slaves back down below. They did not have cabins, just a stinking part of the hold, which even the rats avoided. Stinking bilge water sloshed around their ankles if they did not keep to one end, where a platform for cargo sat. At first he had found the smell incredible but his nose had given up the unequal fight and he no longer noticed it. This deep in the ship, the nights were freezing and the slaves had to huddle together for warmth. Sleep was difficult and, to stop himself going mad in the dark, Kemal made them talk to him. At first they had been reluctant, for he was a former Crown Prince and they but slaves. Yet, as the days passed, they talked more and he learned about where they had come from, their old lives and what it was like to be a slave. He knew about the last part by now, of course. The work was hard, the food was poor and he was wracked with fear for Feray and his sons, as well as horror over the endless blood sacrifice. But, strangely, the night-time talks made him feel better about some of the choices he had made. He'd been tormented by thoughts he had been weak in giving in to Fallon. Yet he had given in to Swane and Dina twice now, first to save Gaelish children and now to save slaves. And he did not regret that. His dignity was not worth anyone's life. A few moons ago he would never have thought that but these journeys were changing him. Perhaps for the better.

The creak of the hatch above stopped his musings, made them all look up. The rest of the slaves scattered, jumping down into the filthy bilge water as soon as they saw who was looking in on them.

"So what brings you to my comfortable cabin?" Kemal asked.

"What? Can't I visit my own brother?" Durzu asked innocently, squatting down and holding a perfumed handkerchief over his nose.

Kemal scratched his unshaven chin. "You would not visit this place unless you had a compelling purpose," he said thoughtfully. "Durzu, you are here because you know what you are doing is wrong. Do you want to be responsible for turning the whole world to Zorva, seeing bloody altars built in every city for children to be sacrificed? You have killed our brothers and now slaughter men we have known all our lives, loyal servants of our father. Do they deserve that fate?"

Durzu spread his hands. "I cannot act now," he said. "We need their blood power to make it across the sea safely. Besides, where you see loyal servants, I see men who have always put their own power and profit first and who would seize the Elephant Throne if they got the chance. This will ensure the Empire will be strong, once we have cleaned out all the deadwood."

"But afterwards. You have to see they will use you and then kill you," Kemal said.

Durzu chuckled. "After all I have done to you, you are actually advising me. In your place I would be cheering on anyone who would kill my tormentor."

"That is where we are different," Kemal said. "I have learned that there are darker things in this world and that the enemy of my enemy is not always my friend."

"Very deep," Durzu applauded. "I shall try to remember that one." He stood up. "Thank you for the talk, brother, I have to admit, I enjoy seeing you like this. The favored Kemal, the golden child, now a filthy servant. It's worth keeping you alive for."

"Listen to me," Kemal cried. "Have men ready to kill those Gaelish the moment we sight land. Give me a knife and I will do the job myself."

"Give you a knife? Now that is one thing I shall not do," Durzu said instantly. "But it has been a pleasure talking to you. I shall use those Gaelish until I stand all-powerful, then I shall dispose of them."

Kemal slumped back, frustrated, as his brother dropped the hatch back down, plunging them into gloom. Slowly the other slaves joined him, but he was hardly aware of them.

Kemal sighed. To think he had the chance to end all this and he had thrown it away. Feray had been right and he wished with all his heart he could tell her so. He knew she would fight to save their sons but surely that was hopeless. He would have to resign himself to only seeing them again in another life.

*

"I still need you to help me," Feray said.

"What do you want me to do?" Ely asked nervously.

"I know that I said you were free and you could do what you wanted but I am asking you, for the sake of my children, to help me when we reach Gaelland," Feray continued.

Their ship had become an accepted part of the invasion fleet, unchallenged by the others and protected by the evil magic of the Gaelish when the storms rolled across the sky. That was another successful step in her crazy plan to free Kemal, but the next step was what to do when they reached Gaelland.

"We have to find out where my husband's men are being kept. Only then do we have a chance of freeing them. I have money but I need someone who speaks good Gaelish and doesn't look like they just left Adana to do the asking. I know it is a risk. And I know that you must have little love for my husband, after what he made you do. But, if you can help us, I would be even more grateful than I am now."

She looked into the girl's eyes, knowing she had no right to ask this but having no choice. Even knowing where the prisoners were held was just another step in a hugely improbable chain of events. Then she had to free them, arm them and – somehow – use them to free Kemal before the Zorva-worshippers sacrificed him. Chances were something would go wrong and they would all die. But, until then, she would keep fighting.

"I will help you," Ely said. "But I cannot promise they will talk to me. I have never been in Gaelland and I must sound more Kottermani than Gaelish."

"We can fix that," her mother said, in Gaelish.

Feray glanced at her and saw the remains of beauty, as well as a familiar look. It was that of a woman who was prepared to do anything to keep her children alive and she felt an instant connection with her.

"Aroaril willing, you will have the grateful thanks of the Emperor," Feray said. She felt a powerful need to go and hug her sons.

Her mother sniffed. "I cannot see us living that long."

"Then why did you come with us?"

"I lost all hope many years ago. But, Aroaril willing, I shall see my home again before I die. What else do we have to look forward to?"

Feray looked her in the eye. "Follow me and you shall find out," she said.

CHAPTER 57

Bridgit woke up right after dawn. She rubbed sleep out of her eyes and saw Kerrin doing a series of push-ups. She yawned. She had not slept well because Fallon had not come to bed that night.

"You shouldn't do those on the cold stone floor. You will catch your death," she said without thinking, then bit her lip.

"I've been doing these for moons now and I am fine," Kerrin replied, between pushing himself up.

Bridgit lay in the warm bed for a little longer, preparing herself for the cold. Old habits died hard and she wrapped a robe around herself and then stirred up the fire, getting it going again.

"When you have finished, we shall go and get some breakfast," she said, watching Kerrin stretching and marveling that this was the same son she had sat with, night after night, listening to him cough.

He pulled a face at that.

"I know it is the same oat porridge that everyone else has to eat but we might be able to find one slice of bacon, eh?" she said with a smile. "What were your plans today?"

"I usually help the recruits, or train with the guards, maybe see what Dad is up to," Kerrin said casually.

Bridgit felt a sudden pang that she did not know what he did every day. How could she have let that happen? He was growing up so fast. Once she would have known everything he did but now she seemed to know more about what was happening in Meinster than what her beloved son was doing.

"Then today we shall do something different. Spend the day together, like the old times."

"All right," he said, without any great enthusiasm, which was a knife to the heart. It was like Fallon had stolen him away. She pushed that thought away. *He will come back to me – they will both come back,* she told herself.

The castle was quiet that early in the morning. Without the old routines of farming and fishing, many of the families from Baltimore had taken to sleeping late, for the lack of food discouraged most of them from much activity and the cold discouraged the rest.

"What do you want to do today?" Bridgit asked.

Kerrin only thought for a moment before replying. "Can we go and see the new recruits? I want to know what they're doing."

"Go out in the snow to watch people hitting each other? Really?" she asked, disappointed. "Would you rather not spend the day finding books to read?"

"Maybe afterwards," Kerrin said.

She sighed. "Right. Well, breakfast first."

They wandered into the kitchens to see a servant working on the porridge, a huge cauldron full that would feed everyone in the castle. The woman had a friendly face and Bridgit smiled at her.

"Smells good," Bridgit said absently as she looked around. She had not been down here since their big feast. "Come on Kerrin, let's find some bacon," she said.

But he had stopped.

"Who is she?" he asked softly. "Mam, I've never seen her before and I don't think we're using servants anymore. And what is she putting in the porridge? That's not a honey jar she's waving over the top."

Bridgit looked at him blankly for a moment, then her brain woke up properly.

"I'm sure it's nothing," she said softly. "But stay behind me." She turned to the woman. "What's your name? I don't think I've seen you before," she said casually.

"This is my first day here," the servant said warmly, turning and busying herself at the bench. "I'm Jen."

Bridgit glanced over towards the kitchen door. It was a few paces away. That was the smart move. Get Kerrin to safety and then come back with some guards.

"Well, I hope you enjoy it here," she said, edging towards the door.

Then Jen spun, a knife in her hand, and hurled it at her.

Bridgit instinctively ducked but Kerrin had grabbed a chopping board and lifted it up, using it as a shield. The knife thumped into it, then Kerrin hauled the knife out and brandished it.

"Get behind me, Mam," he said urgently.

She had no intention of doing that, especially as Jen was advancing on them. "Guards! Guards!" Bridgit screamed.

"Come and get us," Kerrin invited. "I've been training for moons to kill you!"

Bridgit was horrified at that but the woman must have decided that staying any longer was too risky. Instead she raced out of the kitchen, going towards the castle garden.

"After her!" Kerrin cried.

But Bridgit had his tunic in her hand. "Not you, my lad," she said firmly. "Quick, this way."

They raced off to the guard room by the keep's main door, where a handful of men were ready and waiting, led by Jason.

"Jason! Thank Aroaril! Sound the alarm!" Bridgit shouted.

Instantly he grabbed a large bell and began to ring it, while two of his men hauled the big doors shut, slamming the locking bar into place.

"Now, follow me – there's a woman out there who tried to kill us. We have to catch her," she said loudly, over the sound of the bell. She turned back towards the kitchen but he did not move.

"What are you waiting for?" she demanded.

"I cannot leave my post without Captain Fallon's orders. He was most definite about it," he said uncomfortably. "If I do so, he will dismiss me."

"Jason, a woman called Jen tried to kill us in the kitchens and she is getting away while we waste time here!"

Jason snapped his fingers at two of his men and they raced off. "We'll get more guards and I'll warn Captain Fallon," he said. "The gates are all sealed, she can't get away."

Bridgit swore. "Do you really think she was planning to walk out the gates?" she asked bitterly. "She will be long gone. Keep looking and I'll go and tell the Lord Protector myself."

"Who?"

She flapped her hand impatiently. "Fallon. Leave him to me. But for Aroaril's sake don't let anyone eat the porridge until Archbishop Rosaleen has checked it."

*

Bridgit strode down the corridor, ignoring the drafts of icy wind that whistled down after her, Kerrin at her heels. She reached Fallon's offices and paused. "Kerrin, go back to your room," she ordered.

"Mam, I'm not going anywhere. That woman might have doubled back. You need me to protect you," he said.

"I don't need protection." *Although your father might need some protection from me*, she added silently.

Kerrin showed no signs of going and she sighed in exasperation. "Will nobody in this family listen to me? Go and find your Aunt Nola, tell her about the porridge before someone tries it."

But before she could hustle him away, Caley barked from inside. The door jerked open a moment later, revealing Fallon. He was pulling a tunic on and looked as if he had not slept well. Bridgit felt a little flicker of pleasure at the thought he had been suffering.

But he sounded normal enough. "Who sounded the alarm?" he asked urgently, looking down the corridor.

"I did. Because you have lost your senses!" Bridgit snapped, before she could stop herself.

"What are you talking about?" he growled.

Bridgit forgot about Kerrin being there. "Well, Lord Protector, thanks to your foolish orders, we had someone trying to kill us both in the kitchen and they have got away!"

"What? One of Munro's men?" he gasped.

"One of his women actually. Poisoning the porridge and throwing knives at us. But we couldn't chase them because the guards won't obey my orders unless they have been signed by you!"

Fallon's face darkened. "Are you both all right? What happened?"

"No, we are not all right! We haven't been right since Baltimore!" she cried, feeling shaky from the reaction from her kitchen encounter. "And you are not helping at all!"

"Well, if you had listened to me, we could have caught Munro by now and none of this would have happened!"

"Have you lost your wits? Is there something in this castle that rots men's brains? We were attacked! If it wasn't for Kerrin we could be both dead."

"I will find Munro and destroy him. And I don't care what I have to do to get him," Fallon vowed, stepping closer and holding out his arms.

But she was in no mood to embrace him. "Stay back," she warned.

"Stop it!" Kerrin cried, jumping in between them.

Bridgit took a step back, appalled. They had fought before, obviously, but never when Kerrin could hear. As far as he was concerned, they had never had an angry word before. She glanced at Fallon and saw her own horror mirrored in his face.

"What is the matter with you? Why can't you be like you were before?" Kerrin demanded.

"It's not that easy," Bridgit said gently. "We don't have a village to look after, we have a country instead."

"And you have changed too," Fallon added.

Kerrin burst into tears. "But you have to stop fighting! We have enough fighting to do already with other people. I need you to be together, and happy!"

Bridgit went down on one knee and gathered Kerrin to her, feeling the sobs rack his body. She saw Fallon reach out and pat Kerrin's head gently and she felt immensely tired. The baby was a weight in her and she could not carry all this as well. Her son was being lost to her and that could not happen. The needs of the people outside this castle, which had sat on her shoulders for so long, melted away.

"There will be no more fighting. I shall look after you and the baby and leave your father to look after the country. It will be like it was before," she said brightly. A nagging voice in the back of her head told her not to step back like this but she ignored it. She had done enough. More than enough!

"It will?" Kerrin asked, drying his eyes.

"It will?" Fallon asked, looking down at her.

She looked up at him, unable to even muster indignation, let alone anger. Part of her knew this was an emotional decision and she should stop and think for a few moments but the habit of a lifetime could not be denied. Nothing was worth hurting Kerrin.

"The Ruling Council is yours. I am stepping down for my health and the health of the baby," she said tiredly. "You can tell that to whoever you like. Kerrin, help me back to our room. I need to rest."

"Here, let me help you," Fallon offered but she held up her hand.

"You have done more than enough," she told him. "You wanted this country for your own. Well, it is yours now. Do what you want, I don't care. Leave me out of it."

*

"I don't know what sort of poison it is, but it is deadly," Rosaleen said, holding the bottle up to the light. "She put perhaps half in this porridge but just a spoonful would be enough to kill a man. We need to take this out of the city and bury it, even the cauldron, because anything that eats it will die."

"May I?" Fallon took the bottle and inspected the colorless potion inside. It did not smell but it was thick, like porridge itself. "Could you save someone who had taken it?"

"Probably. If I got to them early enough. But at the very least they would suffer unbelievable agony."

"Good to know," Fallon said, slipping it into a pouch.

"What will you do with it?" Rosaleen asked.

"Keep it safe," he said. "Now, to other matters. I will be bringing you men today. You will read their minds for me."

She shook her head. "You know I don't like doing that."

"I don't care what you like. Munro nearly killed us all. You will do as I say."

"How dare you speak to me like that!" Rosaleen cried indignantly. "If not as the Archbishop then as your friend I deserve respect."

But Fallon was already walking away. He was done listening to complaints. It was time to let Berry know who was really in charge.

*

"You will read this out today and every day until I tell you to stop," Fallon ordered.

The assembled town criers looked doubtfully at the scrolls they had been given. Fallon was more than happy with what he had come up with. Anyone caught shouting about Swane or against the Ruling Council would lose their place in the ration queue for that day, so lose a day's food. Anyone who complained lost an extra day. And anyone who helped them catch Munro would get a moon's extra food.

"I want this message spread across the city. Anyone shouting about Swane, or against me, can find their family going hungry. If they like Swane so much, perhaps he can feed them. If they hate me, they don't get food," he said, warming to the idea.

"Lord Protector, we are ready to ride out," a guard called.

Fallon nodded and stood.

"Is that your new title? Lord?" one of the criers asked.

Fallon was about to deny it. It had come from Bridgit as a sarcastic joke but more and more of his men had taken it up and, he had to admit, he had grown to like it.

"You may call me that," he said, then snapped his fingers to Caley and hurried down to the stables. He had a busy day planned. And it was going to be a good day, he could feel it.

*

Fallon had spent the morning kicking down doors and chasing men around the city and had an impressive haul of men as he strode into Rosaleen's church.

The church was full of worshippers and the sight of two score men roped together and surrounded by grim warriors in armor was like releasing a fox into a henhouse. People cried, screamed and scattered in all directions. The sight of Brendan with his bloody hammer was enough to make at least one elderly woman faint. Through the confusion, Rosaleen raced to intercept them.

"This is a church and you would do well to remember that! What are you doing bringing men in here like this?" Rosaleen cried.

"What I told you," Fallon said. "I need their minds read."

"Have some respect!" Gallagher spat, pushing past fleeing worshippers to hurry to his wife's side. "The Archbishop is not some recruit of yours to be ordered around!"

Fallon ignored him and gestured at the men. "Start at the beginning. I need to know what they do."

"How dare you! Get out of this house of Aroaril!" Gallagher grabbed at his arm and Fallon stepped back, hand going to his shillelagh. The church seemed to go silent as they faced each other.

"You would use that on me?" the fisherman asked dangerously.

Fallon said nothing, but neither did he let go of his shillelagh.

"Enough!" Rosaleen cried, stepping in between them. "I shall do what you ask. But bring these men out the back, this is not seemly."

Fallon stared at Gallagher but the fisherman did not drop his eyes, nor his angry look. Fallon was careful not to turn his back on Gallagher as he led his haul of prisoners past the altar and out into the rear of the church.

Rosaleen gave him a glare that would have melted iron then pushed past him to grab the first prisoner. She closed her eyes, her mouth moving silently. Then she released him.

"He knows nothing," she said shortly.

The second man shied away from her and Brendan shoved him in the back.

"Resist and it could go badly for you," Rosaleen warned. "I have seen men lose their minds through this. Relax, and let me into your memories and it will not hurt."

Once again she grabbed the man's head and closed her eyes. The sweating man tried to jerk away but she held him firm. Then, with a revolting noise, his bowels gave way and the stench made them all turn away.

"Aroaril!" Fallon spat.

Rosaleen let go and staggered backwards, her face ashen.

"What is it? What did you learn?" Fallon demanded.

By way of answer, the man giggled and looked around, a foolish smile on his face.

"His mind is gone," Rosaleen said, her voice a croak, then clutched her hand over her mouth and raced away.

"This is your fault, not hers!" Gallagher said furiously, then tore after her, leaving them alone with the prisoners, who were edging away from the stinking one. "What now?" Brendan asked.

"Back to the castle and try something else," Fallon said, then covered his nose and gestured at the man, who was now rummaging in his own trews with an expression of wonder on his face.

"But leave this one behind."

*

"Who is paying you? Who told you to shout about Swane?" Fallon demanded.

Behind him, Brendan twirled his hammer menacingly, letting the man see the stains on its scarred head.

The man sobbed slowly, blood oozing out of his nose and mouth. "I don't know his name!" he cried.

"Not good enough. Tell me something, or I'll have Brendan do the asking. And he's not as gentle as I am," Fallon threatened.

The man's bruised eyes flickered around the room but there was no escape and he sagged in his bonds.

"I don't have a name but I can give you an address," he said dejectedly. "I didn't mean any harm, I just wanted the silver."

Fallon turned away to hide his smile of relief.

"Get hold of Bran. I want two teams ready to go. But we'll have to use the roofline. They'll be watching the streets below," he said.

"Do you think it's Munro?" Brendan asked.

"I bloody hope so," Fallon said fervently. He knew that was unlikely. But, with a little luck, the paymaster might lead him to Munro.

The address led to a small house in a peaceful part of town, nothing too poor but not rich either, the sort of house owned by working men and minor traders. It faded into the background of the city, which made it perfect as a hideout, for it was impossible to move large numbers of men into the area without attracting attention.

But that only applied if you used the actual street. Having practiced moving around on the roofs, Fallon's men brought up the ladders that Brendan had invented and used the darkness to move stealthily into position.

Fallon and a dozen men, all on horses, waited at a nearby street corner, Craddock acting as watchman, while Brendan led men onto the house's roof.

"At least we are getting to know the city with all the searching we are doing. First the Snatchers and now Munro," Devlin whispered.

"Pay attention," Fallon hissed. He could feel his heart pounding and wished he was up on the roof, preparing to break in. With the roof sealed off, a second party led by Bran would gallop up to the back door while Fallon led these men to the front. It was complicated but, if it worked, he reckoned it would be more than worth it.

"Looks like they are both ready to move in," Craddock reported.

"That's it. Give the signal," Fallon ordered another of his faithful Baltimoreans, a grizzled old fisherman called Donnchadh.

Donnchadh blew two long blasts on the horn he carried, then Fallon kicked his horse into movement, its hooves slipping slightly on the icy cobbles, before it built up into a gallop. As he raced down the street, doors and windows banged open, while a series of crashes announced that Brendan's men were breaking into the top story of the house. Devlin, riding at Fallon's shoulder, turned his head.

"Do you think that was the roof giving way under Brendan's weight?" he shouted.

Fallon ignored him, instead watching the front door of the nondescript house. It did not open and he hauled on his reins, his horse fighting to keep its balance, until he could jump down and draw his shillelagh. He did not want deaths – only men captured.

The door was locked but yielded to the second shoulder charge, when Fallon was joined by Craddock and Devlin, and the three of them shattered the lock and burst inside.

There was plenty of shouting upstairs but little light and Fallon stood there, poised, waiting for his eyes to adjust. A few moments later, the back door burst open and Bran and his men poured inside. Upstairs, the shouting had died down and the stairs reverberated a heavy tread.

"That better be Brendan," Devlin whispered, as they moved across to the steps.

"All's clear up here. We've got what looks like a family living here," Brendan said. "We'll bring them down now."

"Search everywhere. Knock holes in everything. There could be hidden rooms anywhere," Fallon ordered, disguising the sting of disappointment with harshness. "And somebody get a fire going and then we'll talk to these people." Maybe they would have some knowledge of who had been here.

But the family, a woman and her three young children, proved to be useless. They were obviously terrified of the armed men and of Brendan in particular and gabbled answers to any question asked of them. They had broken in through a window and were sleeping out of the cold because they had lost their home when they had failed to pay that moon's rent.

"Either Munro is a genius using people such as these or they are who they say," Bran muttered.

"Get them some food and tell them they can stay here. But we need to fix the doors and leave a few men to keep an eye on the house. Maybe Munro or one of his lieutenants will come back," Fallon suggested, more out of hope than anything else. He could see none of his men believed it and he had to bite down on his anger. "Good work. We probably just missed him. But we'll get him next time."

*

"For Aroaril's sake!" Fallon kicked a chunk of broken door across the room and raged back and forth, using every curse he had ever heard and a few he made up on the spot.

Nobody said anything, or met his eyes. Once again his men had swept in and surrounded a house but all they'd found were footprints in the dust, showing that men had recently been there.

"Munro is obviously moving around every day," Devlin said. "Catching him is like trying to find a good-looking sheep in a flock—"

Fallon rounded on him. "If you make another stupid jest, you will not be coming along on another raid," he told him coldly. "I'm not in the mood."

"I'm sick of going on these anyway, and being treated like a fool! I've been right by your side from the beginning and this is the thanks I get!" Devlin snarled, then stormed out of the room.

Fallon shook his head. First Gallagher, then Devlin. Was there nobody willing to stand with him?

"What next?" Brendan asked stolidly.

"Let's see what the recruits are up to and how training is going," Fallon said with a sigh.

CHAPTER 58

"We have to stay off the streets. They are destroying our safe houses one by one and increasing the reward every day."

"How much is it?" Munro asked. "If it's big enough, I shall be tempted to turn myself in."

He raised a few chuckles but it was a mark of how they were all feeling that it only got a small response.

"What is the matter with you?" Munro demanded. "We have turned Berry against Fallon. The seeds we have sown have borne fruit this cold winter. The word is out on the street that you can get free food in the castle by shouting against Fallon and for Swane. Soon they will begin to believe what they shout is the truth and not just something to earn them another bowl of food."

"Aye. We have done our job. Now we need to survive to get our rewards," Jen muttered.

Munro looked around the room and saw from the faces how many of them agreed with that statement, even if they would not say so. He was tempted to chide her but, given she had broken into the castle and risked her life trying to poison Fallon's friends, her courage was beyond question.

"Do you all feel like that? That we should hide in our holes until the Prince and Duchess return for us, like so many moles?" he demanded.

"Fallon will show us no mercy if he catches any of us. He'll turn Brendan loose on us with his bloody hammer until we give up where you are. It just takes one of us to be snatched up and we shall all come tumbling down. And we've made Fallon so angry that our deaths will not be easy," Jen said.

Munro shook his head. "We are no longer staying among the ordinary people. We are staying with merchants who will condemn themselves if they give us up. They know what happens to those who cross Fallon. And we have no choice. Yes, we shall be rewarded beyond our wildest dreams when Prince Swane takes the throne again. But only if he does take the throne. We have split the Ruling Council apart; now is not the time to give up. Now is the time to keep pressing. But, to spare your nerves, let us make this the last meeting for a moon. Devote yourselves to spreading word about how much food is in those warehouses and see if we can't get a riot going, then tell the people that Swane will throw open all the warehouses when he returns, so all can eat until they can eat no more. Go to it!"

He watched his men and woman disappearing out of different doorways, down a variety of streets, and sighed. They were right. The risks were mounting. Posing as the dressmaker had got him into the castle but also meant they now knew his face. Crude but recognizable signs were everywhere in the city, offering ridiculous sums for his head. Many of his old safe houses had been raided and he went everywhere these days with his hood up and a woollen scarf across his lower face. Many in the city also wore that in the cold but when spring arrived, he would have problems maintaining that disguise. Worse, the reward was getting to the point where one of the merchants might just take the risk and hand him in. He dared not spend more than one night with them and often had two or more lined up as safe houses, choosing one only at the end of the day. Still, these men were black marketeers and had nearly as much to fear from Fallon as Munro did.

CHAPTER 59

Watching his new recruits put Fallon in an even fouler mood, because they varied from listless to useless. With most of his experienced men despatched across the country or guarding food warehouses and the castle, these recruits were not getting the right instruction. They would not be ready to fight Kottermanis any time soon. Once again it came back to Munro. Find him, track down Swane and Kemal and they had a chance. But would Munro even know where Swane was? And would Kemal be there? He clenched his fists. It felt like he was trying to fight blindfolded, while his enemies laughed at him.

"Maybe the lads out around the country are having more luck?" Brendan suggested hopefully.

Fallon just grunted.

"It would help if we knew how long we had," the smith went on. "If we knew when the winter storms will end and when the Kottermanis might land, we could work more on these men."

Fallon stood straighter. "Brendan, you are a genius," he said fervently.

The smith cracked his huge knuckles. "One of my many talents," he said.

*

"What are you doing?" Padraig asked.

"We need to make sure this city is ready when the Kottermanis come," Fallon said irritably. "What do you mean, old man? Speak plainly!"

The old wizard sighed. "I had hoped to come and talk some sense into you. You can't do this by yourself. There is too much going on. And what has happened between you and my daughter?"

"Nothing," Fallon lied. "Anyway, I didn't ask you here for a lecture. We need to know when winter might end and when we might see the Kottermanis."

Padraig grunted. "That is far past my abilities. I need help unbuttoning my breeches."

Fallon would have enjoyed making some comment about that a few moons ago and Devlin and Gallagher would have loved it. But he did not have the energy for jokes and Devlin had been banned from meetings, while Gallagher just sat there and glowered.

That set Fallon's teeth on edge. He had asked politely for the Archbishop's help and it had taken a full quarter moon before she agreed to turn up. It was insulting.

"Archbishop, is there any divine help we can get? How long have we got?"

Rosaleen sighed. "I will pray for guidance but I cannot promise anything. Winter's end is hard to predict at the best of times and depends on many things. We don't even know how that will help us, for storms in early spring can be just as destructive as the winter storms. Or we could get half a moon of calm weather in late winter and the Kottermanis sail here without any difficulty."

"I just need any edge I can get," Fallon said cajolingly. Aroaril knew he needed it. There was still no sign of Munro, let alone Swane, and putting more men into the recruits' training had not worked yet. It seemed there were more grumblers than men willing to fight.

"I shall see what I can do," Rosaleen repeated. "Meanwhile, I need to raise with you the issue of using food as a weapon to keep order on the streets."

"What of it?" Fallon asked belligerently.

"In the past quarter moon we have been inundated with people begging for food from the church and we've tried to find a way to feed them," she said.

"That's easy. Don't feed them," Fallon snorted.

"I cannot turn people away from a church when they arrive wanting help, especially those with children!" Rosaleen snapped. "We have little but we have to help all that turn up at our door, or we betray everything we stand for."

"How do you have food? I thought all food supplies had been brought to us for distribution?" Fallon asked suspiciously. "Don't tell me you've been giving your rations to people off the streets?"

Rosaleen pursed her lips but did not reply and he leaned forwards, feeling a now-familiar surge of anger.

"You've been buying food on the black market, haven't you?"

Gallagher slapped the table. "You would do well to remember who you talk to! Show some respect to the Archbishop!"

"I thought I knew who I was talking to. An old friend who would help me. But it seems there is someone different sitting here," Fallon retorted.

"The church has money, stolen and hoarded by Archbishop Kynan over the years, and we have been using it for good," Rosaleen said stiffly.

Fallon shook his head. All this time he'd been trying to stamp out the food hoarders and see if they could link him back to Munro, and the church had been helping them!

"Then do some more good now," he said through gritted teeth. "Give me names and places of the merchants selling you food and we'll pay them a visit."

"I cannot betray those who have dealt with us in good faith. What would that do to the reputation of the church? Besides, there is no evil in those we buy from, only greed."

"No evil? They grow rich and fat while people go hungry!" Fallon said indignantly.

"It is the only way," Rosaleen said firmly. "Your actions have left people starving on the streets. Whatever the sins of their parents, the children deserve better and we have to be able to feed them.

The church has always bought food, now we use it to help others rather than ourselves."

"Well, I order you to cease and turn over your food supplies and money to me, then tell me who has been selling you food."

"And you will put it to better use," Gallagher said sarcastically.

"Fairer use. With money I can put some enthusiasm back into the recruits and with more food I can offer a reward to find Munro. And once I have Munro then he will lead me to Swane."

"And who will feed the starving children?" Rosaleen demanded.

"I haven't cut them off from food, just reduced their rations for a day," Fallon growled. "You sound as though I am personally torturing small children!"

"Well, you are," Rosaleen said. "Your actions are causing them harm and you have the power to stop that."

Fallon sighed. "I do not have the time for this debate. Are you going to give me your food and money?"

"No," Rosaleen said firmly.

"What? You refuse a request from the Lord Protector?" Fallon asked dangerously.

"That was not a request. That was a demand. You might as well have been holding a knife to our throats when you said it," Rosaleen snapped. "You cannot demand anything of us, anyway. We are not subject to your powers."

"Are you really going to turn against me and side with our enemies?" Fallon asked threateningly.

"It is not that simple!" Rosaleen insisted. "I will never stand with the Zorva-worshippers but neither will I stand by and let children suffer when I have the power to help them."

Fallon forced a laugh. "So you would put the lives of a couple of urchins, whose parents are traitors, over the entire city?"

"You are trying to make this a question of black and white answers. But there is only gray in a Gaelish winter," Rosaleen said. "And that is the best answer I can give you." She pushed back her chair and stood, followed a heartbeat later by Gallagher. "I came here today out of respect but, in the future, you will need to come and see me. And you will need to speak to my secretary first."

"And who is that? Gallagher?" Fallon stood also.

"I shall try and find some time for you, but I cannot promise anything, Lord Protector," Gallagher said, putting a sneer into the last two words.

"Well, don't come to me for help, because you won't be getting it!" Fallon snarled as they walked out.

They both ignored him, Gallagher holding the door for Rosaleen and then shutting it behind him.

"That went well," Padraig said dryly into the sudden silence.

"The arrogance of some people!" Fallon muttered.

"Imagine," Padraig said mildly.

Fallon walked to the window and, heedless of the icy draft, forced open the covering to look out over the city, shivering in another day of merciless rain. A gust of it pattered onto his face and arms and he shoved the window covering shut again.

"We got one useful thing out of that," he said, walking back towards the fire.

"Pray tell me," Padraig said, shoving his boots up onto the table.

"Gallagher is doing the dirty work for her, buying food off the merchants. All we have to do is follow him and we will get Munro at last," Fallon said with relish. "Munro can't be getting any food from us. So he has to be buying it from somewhere. And, if he is smart, he is buying it from several of them, to reduce the risk. All we have to do is follow the trail of crumbs and it will lead to his hideout."

"But how do we follow Gallagher?"

"You can use magic."

Padraig sighed. "Well, if I do this, will you at least promise to apologize to Bridgit and make her smile again?"

Fallon chuckled. "A promise easily kept!"

Munro would be within his reach at last! He could nearly taste the feeling of success when he dragged the bastard down into the cells. He almost hoped Munro did not want to talk, so he could enjoy making him.

*

"There goes Gallagher now," Padraig said, his teeth chattering. "Couldn't we find somewhere warmer to wait for him?"

"We can't have any fires. He'll see it," Fallon replied absently.

They had set themselves up in a wreck of a house that overlooked the back of the cathedral. Just in case, Brendan had other teams out the front but Fallon reckoned Gallagher would trust to the alleyways, for the front of the cathedral was always lit up and, even at this time, there were plenty of worshippers around. The only drawback to their hiding place was it being open to the weather – which, after dark, was enough to have ice forming on the floor.

"Send the birds after him. We'll follow at a distance. He's too clever to risk giving this away," Fallon whispered.

Padraig closed his eyes briefly and then nodded. "I have two of them circling overhead. That way one can keep watching him while the other reports back to us."

"Good." Fallon blew on his frozen hands. "Now we know he is going tonight, we can go and get ourselves warmed up."

"About bloody time. I daren't take a piss for fear it might snap off in my hands," Padraig grunted.

A few moons ago Fallon would have made some sort of joke about sex but he was feeling keenly the absence of Bridgit in his bed and it was hard indeed to raise a laugh about that. In fact, every word he thought of just reminded him …

"Come on," he said roughly. "We'll thaw out and then get the horses."

A few minutes later, guided by constant reports from the pair of owls that hovered above Gallagher, they were able to stay two streets back, well out of sight and even out of hearing, as they crossed into the Merchants' Quarter.

"I might have guessed those bastards would have been helping Munro," Fallon muttered.

Padraig merely nodded. They had muffled the horse's hooves with rags so that they moved almost silently through the city. Even the bridles and reins had been worked on, so there was nothing jingling to give them away.

"He has stopped," Padraig said, an owl flying down to his hand. "They are in a small warehouse."

"Guide us in. We surround it," Fallon said. "Nobody is getting out of there, not even Gallagher."

*

Gallagher stared at the merchant Docherty with disgust. "How much do you want for this?" he asked, revolted.

The merchant spread his hands expansively. "There is nowhere else you can buy this and my supplies are running low. I also have risks in moving this around the city. If Fallon was to hear of what I was doing, then I would be lucky to keep my head. I had to put my prices up. Besides, the church will be able to afford it. Just tell the peasants that Aroaril needs some extra help and then you and the rest of the church can stay warm while you enjoy the extra food."

"This is not for us," Gallagher snarled. "This is for the poor!"

Docherty smiled warmly. "It's for whoever you want. Once you buy it off me, you can feed it to the pigs, for all I care. But the price is double what it was last time."

"I don't have enough to buy it all then," Gallagher said, clenching his hands inside his coat to stop himself from punching this man. Once he would have done so but he was a different man now, although one sometimes sorely tested by the path he had chosen. He was tempted to grab this slimy merchant and drag him off to the castle, allowing his ill-gotten supplies to be shared out equally. But then the hungry would starve and, anyway, Docherty had a trio of burly guards, all of whom looked like they would love to use the shillelaghs they carried.

"Well, you can take what you can afford and remember to bring more next time," Docherty said brightly.

Gallagher shook his head before removing his hand from his pocket slowly. He would have liked to be holding one of his knives in his hand but instead he handed over a small bag filled with gold. Rosaleen had given him more than what he'd paid the previous quarter moon, thinking the merchant would put the price up. But not by this amount.

Docherty hefted the bag with another sickly smile and then counted it swiftly before signaling to the guards, who swiftly tossed sacks onto Gallagher's small cart, stopping well before it was full.

"A pleasure doing business with you," Docherty said with a wave.

Gallagher restrained himself and climbed into the driver's seat of the cart. As soon as he was ready, two of Docherty's guards hurried over to the warehouse's double doors and unlocked them, hauling the heavy wood back to let him out. But, before Gallagher could do more than click his tongue to the mule, armed men burst in through the doors, smashing over the guards and shouting at the top of their voices.

Gallagher sat there, stunned, while Docherty and his remaining guard turned to run. But an enormous crash announced the back door being beaten down and a familiar giant figure ran in, others at his shoulders. Docherty's last guard threw his shillelagh aside and dropped to the ground, hands over his head. Docherty turned again but a pair of armed man grabbed him and walked him over to the center of the empty warehouse, kicking him in the back of the legs so he dropped to his knees.

"Evening, Brendan," Gallagher nodded.

"Gall," the smith acknowledged. "You might want to get down from there."

Gallagher nodded and jumped down. "I don't suppose you could just let me go, for old times' sake?"

"No," Brendan said.

Gallagher sighed. "You don't mind if I pray?"

"Go ahead. You might need it. Fallon's coming."

*

Fallon congratulated his men as he inspected the haul. Three guards and one merchant, as well as enough oats to feed the city for an extra day at least.

"What about Gallagher?" Bran asked.

Fallon looked over to where his old friend knelt, praying. He was tempted to speak to him but knew that would not end well.

"Let him walk out of here. But he can leave behind the money, the food and the cart," Fallon said. "This might give Rosaleen second thoughts about dealing with black marketeer scum again."

He turned back to his prize. The guards would know nothing but the merchant could have anything in his fat head. It was all a question as to how to unlock it and how much force might be required. Rosaleen obviously was not going to help. But there were other ways to make men talk. He studied the merchant carefully, seeing the sweat trickling down his face despite the bitter chill in the cavernous warehouse.

"Strip him," he ordered his men, who dragged the screeching merchant up and began to rip off his rich cloak, jerkin and trews.

"Fallon!"

He turned to see an irate Gallagher storming over. A pair of Bran's men stepped in front of him but Fallon waved them aside.

"What is it?" he asked. "Don't tell me you want to beg for mercy for this man?"

Gallagher shook his head. "Do what you want to them. But let me take this food back to the cathedral, where the poor can receive it."

Fallon stared at his friend in shock. "You do realize the penalty for what you were doing here tonight? I was going to let you go. Don't make me change my mind."

Gallagher pointed at the cart of food. "There are children who are depending on that food. We cannot let young ones go hungry because their parents were foolish!"

Fallon laughed, but there was nothing humorous about it. "You are living in a strange world indeed if you cannot see the problems we face. I have a whole city to try and keep alive. And I shall do that best by adding all this food to the city's supplies, and using the gold to pay for blacksmiths to provide us with arms and armor in time for spring."

"Fallon, please, in memory of what we did together, I beg you!"

"That was another man," Fallon said coldly. "Out of respect for him, I let you go tonight. But don't push me too far." He waved to his men. "Escort the Archbishop's man out of here and make sure he does not come back. We have work to do."

He ignored Gallagher's shouts as the former fisherman was hustled out and the doors shut behind him. One benefit was the merchant had had extra time to shiver in the cold, his plump body looking particularly pale in the lamplight. But he was still carrying plenty of extra flesh, Fallon noted sourly, unlike most people in the city.

"Right. You are going to tell us where Munro is hiding," he announced.

"Who?" the merchant blustered.

Fallon signalled and two of his men wrapped a rope around the merchant's wrists and then fed it over a beam, hauling on it until the man's toes were scraping at the floor.

"You may have heard what I did to King Aidan, and to the country's nobles when I caught them in Meinster," he said conversationally. "That was merely practice. I shall test it on you in a moment unless you start talking."

He snapped his fingers and Brendan stepped forwards, his hammer over one shoulder, while Bran produced a long knife, wickedly curved.

"We shall start to break every bone in your body, and then we shall skin you. Or maybe we'll skin you first and then break your bones," Fallon said. "I want to know about Munro!"

The merchant began to sob then, deep wailing gasps that shook his whole body and made the soldiers on the rope fight to keep him upright.

"Oh, for Aroaril's sake, cut off his fingers and see if that gets him talking," Fallon said sharply.

The merchant's eyes snapped open and he gasped down his tears.

"Please, you have to protect me," he babbled.

Fallon smiled in satisfaction. "Tell me everything and I shall keep you safe. But lie to me and I shall see you take days to die," he promised.

"I can give you several houses where others are storing food illegally," he said. "I also know where Munro is staying tonight."

"Then tell me."

"Can I keep my house and my gold at least?"

Fallon stepped closer, so close he could see tears dripping down the man's face.

"Keep your house and gold? I will let you keep all your fingers and toes and no more. Try to bargain with me again and you will lose your balls first of all."

The merchant's bowels let go then, forcing Fallon to step backwards in disgust. "He's staying at my house!" he cried.

Fallon stepped closer, carefully, and patted the man's damp cheek.

"Excellent. Then we are going to pay him a visit."

*

"Are you sure this is a good idea?" Brendan asked.

"No, let's go back and find another, while we wait for Munro to escape," Fallon said.

The smith grunted. "Three of us to grab the man who has been dancing around us for moons?"

"Any more and he will smell a rat. Three guards left with Docherty here, three have to return. Padraig will be leading the others in to throw up a circle around the place. All we have to do is get close enough. He was a dressmaker, for Aroaril's sake!"

"Well, he might have posed as a dressmaker but he killed two of our best men easily enough to free the Duchess and then got in and out of the castle without anyone seeing," Bran pointed out.

"Just let me near him with a shillelagh and he will be nothing to worry about," Fallon promised. "Now, Docherty, are you ready for what we have to do?"

The merchant nodded vigorously and Bran patted him on the shoulder. "Good, because I shall open your fat guts with my knife and let you take a day and a night to die screaming if you try to do anything clever."

"Nothing clever, I promise you," Docherty said hastily.

Fallon pulled a blanket around his shoulders. He was not cold, in fact he burned with impatience and excitement, but it was important Munro, if he looked out, saw what appeared to be three bored guards returning from their job.

"How far?" he asked.

"Just at the end of this street," Docherty said. "When we get there, two of you will need to open the side gate and then we all ride in, hiding the cart in my stables at the back. Munro is in there, under the false floor."

"That better be the only false thing about this story, or you will regret it."

The merchant nodded vigorously. Fallon congratulated himself on ordering the man stripped before being strung up. It meant his clothes had not been completely ruined. Some of the buttons were torn but the thick cloak hid the worst of the damage and it only needed to last for a few moments, long enough to get to Munro.

"What if this is a trap?" Bran murmured into Fallon's ear.

Fallon smiled. "This tub of lard won't give us any trouble. He shat himself at the thought of what we would do to him. It's taken a long time but we've closed enough of Munro's ratholes that he's had to put his trust in this pudding. Anyway, if there is trouble, we just need to keep the gate open. And Padraig will be there with the others in a few heartbeats."

They rattled on slowly, the cart's greased wheels making little noise on the cobbles, until Docherty nodded towards a substantial house on their left, set behind a tall stone wall.

"That's the gate," he said.

Fallon nodded to Bran and Brendan, who jumped down and strolled over to the double gate set in the wall. The ornate ironwork decorating its wooden panels would have cost enough to feed a family for a moon, Fallon thought sourly, as Brendan and Bran lifted the latch and hauled the gates open. Docherty snapped the reins and the horses ambled forwards, their hooves wrapped to protect against the ice and noise. The cart just fitted through the gate and forced Bran and Brendan to wait until it had passed before following them.

In that moment, Docherty reared up on his seat, jumping to his feet on the leather-padded bench.

"In Zorva's name!" he roared into the night, his voice echoing around the small stone courtyard beside the huge house.

Lights were unfurled around the courtyard and men raced out of the darkness, armed with sword and spear. As Fallon quickly counted his attackers, Docherty bent down and whipped out a long knife from a hidden sheath beside his seat and jumped into the bed of the wagon, the blade held high.

"My weakness was my strength. Now you shall die, you arrogant bastard," Docherty snarled. "Die for the glory of Prince Swane and Zorva!"

But Fallon had a shillelagh in his hand and he reacted instinctively, punching the end out to snap the merchant's head back and send him reeling, dribbling teeth. Then Fallon stepped in and smashed the iron-bound end into the merchant's forehead, flipping him back off the cart, where he landed with a soggy thud on the cobbles.

"With me! Padraig, get here now!" Fallon bellowed.

Bran and Brendan joined him on the wagon, which now blocked the doorway and also acted like a little castle. A dozen of Docherty's guards flocked around the wagon, trying to get up, spears jabbing out and swords waving.

Brendan reached down and grabbed one waving spear and simply hauled it out of the man's hands by strength alone. The guard was dragged up onto the wagon bed and Fallon slammed his shillelagh into the back of his neck, ignoring him as he convulsed and then went limp. Bran dodged a spear thrust and kicked out, snapping that man's head back, then jumped high as a sword thudded into the wagon bed, just missing his foot. Brendan reversed the spear and rammed it into a man's neck, deep into his chest, before unslinging his massive hammer.

The guards drew back instinctively at the sight of it and, in the sudden silence, broken only by the moans of the dying, Fallon could hear the clatter of hooves on cobbles.

"Give it up now and you might live! Your paymaster is dead and you will soon follow if you don't drop your weapons now!" he ordered.

They wavered, then one jumped up onto the wagon, only to be met with a swing of Brendan's hammer that caved in his chest with a hideous crack and dropped him back to the cobbles. The others, who had been about to leap up, hesitated again. Fallon was sure they were about to give up when a voice called from the darkness beyond the lamps.

"Get them! They can't stop you all!"

They surged in again and Fallon braced himself, except the cart horses came to their rescue, coming to life, kicking and biting and stamping at the men around them.

Guards fell under their hooves, while Bran hacked the arm off one of the few to reach up to haul themselves aboard the wagon.

Next moment crossbows began to snap, throwing the surviving attackers back, and a rush of armed villagers came around the back of the wagon and swept through the remaining attackers.

"I want that man out there!" Fallon bellowed, pointing into the darkness where the voice had come from.

He jumped down from the wagon, his men flooding forwards at his back. A dazed guard raised a sword but Fallon rammed his shillelagh into the man's groin and shoved him aside for someone else to take care of. His night vision had been spoiled by the lamps but he could see the bulk of the stables and raced towards them, heedless of what might be waiting.

The doors were locked and he looked around for Brendan. "Hammer! Fast!" he roared.

Brendan pounded over and snapped the locking bar with two huge blows and a dozen men shoved the doors open to see another door swinging shut at the other side, leading to another street.

"Hurry!" Fallon called, feeling sick at the thought Munro might escape again. "Padraig!"

By the time they got through the other door, all they could hear were hoofbeats on cobbles as someone made their escape.

"Tell me we have patrols blocking off these streets as I ordered," Fallon said.

Nobody said anything and he clenched his hands around the shillelagh. In the next moment, the hoofbeats seemed to get louder.

"Maybe he's doubling back," Brendan said.

"Spread out. We have to bring him down," Fallon ordered and they blocked the road.

A man on a horse rounded a corner, coming out of an alleyway hanging on for dear life as he seemingly fought with the horse. Fallon braced himself but the horse simply ran up to them and skidded to a halt, despite the rider's best efforts to make it move. The man sat there, jerking the reins this way and that and slamming his heels into the horse's flanks but it refused to move.

He was dragged off the horse and pinned to the ground.

"Get a lamp and let's see what we have here," Fallon ordered. He was elated but had to fight to keep it under control. After all, it might not be Munro. There had been so many false leads and hopes over the past few moons.

Padraig strolled up, wiping sweat from his brow. "Not a bad effort, even if I say so myself. He was nearly too far away but I found his horse and brought it back here for you," the old wizard said with satisfaction. "I don't think he was expecting that."

Fallon clapped Padraig on the shoulder. "You have earned your pay tonight, my friend. Saving our bacon at the gate and now this!"

"I get paid? Since when?" Padraig exclaimed, raising a chuckle from the surrounding men.

"Since tonight," Fallon smiled, as a lamp was brought over and held high over their captive's face. It was streaked with dirt and twisted in a snarl but it was still unmistakable.

"You can have half of whatever we find on Munro!"

*

Docherty still lived, but not for long, and spent his last moments raving his hatred of them.

"You were right and I was wrong," Fallon told Bran. "But, I have to say, he was the most unlikely killer I have seen in a long time."

The bearded guardsman nodded in reply but said nothing. Fallon didn't worry about that. He had much bigger things on his mind. As Docherty had said, there was a false floor in the stable and a cellar beneath. Obviously once it had been full of food but now only a quarter or so was filled with sacks of oats.

"He had to be selling to others. No way a man like him would have lived on oats alone," Brendan said.

A search discovered the answer: a series of parchments detailing payments to five other merchants, goods in kind for delicacies.

"Get Bran in here. I want to find out where these five men live and then pay them a visit. We tear their places apart until we find what they've hidden," Fallon ordered.

He paced over to where his men had been ripping apart Docherty's house, revealing little, but giving them a certain amount of satisfaction. He was tempted to inspect their progress, to delay the pleasure of interrogating Munro a little more, but it was bitterly cold and getting late and tomorrow promised to be a big day of hunting for Munro's spies and, best of all, for Swane.

He walked back to the stables. A line of his men were hauling sacks of oats out to be taken to the nearest food warehouse, while four guards watched Munro intently, even though he was tied to a stable post with so much rope that only his head and feet were visible, although his hands were also poking out. Fallon nodded to Brendan.

"Soften him up," he ordered.

The smith stepped up with a grim smile. Slowly he grabbed Munro's hands and, one by one, broke each finger, until the man was howling and cursing.

Fallon signalled and took Brendan's place.

"We've done this to show we're serious. If we'll break your fingers before we even ask a question, imagine what we'll do if you don't give us the answers we want. Now, you are going to tell us the names of all your accomplices, and where we can find them," he said flatly.

Munro looked up, eyes slitted against the pain. "I cannot do that," he said.

Fallon hit him, smashing punches from either side, hitting out all his frustration and anger, only stopping when Munro's eyes were swelling shut and there was blood running from both his lips and nose.

"Are you ready to talk? Give us the woman who tried to kill my wife? Or do we get out the knives?"

Munro spat blood. "I cannot give you what I don't have. I gave my people their orders and then sent them away. You can make me scream as much as you like but I still won't know where they are."

"Swane," Fallon said. "Give me Swane. Where is he?"

Munro chuckled, then gasped as Fallon grabbed one of his broken fingers and twisted it.

"I can tell you that now, much good it will do you," Munro gasped. "He is beyond your reach, for he has gone to Kotterman, taking back Prince Kemal with him. But you will see him again. He will return in the spring, with an army of Kottermanis at his back."

Fallon became aware that everyone in the stable had gone quiet and was staring at Munro.

"You're lying," he accused.

Munro snorted back blood and spat it out again. "Cut me and burn me if you want. Or get your Archbishop to question me. But my story will not change because it is the truth."

Fallon spun around, looking at the men in the stables.

"Not a word of this is to be breathed outside the castle," he said. "If I hear this on the streets, I will know where to look." He raced out of the stable, his mind racing. He had to get Munro back to the castle for further questioning and leave Bran to clean up this mess. Suddenly the taste of victory had gone sour.

CHAPTER 60

Fallon sat down at the table, ignoring the furious stares he was getting. Gallagher, Rosaleen, Nola, Riona and Devlin all looked like they would like to torture him. Even Bridgit wasn't smiling. It had taken most of the day and a mixture of threats and promises to bring them here. Well, that had to change.

"Last night we caught Munro. He revealed Swane has gone to the Kottermanis and plans to use Prince Kemal to convert their Emperor to Zorva. What is coming for us is not just an army but an army of the Dark God," Fallon said heavily.

He had to wait until the shock had died down, waving his hands for quiet as seemingly everyone blamed someone else.

"Where is Munro? Let us hear what he has to say," Bridgit said, cutting through the chatter. "I, for one, would like to meet the man."

Fallon paused.

"You have tortured him," Bridgit said flatly.

"What else was I supposed to do?" Fallon protested. "I had to make him talk and Rosaleen wasn't helping!"

"Because you insulted both Rosaleen and Gallagher. You should have gone on your knees to them if that was what it took to get their help."

"A fine look that would be for the Lord Protector," Fallon said.

"Does it matter how you look, or whether this country is safe?" she fired back.

Fallon closed eyes that felt like they were full of grit. He could not remember when he had last slept a full night. He wanted to crawl between the covers, embrace Bridgit and then close his eyes and forget all about this for at least a day.

"All right," he said. "I think we can all accept I have made mistakes."

He ignored a snort from Nola and a sarcastic laugh from Gallagher.

"Put aside all that. We have to work together now. Please, I need your help," he said. This was the old nightmares in the light of day, this was Aidan's dying prophecy sprung to life. He could not let his choices doom Gaelland. Whatever it took, he had to undo his mistakes.

"It would have been better if you had said that before you insulted us all, threw aside Bridgit and seized power for yourself," Riona told him.

Fallon leaned back in his chair. "You want to get revenge? Fine, shout at me all you want. I shall just sit here. Let me know when you have finished and then perhaps we can get on with saving the country."

Bridgit held up a hand. "What needs to be done?"

Fallon gave her his warmest smile. "First I need every priest in the land preaching the same message, that Gaelland must unite to defeat this enemy. Everyone must do whatever I say if we are to defeat them and end the menace of the Zorva-worshippers."

He looked at Rosaleen and Gallagher but they just glared at him.

"I know we haven't always agreed over the past couple of moons and I regret that I had to use Gallagher to uncover where Munro was really hiding. But this is Aroaril against Zorva and I need the church to stand with me on this."

"That wasn't what you were saying when you took the church's food and money," Rosaleen said mildly.

"I'll give you the money back and throw in a few sacks of oats for the brats of the useless bastards who were helping Munro," Fallon said angrily. "But I need you to counter the moons of lies that have been spread around this city. You have to preach that I am this country's only hope."

"But are you? And do we even know that Swane is on his way here? The Kottermanis pray three times a day to Aroaril, we saw their devotion. Yet you expect us to believe that Swane will have converted them to Zorva and brought them over by the start of spring?" Nola asked.

"He may not have converted them. But he is on his way and he will have a Kottermani army."

"On the word of Swane's man Munro, who could be lying to save his skin or protect his master, or both," Devlin sniffed.

"He knows he has nothing to gain by lying," Fallon argued. "And we have been unable to find Swane. It all fits. Kemal disappeared and so did Swane."

"But men will say anything to stop torture," Rosaleen observed.

"He would not speak to us until we had put him to the test," Fallon admitted. "But what else did you expect me to do? You would not help me."

"I would not do your bidding, like some dog that you can order around," Rosaleen corrected.

"Well then, help me now. Examine this man and what he has to say."

"But if he has told lies to save himself from pain, they will be mixed up with his real memories and it may be impossible to distinguish between the two," Rosaleen said quietly. "Extremes of pain have a dramatic effect on the mind. He will believe what he told you is the truth, to spare himself from further agony. Anything I get from him will be tainted."

"Besides, how did he know Swane was gone, if Swane has not been here since we defeated him at Lake Caragh?" Gallagher added.

"Since *I* defeated Swane," Fallon said, holding his temper by a slim thread. He knew he had to eat a plateful of shit to get them to help but they could at least hand him a spoon! "He has been receiving messages delivered by a magicked bird."

"Which could have come from anywhere," Rosaleen said.

"It came from Swane, on his way to Kotterman! For Aroaril's sake, will you not help me? What if I am right and they do arrive?"

"What has really changed? We all knew there would be an invasion and we were supposed to be getting ready for it all winter, except you were obsessed with catching the flea that was biting at you, rather than stopping the man with a crossbow who was coming to kill you," Nola said primly. "What is your plan now?"

Fallon resisted the urge to thump the table only with the greatest of difficulty. He forced his voice to become reasonable.

"At best they have a puppet prince to install back on the throne, at worst a Fearpriest to lead them. I need the church to speak for us and the rest of you to run the country while Padraig searches for the Kottermani fleet and I train our army."

"We shall tell the people to prepare for a Kottermani attack and to be steadfast in their faith. But we shall not tell everyone that you are the savior of Gaelland and must be obeyed at all times. Because we have sworn not to lie," Rosaleen said coldly.

Fallon forced a smile. "As long as they help, that is all that matters."

Bridgit slapped the table. "Of course we can look after the running of the country. But we have to be left alone and you can't run around changing what we do."

"If we get through this, I will do anything you want," Fallon promised. He would not let them see his gut-wrenching disappointment. He had been so sure his news would change everything between them and it would all go back to the way it was. Yet his friends were still against him. How had it got so bad?

*

"If the Kottermanis sail in here, we'll send half of them to the bottom of the sea before they can unload their men," the black-bearded Bran said with satisfaction.

Fallon looked at the new defenses around the harbor and breathed out in relief. Here, at least, was some progress. He had promised to send more trained men to help whip the recruits into shape but one or two days would make little difference, while this could change everything.

The protective blockade across the harbor had been doubled in size and strength, Fallon ignoring the protests of fishermen and merchants alike to create a double layer of boats, chained together, with a hedgehog of sharpened floating logs pointing out between them, ready to ram into the bows of any approaching ship and tear a hole in it.

On the bigger boats in the barricade, double-sized crossbows had been rigged up, ready to send flaming arrows into the sails of any Kottermani ships. More of these had been installed on the harbor walls. Fallon could see them pouring a withering fire onto the decks of warships packed with men.

Rocks had also been piled on the walls, while larger catapults waited on the headlands above. They would not be taken by surprise again. Fallon looked around and felt his face crack into an unaccustomed smile. The Kottermani fleet would be slaughtered if it tried to come into the harbor.

"Keep going. Once you're finished here, we need to look at the main walls," he said, patting Bran on the shoulder. "By the time the Kottermanis get here, we'll be ready to send them packing."

CHAPTER 61

"We are going to lose men and ships going into the Berry harbor," Finbar warned.

"We knew we would suffer losses. And nothing good comes easily," Dina replied. "After all, they are only Kottermani lives. And anyone who appears too loyal to the Emperor can lead the attack."

"No, I mean we could be destroyed there. Fallon has strengthened the defenses to the point where we could be defeated," the wizard said.

"Then use magic to break them."

"We shall need enormous amounts of magic for that. And, remember, they have both the church of Aroaril and their own wizards helping them. It could turn into a slaughter."

Dina sighed. They were getting close to Gaelland but sometimes it seemed like new obstacles were thrown in their way every day. "But we need to take Berry. Crush Berry and the country is ours," she said.

"We can still crush it," Durzu said. "We don't have to attack from sea. We can attack from the land side."

"We should surround it and demand Fallon's surrender. That way we capture it intact," Swane added.

"But the nearest port that can take a fleet this size safely is Lunster," Dina warned. "It is a quarter-moon's march south of Berry. That is a long time for Fallon to find some way of stopping us.

And even then, many of the ships will be forced to anchor outside, at the mercy of the seas."

"The solution is simple. We shall split the fleet up, taking only what could fit into Lunster harbor and sending the rest to seize other ports around the country. We will still have more than enough men to take Berry, and the rest of the country will be ours at the same time," Durzu said, leaning over the map.

"You don't know Fallon," Dina said. "If we split up our forces, he will try and defeat us in turn. He could come up with some way of winning."

Durzu chuckled. "I can respect an opponent but this is ridiculous! We have tens of thousands of the Empire's finest soldiers. How many will Fallon have?"

"A few thousand, at best. Most of them unblooded," Swane said. "He only had a few thousand at Lake Caragh. The word we had from our agents in the city is his attempt to create a larger army is not going well. Even if he puts 10,000 up against us, they will mostly be the fyrd – peasants armed with pitchforks and wood axes."

Durzu chuckled nastily. "The Empire's finest will enjoy ripping them to pieces. So, if he tries to meet us we shall destroy him and if he attempts to hold the city we shall bring the walls down around his ears."

"It will not come to that," Dina said dismissively. "As soon as we threaten the people, he will buckle." She watched Durzu carefully for his next reaction. He had been enjoying the sacrifices a little too much for her taste. She saw it as a means to an end, while Swane and Durzu were acting as though it was the whole point. Perhaps it would be better to get rid of the pair of them. One at a time, of course. As long as there were enough men to obey her every order, then it should not be too hard ...

Durzu shrugged. "As I said, no matter what he tries to do, we shall have his measure. But it will be useful to see him bring an army into the field. Because then we shall enslave all who defy us. Nothing will entrench me better as the new Emperor than bringing an army of slaves back to Kotterman. And there needs to be some fighting as well, otherwise there can be no glorious death to explain the disappearance of the nobles and the deaths of my father and brothers."

Dina glanced at Swane, who nodded imperceptibly. "Then it shall be so," she said.

"Good. Now, how many ships can we fit into the Lunster harbor?"

Dina thought quickly. Those were not the kinds of details she enjoyed, for there were always little people to do calculations for her. "We have a hundred ships, I would say we could fit half of them into Lunster harbor, perhaps a few more," she said. "Say sixty of them to be sure."

"That would give us eighteen thousand soldiers to march on the capital and the rest to be spread around the country. Is that enough to deal with Fallon?"

Dina laughed. "About twice as many as we need to crush Fallon. Kemal had less than three thousand and almost defeated him."

Durzu raised his glass. "Then I think we can drink to our new Empire."

*

More than a hundred ships weren't easy to organize, even with the system of flags that the Kottermanis were using. Gemici took advantage of that to add their ship to the mass heading straight for Gaelland, instead of the ones sailing off in different directions.

Feray felt the tension aboard the ship but refused to let it show. As long as she seemed calm, then the others would not panic. Still, when Gemici called her over, it was hard not to keep her heart from hammering. It was one thing to say you had to risk your life. It was another thing when you actually had to do it.

"Highness, I don't think they are heading for Berry. We've taken a course that is too southerly for the Gaelish capital," he said softly.

Feray did not bother asking if he was sure. His knowledge of the Gaelish coast and sailing routes was unquestioned.

"What's the next biggest port where this many ships can put in?" she asked.

"Lunster. It has to be," he replied.

She thought quickly. This could be their opportunity. They had always planned to slip away and use their greater speed to get ahead of the fleet, so they could learn where the Kottermani prisoners were being held and use them to free Kemal. She could not see why they were bypassing Berry but it was too good a chance to pass up.

"As soon as it is dark enough, fill the masts full of sails and head for Berry," she ordered.

"My lady, I don't know how well the ship will cope with that. And, if we leave the fleet, we shall also leave their protection. A storm could strike before we arrive."

"This is not the time for worrying about risks. We just have to do it," she said simply. "Either Aroaril will listen to us or He will let us die. It is in His hands."

Gemici's face twisted. "I would like to think that my skill would have something to do with it, my lady," he said.

She smiled in response. "That was, of course, what I meant," she agreed.

CHAPTER 62

Fallon ducked his head in the bowl and poured a generous measure of icy-cold water over his head. He felt the shock of it wake him up but it could not push the tiredness away completely. The last few days had been infuriating and exhausting. The harbor defenses were completed and, while they had taken resources, men, money and time, he felt much more comfortable knowing they were there. He just needed to sink a dozen Kottermani ships and the rest would be unable to get inside. And, for all their bright armor, they would die like rats once they were bottled up.

But everything else was not going nearly as well. His men around the country were having no more luck than he was in putting an army together. They were working the new recruits harder than ever but their progress was still painfully slow. On the positive side, they had found a pair of Munro's men, although they had proved to know little more and certainly were not senior enough to have met or heard from Swane.

Fallon patted his face dry on a rough towel. He cursed himself for not killing Swane when he had the chance. Or maybe it was Dina who was behind Swane's sudden change from poor opponent to master strategist. There was another one who should have been finished when he had the chance.

He looked into the bronze mirror and had to glance down. He had made so many mistakes. All his life he had wanted the chance to be a hero but it was proving far more difficult than he imagined.

Even when things went right, such as destroying Swane's army and catching Munro, they seemed to lose their luster quickly.

He sighed. There had to be a way to make up for all of this. If he couldn't save Gaelland then he had to save Bridgit, the baby, Kerrin and his friends.

CHAPTER 63

Gemici had taken them into the coast, as close as he dared. The sea was slate gray and sullen but the waves were calm and that was a blessing as it allowed them to launch one of the rowboats. Feray had been tempted to send some of the Gaelish Ely had rescued instead of Ely herself, but while she knew these Gaelish sailors were against Swane and Durzu, she could not be sure they were entirely for her, either. It was a risk but everything was now.

"Keep your heads covered and pretend to be fishermen," Feray told the four sailors who had volunteered to row inside. "Say nothing. Just grunt if anyone asks you anything and hand them silver."

They nodded and she turned to Ely.

"Don't stay long and don't take any risks. Ask a few questions and see if gold loosens some tongues. Your story is you want to get out of the city and find a little farm to buy but you don't want to be anywhere near the Kottermani prisoners. Only talk to the richer-looking people and, if you feel scared, just come straight back and I will go. Now, are you sure you want to do this?"

Ely had been nodding vigorously as she talked but now she stopped.

"I don't want to do this but I will anyway," she said. "You cannot go. If they discover who you are, they will use you as a hostage."

Feray knew that was true but it still felt wrong not to be taking the risk herself. She embraced Ely. "You are a brave girl," she said simply.

She watched the girl descend the rope ladder smoothly, the oarsmen helping her into the rowboat as it rode the small waves in the sheltered side of their ship. She sent another prayer up, that the girl would find someone who would help her. It was all she could do. Everything else was up to Ely.

*

"And who do we have here?" Fallon asked, rubbing at eyes that seemed to refuse to stay open.

"Looks like a spy," Craddock replied. "She was picked up in the market. Speaks with a Kottermani accent and she was asking questions about the men we took off Kemal. And while she doesn't have any ration details, she's carrying a bag of Kottermani gold."

Fallon looked at the young woman who stood shivering before him, flanked by two burly villagers. He had seen some strange people since leaving Baltimore but he doubted this one was a deadly killer. But what was she?

"You don't look like a Kottermani but you don't look Gaelish either. And you must have been asleep for most of winter because you obviously don't know what has been going on in this town," he said. "Are you one of Munro's? Or are you some slave, escaped from a Kottermani safe house?"

The young woman looked back blankly, terror in her eyes.

"Well, answer me! What is your name?"

"Ely," she whispered, eyes downcast.

Fallon blinked. That name seemed familiar to him for some reason but his tired mind could not come up with any connection.

"What are you doing? Who are you working for?" he demanded.

"I am free. I am no slave," Ely replied, in little more than a whisper.

"I don't have time for this," Fallon declared. "There's a score of vital matters that need me before noon. Throw her in a cell and leave her there until she wants to tell us what's going on."

He waved them away and Craddock hustled the girl out of the room. He picked up the first of many parchments, lists of men, arms and armor at Rexford ready to fight for him. It was a short list.

*

Bridgit smoothed her dress over her growing belly and wrapped a thick cloak around her shoulders before going to look for Fallon. Not talking to Fallon was ridiculous and things had gone on for too long. She shouldn't have stepped aside. Maybe the baby had affected her more than she thought or maybe she just needed to step back to see what was really going on. If Fallon was incapable of being sensible, then it was up to her to fix things. As usual. She would just have to stroke his ego a little, flatter him and tell him he was doing the right thing, then gently, gently steer him.

She strode quickly down the corridors, partly driven by a desire to confront Fallon and partly because there was still a fearful wind that whipped through the castle at odd moments, sending shivers down her back. As she got closer, she saw Craddock and a couple of others escorting someone away. She slowed down, not wanting to have them ask her questions, then caught a glance of the woman they were escorting.

"Ely!" She gasped and rushed forwards. "Craddock, where did you find this girl and what are you doing with her?" she demanded.

"She's a Kottermani spy or some such. Picked her up in the markets but she won't say where she's from. The Lord Protector said to toss her in a cell until she agreed to talk."

Bridgit winced. Now even Baltimoreans were calling him that! She glanced over at Ely, whose face showed a mix of emotions.

"I shall talk to her. Give us a few moments," she said.

Craddock cleared his throat uncomfortably. "Fallon said to take her down to the cells, not turn her over to you."

"Well, I am saying different. Who are you more afraid of?" Bridgit demanded, taking a step closer.

Craddock and the other villagers exchanged a look. "We'll just step off this way for a few moments," Craddock said.

Bridgit grabbed Ely's arm and hustled her down the corridor a dozen paces.

"What are you doing here?" she asked urgently. Ely seemed incapable of speech, so she shook her, gently. "Listen to me. I know what Kemal did to you and why you had to run. But I know what you were trying to tell me and I also know that we would not have escaped without Kemal's help. So I don't blame you but I do need to know what you are doing here. Who are you working for now?"

She looked intently into Ely's eyes and saw the doubt and fear warring there.

"I am not your enemy," Bridgit said steadily. "I saw you with the children and I know you have a good heart. But if I have to walk into that room and tell my husband that you were working for Prince Kemal and tried to betray us, you will be in more trouble than you can imagine. So give me a reason not to go in there."

Still Ely hesitated and Bridgit let go of her with a hiss of disappointment. But, as she turned, Ely caught her arm.

"Please," she said. "Did the children all get home safely?"

Bridgit stopped and held Ely's hand. "They are all safe and back with their parents," she said gravely. "Not one of them was hurt."

Ely's eyes closed for a moment, and then they opened and she smiled. "I am working for Princess Feray. We are trying to stop the Gaelish in charge of the Kottermani fleet. Feray thinks if she can get to the prisoners you took, she can free Kemal and stop the Gaelish."

"You mean Swane and Dina? They are in control of the Kottermanis?" Bridgit demanded.

"They are holding Kemal prisoner and using his brother Durzu to control the Kottermanis. If she can free Kemal, she can stop them," Ely said. "I just need to know where the prisoners are."

"And how can you stop a Kottermani fleet with only a thousand prisoners?" Bridgit asked.

"Our ship waits outside and it is loaded with weapons," Ely said.

"Why are you doing this for Feray? Does she have your family again?"

Ely shook her head. "My mother and sister are there but we are not prisoners. We have been freed, and she promises to free all slaves if we can rescue her husband from his brother."

"And you believe her?" Bridgit asked skeptically.

Ely looked her in the eyes. "I do," she said simply.

Bridgit thought swiftly. What to do about it? Fallon hated Kemal. The news that his wife Feray was trying to free him to stop the Kottermani invasion might not win any sympathy. And Bridgit was not sure Kemal *could* stop the invasion, even if he was freed. She looked at Ely, then had the strongest feeling she needed to help her. The last time she had a feeling that strong, it had been looking down at the Duke's ship at Baltimore. That was hardly a pleasant memory but it had been right. She knew how few men they had to stop the Kottermani invasion. Any help was a chance worth taking. It was a risk but then everything was.

"Do you swear on the lives of the children that Feray is going to use those men to stop Swane and not help him?" she asked fiercely.

"On their lives and on the lives of my sister and mother," Ely said immediately, her gaze level.

Bridgit smiled. This felt right. It was a crazy risk and if she thought too much about it, she would convince herself out of it. But the time for being consumed by fears was long gone.

"The prisoners are in my old village of Baltimore, to the south of here. Can you get back to Feray?"

Ely's eyes widened. "If I can get back to the docks," she said.

Bridgit beckoned to Craddock and the other villagers, who hurried over.

"This is Ely. She helped us escape from Kotterman and bring your families back to you. She is working for me now. I need you to escort her down to the docks," she announced.

Two nodded obediently but Craddock looked less than happy. "Fallon told us to take her down to the cells," he said.

"I don't care what Fallon said. I am telling you what you have to do," Bridgit told him. "Now go and do it!"

"Shouldn't we just—"

"I shall go and speak to Fallon now and explain it. Or don't you trust me to speak to him?" she asked.

Craddock held up his hands. "Fine. We'll do what you say."

Bridgit embraced Ely quickly. "Come and find me afterwards," she whispered.

The young woman nodded uncertainly. But whereas before the villagers had taken the girl by the arms and marched her along, now they let her lead them away down the corridor.

Bridgit took a deep breath. She did not know whether this was a stroke of genius or stupidity. But there was no more time to worry about that. She hurried towards Fallon.

*

Fallon looked at the list of weapons they had bought the previous moon and groaned. It was not nearly enough for what he wanted. Even adding in all the weapons they had seized from the Kottermanis and from Swane's men, any attempt to call out the fyrd would result in half of them being armed. Maybe not even that.

A knock on the door broke his feverish thoughts as to how he could find thousands more weapons and he leaned back, hoping it was not another problem.

"Come!" he called.

Then he jumped up from his seat when Bridgit walked in. He saw at once she was wearing one of the dresses Munro had made for them and her hair was pulled back from her face, showing off the lines of her neck. But his eyes were dragged down by the way the dress clung to her breasts and hips. It felt like it had been a long time indeed since they had shared a bed together.

"Fallon, we need to talk," she said gently.

"Of course," he replied. Especially when she looked like that. He sat down hurriedly, because his trews were now uncomfortable.

She sat down opposite him. "You know I hate it when we are fighting."

"As do I. This has been a hard time for all of us and things have been said that are regretted now," he said hurriedly.

She leaned out and he took her hand. "We work well as a team," she said. "And I want you to be there for the baby."

"And I will," he promised instantly.

He looked into her eyes and felt himself relax. Things would be all right now and they would get through this together. Best of all, Kerrin could be returned to his room and he could return to their bed.

"I am sorry for upsetting you," he said. "I have missed you. As though they had cut off one of my arms."

"Only one?" she said with a smile.

He chuckled. "And both my legs!"

"Well, then let me give you a hand. What needs doing?" she asked.

He hoped for an apology but it felt like all of this was an apology and, anyway, actions meant more than words. Some time alone tonight with her meant more than a few words. He pulled a sheaf of parchment across the desk.

"Every bloody town is saying they cannot supply weapons and have only scraped together a few volunteers. We can call the fyrd and everyone will be required to come along or lose their land but will they? After all, there are no more nobles. And, even if they do turn up, we can't arm them."

She grabbed one of the papers and began to read, then pulled the ever-present and much-thumbed map over.

"Let's see what we can do, eh?"

He grinned at her. Just having her back beside him made him feel better. It was as if a weight had come off his shoulders.

They worked companionably, as well as they ever had, and Fallon felt the room grow warmer as they did. He caught her hand and kissed it and looked into her eyes. Now was the time to end the distance between them.

A knock on the door broke the moment and he looked up irritably.

"What is it?" he snapped.

The door opened and an apologetic Craddock stuck his head in through the door.

"I am sorry to disturb you," he said awkwardly. "But I thought you should know that the girl has left the harbor in a rowboat. She was asking if she could have her money back before we let her go but we didn't have it. I hope that was all right."

Fallon sprang up. "What girl? What money?" he demanded.

Bridgit also stood, her chair rasping on the floor. "Thank you, Craddock. That will be all," she said crisply.

Craddock's eyes flickered to Bridgit, and then he nodded.

"Answer my question!" Fallon snapped.

"You know, the girl Ely. The one just in here, that we found in the marketplace. We brought her down to the harbor and a rowboat took her out," Craddock said hurriedly, his hand on the door.

Fallon stared at Craddock in bewilderment. "Harbor? The one I said to put in the cells? What in Aroaril's name are you talking about?"

"You need to go," Bridgit told him firmly.

"Yes, I have to go," he agreed and turned for the door.

"Don't bloody well go anywhere!" Fallon boomed and the villager froze, guilt written plain on his face.

"Craddock, tell me exactly what happened," he ordered.

"He doesn't need to do that. Craddock, you can go, I shall take it from here," Bridgit said crisply.

Fallon saw the relief bloom on Craddock's face and again the villager reached for the door and his fury ignited.

"Don't bogging well move!" he roared. "Not until you tell me what is happening!"

Craddock froze again, his eyes darting between the two of them, anguish on his face.

"Craddock, you can go," Bridgit insisted. "It does not involve you. Go, man!"

Fallon could see that Craddock wanted nothing more than to go. "Get out of here," he said angrily, waving his hand. He didn't really need Craddock anyway, he could guess what had happened.

Craddock wrenched open the door, gave an apologetic smile to both of them and then slammed the door.

Fallon wiped that from his memory as he turned on Bridgit. "You let her go, didn't you? Why? Do you delight in making me look like a fool?"

She crossed her arms. "How about you calm down, sit down and I will explain it to you?"

He flung himself into a seat and glared up at her. "Go ahead. I'm listening."

"Are you?" she demanded. "Or have you already made up your mind and you just intend to shout?"

"What do you want me to say?" he snarled. "I am not the one in the wrong here!"

"The one in the wrong? So you have already made up your mind!"

"That's not what I said and you bogging well know it!" he bellowed.

She turned away then and burst into tears. Instantly his anger dried up and he stood uncertainly.

"What is it?" he asked awkwardly.

She held up her hand, while using the other to cover her face.

"Stay away from me," she said thickly. "Do you think I am some sort of traitor, trying to help Swane regain power?"

"No," he said uncomfortably. "It's just maybe the baby is affecting your brain, making you do silly things—"

"Oh, so it's the baby's fault?"

"No," he said, feeling empty inside, the anger burned out and only ashes remaining in his chest.

"That girl was the one who helped us escape from Kotterman and I think she can aid us again. I was going to tell you about it but you had your own problems. I try to come here and help and this is the thanks I get. Well, I can't take this anymore!"

Her voice rose as she finished and she rushed for the door.

"Bridge, wait, please, let me talk," he pleaded, hurrying to cut her off but she just shook her head, tears pouring down her cheeks.

He still tried to get the door but she was too quick, ripping it open and disappearing.

"Wait!" he cried but she ignored him, hurrying away, weeping.

He hurried after her, only to collide with the grizzled old fisherman Donnchadh. "Fallon! There's a message here from Lunster! You have to read it," he said urgently.

Fallon tried to sidestep him but Donnchadh followed, waving a piece of parchment in his face. They danced like this across the corridor, Donnchadh showing an unexpected ability until Fallon slipped past. But, although he raced down the passage, Bridgit had made it to their room and barred the door. And nothing he said made her open it.

He leaned against the wall and hit his head several times with his open palm.

"Brilliant work, some of your best," he told himself.

CHAPTER 64

Feray helped a shivering Ely back on board and embraced the young woman.

"Thank Aroaril you're back," she said. "What happened? Did you find what we need?"

Ely accepted a steaming mug of tea from her mother and a blanket around her shoulders from Gokmen. "I was captured in the market and taken to the castle. They were going to throw me into the cells but I ran into Bridgit, the leader of the Gaelish that escaped from Adana. She recognized me and agreed to help."

"Really?" Feray asked. She was instantly suspicious, her mind racing. *Why would the Gaelish help us?* And yet she also felt a brilliant shaft of hope. *Is this the answer to my prayers?*

Ely sighed. "I didn't believe it either, but she sent the guards away, then had them escort me back to the harbor, where we rowed out. She told me the prisoners were being kept at Baltimore, a village to the south of here."

Feray paused. "And did you believe her? Are we perhaps going into a trap if we go there?"

Ely swallowed a mouthful of tea and shook her head. "She meant it. I know her, from Adana. She was telling the truth."

Feray turned away for a moment, giving herself space to think. Although, when she did, she realized there was no choice. They had to press on and hope for the best. If this did work out, perhaps

Bridgit could be an ally. Maybe they could achieve something where their husbands had failed.

"Set course for the south. We shall free the prisoners and then use them to free my husband," she announced.

The crew cheered and rushed to obey and she smiled and patted Ely on the shoulder. Inside, however, her stomach was churning. This was a house built on pillars of sand. A gust of wind and all would come tumbling down.

*

Gannon looked out over Lunster town, as he had done almost every day of his life. It was strange to think he was the master of the town now. Well, not quite, for he was just holding it for Bridgit and the others on the Ruling Council and sent regular birds to them asking what he should do.

Still, he felt a sense of ownership when he looked out over the town. Dawn was arriving earlier each day and there was less of a vicious chill in the air, saying that spring was on the way. The best thing about winter was the smell was better. Warm weather brought the real fragrance of Lunster out but the cold seemed to mask it better. Or maybe his nose was just blocked.

He looked out towards the forest and enjoyed the way the early sun lit up the trees, casting strange shadows. He gazed out towards the sea – and his mouth dropped open. There was another forest out there. Of masts. Kottermani masts. He opened his mouth but nothing came out. It was like one of those dreams where you could not sound the warning. Then the first ship appeared at the entrance to the harbor and the spell was broken.

"Sound the alarm!" he bellowed.

A turn of the hourglass later his own men, three score of them, were easily mustered, but only half a dozen of the hundreds of new men he'd been training were standing there.

"Where are the rest of them?" he demanded.

"Scarpered, sarge," one of his men said. "Said they was going back to their families."

Gannon was tempted to go and drag them out of their homes but the first of the Kottermani ships was already at the docks, swarms of heavily-armed soldiers blocking off the jetty. The plump harbor master had run, along with his staff, and the place was deserted. Just one of their ships had more men than he could hope to handle but there were dozens more behind, slowly flooding into the harbor.

That was bad enough but there was one thing that made it even worse. He recognized the flag fluttering at the mast of the largest ship. King Aidan's flag, now Prince Swane's symbol.

"Right," he said. "We need to send a message to Berry and then we need to get out of here."

"Sarge, what are we going to do when we get to Berry? There's enough men and ships here to take the whole bloody country," someone asked.

"That's not our problem. We just need to get back there and obey orders," Gannon said sharply. "Bridgit will know what to do."

*

"Bridge, they're calling for you. There's a full meeting of the Ruling Council, with Rosaleen, Padraig and everyone," Nola called through the door.

Bridgit lay on the bed, hands over her eyes. "I'm not coming," she said.

"Bridge, it's really important. There's a message from Lunster. We need you."

She did not remove her hands. "I'm sick. I might come later," she said.

Nola was still saying something from the other side of the door but Bridgit ignored her. She felt worse than she had that time in Kotterman, when she learned she was pregnant and had been unable to get up for days. Running Berry was destroying Fallon, destroying the man she had once known, and she hated that, hated fighting with him, hated feeling like they were trying to hold back the tide with a bucket of sand. Her emotions were swinging and surging as the new life grew inside her and she could not face Fallon at the moment, let alone her friends. He would beg forgiveness and she would have to agree, because everyone was expecting her to. But she didn't feel like forgiving him. How could he yell at her like that, when she was pregnant?

Worse, if she went back in there, she thought she might burst into tears and she could not bear that right now. She rolled over on the bed, clutching one of the pillows to her chest. She could not even call for Kerrin, because he'd want to know what the matter was. No, better she just stayed here for a while, until she could get her thoughts together. There had to be a way to get the old Fallon back, the old Brendan, the old Devlin and the old Gallagher.

*

"Where is Bridgit?" Fallon asked.

Nola shrugged. "She says she's sick. She might be along later."

There was an awkward silence and Fallon was tempted to confess all, or to leave here and rush down to speak to her. But then he looked down at the message from Lunster, brought by a magicked bird, and shook his head.

"We shall miss her advice. But we have to make decisions now," he said.

"Where is Padraig?" Devlin asked. "Should he not be here too?"

"I am here," the old wizard said, hurrying in, his face looking gray and lined. "I was just completing a task."

"And?" Fallon asked.

Padraig shook his head. "Nothing for miles," he said.

"Well, do you want to stop being mysterious and tell us what this is about? Life or death, your message said," Rosaleen asked sourly.

"More death than life, I fear," Fallon said grimly. "We received a message from Gannon, down in Lunster. A Kottermani fleet of more than fifty ships has entered the harbor and is taking over the town. The men Gannon tried to recruit to form a new company deserted and he was forced to ride out of Lunster as fast as he could. He estimates at least fifteen thousand Kottermani soldiers there, probably more."

He let the shocked and horrified noises die down before turning to Padraig.

"So they are definitely not sailing for here?"

"Not unless they are invisible. There is nothing around," the wizard insisted.

"We'll keep the harbor on full watch anyway," Fallon said. "We have sent messages to every other town. Any word back yet?"

Padraig shook his head. "We should get a clear picture soon enough. They will all send out birds to search their areas, to see if there are any more ships approaching their areas."

"Why Lunster? Why not here?" Brendan asked.

"Maybe they've seen what we've done. If they tried to force their way into the harbor we would have slaughtered them. This way they have a safe harbor in case of storms and can march their army here within a quarter moon," Fallon said grimly. "But that is not the worst of it."

"How could it get worse?" Riona asked.

"Munro was right. Swane is with them and his flag is flying on one of their biggest ships. Somehow he has persuaded them to fight with him, which means he must have Prince Kemal there as well, so we have nothing to use against them."

He looked around the table and took no pleasure in the horrified looks.

"What can we do?" Rosaleen asked. "What do you need from us?"

Fallon felt like laughing. Except he didn't. "We have to march out and meet them because we can't wait here. They would smash through the walls and slaughter the people. Our only hope is to somehow take out Swane and the Emperor, or whoever is in charge of the Kottermanis. With them in our hands, we can make them surrender, just like we did with Kemal before."

"But even if we recall every man we sent out, we wouldn't have enough to try that," Brendan said, his voice hollow.

"We have to try it, and trust in Aroaril," Gallagher said.

Fallon bit his tongue. "We have to call the fyrd. I know I said we could not send untrained men in against the Kottermanis but we have no choice. We shall try and protect them with our trained men but we have to create the illusion of a big enough army that the Kottermanis will stop and deploy. Then a small party can attack wherever their leaders stand and capture them."

"And how will we know where that is?" Riona asked.

"That will be the trick," Fallon admitted. "We have to find somewhere between Lunster and here where we can hide a small party, enough to deal with any guards but not so big that they can be found."

"And who is going to lead that? If it goes wrong, they will be killed or, worse, caught and sacrificed," Nola asked sharply.

"It sounds like a task for me," Brendan said.

"No!" Nola cried immediately.

Brendan shrugged. "It's what I'm good for now. And I give them the best chance of succeeding."

Fallon held up his hand. "We need to call the fyrd first, and then find somewhere where this might work. Then we can think about calling for volunteers. Nola, can you and Riona send the word out for the fyrd to assemble. It is every man's duty to be outside their closest city gate with a weapon at dawn tomorrow. Anyone who doesn't turn up won't receive their food ration. That should get them out of bed."

"But will they fight? Will they stand or just run away?" Devlin asked pointedly.

"That's where you come in, Rosaleen. You have to fire them up, explain this is a fight between good and evil. They have to march out there knowing they are fighting for their wives and children, friends and family."

"Of course. I know what is at stake."

"I'll summon all our men back," Padraig offered.

"Make sure they call the fyrd too," Fallon said.

The old wizard's eyebrows shot up. "Can we get that many men through the gateways?"

Fallon grimaced. "Tell them to at least bring back a hundred men in their prime, all with some sort of decent weapon. We'll hide the fyrd behind my men and maybe we can get away with this."

"We shall triumph," Gallagher declared. "Aroaril will not let us down in our time of need."

Fallon nodded, not entirely agreeing with the words but the sentiment was good, and at least nobody was arguing. They were all doing their best to help. Unlike the events of the last moon. If this was what it took to get them back on side, he could not help thinking maybe it would have been better if the Kottermanis had turned up a moon ago.

"We cannot lose now, not after all we've been through," he said.

CHAPTER 65

Dina shuddered as she looked at her former home, the manor house of Lunster.

"It is a solid building," Durzu said.

"It is a pus-filled boil on the arse end of Gaelland," Dina corrected him. "I made it almost acceptable but there are far better places to live. The sooner we are out of here, the better."

Durzu chuckled. "Sadly, we have to take our time. Your streets are too small and your port too badly designed. It will be two days to move everyone through. At least the cold is helping us in one way, for the road north is nice and hard."

"It's a mud pit during spring and autumn," Dina agreed. "And the smell! It's bad enough as it is but add in some warmth and it is impossible to live with."

Durzu did not answer but instead his gaze flickered over her shoulder, towards the front gate of the manor house.

"What's that noise?" Dina asked, turning her gaze on the disturbance that had been growing louder while they spoke. "Kane, go and find out what it is."

The guard captain hurried off, returning with a merchant and a bishop, both of them dressed in clothes that looked too big for them. Dina could not remember their names and couldn't be bothered to try.

"What do you want?" she snapped.

"We are glad to see your grace back again in Lunster," the merchant said, bowing floridly, his clothes flapping around him.

"Are you sick? Or have you stopped eating?" she asked irritably.

"That accursed Fallon put us on rations," the bishop replied, adding his own bow. "We had to eat exactly the same as ordinary people!"

"How terrible for you," Dina said, feeling bored. "Now, we are busy, so tell me why you are here and then go."

"Your grace, we have welcomed you with open arms. So, we pray that you will help us with what is happening," the bishop said.

"Do I have to ask?" Dina hissed. "Get on with it!"

"All the town's food was in a series of warehouses. Your allies have been helping themselves to this food."

"We face a march to Berry through uncertain weather if we are to destroy Fallon and free you all from his tyranny," Durzu said. "Of course my men need food."

"But, your grace, the people will starve," the merchant said. "That is all our food."

"Sacrifices must be made," Dina said.

"And this order that all women must present themselves in the town square tomorrow – what is that for?"

"My men have been on board a ship for more than half a moon, and away from their families for twice that. They need female companions before they begin," Durzu said. "Tell the women to bathe before tomorrow."

The merchant's face went white. "But, you cannot be serious!"

Dina snapped her fingers and Kane was at her side a moment later.

"Take these fools into the town square and flog them to within an inch of their lives. Then they will see how serious we are. We don't have time for foolishness. Anyone who does not obey our orders will die."

The shrieking merchant and bishop were dragged away and she turned to Durzu with an apologetic smile.

"Everything will be ready for you," she promised.

CHAPTER 66

Bridgit tried to ignore the hammering on the door but it refused to go away. Finally she unlocked it and opened up, ready to slam it in Fallon's face.

"Thank Aroaril you opened up when you did, because it felt like my bloody hand was going to fall off," Padraig said, wringing his fingers.

"What do you want?" she demanded.

"A fine greeting for your father!" He gave her a half-smile but then it faded. "You look terrible but I'm afraid we need you."

"Why? What has Fallon done now? And why do you think I can do anything about him?" She swallowed hard at those words, for she could not bear to face her husband at the moment. In fact she could not think of a time when she *did* want to face him.

Padraig looked, if anything, even grimmer. "It's not about Fallon," he said softly. "Swane is here."

She felt as though someone had thrown a bucket of cold water into her face.

"Where? When?"

"He's landed at Lunster with thousands upon thousands of Kottermani soldiers. And our men at the other ports are reporting the same thing. Eight ships at Lagway, a dozen at Meinster – they are landing everywhere."

For once there wasn't a chill breeze whistling down the corridor but Bridgit shivered nonetheless.

"What are we doing?" she asked.

"Everything we can. But we need you."

She grabbed a cloak from the hook beside the door. "Then we are wasting time, old man. Hurry!"

Padraig snatched his hand back as she made a grab for it to hurry him along.

"That's my door-knocking hand. Do you know how sore it is?" he complained.

Bridgit ignored his attempt to make her smile. All of the confusion, frustration and anger of the past few moons had melted away and in its place was a steely focus. Nothing else mattered more than stopping Swane. It was just like she was back in Kotterman, utterly determined to escape and bring her people home. Whatever it took, Swane would be defeated. Already her mind was racing for ways to stop him. It was a good feeling. She almost wished Swane had come earlier.

*

Fallon swallowed a mouthful of water and wished he could just pour it onto his head. Anything to keep him awake. The energy that had filled him at the news of Swane's landing was draining away after a full day of preparation. They had found two possible sites to meet the Kottermani army and he planned to ride out tomorrow to inspect them himself. Meanwhile everyone was getting a better picture of how the Kottermani net had been thrown around the country. Every port either had Kottermani ships moored in their harbor or a small fleet closing in on them.

Padraig and his wizards were hard at work bringing men back from across the country, as well as keeping an eye on the Kottermanis at Lunster. As far as Fallon was concerned, they could land as many troops as they wanted at Meinster and Lagway and the like. There was no way those troops could get to Berry soon enough to affect anything. It was all about the main fleet at Lunster. And the news was horrifying there. Padraig's watchers were reporting ugly scenes in the town, with people trying to flee and being dragged back and slaughtered. Bodies were staked out across the town square, while theft, fire and rape was rife as the Kottermanis were turned loose on the people.

It was terrible to hear but the news could also be used. There was no doubt this was not a force to free Gaelland, as Munro's persistent rumors claimed, but to punish it. There was nothing they could do for Lunster but at least its example could be used to inspire the rest of the country to rise up and fight.

Already Rosaleen and her priests were preaching that message at every church up and down the land. The forces of evil were here and it was time for all men to stand up and defend Gaelland. Similar scenes, albeit on a smaller scale, were taking place at the other ports where Kottermani ships had landed. Roads away from the coast were choked with refugees, heading inland to an uncertain future. That was going to be difficult to deal with later but they could not spare time to worry now.

There were some people leaving Berry already, but these seemed to be mainly the richer merchants and Fallon was happy to see them go. They could slink back later and beg his forgiveness. He did not trust them and did not need them. It was the ordinary people who would save the day here. Besides the message going out from the churches, town criers were striding through the streets, announcing that an army of darkness was coming and it was every man's duty to defend the capital. The fyrd was being called and they had to live up to their oaths.

He stared again at the map, trying to decide which of the two sites would be best to choose for the ambush. They needed time to get there and of course the better site was further away. But the Kottermanis were tied up in Lunster and maybe there would be time—

"Look who I found," Padraig announced, walking into the room.

Fallon looked up and his tiredness fell away as he realized Bridgit was with the old wizard. He walked over, his mouth dry despite the water he had just drunk. He was very conscious that everyone in the room was watching them.

"Bridge, I am so sorry—" he began.

She lifted her hand. "We can talk about that later. Now we need to destroy Swane. Where are we?"

Even though they were in a terrible situation, he could not stop the smile that filled his face.

"We are much better, now we have you," he said.

She smiled briefly. "You have lost none of your blarney, I see! Where are the Kottermanis and how are we going to send them packing?"

"The same way you beat Kemal," Fallon said.

She smiled again, more broadly this time. "Well, at least you have a good idea. Now let's see what I can do to help."

He was going to take her arm and show her to his seat, but then he could not stop himself and hugged her instead, to the cheers and claps of their friends.

"See, trust in Aroaril and He will make sure all is right," Gallagher declared loudly, while Devlin laughed and patted him on the back.

Out of the corner of his eye, Fallon even saw Nola lean over and hold Brendan's hand.

"This isn't helping stop Swane," Bridgit whispered in his ear.

"Yes, it is. It is helping me," he said thickly.

He felt her arms tighten around him.

"Why did we fight?" he murmured. "I am so sorry. For everything."

"As you should be," she said. "But we can talk about that later. Now let me go and let's see what you have been up to."

He hugged her for a heartbeat longer and then let go. Everything would be fine now, he could feel it.

*

Fallon shivered a little in the pre-dawn chill and reached out to put his arm around Bridgit as they walked down to the castle stables with Kerrin and their friends. Saddled horses and a pack of trusty Baltimoreans were already waiting for them. This was the moment when they would rally the city and ready the fyrd to take on Swane and the Kottermanis. Everything they had worked for had been for this moment. Dawn was a little way off but Fallon had not slept much that night, although not because he'd been allowed back in

Bridgit's bed, much as he would have liked that to be the case. No, they'd been up all night planning instead, trying to work out how to organize the tens of thousands of men who would make up the fyrd. It would be almost impossible to direct and they would have to divide them up into rough companies, led by an experienced man. That sounded easy enough but every man they took out of the front line to look after the fyrd made it more likely that the fyrd would be needed to fight. He thought they had it worked out and they had snatched a few hours of sleep, although he reckoned it was only a matter of time before he and Bridgit could apologize to each other where it really mattered, in the bedroom. As far as he was concerned, the argument was not over until then.

Having Bridgit beside him again was the best thing about that morning but a close second was the crowds packing the streets as they rode to the north gate. It was a fantastic display in the pre-dawn darkness.

"Why are there so many women and children here?" Bridgit asked.

Fallon looked around at the crowd. "They've probably come to give their men support. A good thing too, because they need to be thinking of their families when they march out to face the Kottermanis," he replied.

"It's going to be a desperate gamble," Bridgit said. "If Brendan can't grab the Kottermani leaders then you're going to have to fight them. And while you might have a slight edge in numbers, each one of theirs is worth three of the fyrd. Most of them aren't even armed."

"I know," he agreed. "But look at our villagers from Baltimore. They were just farmers and fishermen and they are now some of our best fighters."

"Because you trained them for moons, then led them through a series of battles," Bridgit pointed out.

"But they are the same inside. When they have something to fight for, they are capable of great things. And these men will have everything to fight for."

She did not say anything, which he knew meant she disagreed but did not want to say anything to disturb the fragile peace between them.

"And you have me," Kerrin said.

Fallon reached across and patted his son's shoulder. "If I had a hundred of you, we would send those Kottermanis running," he said.

They allowed themselves to be carried along by the crowd to the north gate and then outside. Fallon turned their horses then, moving them away to the side, staying close to the wall, where they were joined by the rest of the Baltimoreans. Wagons full of weapons were parked there, ready to be handed out to the most likely looking men.

"Where are they supposed to form up?" Bridgit asked.

Fallon watched as the crowd still flooded forwards, keeping tight to the road.

"Right here," he said. "But it will take forever to get the women and children back into the city. We have to make them form some sort of ranks. Come on, Padraig, I'll need your help to be heard over the noise of this lot."

He spurred forwards, Brendan and a handful of Baltimoreans behind him and Padraig at his shoulder. Dawn was breaking and the weak sunlight showed an unbroken line of people heading into the distance.

"Where are they going?" Brendan rumbled.

Fallon swallowed, his good feeling evaporating as fast as the morning mist.

"They aren't here for the fyrd. They are running, getting out of the city," he said through a dry mouth.

"Well, we have to stop them. That is our army running away!" Brendan said indignantly.

Fallon tapped Padraig on the shoulder and the wizard nodded. "Stop!" Fallon roared, his voice echoing across the countryside. "Come back!"

But he might as well have been talking Kottermani for all the notice the crowds took of him. He kicked his horse forwards, Brendan and the others following him, plunging into the rush of people as if they were riding through a river. Men, women and children parted for them and they formed their horses up across the road as a barricade.

"No further!" Fallon called angrily.

But they just flowed around them, breaking apart and reforming on the other side. Fallon nudged his horse forwards and grabbed a tall man by the jerkin.

"Where are you going? Why are you running? Don't you understand that Swane will sacrifice your children to Zorva and hand your wife over to the Kottermanis?" he asked, his voice back to normal now.

The man shook himself free. "So you say. But the word on the street is Swane will open the warehouses and we will all feast!"

Fallon stared at the man in shock. How was that the message on the streets? Somehow Munro's men were still spreading their lies and people were preferring to believe that than the truth of what was happening in Lunster? He wanted to argue but the man was gone, so he grabbed another instead.

"Fight? I saw what happened when you fought three thousand of them. Now there's ten times as many coming. The only way to live is to run," this man said.

"And how long will it be before they catch you?" Fallon called angrily, but the man was gone, back into the flow. "You will regret this day, you coward!"

He turned to his friends. "Were they not listening to the town criers and the priests? What is the matter with them?"

"They were listening too well, it seems," Craddock said. "They have never held a weapon and are terrified of facing the Kottermanis. At least we spent one day a moon training. I'd wager these city folk never even thought of being called out for the fyrd."

Fallon shook his head in disbelief. "Well, we can't lose any more. Get those gates shut. All of them. If this is happening here, the other gates are the same. Quick now!"

They eased their horses out of the refugees while Brendan went to close the gate, rejoining Bridgit and the others.

"They are running. Too scared to fight," Fallon said gruffly, covering his fears. "This will be good in the long run. We won't have as many men in the fyrd but the ones who will be left will be fighters, ready to stand up to the Kottermanis."

He could see she did not believe him but he could not blame her. He did not really believe himself.

The gates took an age to close, allowing hundreds more people to rush off into the countryside, to Aroaril-knew-where. Even then, the streets around the gates were full of families and it took even longer to get them to move back to their homes. Scores threw down their bags and waited by the gates, obviously hoping for another chance to get out. It was impossible to tell how many had left because some of the remaining townsfolk were hiding in their homes. But Padraig sent a few birds out to look over the countryside and reckoned perhaps two in ten had gone, maybe a little more.

"Leave the ones by the gate there," Fallon declared. "After a day of being hungry, they will think again."

"But what do we do about the fyrd?" Devlin asked.

"Send the town criers around. Only this time they can assemble in the square outside the castle at sunset," he decided. "And tell them that anyone who comes along will receive a double ration for their family." He gave them a smile. "After all, there's far less people to feed now."

Nobody smiled back. He could feel their tension. The feeling that they had a way to win was slipping away, although Gallagher was still insisting that Aroaril would provide an answer. They just had to trust and hope.

"I'll trust when I see that square full at sunset," Brendan said.

"You have nothing to worry about. Rosaleen and the others are out there, telling the people what they have to do," Gallagher said confidently.

"Order our new army to parade there as well. That will make it look more impressive," Fallon ordered. "If they see thousands of other men, then the waverers will be more inclined to join in. I reckon there'll be hundreds who wait and watch before coming along."

The others agreed but Fallon caught Bridgit's eye and her expression said it all: they were clutching at straws.

"Padraig, ride with me," he said. "I will appeal to the people myself. Maybe I can bring some more out."

"Are you sure that is a wise decision?" Bridgit asked delicately.

He laughed hollowly. "Probably not. But I cannot just stay here and hope. I have to fix this."

*

In the end, Gallagher, the black-bearded officer Bran and a score of men came along with him, while Padraig pleaded tiredness and gave them a pair of younger wizards instead. With his voice magically enhanced, Fallon rode slowly down the streets, calling out the men he knew were hiding in the houses.

"The forces of Zorva are at the gates. They will sacrifice your children to their foul God and hand your wife over to the Kottermanis. Then they will take you back to their desert and work you as a slave. But you can stop this. Just stand with me and you will live in freedom. Come to the square at sunset! All true men of Gaelland, you are needed now. Captain Fallon, the man who freed you from the snatchers and witches, who ended the rule of evil King Aidan, who saved you from the Kottermanis, needs you to join him!"

He called out his little speech, or variations on it, down more streets than he cared to remember. But he never felt like the people were really responding. Once he would have drawn an adoring crowd. Now they stayed away in their homes. A few came out to listen, but not many. Little more than a hundred lined up behind him and some of those seemed to slip away as fast as they joined. Fallon watched a man walk out, a wood axe over his shoulder, only for his hysterical wife to drag him backwards, shrieking at him.

One man spat in the street and turned back to his house, while a handful of others jeered at Fallon out of windows.

"Stand with me now! Swane is back, wanting to doom you to a life of darkness. But together we can destroy him!"

A few children came out to see what was going on, only for mothers to hustle them back indoors.

"Are you not scared for your children? It is time to fulfil your oaths and defeat the invaders, the ones that stole children and sacrificed them to Zorva!"

"You will lead them to their deaths, Fallon, and for what?" a woman yelled at him. "Swane will feed us!"

"He will feed you to his Dark God!" Fallon snapped back.

But she just slammed the door shut.

Gallagher joined him, promising Aroaril's favor and help in the coming battle and how they would defeat evil for all time and start a new era of plenty for all. Fallon was grateful for the help but even he found Gallagher's promises hard to believe.

As he went on, he found himself faltering. He had visions of leading a huge crowd back to the square, the way he had done when he had defeated the snatchers and rescued the families. But he barely had a company.

"Still, we made some of them think. They'll come along at sunset," Gallagher said confidently.

Fallon ordered his men to spread out alongside the pitiful column, so the few he had found did not have second thoughts or decide to disappear down a laneway. He looked at the sinking sun and sighed.

"Well, we shall know soon enough," he said.

*

Fallon looked out at the square and saw all his hopes go up in smoke. It was his darkest dream come true. A huge army was bearing down on them and what did he have to face them with? His loyal men and little else.

Casey, who had been trying to train the new army for him, clattered up the steps, his normally youthful face lined with worry.

"A little over a thousand, sir," he reported. "That is the fyrd and your new army."

"Including the new army? We have been feeding the bastards all winter and this is the way they repay us?" Brendan snarled.

Fallon did not have an answer and neither did anyone else. He felt sick – a hollow feeling in his stomach.

"What about our other men, the ones from towns like Rexford? They could march men here. These city folk don't have the same connection to their lords the way the country has. Out there, the oath of fyrd means something. They should have answered," Gallagher suggested.

Bridgit was the first to break the awkward silence. "We have been talking to them all day. They are bringing back a handful, no more," she said. "We can expect no army from there."

"Maybe there was not enough time, or the streets here were too crowded," Gallagher said. "We need to tell people to come back again, at dawn. And we'll have priests riding through the streets overnight, telling them their duty."

Fallon thumped the wall. This was his fault. Aidan had been right. He had doomed Gaelland with his choices. If only he had concentrated on training the men. If only he had caught Swane. If only …

"We should just trust in Aroaril. Something will happen overnight," Gallagher said.

Fallon shook his head. "We're done," he said hollowly. "All we can do is find a way out of this mess I've landed us in."

CHAPTER 67

Feray was less than impressed with her first sight of Baltimore when the ship rounded the shingle hook and sailed into the bay. She knew Fallon and Bridgit came from here and thought it would reflect that. It would be simple, of course, but there would be a certain nobility to it. Instead it looked like a grubby fishing village. She gripped the rail to keep herself together. Was this to be a trap or the start of new hope? She fought to keep her fears from her face. She could not alarm her children.

Men poured out of the huts and lined the shore as the unmistakably Kottermani ship slowed to a stop, the anchors thrown out to keep it steady in the center of the small bay. She stifled a gasp of relief as she recognized some of them and her legs felt a little shaky with the release of tension.

Feray made sure both she and her boys looked their best before they were rowed ashore, aiming for a cluster of men standing apart from the others, men who stood with the bearing of senior officers. Gokmen and Gemici sat with her, while her oarsmen were the biggest men on board the ship.

The men on the shore watched in silence as the rowboat crunched into the beach and four burly oarsmen leapt into the water to drag it higher, so Feray and her sons could step onto dry land.

"Welcome! Princess Feray, what brings you to Baltimore?" A slim man stepped forwards and it took Feray a few moments to recognize Abbas, her husband's once-plump adviser and spy, captured in Berry.

"Greetings, Abbas. I am here to bring you all back to honor and favor. Who is your commander here?"

Abbas's eyes flickered to a pair of men whose impressive moustaches had survived the Gaelish winter.

"Boluk-bashi Mahir, the bravest man in the army," Feray said, "and Corbaci Nazim, who won the battle of Berry for my husband, only for a despicable trick to snatch victory away at the last moment. I am glad to see you."

Nazim snapped a command and the men around him all dropped to one knee. He, Abbas and Mahir followed a heartbeat later.

"Highness, what are you doing here? What has happened?" he asked.

Feray looked out across the sea of bowed heads and nodded in satisfaction.

"Is there somewhere warmer to talk?" she asked.

*

They were taken to the largest building in the village, still a place of low beams and a dirt floor, which smelled faintly of vomit.

"I am sorry, High One," Nazim apologized. "It was like this when we found it."

She dismissed the comment and quickly explained what had happened: how the Gaelish had secretly taken over, controlling the Emperor and installing Durzu as the leader.

"They will sacrifice my husband and his father to Zorva and then plunge the world into darkness, unless we stop them," she finished powerfully.

Mahir and Nazim exchanged a look.

"And how are we to do that, High One?" Nazim asked cautiously.

"I have weapons in my ship's hold. We shall march after the main army. You know the army, you know passwords and habits. And your men are former comrades of many of those men who are now serving Swane and Durzu. You can get us into the camp, where we shall free my husband. Once he is with us, we shall destroy the Gaelish Zorva-lovers and free the Emperor. You shall be hailed as heroes and rewarded."

Nazim said nothing. Abbas was the one to break the silence. "High One, we cannot go against the Emperor. If he gives us an order, we must obey," he said. "And we only have your word that it is the Zorva-worshipping Gaelish behind Prince Kemal's fall and Prince Durzu's rise."

"What else could it be? You dare to doubt the Princess?" Gokmen roared, his face turning red.

His anger had no effect on Nazim. "Abbas is right. I was only a corbaci but I know how the Empire works," he said. "Our loss at Berry has disgraced us. If the Emperor heard of it, then I can see why Prince Kemal was removed from his position and his brother installed in his stead."

Feray locked eyes with him. "Do you think I would have sailed here with a small shipload of men, and with my sons, if it were that simple? All that we hold dear is at stake. I come to you, offering you the chance to regain honor and position, and you question me?"

Nazim held his head high. "I mean no disrespect, High One. But I have kept these men alive through a Gaelish winter. If I am going to order them to die, I want it to be for the right reason. We lost the battle and our honor with it. It is up to the Emperor what to do with us."

Feray stood. "Come, Gokmen," she said. "I can see I made a mistake here." She glared at Nazim. "I shall march after them by myself. You might want to live in a world ruled by Zorva but I will fight to my last breath to stop that. And what message would you like me to give to Prince Kemal when I see him? How would you like to be remembered to him?"

Nazim jumped to his feet.

"High One, I meant no disrespect, I was just—"

"If my husband was here, would you obey him without question?"

Nazim hung his head. "Yes, High One."

"If he is dead, that makes his eldest son, my boy Asil, the Crown Prince and heir to the Elephant Throne. Is he as good as the Emperor for ruling on your fate?" she challenged, her voice lashing at him.

"High One, I—"

But she would not give him the chance to get a word in.

"Prince Asil, what do you say?"

Asil crossed his arms, the very picture of his father. "My father is in the hands of Zorva-worshippers. When we meet again in Aroaril's realm, shall I tell him we had the chance to rescue him and yet we were let down by cowards?"

The three of them stared at Asil, then glanced at each other before Mahir, Nazim and Abbas fell to their knees.

"If our lives can free Prince Kemal and end the threat of the Zorva-worshippers, then that will be a small price to pay," Nazim said thickly.

"What are your orders, High One? Command and we shall obey," Abbas added.

Feray glanced at her son, letting him know with a look how proud she was of the part he played. They had rehearsed this many times on board the ship but he had done just what she wanted.

"Launch every boat you have. We have to get every weapon off the ship and then decide how we are going to catch up with the Zorva-lovers."

*

"We shall make slow progress for the first few days, for the men need to regain their fitness after all that time on the ships," Durzu said. "But then we can easily make twenty miles a day on good roads."

"The quicker the better," Swane agreed. "I have been too long away from my father's throne."

They had left Lunster behind, with just a small company of five hundred to watch the ships. Dina had not wanted to leave even that many but, after what the Kottermanis had done to the town, it was necessary. Two days of rape, theft and murder left the remaining residents in an ugly mood and it would not do to take Berry and return to find half the ships burned by an angry mob.

"We can clean out the city on our return, making sure any who defy you are removed as slaves," she said. "But we need to get to Berry as fast as possible. We cannot give Fallon time to prepare his response. He lured us into a trap at Lake Caragh and he will seek to do the same again here."

"With what? He cannot stand against our might," Durzu chuckled.

Dina acknowledged the size of the Kottermani army with a nod. Over seventeen thousand battle-hardened veterans was more than Fallon had ever faced. But she did not want to take a risk.

"What is the word from your agents in Berry?"

"Sadly, our best man was captured," Dina admitted. "But we have sent messages to others and we should know by dawn."

"Cheer up," Durzu said with a smile. "All we need to do is ride up to the capital and then divide the spoils, before enjoying the execution of our enemies."

Dina bowed her head. After that she could work on her own plans. First Swane, then Durzu. Only then could her victory be safe, and complete.

*

Kemal shivered. Not at the cold Gaelish wind that whistled off the water but by the feeling of having silk clothes against his skin again. He had been taken off the ship, washed and allowed to dress so he no longer looked like a slave. But he was just as much a prisoner. Durzu had made the Emperor give orders to his guards, who watched them both. He was with his father but he might as well have been riding with a dummy. The Emperor never said a word, nor reacted when Kemal tried to speak to him. And the guards were always there, so he had no chance of escaping from Durzu. And if he did, who could he appeal to? All the nobles he remembered were gone.

Still, he was off that damned ship so maybe there was a chance. Durzu and his Gaelish allies thought they had already won. But maybe Fallon could spoil their plans and give him a window of opportunity. Kemal smiled to himself, a little, at the thought of needing his erstwhile enemy to help him. There was little else to smile about.

CHAPTER 68

It had been a long day and even a quick bowl of stew did not revive Bridgit much. She could see the others were much the same and the temptation was to go to bed, try to forget what had happened and hope maybe things would improve in the morning. But time was running out.

"We can still try our plan. It is the only one that stands a chance. If we can put five thousand men together that will be enough to get the attention of the Kottermanis and, once we have Swane and the rest of their leaders, numbers don't matter," Gallagher said.

"Except we don't have that many. We have about two thousand men who fought with us at Lake Caragh and a few hundred others, at best. Our men will be slaughtered in a hundred heartbeats by the Kottermanis," Fallon said tiredly.

"Can we make it seem as if we have more men with magic?" Nola asked.

"Yes, we can," Padraig said. "For about two hundred heartbeats. Then they will all disappear."

"We could hold the walls. They were scared of what we did in the harbor. We can do the same with the walls," Devlin offered.

Fallon scraped grit out of his eye. "Too much wall and not enough men. We would need five times as many to hold such a long wall. And if we had that many we could march out and meet them."

"The castle then. We hold the castle," Devlin continued.

419

Bridgit ignored Fallon's careful explanation of why a defensive battle could not work. All they were doing here by talking was wasting time. The solution was obvious: they had to get the people to rise up. Even an army as big as the Kottermanis could not hope to stand against a whole city. And, in the tight confines of the streets, anything could happen. They had proved that once, already. The question they should be asking was how to get the people to rise up in fury and fight. It could be done – they had been ready to do that the day Aidan had been executed, but it had slipped away during a cold winter. She thought she had a way of making them fight but it was a crazy idea, one that scared her and went against every instinct she had. But maybe it was the only way. Still she hesitated. There were too many things that could go horribly wrong.

*

Fallon shook his head at Gallagher's fresh suggestion that Aroaril would provide and they should pray all night for a way out of this dead end. Whatever was put forward had the same ending. They were all dead and Swane triumphant. He only had one thought now, a crazy idea, which scared him. But it could save almost everyone's lives. He wanted to say it but the words would not come.

He glanced around the table and saw Bridgit absent-mindedly rubbing her gently swelling belly. Such a simple act made his stomach twist and he came to a final decision.

"I know what to do," he said, and the words set him free. He felt himself relax, for the decision was made now. They would have to go along with it, for he would not be turned aside. He looked around the table as they all leaned forwards excitedly. He locked eyes with Bridgit for a moment and it was as if she already knew what he was going to say. He cleared his throat.

"We are all agreed the only way to victory is to use some distraction to kill Swane and Dina. I will be that distraction. I will wait here in Berry, with a few volunteers. Swane and Dina will not be able to resist their prize. I shall lure them in close and then kill them with crossbow bolts from the wall."

"Are you crazy, man? The chances of that working are tiny!" Devlin was the first to react.

"I shall have the crossbows hidden and the quarrels will be made out of solid metal, so the Zorva lovers cannot affect them with their dark magic. And I shall coat the heads in that poison we took from Munro's agent, the woman who tried to kill us with porridge. Even a scratch will kill them," Fallon said calmly. "Once they are dead, the Kottermanis will have no puppet ruler and will need to deal with us. In one stroke, we go from defeat to victory."

"You are gambling everything on a poisoned quarrel," Nola said.

"Because there is no other choice," Fallon said. "But I know how risky it is. I will only stay here with a small number of volunteers. Everyone else needs to get on the captured Kottermani ships and get clear. Padraig can use his magicked birds to see what happens with me. If all goes well, then you can come back to Berry. If not, head for Cavan's island. There you can make a new life, away from the evil here."

"But, even if you kill Swane and Dina, there is no guarantee the Kottermanis will deal with you. Prince Kemal hates you," Brendan warned.

"Aye. But we don't know he is even in charge. But, if he is, he will be content with just taking my life. Swane and Dina would not stop until all of us are dead."

"This is madness," Riona said flatly.

Fallon shrugged. "Madness is all we have left. You all know how good I am with a crossbow. Get Swane and Dina within fifty paces of me and they are as good as dead. I will hit them – and that is all we need. Once they are gone, everything changes. I can try and make a deal with the Kottermanis. Even if they rule, at least there will be no more sacrificing children."

"Except you will be dead as well," Bridgit said.

Fallon swallowed. "And that is a small price to pay for knowing you are safe," he said. "And after all I have done, it is a fair price to pay. I was the Lord Protector and failed to protect the people. They won't even fight for me against the evil that's coming. And I killed Cavan. If I had not done that, we would not be in this mess." He swallowed down bile at the thought, his throat almost closing over.

"But I will not be looking to die. I want to kill those two and then offer a deal to the Kottermanis. We could still all walk out of this with what we wanted from Kemal – the chance to run Gaelland like we did Baltimore, just sending tribute to our lord but being left alone otherwise."

The others were all shouting now, trying to protest, but he just held up his hands until they eventually fell silent. Bridgit looked at him and twitched her head. He sighed and stood. Of course she wanted to talk but he would not step back from this plan. It felt too right. He joined her on the other side of the room, conscious that the others were all trying to hear what they were saying.

"You know this will not end well. Even if you kill Swane and Dina, whoever rules the Kottermanis can't let you live. You are too dangerous," she said. "What about me, Kerrin and the baby? Don't you want to be there for us?"

Fallon stroked the hair back from her face. "I am not the man I was, nor the man I wanted to be. I am no longer worthy of you. I have to put my fate in Aroaril's hands. If he finds me worthy, then I will survive and I have a future. But my life is a small price to pay for you being safe."

She kissed his hand and looked into his eyes. "I want us to be a family again. Can you not turn your back on your guilt to do that?"

He wanted to say yes but it would be a lie and he could not lie to her. "I wish I could, with all my heart. But I am only half a man. Please, Bridge, if you love me, you will let me do this."

She looked at him for a long, long time. He could see she was about to say something, but then she just nodded, her eyes filling with tears as she hurried back to the table. He followed, much slower, seeing his friends watching him expectantly.

"We don't have another choice. Swane and Dina must be stopped and I can do it. And if it goes wrong, at least I can look Cavan in the eye when I see him in the next life," he said.

"Well, you shall not be alone. I will stand with you," Brendan said immediately.

"Brendan!" Nola cried.

The big smith turned to his wife, a gentle smile on his face that reminded them of the old Brendan. "It is all I am good for now," he said. "I know you and the girls are safe and that's all I ever wanted. I am no longer fit for living, only for dying. I cannot put down my hammer. They will have to rip it out of my dead hands."

Fallon clasped his friend's shoulder. "I should be honored to have you beside me, my friend," he said.

"This is insane! This is the craziest thing I have heard from you, and I have heard plenty!" Nola cried, her voice almost hysterical. "Bridgit, tell them!"

He felt everyone's eyes swivel to Bridgit and he joined them. She was staring down at the table but, when she looked up, her tears were gone. Still, she would not meet his eyes.

"Fallon is right. There is no other choice. The people will not stand with us and we cannot defeat this army by any other means. We do not have enough time to show the people how bad Swane truly is," she said dully. "I hate it but we have to do it."

There was no uproar this time, instead a deathly silence, broken only by Nola's sobs. Fallon closed his eyes. How had it all gone so wrong? How had it come to this? A vision of Prince Cavan came to him and his eyes snapped open. Bridgit, Kerrin and the baby would survive. That was all the comfort he needed.

"No!" Gallagher howled suddenly, jumping to his feet. "It cannot be like this! It must not end like this. We need to get together, to pray for guidance. There is another way—"

Fallon strode across to his friend and embraced him.

"If this is all part of a plan, then so be it," he whispered into Gallagher's ear. "But it has to be done. Bad things happen. My friend, you know that more than most."

He pulled his head back and saw the horror on Gallagher's face. "But all you need is to believe in Aroaril," the fisherman whispered.

Fallon squeezed him harder. "There is another side and they believe hard, too. We are not puppets, dancing to the tune of a God. We are men and we make our own choices. My mistakes have led me here and this is my chance to make amends."

Gallagher's eyes cleared. "Then I shall stand with you."

"No. For you are the only man who can find Cavan's island for everyone. They will depend on you. I will depend on you. If we fail, you have to succeed."

"I can't believe it has to be like this," Gallagher said. "We don't deserve this, after all we have been through."

"You didn't deserve to lose your wife and boys either. But you did. Now you just have to swallow it down and get on. Understand?"

He let Gallagher go and the fisherman slumped into his seat, his head in his hands.

"This is a joke," Devlin said slowly. "Come on, the pair of you. Have a laugh and prove to us that this is a joke."

Brendan laid a huge hand on the farmer's shoulder. "There is no jest. We are deadly serious," he said.

"But it has to be a joke. A bad one, but still a joke. How could you think to end it this way?"

"Because as much as we like to laugh, sometimes life brings you to tears," Brendan said gently. "If you want to help me, tell jokes to my daughters. Make them smile again, when you find Cavan's island."

Devlin's face was aghast. "How can I laugh about the death of two of my best friends?" he whispered.

"You must find a way," Brendan said remorselessly. "Make my girls laugh again, or I shall know about it." He buffeted Devlin on the shoulder again but the farmer merely shook his head.

"I cannot leave," he said. "I will stand with you."

"Now you are jesting. And this is not the time," Riona said.

Devlin reached out and clasped his wife's hand. "I am sorry, my love. But I cannot turn my back on my friends. I could never smile again knowing I did not stand with them."

"Devlin, this isn't funny," she snapped.

He raised her hand to his lips. "I know," he said. "When you were taken, I could not laugh. When you returned I tried too hard to laugh. But I am not the same as I was. I don't want to, but I need to do this."

She snatched her hand away and stared at him.

Fallon cleared his throat, breaking the uncomfortable silence. "This is not the end," he said. "The poisoned quarrel will finish Swane and Dina and we can all laugh about this later."

Nobody looked even remotely like laughing, although both Nola and Riona were glaring at Bridgit. But she was just staring at the table.

"Come on. We need to get back to work. We have to see who'll stand with us against Swane and Dina and then plan the voyage to Cavan's island," Fallon said.

"It should not be like this," Rosaleen said slowly. "What if we can think of something better?"

"Then do so," Fallon said. "But make it quick. The Kottermanis are marching and will be here within a few days."

*

As soon as Fallon had walked out of the room, Bridgit grabbed hold of Padraig's arm. "I need you to send a bird south," she whispered.

Her father's face crinkled in confusion. "But we are already watching the Kottermani advance," he said.

"No, further south. To Baltimore. I need to know what is happening there, but only for my ears."

He gazed at her for a long moment, then nodded. "You know I will. Whatever you need. But, tell me—"

She placed a finger on her lips. "Come and see me afterwards and I will explain everything," she whispered.

He looked at her strangely but she ignored him and pushed back her chair. "I need to go and talk to Kerrin, before he hears any of this talk around the castle," she announced.

"Bridgit, you will really let this go ahead?" Nola asked, her eyes red-rimmed, her voice cracking.

"It makes my skin crawl," Bridgit said. "But I can see no other way. The people are not with us and we face a choice between life and death. How can we not choose life? One day we can return, once the people are sick of Swane's evil, and lead them again. But now we would just be signing our own death warrants."

"But letting them die? Devlin, Fallon and Brendan?" Riona groaned.

"They have to do it," Bridgit said. "What they have been through has left its scars on them. They are not the same men they were. And maybe that is a lesson for Gallagher."

"How do you mean?" Rosaleen asked, bristling.

"Fallon and Brendan could not find their way back again after what they were forced to do. Don't let their fate become yours," she said. "And now I really must find Kerrin."

She left them sitting there, stunned. She had to find Kerrin fast, or otherwise he would hear the news directly from Fallon and that would not do. She took a moment though, leaning against the wall to get control of herself. She felt like panicking, like rushing after Fallon and forbidding him from doing this. Even riddled with guilt as he was, even lost as he was, she knew he would not go against her if she pushed hard enough. But he was right in one way. She could not see another way of defeating Swane and the Kottermanis. It was a crazy plan, a ridiculous plan but, try as she might, she could think of no other. The thought of raising Kerrin and the new baby without Fallon wrenched at her heart and almost set her to weeping. But she took a deep breath. That time on the ship sailing back to Gaelland had taught her to do what was right, no matter the cost. This was the only way. And, besides, there was always hope. She just had to explain that to Kerrin.

CHAPTER 69

"I had never been with a woman with blonde hair before," Durzu said lazily, lying on his back. "Are all Gaelish women like you?"

Dina smiled. One day manipulating men would get boring but that day had not arrived yet.

"You will never find anything like me," she purred, running her hand through his thick chest hair. "And I have never found another man like you."

She watched him flush with pleasure. Men were so stupid! Now he was bound to say something about Swane.

"Better than your boy-King?" he asked.

"As different as night and day," she assured him.

She watched him relax and closed her eyes briefly. It was an unpleasant task but necessary. Use Durzu to get rid of Swane and then remove Durzu.

"We might have to get rid of him," she said softly. "He is becoming lost in his pursuit of dark powers. I am worried that he might seek to take more than just Gaelland. Zorva does not permit sharing of power."

Durzu sat up. "What has he said?" he demanded.

"Nothing yet," she said. "But we should not let our guard down."

"Oh, there is no danger of that," Durzu said, reaching for her again.

She smiled warmly. She had achieved what she wanted. Now it was time to go back to work.

"We cannot catch them, High One," Nazim said sorrowfully. "Our men have been weakened by a winter in this village, on little food."

Feray wanted to demand that he do more but it was obviously impossible. All of the men looked far thinner than she remembered and while they all bowed and smiled whenever she came close, it was obvious winter had taken its toll. The marching left them exhausted at the end of each day and although they had brought all their food with them, there was little to spare. They had become used to catching fish each day to eke out the oats they had. While they had found a handful of domesticated animals in the nearby woods – obviously missed by the original Kottermani attack – that was nowhere near enough for so many men. The other problem was a lack of armor. The cases of swords and barrels of spears they had loaded onto the ship in Adana, combined with a series of crude weapons that the men had made for hunting and fishing over the winter, meant all had some type of weapon. But none had armor, let alone a shield.

The long, cold winter had left them all far paler than the crew she had brought with her. That was another concern. If they did manage to catch up with the Kottermani army, it was going to be nearly impossible to pretend they were just another regiment. They would be spotted immediately. But what could she do but press on? There was no other choice.

"What is that, High One?" Gokmen called, interrupting her thoughts.

She looked up to see a bird circling above her head.

"Get away!" Gokmen roared, leaping up and swiping at it.

The bird evaded him nimbly but still circled Feray.

"Is it dark magic?" the former slave master asked. "If only we had bows!"

"I think the Zorva-worshippers would have called for more than a pigeon if they wanted to harm me," Feray said and extended a hand.

Instantly the bird flew down, landing on her palm and lifting its leg, to which a small scroll was tied.

"A message. Perhaps our prayers for help have been answered," Feray said, stroking the bird gently. She read carefully and closed her eyes for a moment to whisper a prayer of thanks. Her eyes snapped open and she smiled. "Find me something to write with."

CHAPTER 70

Fallon inspected the ranks of men before him.

"I have to give you a choice," he told them, his voice carrying clearly to even the back ranks, thanks to some help from one of Padraig's wizards.

"The people have deserted us. Our new army has run away. The fyrd has not risen and we don't have enough men to defeat the Kottermanis. Our only chance is to kill Swane and his witch Dina. If we do that then we can make a deal with the Kottermanis and we all win. Everyone comes back and life can go on. I shall use myself as bait and when they come in, kill them with crossbows. I just need a few men to stand with me, to make it look like there is an army of us, enough to bring Swane and Dina in close."

"We will all stand with you," someone shouted. Fallon looked along the line to see Bran there, the bearded guardsman pushing his way out of the ranks.

"I cannot risk you all, because it could go wrong. If Swane and Dina don't take the bait, or the Kottermanis don't want to do a deal then we shall be fighting for our lives. I know I can kill Swane and Dina but the rest I can't control. I don't want your deaths on my hands."

"I will not leave my captain to die. If you go, then I go too," Bran bellowed, and there was an answering rumble from the other men. "I cannot live in disgrace, knowing my life was bought with your death. I will stand with you," the officer declared, walking over. Brendan held out his hand and Bran clasped it.

Next moment more men, ones and twos at first, then a wave of them, came forward. .

"Don't all do this," Fallon called. "You could die in battle or, worse, on some foul altar to Zorva, or torn to pieces by Swane to terrify the people into never rising against him again."

The rush of men slowed to a trickle.

"There is no disgrace. You can have wives, families, hope for a life ahead of you. Take it," he called.

After some milling around, perhaps three hundred remained with him. He looked over them with mingled pride and fear. There were some real surprises in there as well: Fitz, the skinny thief that Bridgit saved, Gannon, arms crossed as if daring Fallon to send him away, and Brasso, Casey and many others that he had trained from farm boys into warriors.

"Are you sure? Sleep on this, for this is your lives," he urged them. "Even if it goes wrong for the rest of us, one day there will be a chance to return, to get revenge and to help the people rise up against Swane's evil. You will be needed then."

"We shall be here tomorrow, to get ready," Bran promised. "If your plan is to work, we need to show the people that we are not afraid. And we shall give Swane nightmares."

They raised a defiant cheer then and Fallon had to turn away. "This has to work," he said.

Brendan put a thick arm around his shoulders. "It will work, or we die trying," he said.

*

Fallon inspected the quarrel carefully.

"I had to make it smaller and thinner than the usual one, because the metal shaft is far heavier than even oak," Brendan explained. "The flights are also smaller, and as thin as I dare make them."

"You have made far too many," Fallon said, gesturing at the table. "I only need two."

"But you will need to practice with them first," Brendan warned. "They will fly differently to what you are used to. We need to set up a target outside the main gate and—"

"No," Fallon interrupted. "I shall practice here, where none can see. Don't forget there are still plenty of people out there who would be happy to see Swane back. It just takes one of them to send a warning and the plan falls into a heap."

"It can still do that," Brendan said.

"Look, we'll have three crossbows there and ready. I might miss once but that's it," Fallon said. He placed the quarrel down carefully. "I'll be back later, when it's dark, so none can see what we are doing here. Are you sure you wouldn't rather be on the ship with the others?"

"No," Brendan said.

Fallon grimaced but patted his big friend on the back before heading out to check on the progress of their other preparations. It was essential to give the Kottermanis the impression they were planning to hold the city walls, so half the crossbows from the harbor had been set up on the wall around the southern gate, where the Kottermanis were most likely to arrive. The other half had been taken to the castle, in case things did not go as planned, in which case they could be turned on the vengeful Kottermanis. Fallon supposed there was a chance they would merely enslave him but he doubted that. After what Bridgit had done, they would not want a troublemaker like him loose in their country.

More than a score of the crossbows had been lashed to the old city battlements and he watched sweating men attach the last one, bashing iron pins into crumbling mortar and then using them to fix the tall wooden base into place. He gave them a nod and walked on. It was convenient for what they wanted but the state of the wall was a worry. Years of neglect and harsh winters had left much of the mortar feeling like sand. Chunks of stone could be pushed away by hand and sentries had to be careful not to send pieces tumbling. It would prove to be nothing more than an inconvenience to the Kottermanis. The castle was better, of course, because it had been cared for. But he did not have enough men to hold the castle.

Fallon walked along the city wall and looked out at the sleepy countryside. Nothing moved out there. The other two gates had been locked shut, Brendan and teams of men nailing huge planks across them. Partly to keep the Kottermanis out but mainly to keep everyone else in. Crowds of refugees heading in all directions would just tell Swane and Dina that he had no hope of holding Berry and they would be alert for a trick. He smiled to himself. They would still expect a trick but, once they were inside crossbow range, nothing was going to save them.

*

"The men are making excellent progress. The Kottermanis have thick screens of scouts out in all directions. If Fallon is planning an ambush, he is doomed to fail, for they are checking everything bigger than a rabbit hole," Kane said.

"So, the Kottermanis are ours now, eh?" Swane asked with a smile.

"They might as well be, sire," Kane replied.

Swane turned and winked at Dina. "True enough, though! They are ours in all but name and once we have Berry, even that will change."

She smiled at him, although it was becoming harder to do so every day. "What is Fallon doing? Is he marching to meet us?"

Kane shook his head. "The prisoners we have captured all claim that he has summoned the fyrd, but they all ran rather than fight for him."

"Oath-breakers!" Swane spat.

"Yet they serve us by doing so," Dina said mildly. "Does that not make them your followers?"

"Still, they should be punished. We should sacrifice some to Zorva and send the rest as slaves back to Kotterman. If they had truly been my followers they would have fought against Fallon from the start. They are merely untrustworthy cowards."

Dina stroked his arm. "Yet a King can also be merciful," she said.

Swane jerked his arm back. "There will be no mercy when I reach Berry. There will only be revenge."

Dina bowed her head. That would never do. Munro might be in a cell but he had done magnificent work. Berry was like rotten wood, ready to collapse at the slightest touch. The people would fall for Swane, if he let them. His lust for revenge would ruin all that. She would have to steer him carefully for the first few days when they were back in the capital. Handled carefully, their rule would be secured and then he could indulge his lust for revenge quietly, over time. She felt like shouting sense into him. Without her, where would he be?

*

"It seems your people are fleeing your capital rather than waiting for you to arrive," Durzu said, inspecting the hundreds of refugees that had been swept up.

"Where did you find them all from?" Dina asked. She had worried Durzu might betray their new relationship somehow but those years in his father's court had obviously enabled him to perfect the art of keeping secrets.

"We took your worries about Fallon seriously, so we have had strong patrols sweeping out for miles, to make sure we are not outflanked. They keep coming back with them. Most have run out of food and are begging for more. What should we do with them?"

"We have to bring them along, so they can witness our triumph," Swane said. "And then we can decide how they shall be punished for their disloyalty."

"Are we to feed them?" Durzu demanded. "I want my men fresh and ready for battle if Fallon marches out."

"Throw them a few scraps," Dina suggested. "When we arrive, they will be grateful for anything we give them. Besides, we shall arrive in the next day or two, will we not?"

"Easily," Durzu confirmed. "The only thing slowing us down is the need to watch out for an ambush. I have been keeping our pace down for that reason. But there is no longer anywhere for them to ambush us, it is open, flat country from here to Berry. We shall march fast and hard and surprise them by arriving a day earlier than they expected."

"Fallon will have something planned. But we shall be ready for anything he tries," Swane predicted.

"Then we shall have the Emperor name you as his heir and we shall rule Gaelland for you, while you are in Kotterman," Dina told Durzu.

She smiled at the pair of them, feeling the undercurrent of tension between them. Still, as long as she was there, that would not get out of hand.

CHAPTER 71

"Are you ready?" Fallon asked, trying to keep his voice casual.

Bridgit looked up from a pile of papers. She scraped them into a rough pile and stood, stretching her back.

"I think all is ready," she said. "But I am haunted by the thought of missing one vital thing."

He smiled in agreement. Time and again he had gone over things in his mind, searching for another way – but he just kept coming back to the plan of the poisoned quarrel. He had expected Bridgit to come up with something else, or to flatly refuse to allow him to go ahead. At first he had been relieved she had accepted his plan. But, as the Kottermani army got closer, everything was changing.

He was torn between wanting to wipe out his guilt and being able to see the new baby and watching Kerrin grow to manhood. Sometimes he felt like rushing to Bridgit's side and announcing they would all flee the city and trust to the secret location of Cavan's island to protect them. Yet he knew what Swane and Dina were like. They would not be content with merely seizing back Gaelland. And they had magic, both from their tame wizards, and the dark magic from the blood sacrifice. Not even Cavan's island was safe from that. He wanted to talk out his fears and self-loathing but could not find the words. He wanted Bridgit to tell him he could not sacrifice himself like this, he wanted her to beg him to save himself. *There's a part of me that came up with this plan just to hear that from her*, he realized.

"Are you all ready?" she asked.

He sighed. "Bridge, you know I don't want to do this," he said awkwardly.

She turned and he saw the mask she'd worn since he had announced his poisoned quarrel plan crack.

"I don't want to do this either," she whispered. "The thought of life without you is tearing me apart."

He was at her side a moment later and held her close. If he closed his eyes, then perhaps he could pretend none of this was going to happen.

"I am so sorry for everything," he said. "I wish I'd never picked up that cursed last quarrel and landed us in this mess."

"Hush," she said, reaching up to touch his mouth. "We are here now. Wishing we could change the past can't help anything."

"How is Kerrin?"

He saw her face twist. "He is terrified for you but I have explained everything to him and he has agreed to go along with the plan," she said. "He will need to see you one last time but I have tried to keep him away because it's upsetting him too much." She sniffed. "I feel much the same way. Sometimes I think I can hold it together and then I want to run to you and say this is madness, that we should all go, and hope Rosaleen and Padraig can hide us from Swane and Dina."

Fallon tightened his arms around her. "I feel exactly the same way," he said.

She looked up at him, her eyes shining with tears. "This plan terrifies me. So much can go wrong. And yet there is a chance we can end up triumphant. I try to see that in my mind but it is washed away by all the things that can go wrong. I dream of seeing you dead and I don't know if I can go on when that happens."

Fallon kissed her head and her face, kissed her tears. Hearing his own fears come back at him strangely made him feel much better. This was something he was finally familiar with: Bridgit was worried and he had to reassure her that everything was going to be fine.

"This is what we have to do. And I will make it work," he said. "I have spent my life practicing for this day. All that time in Devlin's field loosing crossbows – it has all led to this. I will not fail."

Now it was her turn to tighten her arms around him. *Here it comes. She will beg me not to do this.*

"Whatever happens, don't kill yourself," she begged.

"What?"

"It is a mortal sin. You cannot take your own life. I know the thought of being captured by Swane or the Kottermanis must be horrible – it gives me nightmares because I know they are a cruel people. But I want to see you again after this life. Don't anger Aroaril by ending your own life."

Fallon hesitated. This was not what he had expected. She was relying on him to protect her and he couldn't let her – let any of them – down. He straightened his back. Death was what he deserved for killing Cavan and only sacrificing himself could atone for that. But there was dying and there was dying. He remembered the tales of how Sean and Seamus had died in Kotterman. When it came down to it, could he really throw himself on his own sword? Still, if he fought hard enough, they would have to kill him instead. That was by far the better option.

"I won't," he said. "I swear it." After all, it was easy enough to say here.

"I pray every night that I will see you again. I know it is possible and I have offered Aroaril everything in exchange for that," she said softly.

He kissed her again. "After all I have done, I thought you might be happy to see the back of me," he said, trying to add a smile to it.

She kissed him back, fiercely. "Just because you are a bonehead sometimes doesn't mean I don't love you. That has never changed. Besides, if you could put up with my madness for so many years, why can't I do the same thing?"

He closed his eyes, so he would not cry, and held her tight.

"I just want to live quietly, with you, Kerrin and the baby," he said. "I see now that I am not the hero I wanted to be. Nor the hero that Gaelland needed. I have left death and destruction behind me at every turn. You will rule far more wisely on Cavan's island. I would be happy to follow your orders."

"Now you say it!" she said.

"I am sorry. You deserve better."

"Now that's enough!" she said, squeezing him suddenly, making him open his eyes. "You have done your best, in a world gone mad. And there is still the chance that all will end happily."

He forced a smile to his face. "That is right," he agreed. "All I need to do is put two quarrels into a target, something I have done a thousand times before."

"Kerrin is sleeping in his own bed again tonight," she said. "You are coming back with me."

He kissed her, unable to say anything.

"Just stay alive. Do that for me," she begged.

"Anything you ask," he said, wishing he could believe in it.

*

"Kottermani scouts are here!"

The thumping on the door woke Fallon from a dream where he was being chased through the castle by the men he had led to their deaths, as well as a sorrowful Cavan. He sat up and rubbed sleep from his eyes, wishing he felt more ready for this, that he had another ten thousand men, that he was still home in bed in Baltimore and his biggest problem was getting Sean and Seamus to stop drinking. He swung his legs out of the bed and Bridgit grabbed his arm.

"You don't have to do this. There is still time for us to run," she said.

He blinked his eyes clear. It was strange but it felt as though she was almost talking to herself as much to him. He was sorely tempted, then the dream returned to him and he shivered. He *knew* he could never be free of his guilt unless he did this.

He rolled back and embraced her. "I swore I would keep you safe and so I will," he said. "And this is the only way."

She hugged him tight. "Aye. You are right. This is the only way," she agreed.

The sadness in her voice struck him to the quick. There was only one way forward now.

"We shall see each other again. It will only be a few days," he said briskly. After all, that might even be true.

"Fallon!"

The hammering at the door got louder and he kissed her. "We'll get you away now, before those bastards get close enough to see you," he said. "Are you all ready?"

"As we can be," Bridgit said, her voice muffled.

He could see she was crying but they had said all they could last night. Now it was up to luck, skill and maybe Aroaril as to what happened next.

CHAPTER 72

"Take care of your mother, and the new baby. Remember the good things I taught you, and not the swearwords," Fallon said awkwardly. What could you say to your son at a time like this?

The ships were already being towed out of the harbor and towards the open sea. Only Bridgit's remained. This was Baltimore's ship and Fallon could see so many familiar faces, from Gallagher to Rosaleen and Riona.

Devlin was sitting down on the dock, his head buried in his hands, seemingly unable to even watch. Likewise, Nola and her daughters had gone from the ship's rail after a teary farewell to Brendan. Fallon had half-hoped his big friend would break down too and agree to leave but he had merely hugged his wife and kids and then picked up his hammer again.

"I should be with you, Dad," Kerrin said, his voice muffled from where he was pressed into Fallon's chest.

Fallon lifted his son's head. "That you cannot do," he said gently. "Son, you are the best part of me. If I do nothing else good in my time on this earth, you are worth it alone. Knowing you and your mam and the baby will live long and happy lives is what keeps me going."

Kerrin hugged him harder and he held his son back, feeling the muscles that had not been there last summer. "I am sorry for dragging you through this but I can only do this knowing it is keeping you safe."

"I will save you, Dad. I will," Kerrin promised.

"No, you will keep your mam safe," Fallon told him.

"No, I can do both," Kerrin insisted, then Bridgit gently pulled him back.

"Take Caley on board," she said. While Kerrin talked to the dog, Fallon faced her.

"Well," he said.

"Well yourself," she replied.

He found there was nothing more to say. They had said so much last night. The time for words was done. It was too late. Instead he held her, trying to drink her in, feeling much as he had done when she had arrived back from Kotterman.

"I shall see you again. Stay alive!" she whispered in his ear, and then she was gone, turning away and hurrying Kerrin off.

"But, Mam, Caley won't move!" Kerrin protested.

The dog sat resolutely.

"Go on," Fallon commanded but when she stood, it was just to move behind him, and sit back down again.

"No, you fool. There will be no food and playing this time," Fallon told her, but she just looked up at him.

"She has to stay with you, Dad. She will keep you safe. I told her so," Kerrin declared.

Fallon picked the dog up, intending to deliver her onto the ship, but Kerrin held up his hands.

"No! You can't, Dad! Without her, you won't live!" he cried, his face panic-stricken.

Fallon glanced over at Bridgit and she nodded imperceptibly. He put Caley down and then watched Kerrin and Bridgit hurry up the gangplank. Immediately it was thrown back onto the jetty and the rowboats began to move it away from the docks.

Friends waved down from the deck but Brendan and Fallon did not wave back. It was all Fallon could do not to lose control. It felt like his heart was sailing away. Devlin got up and joined them and he squeezed his friend's shoulder.

"They will be safe. That is what matters," Fallon said hoarsely.

"Yes, they will," Padraig said from behind him.

Fallon spun. 'What are you doing here, you old idiot?" he growled. "I thought you were looking after Bridgit and Kerrin?"

"They can look after themselves. You are the one who needs me," the old wizard said with a half-smile.

Fallon put his hand on Padraig's shoulder. "You know what we risk?"

"Things are more likely to have a happy ending with me here," Padraig said. His eyes looked clear and steady and he appeared to be a man at peace with himself. Which was more than Fallon could say. "Now are you going to stand here moping or do we get it done?"

Fallon smiled. "I am glad to see you, old man, and to have you with me."

Padraig sighed. "Are we going to sit around, have a hug and good cry, or are we going to do this thing?"

Brendan agreed hoisting his hammer over his shoulder. "Aye. I really feel like killing some Kottermanis."

"But first let's kill the bastards who started this all," Fallon said, and his grief was replaced by a cold anger.

CHAPTER 73

By the time they got to the wall, there was a ring of Kottermani scouts around the city. Any thoughts of trying to get away were now gone. Most of the remaining townsfolk were locked in their houses, knowing that trouble was looming, but a few hundred brave or foolhardy souls had crept onto the wall – keeping well away from Fallon's men around the South Gate – to watch what was happening.

Of the three hundred-odd men who had volunteered to stay back to see Swane killed by a poisoned quarrel, nearly half were on the wall here. Another fifty were at the castle, while the rest were lining the route back, just in case one of Munro's men tried to block their escape with a burning wagon or something else.

Fallon made a point of clasping hands with every man. "No matter what happens, know you are the bravest of the brave. Aroaril will welcome you and children will sing your name for what you do today," he told them, time after time. Finally he made his way to the actual gatehouse, merely a raised battlement over the gates.

"Are you ready?" Brendan asked as he got there.

Fallon stretched his shoulders. "Those metal quarrels are not the same, that is for sure. But I have the hang of them now. The range is reduced, because the string cannot generate enough power. Still, they fly true. You did a fine job, my friend."

He gestured down to where Devlin sat below a merlon, three loaded crossbows beside him.

"They will think I am going to use the big bows, so they won't expect anything smaller. And they will also think their magic can protect them. They won't expect this."

The Kottermani army was flooding forwards now, regiments moving smoothly out to either side to form a huge mass pointed right at Berry.

"There was no way we could have stood against so many," Bran said softly, watching the perfect lines engulf the city.

"Just three hundred against a whole army. That could be quite a tale. It will be a legend, one day," Fallon said, offering them the ghost of a smile.

"If I can sing it, I will be a happy man," Devlin announced.

"If it's you singing it, none of the rest of us will be," Padraig said with a wink.

Fallon looked up at the sky. He had half-expected hail, or at least rain. But it was one of those rare spring Gaelish days where the sun was out and the sky blue. There was little warmth in it, but it was better than what they had fought in before. And at least there would be no danger of the crossbows misfiring on such a day. It felt like time had slowed and every sense was heightened. Every breath was impossibly sweet, even the birds circling gently overhead looked beautiful. He stared at them. What were they doing up there? He looked around to ask Padraig but the wizard had wandered further down the wall.

"Here they come," Brendan said grimly.

Fallon stopped looking at the birds and focused on the Kottermani regiment marching straight up the road at the gate. Already they were only about a hundred paces away.

"That's close enough," he said and signalled down to where Bran stood beside a pair of wall-mounted crossbows.

Bran waved back and an instant later the crossbows rocked back on their makeshift supports, sending double-sized quarrels out to slam into the ground beside the road, sinking half their length into the frozen earth.

The message was unmistakable, a warning rather than an attack, but Fallon worried that the Kottermanis would just keep coming, forcing them to retreat to the castle and try again.

After all, there had been no talking before Lake Caragh, Swane had just sent in his men. But, to his relief, the regiment slowed to a stop. They formed perfect ranks but, from on the wall, Fallon could see messengers running back towards the main mass of the Kottermanis.

"They do want to talk. Thank Aroaril for that," he said.

"I just hope He looks as favorably on our plan to use poison to kill Swane and Dina at a parley," Brendan rumbled.

Fallon wiped sweaty hands on his trews and adjusted the belt on his mail shirt, so the weight did not sit so heavily on his shoulders.

"Over there!" Bran called from down the wall.

A small party of mounted officers skirted the motionless regiment and rode towards the walls, their hands out to show they meant no harm. Fallon spotted a Gaelishman in the middle of them, a man with a slightly familiar face, but he could not place the name. He was the one to hail them.

"Fallon!" he shouted.

"Well, he knows me at least," Fallon muttered.

"What do you want? And why do you come here with an invading army?" he shouted back, mainly for the benefit of the people listening further down the wall.

"I am Captain Kane, the emissary of King Swane and the Emperor of Kotterman, who is here to put an end to your crimes and return the throne to its rightful owner!"

"Here to put up altars to Zorva and sacrifice children!" Fallon roared back. He glanced at his friends. "Do you remember a Kane? Wasn't he some captain of a minor noble's guards?"

"Means nothing to me. He's probably the last one they have left," Brendan muttered.

"You are commanded to open the gates and surrender now. You will receive a fair trial for your crimes and your men can expect to merely be sent into slavery. Open the gates and nobody need get hurt."

"I will only open the gates to Swane and Dina," Fallon bellowed back, "not to their lackey."

Kane rode a few paces closer. "Don't be a fool. I have more than enough men to kill you all," he shouted. "And hundreds of innocents could die in the fighting. Do you want that on your conscience?"

Fallon leaned over the wall. "I have more than enough men to slaughter yours," he fired back. "If you want to save lives, then bring up your so-called King. I will only open the gates to him. Or is he too much of a coward to talk to me? Is he too sunk into evil that ordinary people dare not look at his face?"

Kane stared at him for a long time before turning his horse and signalling to his companions, riding away without another word.

"Do you think he bought it?" Devlin asked.

"We'll know soon enough. If that regiment starts running, we'll give them a volley and then get back to the castle as fast as we can," Fallon said. He was trying to look calm, although inside his stomach was churning and his heart pounding. Should they have just tried this at the castle? But that would have yielded the city to the Kottermanis and they would have nothing to negotiate with. He leaned on the crumbling merlon and tried not to tap his fingers nervously.

Kane and the other officers rode past the regiment – and kept going.

"They might have a trap for us as well," Brendan said.

"Thank you, my friend. I was far too calm as it was," Fallon said sourly.

*

"It's a trap," Dina said instantly. "He has something planned. Those crossbows on the wall must be part of it."

"He cannot harm me," Swane said confidently. "If they try to turn those on us, I shall destroy them. All will see my power and none will dare to stand against me again."

"It is still too much of a risk. We should send columns to the east and north gates and surround him. We don't have to play his games."

Swane smiled. "And yet I do. The challenge has been laid and the people must see how I respond. My father would never let this stand."

"Then you can go alone. I will have no part of this," Dina said.

He turned to her and she had to force herself not to take a step back at the look in his eyes. She had despised him many times but this was the first time she genuinely feared him.

"You will be beside me. We shall face Fallon's ridiculous trap and destroy it, then him. We will show we are not afraid of anything but that this country should be afraid of us." He leaned in close and whispered in her ear and it took all of her self-control not to avert her head. "And it will also send a message to our allies, so when the Emperor announces me as his heir, nobody will question me."

Dina merely nodded. There was nothing else she could do. If Durzu heard these words then things could fall apart quickly. Swane was out of her control now, and that was dangerous indeed.

*

"Here they come!" Fallon pushed himself up from the merlon and pointed to where a new party of riders was making their way towards the wall.

"They have fallen for it, the arrogant bastards. They must think we are idiots and they can outwit us," Brendan snorted.

"Well, we are desperate," Fallon pointed out. But, behind the wall, he was stretching his fingers and warming up his arm and shoulder.

"Dev, get the poison ready," he said softly.

The farmer carefully poured the thick liquid onto the heads of the three crossbows, laying them gently down, pointing away from everyone. Fallon felt a fierce satisfaction at the thought of sending that poison back down at them.

"This is for our children. For all we have gone through," Brendan said. "This is for us, Fallon."

Fallon ignored him. He was slowly blocking everything else out, concentrating on the shot he had to make. Kane had ridden to within thirty paces, a ridiculously short range usually. Yet there had never been as much riding on one shot. He calmed the frantic thoughts in his mind and breathed slowly through his nose, getting himself under control. Even a faster heartbeat could spoil everything, for he needed to loose in the space between letting out one breath and taking another.

The little party came into focus and he studied each one. There was Kane and a pair of guards, each carrying a large shield, as well as the wizard Finbar, the traitorous Duchess Dina and Swane himself.

He watched them ride closer, willing them to keep coming. Unlike before, they stopped some fifty yards away. Still an easy shot, but not quite the certainty from before. No matter, he told himself. His whole life had been in preparation for this moment. Padraig rejoined him.

"Fallon! King Swane is here. Now open the gates, fall on your knees before him and you shall have a quick death!" Kane thundered.

Padraig nodded and Fallon shouted, his voice booming magically across the wall. "And what happens to the people of Berry? And of Gaelland? Will they be forced to bow to Zorva, to hand over their children for blood sacrifice? Tell me *King* Swane. Let us hear it from your mouth, not from your tame lackey."

"Gaelland is not your business. It is mine!" Swane barked, his voice also magically louder. "I am here to rescue these people from you and your band of traitors."

"You are here to enslave them!"

Swane pointed up at the wall. "I am not here to bandy words with a traitor. Either open the gates or prepare to be destroyed."

Fallon waved, and noted how the little party tensed, as if they were expecting an attack. But, instead, his men began to open the huge wooden gates. As he had expected, they instinctively looked there, no doubt wondering if something was coming out of the gate, or if this was indeed a surrender.

Fallon held out his hand and Devlin slapped the butt of the first crossbow into his palm, as they had practiced a score of times the day before.

The familiar feeling of the polished wood calmed Fallon even further and he whipped it up into his shoulder, sighting down at the group, centering in on Swane. The foul Prince looked up at that moment and Fallon breathed out and began to squeeze the trigger. As soon as the quarrel kicked away, he cursed himself. He had loosed Brendan's metal quarrels time and again in the castle garden but while standing on the ground. He had never aimed them downwards. The heavier quarrel dropped far faster than a normal one would through the air and it also wobbled in the air. Over thirty yards it would not have mattered but the extra twenty yards made all the difference. He had aimed at the center of Swane's chest and now it looked as though it would hit his belly. That would still be enough to kill him, even before the poison did its work, but then Swane pulled on his reins, trying to turn the horse, and its head came up – right at the wrong moment for Fallon. Instead of plunging into Swane, it smashed into the horse's skull, killing it instantly.

Fallon snarled a curse and dropped the empty crossbow, beckoning to Devlin.

Down below, Swane's horse had collapsed and Swane jumped clear. He was still an easy target as the little group milled around, turning their own beasts to flee or trying to protect themselves.

Devlin smoothly slipped the next crossbow into Fallon's hand and he sighted again on Swane. He would not miss again.

*

"Get me out of here! Protect me!" Swane shrieked.

Finbar raised his hands then dropped them, his eyes wide. "They are blocking me!" he cried.

Swane could not waste more time on him. He could sense another quarrel was coming soon and Zorva's power could not stop it either. He had tried to block the last one and felt the terror as it refused to obey him.

He grabbed for Kane's hand.

"Shield me with your body. Quick!" he ordered.

Kane hesitated and Swane saw the guard captain's eyes flicker across to Dina before he extended a hand down and began to pull Swane up, *behind* him, not in front. Swane reacted instinctively, tearing his hand free and dropping down. A heartbeat later, another quarrel smashed into Kane's back, right where Swane would have been if he had allowed himself to be swung up into the saddle.

The guard captain did not even have time to scream. His body was flung forwards by the brutal impact, going limp as his spine was smashed to shards. Swane grabbed hold of the twitching leg and flipped it out of the stirrup, letting the body drop down on the other side. He swung himself up into the saddle and then released Zorva's power into the beast, making it break into a mad gallop, faster than it had ever gone before, back towards safety. Behind him, the rest of them were also racing for cover but he did not care about them. His first thought was saving himself, his second was why Kane had acted like that and what signal Dina had given the man – and then he wondered if Fallon had another quarrel. He could not resist turning his head to look.

*

Fallon raised his last crossbow, trying to clear his mind of his two misses. Already there was no chance of making sure Dina was dead. At least he could still get Swane and redeem himself. Strangely, although the foul Prince was more than eighty yards away now and galloping madly, he liked this shot more. It allowed him to think just about where the bolt needed to go, not anything else. But as he nestled the butt into his shoulder and judged where Swane would be, the Prince glanced back. Instantly Fallon's vision seemed to swim and it felt like he was aiming down at Prince Cavan, not Prince Swane. He was horribly reminded of the night when he thought he was saving Bridgit by killing Swane in the castle garden, only to learn he had murdered his friend and Prince instead.

It took him a heartbeat to crush the guilt and anguish and loose, feeling the butt kick into his shoulder as the poisoned quarrel snapped out. He held his breath while Devlin poked his head up from the battlement to see where it would land. All watched it arc through the air and sweep down – and keep dropping. Fallon cursed himself again. A normal quarrel would have flown higher and truer but the heavy metal quarrel dropped like a stone, aimed right where Swane's shoulderblades would be – except it fell a yard behind the horse and vanished into the dust, right where Swane would have been a heartbeat earlier.

"Loose! Everyone! Aim at Swane!" Fallon roared down the line.

His men took a moment to snap out of their shock. Their plan had failed. They bent to the giant bows and released but Fallon knew before the quarrels even came down that they would miss. Besides, these were wooden quarrels and Swane turned to use his powers to swat them out of the sky like so many pesky summer flies.

"What the bogging hells do we do now?" Devlin asked.

Fallon tossed down the third empty crossbow.

Swane and the others were disappearing out of range now, beyond the motionless regiment of Kottermanis. Except they were no longer motionless, they were moving, marching swiftly towards the gate. And he did not have a single loaded crossbow left.

"Back! Back to the castle!" he roared, his voice ragged.

"I've got the poison. There's still some left, so we can try that again at the castle gate," Devlin said.

Fallon forced a smile to his face. There would be no second chance. Swane would not be so foolish. There was only one thing left to do and that was see if he could exchange his men's lives for his own. He felt sick. How could he had missed? If only he had run with Bridgit ...

They clattered down the stairs and hurried back towards the castle. The men along the route watched them approach with hopeful faces, which fell like stones when they saw Fallon shake his head.

"We'll hold up in the castle and try again. Nothing to worry about, lads," Fallon told them, hating himself when they smiled back at that.

"Doesn't look good for us, does it?" Devlin said.

"We could use a joke about now," Fallon admitted.

The farmer sighed. "I cannot see anything to laugh about now. But at least I'll be with my friends at the end."

Brendan slapped him on the back. "We can still beat them. They still have to get into the castle."

"Stay strong. We can still get through this," Padraig said. Of all of them, he seemed the most calm. Fallon wondered if he'd found a flask of something.

Fallon exchanged a look with Devlin. "There is still a chance," he said. "I might be able to get the rest of you out alive. Slaves, but alive."

"And how can you do that? Hand yourself over to Swane?" Brendan asked. "Piss on that. I would rather die than live like that."

"Besides, I fear they're not going to give us the chance. I don't think Swane liked nearly being turned into a pincushion," Devlin added.

*

452

"How did that happen?" Swane screamed, his eyes wild.

Dina reined in her horse, trying to control her hammering heart. She had seen her chance to get rid of Swane out there, given Kane the signal that should have put Swane at Fallon's mercy. But somehow Swane had sensed that and survived. Now she had to do the same.

"I told you we should not have gone out there. I knew it was a trap!" she declared hotly, matching his fury with some of her own. But it only turned his attention on her.

"What was Kane doing? And what did you tell him?" Swane snarled.

"Nothing! He was an idiot and he paid the price with his life," she replied swiftly.

"I would have paid the price," Swane said with a rare fury.

Dina said nothing, seeing he was not to be reasoned with in this mood. Fortunately for her, Durzu rode up at that moment.

"What happened?" he demanded.

"Betrayal!" Swane yelled, froth at the corner of his lips.

Durzu nodded. "Then we shall kill them all," he said grimly.

"No!" Swane cried.

Durzu turned, the look of surprise on his face almost comical, except Dina knew her own face must look the same.

"Not kill them?"

"I want as many alive as possible. Death is too easy for them. And I don't want Fallon to die until I am ready."

Durzu smiled grimly. "Then it shall be as you say."

He turned to the nearest regiment and roared out a series of orders. Instantly they began to run towards the city, followed by another, then another, while a fourth prepared to follow and a fifth began to line up as well.

CHAPTER 74

"How are we going to defend the castle, sir?" Bran asked.

"Casey, take fifty men and watch the back wall. I think they'll go for the front gate first. If you see anything, pull back to the main keep and send word to me."

"What do we do?" Devlin asked.

"We'll line the walls and try and get Swane to come in close again. If they won't talk, then we have to make them talk. They can take the outer walls but they'll struggle to get into the keep. If we hold on for long enough, they'll have to speak to us. And then I can make a deal. Meanwhile, we'll hit them with everything when they're in the square. If they bring up archers then we pull back to the towers and gatehouse. These walls were built for a reason. Let's use them."

They hurried away, looking purposeful and he strode up onto the wall, keeping his hands behind his back, so nobody could see them shaking. His mistakes had doomed all these men, Gaelland's best. All that was left was to try and save a few of them.

He spotted Padraig, sipping from a small flask.

"What are you doing?" he snapped. "I thought you said you wouldn't touch another drop until your dying day?"

Padraig swallowed, his eyes screwed shut with pleasure. "Well, now, I think this probably counts as it," he said, with a wink. "For me, anyway. But if I have anything to do with it, then not for you."

"Well, you were the one who came here. You could be sailing off to a life of luxury right now."

"Are you mad? An island run by my daughter? I'd rather be here!"

They shared a laugh, Fallon enjoying that his men were listening and joining in. The laughter swelled as the joke was retold along the wall – and then it died as the first Kottermanis rushed into the square, shields held high. Fallon watched as they flooded into the open space, spreading left and right to form a long line. Fallon knew the square could hold tens of thousands. But two regiments of Kottermanis seemed to fill it rather rapidly.

"Will they wait and talk?" Padraig wondered.

"No," Fallon said grimly, as the massed ranks advanced again, shields locked tight.

He turned left and right and waved his arms. "Don't wait! Loose!" he bellowed.

The rest of the double-sized bows launched their long missiles. Some bounced off the cobbles before slamming into legs, others sailed high over the Kottermani heads – but most thumped home into the packed ranks, driving through shields and armor to send men flying.

The gaps filled up as fast as they opened and Fallon cursed the Kottermani discipline. Regular crossbows began to loose now, the sound of iron heads striking steel helms and wooden shields a mixture of thuds and bangs. A litter of wounded and dead was being left behind but the Kottermanis still kept coming. The big bows had reloaded and again sent their long missiles streaking out into the tight ranks, punching men over two at a time. The Kottermani advance began to slow and he hoped they might turn this back. Then he cursed again.

A third regiment entered the square and this one had bows in their hands, not shields.

"The men behind! Aim at them!" Fallon shouted, cupping his hands around his mouth to be heard over the noise of battle.

But although the crossbowmen responded, their rate of fire was too slow. The Kottermanis ran forwards, catching up to the first two, heavily armed regiments swiftly. They were barely a hundred yards away and Fallon knew what was coming next.

"Into the towers! Quick!" he roared.

A few men paused to loose one more time before breaking apart and heading either to the towers on each corner or the main gatehouse. Fallon made sure all were going before joining them. He saw the Kottermani archers stop and bend their bows and then abandoned all pretence of dignity and sprinted for the open doorway. He slid the last pace, Brendan throwing out a huge arm to stop him. He could hear the ominous rush of the arrows and then it sounded as though hail was striking the castle. He turned to see white-feathered arrows bouncing off the battlement.

"Well, we're safe enough here – but how do we stop them now?" Devlin asked.

Fallon strode over to the arrow slits, designed to give an arbalester a safe place to aim down. Some faced out across the square, others aimed only downwards, covering the gate itself.

"I want five men to load for me. The rest of you, find yourself one of these and begin to pick them off," he ordered. "They don't have a battering ram, so they're going to struggle to get into those gates."

"Yet," Devlin muttered.

Fallon ignored him and accepted a loaded crossbow. He eased forwards to see the Kottermanis break ranks and race towards the gate, no doubt thinking themselves protected from defensive fire by the arrows that still clanged and clattered off the stonework. It would be a lucky arrow indeed that got into one of the downward-facing arrow slits in the gatehouse and, even if they did, the stonework was angled so that an arrow from below would waste itself on the ceiling, rather than strike the man there.

Fallon hefted his borrowed crossbow and suppressed the urge to curse himself for his earlier failure. Nobody had paid the price yet but it was surely a matter of time. The only thing was to hurt these Kottermanis and keep hurting them until they backed off and talked.

He sighted on an officer and released smoothly, watching the quarrel smash the man backwards. He held out the empty crossbow and it was taken by one set of hands, another loaded one pressed into his palm. Again he sighted and this time picked off a tall man with a huge moustache, sending the quarrel into the middle of his face and spreading the moustache across the square.

More Kottermanis were pushing forwards now, big men with axes who swung them furiously at the thick timbers of the gates. Fallon picked them off, one after the other, every shot going exactly where he wanted it to, as if to mock him for his earlier failures. The men behind him reloaded swiftly, so there was a never-ending supply of loaded crossbows. The Kottermanis had to step over their dead and dying comrades now to reach the gates, and even using screens of men with shields held high could not stop Fallon. The round shields did not link together properly and he sent quarrels through seemingly impossible gaps, throwing back yet another man in a spray of blood.

Archers targeted the arrow slits and the sound of steel crashing into the stone was never-ending. But they had to be right at the gate to loose at the arrowslits and there was no room for them there. Fallon ducked as one managed to fly through, but it merely struck the ceiling above him, crushing the arrowhead, then bounced, spent, off his shoulder. He leaned down, sighted and put a quarrel into the space between an archer's neck and chest. The man sank down but Fallon did not give him a second glance, instead holding out his hand for another weapon.

"This can't be their only plan," Padraig said. "They won't be able to get near the gates soon."

The thunder of axe blows had changed to a mere patter and Fallon paused, out of targets for a moment.

"We're beating the bastards, lads!" he shouted, before bowling over yet another axeman.

The axemen fell back then and Fallon straightened up, his earlier fears replaced with exultation, only for Bran to call out a warning.

"They are bringing up rams now!"

Fallon joined him at one of the narrow slits looking out over the square, to see a fourth regiment arrive, dragging along a pair of trees suspended on ropes.

"We'll pick them off as well," Fallon said confidently, then grabbed Brendan. "Take ten men and check the gate. We can't be trapped in here," he said.

He took over one of the forward-facing slits and loosed at the men carrying the rams, although there were scores of men with shields clustered around them. Crossbows from the gatehouse and the two towers felled a handful of men at the rams, but there were plenty of others to take their place and Fallon changed back to the downward-facing arrowslit as the rams arrived and the Kottermanis raced them up at the gates, swinging them so they crashed together into the wood, a sound that echoed through the gatehouse.

Fallon loosed as fast as men could hand him a crossbow and the swingers soon joined the axemen in screaming piles outside the gate. But each crash was getting louder and he didn't like the sound the wood was making as it tried to withstand the attacks.

There was a gap between the Kottermani helms and the neckline of their armor. It was a small target but to Fallon it seemed as easy as sinking a knife into a lamb chop on his plate. If he struck at the back of the neck they dropped instantly, if he struck at the side, sinking the shaft deep into the neck and down into the chest cavity, they dropped kicking and writhing and if he struck at the front they staggered around, painting their fellow soldiers in crimson before they fell.

"Fallon!" Devlin hit him on the shoulder and he cursed as his quarrel flew wide, sinking into a tree trunk instead.

"What?" he snarled.

"Horns," Devlin said simply.

Fallon tossed the empty crossbow back to his loader and followed Devlin to the doorway, where the noise from below was not as intense. Sure enough the warning horns were sounding. He risked a look back towards the keep and saw men standing there, waving frantically.

"That's where that other regiment got to," he said grimly. "We'll have to get back to the keep." He grabbed Padraig. "Send word to Casey to pull back to the keep and barricade the door in from the kitchen garden. They can only fit two men at a time there, so he should be able to hold that easily enough."

The old wizard nodded and slipped away, picking up one of his magicked birds from where they sat patiently on an arrowslit facing into the courtyard.

"But how do we get back to the keep through that?" Devlin asked, gesturing out to where white-feathered arrows seethed on the battlement and cobbles like a steel-tipped rain. "We'll lose half our men to those arrows."

Fallon spat. "Only one thing for it," he said. "Stop! All stop!"

The crossbowmen at the slits and the loaders all paused, staring at him in surprise.

"We have to let them break in. Once the gates crack, the archers will stop for fear of hitting their own men. Then we can run," he called. "Pass the word to the towers to be ready to run when the gates go."

"But Fallon, won't the Kottermanis be inside then? We'll have to be fighting them," Devlin said.

"I know," Fallon agreed. "But that's a smaller risk than the death from above."

The crossbows were stacked by the wall, for they were just weight to slow a man down. Instead the men gathered by the two doorways, listening to the renewed Kottermani assault on the gates. Fallon watched soldiers pick up fallen axes and rejoin the attack on the gates, emboldened by the sudden lack of defenders.

"Hurry up," Fallon urged. There was a Kottermani regiment loose in the back of the castle and it was surely only a matter of time before they cut off the retreat to the keep.

The trunks swung again and there was a screech of tortured wood, then a cheer from below, a sudden shove of men pushing forwards.

"Now!" Fallon roared.

Arrows still fell on the battlements but the deadly missiles were no longer falling on the small square behind. Fallon's men raced down the stairs from two sides, heedless of the steep stone steps. Fallon could see Brendan and his men fighting the first of the Kottermanis to get through the gate, the giant hammer rising and falling pitilessly. Fallon's men, led by Bran and Devlin, crunched into the sides of the Kottermani advance, bottling them up at the gate, while the next rush raced back towards the keep, joined by the men from the towers. The piles of dead men in front of the gate, not to mention the discarded rams, blocked much of the entrance. The surviving Kottermani officers were making their men drag open the second gate, rather than join the attack. Fallon was last out, a loaded crossbow in each hand. He stamped down the steps, then paused halfway down, triggering both weapons into the mass of Kottermanis before rushing down to join Brendan.

"Back! Run!" he roared.

One of his men turned to do just that and took a Kottermani sword through the neck. Before the Kottermani could even withdraw the blade, a furious Fallon hacked through his wrist. Clutching his stump and spraying blood, the soldier vanished into the press. Brendan's hammer swung sideways, forcing Kottermanis to jump backwards and the last of the Gaelish ran. For a heartbeat Fallon thought Brendan would stay, fighting to the last, but he grabbed the smith's arm and Brendan turned as well, the pair of them pounding towards safety, Kottermanis hard on their heels.

Fallon could hear their pursuers, the slap of their leather boots on the cobbles, could almost feel their breath but he was not going to leave Brendan behind. Then there was a shout and a clatter and the nearest chasers went down in a heap. He saw Padraig waving but did not have time to wave back his thanks. He could also see Devlin forming the men into a battleline, leaving a small space for them to run into. His breath was rasping in his throat and he could hear Brendan panting but they raced to safety, men closing behind them. He spun to see the Kottermanis had slowed to a stop ten yards away, waiting for more men to thicken their ranks before they attacked.

"Back!" Fallon tried to shout but he was out of breath and he had to suck in air before it came out properly.

Tired as he was, he was still proud to see his men retreat as he had taught them, in perfect lines, the edges curling back to protect their flanks. He risked a glance over his shoulder to see the gates into the keep just a few paces away.

"Every second man, back inside, ready on the doors!" he called, his voice still ragged.

But as soon as they did so the Kottermanis charged, seeing their chance for slaughter slipping away. The two sides crunched together, hacking and shoving and stabbing. Fallon saw one of his men go down and stepped into the space, jabbing his sword out at the Kottermani's eyes. The soldier raised his shield and Fallon kicked him in the knee, feeling the cartilage crunch beneath his heel.

The man staggered but instead of pursuing, Fallon stepped back, keeping with the line. The temporary safety of the keep was just a few steps away and yet the Kottermanis, after suffering under the crossbows at the gates, were not ready to let them go. They attacked furiously, remorselessly. But these were Fallon's best men, veterans of battles at Berry and Lake Caragh, and they fought back grimly, swords and shield and mailshirts taking the brunt of the blows as they retreated. Fallon had no shield and had to block an axe coming at his head, and then the Kottermani attacker punched out with his shield, driving Fallon backwards. He staggered and nearly fell but one of his men stepped in to save him, shoving the Kottermani with his shield and then slashing open the man's throat with a ferocious stab.

"My thanks!" Fallon called, then recognized the man was Gannon.

The bald sergeant's face twisted in something close to a smile. "Still don't trust me?" he asked.

"With my life. Although that's not worth much right now," Fallon said with a smile.

Brendan saved them all again. With the Kottermanis right on top of them, preventing the doors being shut, the big smith waded into the battle, hammer flying. His first blow swept three men aside, two of them with crushed skulls, then the reverse sweep sent another two flying. The Kottermanis instinctively drew back a pace and the last of the Gaelish scampered into the keep, where Devlin had teams of men already swinging the doors shut. But the Kottermanis surged forwards again and blocked the doors before they could properly close.

"Get your shoulders into it!" Fallon roared, grabbing hold of the door and throwing his weight against it. For a long moment the two sides were locked evenly, then Brendan shoved against the right-hand door, inching it backwards. The Kottermanis became crushed and then both doors were moving as the Gaelish got the upper hand. The Kottermanis cried out as they fell and were trampled on, or caught by the doors. Fallon flinched as a sword thumped into the door by his hand, then a Gaelish spear rammed into the mass, drawing a scream of pain. The two doors slammed shut, mangling several Kottermani hands as the wood clashed together. Devlin and two others swung the locking bar down and then they all stepped away as the doors shook from the furious Kottermanis.

"That should hold them for a bit," Fallon said. "Now we've got the chance to make a deal."

But, no sooner were the words out of his mouth when the doors began to shiver with the sound of axe blows.

"I don't think they want to talk," Devlin muttered.

The Gaelish backed away from the door. Fallon looked around and realized the castle's defenses began and ended at the wall. There were no arrow slits here and the only windows were high up. Worse, the corridors were wide and open around here.

"Fall back," he ordered. "Line up at the corridor to the stairs back there."

His men obeyed without question but he could see the fear on many faces as the doors slowly splintered under the Kottermani axes. The corridor he had picked was only wide enough for five men at a time but it was one of many out of the entrance hall. Once through the doors, the Kottermanis could go around them, heading towards the throne room or the servants' wing and then come from around the back.

"I am sorry, lads," he said aloud.

They all stared at him but he could not face them.

"You trusted me and I have led you to this. I am more proud of you than if you were my own sons. If you want to step away now, make for the cells. Shut yourselves in and pretend you were my captives, dragged off the streets for defying me. You can survive that way. Gaelland needs you. Dying here will do no good."

There was dead silence to his words, although it was broken by the rhythmic chopping at the doors.

"Nobody is running," a thin voice said from the back.

Everyone looked and Fallon was surprised to see it was the skinny thief, Fitz.

"How can we turn our back on everything we believe in? How can we go on, knowing we cowered and hid while everyone else died? Gaelland does not need men like that," he said, his voice gaining in power as he went on.

"Go back to what we had before? Groveling to bastard nobles like Dina and Swane? What sort of life is that?" Gannon added.

"We'll stand here and make those bogshites wish they had never stepped foot onto Gaelish land," someone else called and then they were all shouting their defiance, taking strength from their noise as it drowned out the assault on the doors.

Fallon had to look at the floor until he could get control of himself. "You are all as full of blarney as an egg is full of meat," he shouted finally. "But, Aroaril save us, I love you for it!"

They cheered him and themselves then, trying to chase away the fear that Fallon could feel was hanging over them. Not that any would admit it.

Fallon grabbed Bran and sent him and a squad to find Casey and bring his men back. He could not bear the thought of them being surrounded and lost. At the very least they all deserved to die together.

In the next moment the locking bar on the doors split and a flood of Kottermanis raced inside, shouting in their own tongue. The Gaelish met them with a shield wall, just five men abreast at the entrance to the corridor, and threw them back. Just as Fallon had taught them, the front rank held their ground and the ranks behind lunged and thrust at the Kottermanis, who crammed into the doorway and squeezed the life out of themselves. More and more pushed forwards but there was no getting through, the Gaelish and the Kottermanis at the front were packed so tight they could not use their swords. They were so tight that some of the corpses could not even fall, just stayed upright, a barrier of flesh to those behind.

Fallon did not have to do anything, just watch as his men stopped the advance dead. But he could see Kottermanis vanishing off to either side and could sense them racing through the castle, searching for a way around them. He could stand it no longer.

"Fall back! Back to the stairs!" he roared.

There was no question of turning and running this time. Not even Brendan could force back that press of Kottermanis. Fallon called out the time and, pace by pace, the Gaelish eased back, the Kottermanis baying for blood as they tried to crack open the shield wall. Gaelish fell with every step, Fallon feeding fresh men into the line all the time. The corridor was treacherous underfoot as blood, brains, entrails and shit slopped across the slates but the Gaelish had the best of the footing, while the Kottermanis were continually slipping on the foul morass.

Fallon risked a glance over his shoulder. They were almost at the heart of the keep: the main stairs, two sets that met on the first floor. Here several corridors came together and opened right up into another hall. He could see Gaelish already fighting to hold back Kottermanis in several of those. He grabbed Devlin.

"Take another two score over to help," he ordered.

The farmer collected a group and raced off and Fallon looked around, hoping to see some way out of this. But there was nothing.

"Join the line," he shouted and the men who had made it out of the corridor took up position at either side, widening the line as they fought their way out. With a little luck they could still fight their way back to the stairs and block the Kottermanis there.

But it did not work that way. The pressure of the Kottermani advance was so powerful, they burst out of the corridor like a cork from a bottle, brushing past Fallon's hastily assembled flank guards. In an instant, there was just a thick knot of Gaelish fighting on three sides, and handfuls of men fighting back-to-back, surrounded by Kottermanis and vanishing with every heartbeat. Fallon felt the pain of every one and it filled him with a colossal hate for himself. But he could only take it out on these bastards.

Fallon blocked a savage thrust and rolled his wrist, cutting down onto the soldier's arm, tearing the muscle and breaking the elbow. The Kottermani reeled away but was instantly replaced – by an axeman this time, who swung powerfully, a blow that would have torn apart Fallon's ribs if it had landed. But he stepped backwards and then jumped forwards, ramming his blade into the soldier's mouth and out the back of his skull. The Kottermani fell, ripping Fallon's sword out of his hand but he reached out and grabbed the falling axe. He hefted it experimentally. It felt quite like a shillelagh, except for the heavy iron head at one end. But it was balanced well and he instinctively held it in a shillelagh grip.

The first Kottermani to come close took a swift jab to the jaw. Because it had the axehead at the end, it didn't break the bone but instead ripped the whole lower jaw away. Before that man had collapsed, unable to even scream, Fallon smashed the butt into another's nose and then adjusted his grip, swinging the axe in a wide arc so it crunched into Kottermani ribs, with a sound like a lamb carcass on the butcher's block.

The Kottermanis drew back slightly and he beckoned them onwards. "Come on!" he roared.

Movement out of the corner of his eye made him turn. Brendan was on his right side, spattered with blood. He turned back in time to see a Kottermani jump at him but the axe sang out and took the Kottermani's head off, sending it looping lazily into his fellows. Fallon jumped back as the headless corpse collapsed at his feet, spouting blood all over the floor.

"Come on!" Fallon shouted again as the Gaelish backed towards the stairs, the Kottermanis trying to get around behind them. Fallon had no idea of what was going on now, his world had shrunk to what was in front of him.

Kottermanis tried to catch him unawares but the axe felt as light as a shillelagh in his hands and he mocked them and then killed them if they came too close. He was invincible. They were too slow and weak for him. It almost felt like magic. By contrast, Brendan did not say anything, just crushed ribs and chests and skulls, his work-toughened arms seemingly tireless.

"Fallon! Fallon!"

Fallon finally heeded the urgent shouts and glanced over his shoulder to see Padraig on the first step, pointing over to the right. Gaelish pushed past him, taking his place, but he could not see what the wizard was worried about and so he jumped up three steps, to give him a better view.

The feeling of invincibility drained away and he became aware of a fire in his shoulder, aches in his wrists and back and the way he was panting for breath. Half his men were down and many of the others had taken some kind of wound. Worse, Casey, Bran and Devlin and their surviving men were being pursued up the other flight of stairs, unable to hold back the Kottermanis. For every one of the enemy soldiers they cut down, two more sprang forward to take their place, while every Gaelish who fell was one less in the line.

Fallon sucked air into his protesting lungs. "Back to the landing! Now!"

His men ran, or at least the ones who still could. The wounded tried to help each other up the stairs, while a knot of men, led by Brendan, held the Kottermanis off at the bottom of the steps. Fallon could not bear to see his friend die, so raced down the stairs and smashed his axe into a Kottermani face. As the man was flung backwards, he grabbed Brendan's shoulder and hauled at the big man with all his strength.

"Move! Now!" he roared.

Brendan took one step back and a slim figure took his place, the mailshirt sitting awkwardly on his thin shoulders.

Fallon recognized Fitz as the thief slashed wildly around him with his sword. He took a sword blow on his shield and mangled the Kottermani soldier's hand with a return blow, then an axe hit his shoulder and he vanished under a press of stabbing swords.

Brendan looked like he was ready to jump back into the unequal battle. The last handful of Gaelish at the base of the stairs were being dragged down, but Fallon grabbed his friend's arm and swung him around so he could see the other flight of stairs, where more Gaelish fought desperately to survive, including Devlin.

"Devlin!" he roared and Brendan nodded.

Fallon ran up the stairs. It occured to him that they were all dead men walking and saving Devlin from one set of Kottermani swords, merely to die at another set, might be pointless. But while he had breath he was determined to keep fighting. He passed his wounded men as they struggled up the stairs, some of them giving up their futile efforts to escape and turning back to be swallowed up in the advancing wave of Kottermanis.

At the top of the stairs, Gannon and a grim-faced, bloodied line of Gaelish waited, opening up to let Fallon and a puffing Brendan through.

Fallon did not stop but pounded across the landing and down the other flight, to where Casey, Devlin and a dozen others backed up the stairs, their Kottermani pursuers being slowed by the many corpses and screaming wounded littering the staircase.

Even as Fallon watched, Devlin was driven back against the railings by a muscular Kottermani swordsman. With a roar that went almost unnoticed in the chaos of battle – the screams, shouts and smashing of steel – Fallon flung himself down the stairs, burying his axe in the swordsman's side. The man folded over and Fallon had to use all his strength to rip the blade free of his flesh, a glistening chunk of rib flying out of the wound as he did so.

Another Kottermani tried to take advantage of this but Devlin thrust his sword up to protect Fallon – and the Kottermani blade shattered, a chunk of it piercing Devlin's right forearm. Fallon used the butt of his axe to smash the disarmed swordsman in the face. He flipped backwards, hit the bannisters and toppled over to hit the stone flagstones with a soggy crunch that was almost lost in the howls and bellows.

Devlin swore furiously, his sword dropping from nerveless fingers. He reeled backwards to sit down heavily on a step, staring at the dagger-sized chunk of steel protruding from his arm. Three Kottermanis closed in on them and Fallon hefted his axe.

"Get out of it," Devlin cried.

"Bog that," Fallon said and prepared for one last axe blow.

Then Brendan tore past them, his hammer a blur as it picked two Kottermanis up and flung them down the stairs. Fallon slashed his axe up between the legs of the third, the Kottermani's agonized screams cutting through everything else.

Kottermanis still threw themselves at Brendan. He caved in the head of the first, then the second tackled him around the chest. He flung his hammer at another, the weapon stoving in the Kottermani's helmet before bouncing away down the stairs. Brendan reached down at the man who held him and plunged his thick thumbs into the man's eye sockets, thrusting them through the eye and into the brain beyond. Fluid and blood sprayed over his face as the Kottermani convulsed and shook in his hands. He tore his hands free and stepped back to avoid a sword thrust, instead grabbing the swordsman's arm and leg. He lifted the Kottermani up and snapped his spine by driving him down onto the point of his knee. From that position he surged up, inside the swing of another blade and grabbed the man around the neck, squeezing with all the power of his huge hands. The Kottermani beat helplessly at the big smith until, with a crack of bones, Brendan flung the corpse away.

Now the Kottermanis did draw back a pace, but Fallon could see they were massing for a charge that not even Brendan could withstand, certainly not without his hammer.

"Brendan! Get Devlin clear!" he bellowed.

The smith's head snapped around and for a heartbeat Fallon thought Brendan was going to ignore him, but then his eyes cleared and he hurried to Devlin's side. Fallon stepped forwards, ready to give them time to get clear but Casey blocked him.

"Get them out of here, sir," he said calmly.

Fallon looked into the young guardsman's eyes and knew what that meant. Casey, the lad who'd wet himself when Fallon had taken them into Killarney, was now announcing he was going to give his life for them in the same tone of voice a man might ask his wife to pass the salt at the dinner table. He nodded and Casey saluted with his reddened sword before taking his last five men and driving into the mass of Kottermanis.

Brendan picked up Devlin and hauled him up the stairs. Fallon followed, up towards where his last men were throwing every Kottermani attempt to gain the top of the other stairs back.

They were his best and biggest, the brave and the bastards, the ones who wouldn't give in, even when a thousand Kottermanis were baying for their heads. He watched Brasso, the guard who had saved them all the night Kemal had attacked, fighting with sword and shield like he had been born to it, every blow throwing a foe back. And Bran, his beard now soaked with blood, laughing at the Kottermanis as he killed. And Gannon, fighting like a madman, flinging swordsmen in all directions.

"Back! Follow me! The stairs are lost!" Fallon roared.

They fell into step with him as though they had practiced it a hundred times before, the last score of his men holding the corridor against their enemies as if the Kottermani veterans were a pack of small children. Fallon fought with them, the handle of his axe sticky with blood, unaware of where they were and not even wondering when the end might come. The world had shrunk to what was in front of him. The Kottermanis seemed ridiculously clumsy and even when they had him at their mercy, kept slipping over or just missing.

"Fallon! The king's rooms! We can head down and try and get out the back!" Padraig cried.

Fallon doubted that was possible but there was nothing better to do, so they backed down that way. He buried his axe in a Kottermani head and stepped into the room he had made his office, Bran slamming the heavy door shut. A pair of Kottermanis were trapped on their side of the door but they only lasted a heartbeat, Brasso cutting one down, Gannon the other.

Devlin opened the secret door, the one that led down to the dungeons, then slammed it shut. "They're already down there!" he cried, despair in his voice.

Fallon shrugged. He had not expected to get away. He almost smiled at the way life had come full circle. He had cornered King Aidan in here and Swane had escaped. Now Swane had him cornered and there would be no escape.

"Block the door, shove the desk against it," he said.

Devlin and Brendan quickly obeyed, although the smith did almost all of the work. Meanwhile the rest of them formed a semi-circle around the main door, which was already shivering under the assault of the Kottermanis. The office was a large, comfortable room but it seemed very full of men. Most were panting with exhaustion, their swords blooded and blunted, their mail scarred and dented or even torn. Only a handful still had their shields or the strength to raise them. Padraig looked the worst of them all. He was reeling, his face gray with exhaustion.

"Getting too old for this," Fallon told Padraig.

"You or me?" Padraig answered, giving him the ghost of a smile.

Fallon slipped his arm around the wizard and helped him over to the chair beside the fire. He went to drop the wizard on the cushion, only for it to give a soft bark. He then saw Caley there, tail thumping against the chair, eyes bright with concern.

"You silly mutt," he said. "You should have hidden somewhere else. You really should have gone with Bridgit. Stay here and get out later. Talk!" At the word, the dog buried her nose in the chair and appeared to be nothing more than a black cushion.

"I'm done," Padraig said softly. "Leave me here."

"Don't be ridiculous," Fallon said, but there was no conviction in his voice. Padraig did look terrible. There was nothing to him, the flesh had melted off him.

"What have you been doing?" he asked.

Padraig reached up and patted his face. "What I had to. I am proud of you, son. And thankful that you were there for my daughter. I was glad to repay some of that debt today. Now let me die in peace."

"What?"

But Padraig had flopped down next to Caley and was whispering softly to the dog.

Fallon grabbed his arm. "Tell me what's going on!" he demanded.

Padraig patted Caley and looked up. "Thank you for this chance to repay some of my debt. Now, stay alive. That will tell Bridgit I kept my word. Farewell, son."

"Wait! What is—" Fallon clutched at Padraig but the old wizard was gone. He stared at the slight smile on Padraig's face, trying to make sense of it all.

"Fallon!" Devlin called out.

He dragged himself away, telling himself that it was just sweat dripping down his face and making his eyes burn. "How's the arm?" he asked Devlin.

The farmer held it up gingerly, blood dripping down his fingers. "Take that out, bind it up and give me something. I'll not face them unarmed," he said.

Fallon looked at Brendan and was horrified to see how blood-covered the smith was. He looked like a walking corpse, although hardly any of it was his.

"I'll hold his arm, you pull it out," he suggested.

Brendan nodded and took hold of the jagged steel. With a quick jerk, he hauled it out of Devlin's arm, making the farmer gasp with pain. Fallon tied a scrap of tunic around the wound while the smith looked at the Kottermani metal.

"Here's the problem," the smith said, turning the broken blade over in his gore-encrusted fingers. "The sword maker didn't fold the steel right. It should not have broken like that. I could have done a much better job. I just need my hammer to beat it out right—"

Then he dropped the fragment of sword and Fallon saw the horror on his face as he contemplated his hands. Brendan looked up and Fallon saw the fury had gone from his friend's eyes. Instead it was replaced by tears, which cut their way down the blood on his face and trickled into his reddened beard.

"I don't want to do this anymore," he whispered. "I don't want to kill. I want to make things. I want to hold Nola and the girls and tell them I am sorry." Then he was weeping, deep, heartfelt sobs that made his huge frame shake.

Fallon had no words, just reached out and clasped his friend's shoulder. Devlin reached out with his good arm and hugged the smith.

"I'll stay with him. Until, you know," the farmer whispered.

Fallon nodded, still not trusting himself to speak.

"We did some good, didn't we?" Devlin said, obviously trying not to make it a question.

"We did," Fallon said, attempting to smile. He didn't believe it but he knew Devlin needed something.

"I'll see you later," the farmer said.

"Aye. Later," Fallon agreed.

"Fallon! They're coming through!" Gannon warned.

Fallon patted Brendan's shoulder, wishing he had said more to the man, wishing he had time to grieve, wishing he had time. The secret door was also splintering and *later* seemed to be coming much faster than he wanted.

"I need six men back here!" he called, surprised at how steady his voice came out. The six closest, led by Brasso, formed a line behind the desk, which was now being nudged away from the door with each blow from the other side.

Fallon went to the other door, not wanting to see his friends die. He pushed his way between Bran and Gannon as the main door finally gave way. There was nothing to say, so he did not waste words.

Yet there was time to notice the Kottermanis who burst in were not carrying swords or axes but instead thick clubs. Others carried the small crossbows, like the one he had given to Kerrin.

And the quarrels they launched were blunted, knocking his men down without sinking into their flesh. But Fallon did not let that bother him, leaping to meet them with axe held high.

The axe bit deep into a neck and he whirled it around his head, heedless of the blood that sprayed off the edges, and thumped it into a chest. It did not bite nearly as deeply as before and he could not get it out of the shrieking Kottermani. A club cracked down on his arm, numbing it, and he let go of the axe, fumbling for his dagger. But another club cracked across his head and sent him stumbling backwards to crash into the chair. His vision was clear and his mind was working but it seemed to have lost all connection with his body. He wanted to get up and rejoin the fight but his legs and arms would not obey him. He wanted to embrace his friends but could not move as clubs felled both Brendan and Devlin. He wanted to talk to Padraig but the wizard was unmoving beside him. He wanted to comfort Caley as she whimpered softly in the chair behind him but he could not even manage that. He could feel a tear trickling down his face as he saw the last of his men go down to lie in the gore and the best he could manage was to blink it away. Instead he slumped there, waiting for death.

Except it never came.

At an order from an officer, the Kottermanis began binding his men's hands and feet. Any that struggled were silenced with another swift blow.

When they came for him he tensed himself to fight but his treacherous limbs would not do anything as a pair of stone-faced Kottermanis lashed his wrists and ankles together. He wanted to ask them for death, rather than be handed over to Swane, but the words would not come. They even bound Padraig.

Fallon glared at them, wishing he could talk and wishing he knew Kottermani. He deserved death. He had failed his men, led them to their deaths, and he'd let Aidan's prophecy come true. His mistakes had doomed Gaelland. He wished with all his heart he had never tried to be a leader. He closed his eyes and let the darkness take him.

CHAPTER 75

"Do you know how long I have dreamed of this moment?"

Fallon opened his eyes reluctantly. Everything ached. He half-hoped this was a bad dream but he suspected he could not be so lucky.

He blinked his eyes open to see Swane and Dina standing in the center of the room, a third man at their side. For a heartbeat he thought it was Prince Kemal, then realized it had to be a relative of his. The face was similar but had a different, crueller cast to it. If such a thing was possible. He looked around the room and saw his men were lying or kneeling in lines closer to the secret door to the dungeons. Kottermani guards with bared blades were standing behind each one, with two guards behind Brendan.

"Just get it over with," Fallon said tiredly. "Kill us and then gloat over our corpses."

Swane chuckled, his face alight with glee. Fallon hated that he looked so similar to his beloved Prince Cavan.

"Nothing so easy for you, I am afraid," Swane said triumphantly. "Not after what you did to my father. The people must see what happens when you rebel against me. The tale will terrify children for all time!"

"Your face alone would do that," Fallon retorted.

He had hoped to provoke the Prince but Swane merely laughed. "Nice try. You want to make me kill you. But nothing will make me give up my revenge."

"Maybe you can even get a younger wife out of it," Fallon said. "You do know Dina's killed every man she's been with? You'd do better with a snake in your bed."

This time Swane did not laugh quite so heartily, and a shadow chased across the face of the Kottermani Prince. Dina, however, stepped forwards.

"You talk big, for a man whose life is measured in turns of the hourglass," she sneered. "You will beg for death at the end and we will laugh at you."

"As the rest of Gaelland laughs at you?"

Dina strode forwards but Swane caught her arm. "He is not to be killed. Not until I am ready," he warned.

She smiled dazzlingly, the smile that Fallon remembered bitterly.

"Don't worry. I want him to suffer but I won't kill him," she promised.

Swane let her go and she walked across to stand by Fallon.

"We shall find your wife and brat. And all the other families. Every man, woman and child who helped you will be slaughtered and they will go to their graves knowing you were the one who betrayed them. You will be haunted by their screams as you slowly die."

He ignored her, keeping the terrible fear that she would indeed do that buried deep inside of him. He would not give them the satisfaction of seeing his terror.

"Lost your smart tongue now?" she asked, then grabbed his hair and rammed his head against the chair. From out of nowhere she produced a tiny knife, no longer than a finger but shining bright.

"I won't kill you but maybe I will take your eyes. Leave you blind and screaming. How would you like that?"

Fallon refused to look at her. If she was going to take his eyes, he would not let his last sight be of her. Her fingers tightened in his hair and tried to twist his head to face her. "Look at me! Beg for mercy! Beg, curse you!"

Suddenly there was a ferocious growl from the chair and Caley sprang up from behind Padraig. Caley, the kind, gentle dog who had slunk away rather than threaten Kemal, leaped for Dina's face. Her teeth closed on the Duchess's cheek and Dina went over backwards, screaming, as Caley ripped at her face.

The Kottermanis did not even wait for orders, they just sprang forwards, their swords chopping down brutally into Caley. The dog's growl turned to a yelp, and then there was silence, just the butcher's noises as they made sure she was dead.

Fallon kept his eyes closed tight, his throat closed off with grief. He had seen his men die by the score but this was somehow worse. An act of suicidal bravery to protect him and the waste of a true and loyal friend. If he had a weapon he would have made them pay for his dog tenfold.

Dina's screams cut through the red mist in his head and Fallon opened his eyes to see her being helped up. Her right cheek was in tatters, hanging away from her mouth, while her nose was sliced open, drooping the other way.

"Heal me! My love, heal me," she slurred through a blood-filled mouth, clutching at Swane.

Swane slapped her hand away. "You have what you deserved," he said coldly. "You wanted your ally Kane to have me killed by Fallon, you plotted against me and I have outgrown you."

"No!" she screamed, and even Fallon shivered at the intensity in that word, the depth of feeling in her voice.

"Take her away," Swane said dismissively.

"Please, sire," she begged, holding out her hands. "Let me show you what I can do for you—"

"You are ugly and traitorous. One I could accept, but not both. Begone!"

She tried to protest but, at a signal from the Prince, guards hustled her out of the room, her screams echoing as she was dragged down the corridor. Fallon kept his eyes on Swane, because he could not bear to look at the twisted, furry body that lay near his feet, blood leaking out of her many wounds.

"Throw them in the cells. They can starve there for a day or two until we are ready to give them the end they deserve," Swane said.

CHAPTER 76

Fallon did not know whether to be pleased or upset that another two dozen of his men were already waiting in the line of cells, especially as most of them were wounded. Their wounds had been treated and, from what Fallon could see, treated well. But, again, maybe it would be a kindness to let them bleed to death rather than go to whatever foul fate Swane was dreaming up for them.

He could not check on them, because he was shoved into a cell by himself, although he could hear them and he had a good picture of how many were out there. Each voice he heard was familiar to him, but it was the voices that were missing that struck to the quick. All gone because he had missed those quarrels. Fitz. Casey. Padraig. Caley. Gone. He wanted to weep but he did not want them to think he was afraid.

A guard wordlessly slapped a clay cup of water on the floor and he realized he was desperately thirsty. He tried to pick it up but could not manage it with his hands tied.

The cells stank of sweat and fear and he fought to calm his mind, forget about the aches and pains all over his body and try and send a message of love out to Bridgit, Kerrin and the baby with his mind and heart.

He was already struggling when the door on his cell was wrenched open with a screech of tortured metal hinges. He looked up instantly, his heart suddenly racing, to see another figure shoved into the cell. This man was sent sprawling onto the ground, where he lay limply. Fallon wriggled over and took hold of the man's arm.

"Let's get you up," he said. "Where did they take you? Are you hurt?"

The man turned over and Fallon found himself staring at Prince Kemal. "They took me from here. I am not hurt but you soon will be," the Kottermani said softly, his face unreadable.

Fallon let go of Kemal's arm. All too quickly he remembered how he had crushed the man's toes, beaten his face in and threatened to skin his son Orhan. And now here they were together. And Fallon's hands and feet were tied. And now Kemal was reaching for him.

*

"We suffered heavily today. A regiment either dead or maimed. Against a tiny force," Durzu said in disgust.

Swane spread his hands. "Perfect. It is what we needed. A treacherous attack by a group of rebels in the castle itself. Almost all of the nobility, along with beloved Prince Kemal, were slain. A heartbroken Emperor names you as his heir then succumbs to a Gaelish illness, made worse by his grief for his son. You return to Kotterman with a perfect story, a new piece of the Empire, leaving me just a few regiments to keep our foot on the throats of Gaelland, and we both live happily ever after. Enough died that none back in Kotterman can question the intensity of the fighting."

Durzu chuckled. "I like your fortune-telling abilities! You were right that Fallon was going to try something, but it seemed a pretty disappointing plan. Lure you in and kill you? What did he really hope to achieve?"

"My death. That is all he wants," Swane said, struggling to control the anger that coursed through him. "That is all he has ever wanted."

"But surely there had to be more behind it than that?" Durzu persisted.

"Who cares? He failed and all that remains is to show the treacherous curs in Berry that they must never dare rise again.

They will fear me and realize the price of defiance is more than they are willing to pay."

"Fear you?" Durzu asked, but Swane could hear an edge in his voice.

"I shall rule here in your name," he said.

"Just you? Not Dina? You will not reconsider and heal her? She has provided much help to your cause."

Swane felt a new pulse of anger at Durzu and Dina. He knew she had bedded the Kottermani Prince. He had even read her disloyal thoughts, since Zorva provided him with much more than just raw power. He had wanted to cut himself free of her some time ago but she was still a fire in his brain. Every time he made up his mind to step away, she drew him back with a word or a gesture. It disgusted him how much she could control him. She was lover and mother and the lines became more blurred with every passing day. It had been a relief when she'd been attacked. Having her face ripped away had broken the spell she had over him.

"We do not need her," he said dismissively.

He watched Durzu carefully and the Kottermani merely shrugged and moved on.

"How do I reward the men who fought today? And how do we secure the city?" he asked.

"Give them a night in the city. There will be food, drink and women out there somewhere. Let them have what they want. Tomorrow we can bring in fresh regiments. Then we can start going through the city and teaching the people a lesson they will never forget. They can all watch Fallon die slowly."

"And his men? And my brother?"

"They can all die on my altar," Swane said softly, relishing the prospect. *And you will die with them too. Then it shall all be mine.*

*

"You tortured me and threatened my wife and children," Kemal said.

Fallon wondered if sending Kemal into his cell was Swane's idea of a joke.

"Yes, I did. And I would do it again to get my wife back," he said, meeting Kemal's eyes.

The Prince had definitely suffered since they had last met. His skin was sallow, he had lost weight and his eyes were deeply shadowed.

"I thought you were the embodiment of evil and all I dreamed about was revenge on you. Probably why Durzu thought he would throw me in here with you."

"Well, looks like all your dreams have come true," Fallon said levelly.

Kemal sighed. "It goes to show how you can be wrong. I cannot forgive you for what you did to me, but you were a man trying to save his wife. Mine is a prisoner of my brother and Swane and there is nothing I would not do to get her back, nor no limit to the revenge I seek on those evil bastards."

"How nice. We have something in common," Fallon said dryly.

"Here. Let me help you." Kemal's hands were tied but nowhere near as tightly and he was able to pick up the cup of water, which he offered to Fallon.

Fallon sat there, too shocked to respond.

"Do you want to drink?" Kemal invited.

"I thought you'd only want to poison me," Fallon said, drinking deeply. The water felt like nectar going down his throat.

Kemal put the cup down carefully. "Much has changed since we last talked," he said.

Fallon looked around the cell and laughed bitterly as Kemal sighed. "I think we can agree we both made mistakes. We are going to pay for it with our lives and we can only pray to Aroaril that our families do not join us."

That stopped Fallon's laugh instantly. He had been trying not to think of what Bridgit and Kerrin were up to and if Swane was going to be content with his death alone. He hoped so but he dared not ask, for Swane would only try harder to find them.

"I thought you were with Swane," he said. "Has he betrayed you? Does this mean he is now the Emperor of Kotterman as well?"

Kemal slumped back against the wall. "I was never with Swane. I was captured by him and forced to watch as he slaughtered children. Now he has my father in thrall and my ambitious younger brother thinks he can use him to get the throne."

"And all he will get is his heart ripped out and given to Zorva?"

"You have it," Kemal agreed. "Soon Swane will be ruler of the mightiest Empire the world has ever seen and who knows what he will do after that?"

"Well, I don't think we need to worry about it, do we? It's not like we are going to be alive to see it," Fallon said sourly.

"So you are just going to let him rule your people?"

"They chose him over me," he said. "They had a chance to stand with me and they turned their backs."

"They will be regretting that soon enough," Kemal said.

"I'm sure we'll find that very comforting," Fallon grunted. "So, are we going to sit here and plan our escape and revenge on Swane?"

"We can try, at least," Kemal offered.

Fallon thought about that for a few moments. He knew the cell bars were solid and the guards outside outnumbered his men two to one. Still, it might do to pass the time.

"You have a chance, you know," he said. "Your wife is a very smart woman and there's no give in her, while your sons are fine lads. If Swane turns his back on them, they'll be away. And no doubt she has friends in the Empire."

"She does," Kemal agreed. "And I know only too well that Bridgit will not be easy for Swane to find. She looks harmless enough but she's always thinking."

"That she is," Fallon agreed. He leaned against the wall. "Do we rush them when they bring the water? Grab a knife and cut our bonds and then free the others?"

Kemal edged closer to the bars and looked out.

"I can see maybe a company of guards," he reported. "And they don't look like they plan to go to sleep." He looked out the other way and cursed in Kottermani.

"What?" Fallon asked.

"My father's guards. Three of them. They are more of the men we lent to King Aidan."

Fallon snorted in disgust. He remembered only too well how hard those Snatchers had been to kill.

"Looks like Swane doesn't want us getting out of here until he is good and ready," he said.

CHAPTER 77

Swane inspected the room full of men – and one woman – with ill-disguised anger.

"So where are the rest of Fallon's friends? We have killed or captured a few hundred, but thousands fought against me at Lake Caragh. Where are they? Where are their families?"

"They sailed away, sire. We could not find out where," Munro said, bowing hastily. He was still bruised and his hands were almost useless, but he, along with a score of others, had been freed from the cells when they'd been cleared for Fallon and his surviving men.

Swane exhaled. "Wherever they go, they will find Kottermani ships waiting. But they will not be allowed to escape. I have suffered and so everyone must suffer more."

"I shall send out word. As soon as they land, you shall know, sire," Munro promised.

Swane smiled with satisfaction. "Your service to the crown will be remembered," he said. "In a city ruled by traitorous scum, you have stood strong and helped restore me to the throne. Now is the chance for our revenge. Every person who tried to betray you, every one of them who ignored you or said that Fallon was the future. I want them punished." He clenched his fists, raising them to the roof. "I will give every one of you a squad of Kottermanis. You point out the scum and they will give them a beating they will never forget, then take them into slavery. Assemble our new slaves at the warehouses. Use the ones that were holding the food. The food you can bring here to me. All of it. Only those who serve me will eat. The rest can starve. And, when you return, it will be to all the gold you can carry."

"Sire, what if we are not sure if someone supported Fallon or was just afraid to stand against him?" the woman asked.

Swane raised his fist again. "It is all the same to me," he snarled. "They allowed my father to be killed and that bastard Fallon to sit on my throne for moons. They need to be taught a lesson. Go out there and give it to them."

He turned to Durzu and the Prince stepped forwards. "There are squads of my men assembled in the courtyard. They do not speak Gaelish but they know to obey you. Merely point them where to go and single out the ones you want punished. They will do the rest."

Swane watched Munro's men hurry out and smiled thinly at Durzu.

"Now for the next ones. Follow me."

"Next ones?" Durzu growled. "I thought we were going to discuss the ceremony where my father anoints me as his heir and announces you will rule Gaelland in his stead?"

"All in good time. We have to set events in motion first. Give your men time to digest the news of the death of so many nobles in that battle in the castle," Swane said, patting Durzu on the shoulder. "Trust me. I have taken you from disgraced younger brother to the brink of the Emperor's throne. Let me finish the job properly."

He steered Durzu down a castle corridor, to where a score of the city's most prosperous merchants waited. Swane knew most of them by sight, if not by name, and could not help but notice most seemed much thinner than when he had last seen them. They all bowed floridly as soon as they entered.

"Sire, it is good to see you back. You do not know what a trial it has been living here without a proper ruler," one announced.

Durzu stood stiffly by the door but Swane did not stop, instead walking right up to the merchant. He backhanded him across the face, sending him stumbling into his fellows.

"You complain to me of difficulties?" he hissed. "You grew fat off my father's table and then, when he needed you, you abandoned him! You helped the traitor Fallon and did nothing to save my father!"

"Sire, there was nothing we could do! Fallon had thousands of men—" another merchant stuttered, as the first regained his feet, a livid red mark on his face.

"Silence! I do not want to hear excuses. I want a thousand gold pieces from every one of you. I don't care where you get it, or how you do it. You will pay, one way or another. Get me the money or die with Fallon in front of a crowd. Now get out of my sight before I decide to make an example of you."

Durzu had to stand aside as the merchants flooded for the door. "That is a lot of gold," the Kottermani said. "What do you intend to do with it?"

Swane laughed lightly. "Well, half will go to you, as a down payment on a tribute. Slaves and gold, as I promised. Now, shall we go and discuss how the Emperor will announce you as his heir and me as Gaelland's ruler? Just as I promised?"

Durzu smiled and nodded and Swane held out his arm, indicating the way to go. Truly, this was a good day.

*

Dina looked at herself in the mirror and could not stop a tear squeezing out. Her face was covered with hideous, weeping wounds. The Kottermanis had cleaned her wounds, stitched them up, and given her a mouthful of poppy juice, which had taken away the pain. But nothing could help the emptiness inside. She had been on the cusp of victory. Durzu would have killed Swane and then left her to rule Gaelland. All she had to do was watch Fallon die, then Swane die, and then enjoy the spoils of all her hard work. Except it was snatched away from her by some filthy animal and Swane, the ungrateful bastard. He could have healed her! She had seen how his face had changed through magic. These few wounds should have been nothing to him.

It was all Swane's fault. If only he had done what he was supposed to. And if only the Kottermanis had checked that cursed chair! She did not blame herself. After all, she had waited a long time for revenge on Fallon. No, it was men who had done this to her. But she was not finished yet.

Shouts and screams from outside on the street interrupted her brooding and she turned from the mirror to the window. Something was happening out there but she could not see what. Not knowing what was going on had always infuriated her and this was particularly annoying, given she should have known everything that was happening in Berry.

She grabbed a bell and rang it. She had taken two of Kane's surviving guards, not caring whether Swane would approve or not. There were many people who still owed her favors and she would see them called in, once she had recovered. Maybe she could not use her face to sway men but gold could work just as well.

"Find out what is happening," she ordered the guards when they finally arrived. Talking was still very painful and her voice was slurred, although whether from the drink they had given her or the wounds to her cheek, she did not know or care.

The pair of them sauntered away and she nearly ground her teeth in anger, although that would have just hurt her face. They would treat her with the proper respect when they were paid, she told herself. They were not long away though, which soothed her raw anger.

"Kottermanis are rounding up people. Munro's men are with them and they are dragging men and women out of houses and beating anyone who tries to stop them," they reported.

Dina slammed her hand on the table. This was exactly what she had feared! Swane had forgotten their plan for winning the people over and gone straight to retribution. If only she was there. She stood and hurried downstairs, not bothering to explain her actions to the guards or waiting to see if they would follow.

Half the street was deathly quiet as people cowered in their homes, while the other half was chaos as men and women shouted and screamed as their husbands or wives were dragged out into the street and beaten by hard-faced Kottermani soldiers, who then tied their hands and fastened them with a rope around their neck to a line of similarly bruised men and women. Screaming children were thrown into the gutter by soldiers, while any adults who tried to stop their loved ones being taken away were left bleeding in the street by a succession of blows and kicks.

"This is the fate for all those who defied Prince Swane! You are all traitors and you must beg for his mercy!" the Gaelishman leading the Kottermanis shouted.

Dina hurried over. "What are you doing?" she demanded.

She died a little inside when the Gaelishman turned to face her and shrank from her, face creasing in revulsion.

"Who are you to defy King Swane?" he snarled. "What disease do you have?"

She drew herself up. "I am the Duchess Dina and you will treat me with respect!" she trumpeted.

He spat at her feet. "You are a hideous old crone and I shall give you ten heartbeats to get out of here before you suffer the same fate as the other traitors. The Kottermanis want slaves and they might even take one as ugly as you."

She drew outraged breath to scream at him but the eager look on the faces of the closest Kottermanis changed her mind. Instead she fled for the sanctuary of her townhouse, bolting the door behind her. Swane was on his own. If he did not want her help then he could shrivel up and die for all she cared. Although, actually, it would be good if he could do that.

*

Men were hard at work in the square outside the castle. Wood was sawed and hammered and a large stage was being built against the castle wall, while bales of cloth were arriving on wagons and being piled haphazardly beside it to cover the raw wood in something prettier. It would contrast with the cobbles, which were stained with blood from the vicious little fight at the gate.

Durzu inspected progress with a broad smile on his face. It was crude compared to what would have been done in Kotterman but all could see that something important was going on. And that was all that mattered. All his dreams were coming true. His father, the Emperor, just had to anoint him as the successor and everything was complete. He had used that Gaelish fool, Swane, to get him this far. Now it was time for Swane to die. His usefulness was over and he was too dangerous to have around. No, far better to kill him and then force his wizards to manipulate the Emperor. Then, in a few days, the Emperor could be quietly killed. He would leave one of his friends in charge of Gaelland, with five regiments to keep the peace, while he went back to Kotterman to enjoy real civilization – and some warmer weather. The sun was out but there was no heat in it here.

He shivered and it made him think of Swane. The way he had cast aside Dina had been the final proof Swane planned to betray him. But soon he would be dead and that would be an end to the troubles on this pathetic little island. He turned – to see Swane come storming towards him, a furious look on his face.

"Your men are refusing to obey orders!" Swane snarled. "I want them killed for that!"

He growled as Durzu took his arm and hustled him further into the square, away from the teams of workmen, but Durzu ignored his tantrum. He was bigger and stronger than the Gaelishman and he only stopped walking when they were out of immediate earshot.

"Do not talk to me like that in front of your people," he hissed. "Do you forget our places?"

Swane tore his arm free. "I forget nothing," he said. "But you promised your men would obey me as I secured this city. They are refusing and I want them dead for it."

"Refusing to obey an order? What order? What men?" Durzu demanded. Swane's arrogance was becoming far more than an irritation now.

"We have to secure the churches. They were supposed to go into the churches and remove all the priests and either kill them or add them to the slave warehouses."

Durzu shook his head in disbelief. "Are you mad? Attack the churches? Why?"

Swane glared at him. "Have you lost your mind? Have you not forgotten who we owe our power to? The churches of Aroaril will forever be our foes. We have to crush them before they realize what we are."

Durzu imagined Swane slowly dying and it helped him keep his temper. "My men still worship Aroaril," he said icily. "Three times a day. Ask them to attack churches of Aroaril and of course they will take a step back. Do you want them to turn on us?"

"Well, what do you suggest we do? We cannot leave those churches untouched, to rally opposition against me."

"Don't you have men of your own? Use them," Durzu said disdainfully.

"This is not part of our agreement. I must have control of your men. How else can I rule the country?" Swane insisted.

Durzu was about to dismiss him outright before he remembered he was not quite ready to dispose of Swane.

"Once I am named as my father's heir, then we shall have more freedom," he said smoothly. "The very day after, I shall order the regiments that attacked the castle to serve as your own. You can do with them as you wish."

Swane did not look happy but after a moment he nodded and turned away.

"The churches can do nothing," Durzu added. "We have ten regiments inside the city and another six outside. Against that, who can do anything? Why don't you go down to the east gate, where the refugees are coming back, and take their obeisance?"

Swane did not answer him and kept walking. Durzu watched him go sourly and then signaled to his guards, who moved to his side instantly.

"Make sure you have the items I ordered with you at all times. The next time Swane defies me will be his last."

CHAPTER 78

"I wish to Aroaril I'd listened to Bridgit more," Fallon said.

"Don't let her hear that. She'd never let you forget it," Kemal said, with the ghost of a smile.

"The mistakes I have made. Why did I think I could get rid of Swane with a poisoned quarrel? It was madness!"

"Well, it might have worked. And then you'd only have my brother to deal with."

"I had to stand there and watch my men die. And now I am waiting for Swane to kill the rest of them and, if I am lucky, finish me off first. I killed Prince Cavan. It was my quarrel that ended his life. I deserve what is coming."

"Nobody deserves to be sacrificed to Zorva," Kemal said bitterly.

"I almost welcome the punishment to come."

"Well, what does Swane deserve, then? What do I deserve? Where does it all stop? I let my hatred consume me. I could have sailed back to Kotterman with your deal and none of this would have happened." He closed his eyes for a moment and sighed. "Yet it all goes further back. I stole your families from their homes. Yet King Aidan was the one who pointed me in your direction. He turned to Zorva and unleashed an evil we had not seen for many years, although he was only doing that because we wanted his country. Ultimately, is all of this my father's fault? Or Aidan's? There is so much blame going around – no point in taking it all for yourself."

Fallon grimaced. "Is that supposed to make me feel better?"

Kemal shrugged. "Or just pass the time."

"I look forward to death," Fallon whispered. "I look forward to the cowards who deserted me learning that their lives will become eternal misery with Swane as ruler. I want them to wish they had stood by me. I want them to regret they abandoned me. I want them to hear rumors of a secret island, where Gaelish live in peace and happiness, ruled by a wise woman, and I want them to cry bitter tears at the thought of it."

"That's not going to do you much good though," Kemal observed.

"And I hope that Cavan can forgive me, when I meet him again. I hope that dying like this will atone for my sins."

Kemal shook his head. "I know we both worship Aroaril but the way you Gaelish go on, sometimes it doesn't seem like it!"

*

"What do you think they'll do to us?" Brendan asked, looking in vain out of the cell in the hopes of spotting a friendly face. He knew Fallon was further down the line of cells but couldn't see him.

"Best not to think about it," Devlin replied, cradling his forearm.

"How's the arm?"

"Just wonderful," the farmer snapped. "How do you think? It hurts like a bastard."

"I'm hungry. Do you think they'll feed us? I could chew my own arm off."

"If this one hurts any more, you can chew it off for me," Devlin told him.

Brendan sighed gustily. "Do you think we'll be judged for what we've done? Will Aroaril look on us as evil?"

"Brendan, we have been fighting Zorva all this time," Devlin said irritably. "What else does He want from us?"

"I killed a lot of men. And I enjoyed doing it," the smith said miserably. He turned his hands over, which were still covered in dried blood and worse, although it was slowly flaking away.

"You should have killed more. Like Swane and that Kottermani Prince that was kissing his arse. If we can just take him with us, I'll be happy."

Brendan shook his head. "I can't do it anymore. Even if Swane was here, and I had my hammer, I could not kill him. I have killed my last man."

"I wouldn't count on that. You're talking me to death right now," Devlin grumbled.

"You should not have stayed. I had lost Nola, there was nothing to keep me. But you had Riona and the kids."

Devlin shook his head. "We've been through too much for me to walk away. I would have been less than a man, not fit to stand beside my family if I had left you."

"Even though it means your death?"

"Well, I'd be happier to be going home. But at least I can die beside my friends. Not many can say that."

"I just wish I could see Nola and the girls one last time. Tell them I'm sorry."

"You'll see them again," Devlin said gently. "And they will understand. And that is no joke, my friend."

*

Fallon knew time had passed, although it was hard to tell in the cells. They couldn't see the light and the only way to judge time was when the guards were changed. It seemed like an age and yet no time at all. But he felt this time had changed him, given him a chance to look back over his mistakes.

"I wasn't really suited to rule a country. I thought I knew how, because I could run a village. But they're not the same thing. Bridgit had more of an idea than me, I see that now. Although it's a bit late," Fallon said.

"Don't waste your time worrying about mistakes you made. It's not as if you can go back and change them," Kemal said tiredly.

"But there must be things you would do differently, if you had another chance," Fallon insisted.

"Of course," Kemal shrugged. "But wishing for another chance is not going to get us out of this cell, nor change what we did. Besides, my second chance would not have ended well for you."

"Really? We have sat here for the best part of two days talking and you would still want to go back and have me killed?" Fallon asked, amused. "Maybe I should ask you to kill me as a favor then, and rob Swane of the pleasure."

"No," Kemal said. "I could not do that. Actually, if I had a second chance, I would like to start from here. It would be better this way. Now, after what I have experienced, I know what it is like to be a slave and what true evil looks like. I would be a far better Emperor and more besides."

"Great, now all we need is to get out of here and put you back on the throne," Fallon said lightly.

Kemal nodded slowly. "When they come for us. We'll pretend to be too tired to get up and we'll strike then."

Fallon shrugged. "We have nothing to lose," he said. "I'll take the ones to the left, you take the ones to the right."

Almost as soon as he had finished speaking, a trip of guards appeared at the cell door.

"It is time," one said in rough Gaelish.

The door was opened and the guards strode in. Fallon let them help him up, then tried to headbutt the nearest guard. Kemal, meanwhile, flung himself at the other two. But Fallon was struck in the stomach, air whooping out of his lungs, while Kemal went down under a flurry of blows.

Fallon was only just aware that his friends were all being dragged out of their cells as well and roped together. He closed his eyes, knowing he would not see them again in this world.

*

Swane inspected the square with pleasure. The city was his again, without a doubt. The returning refugees had been carefully sorted, with several hundred dragged away to join the ranks of slaves. The merchants had produced the money, as he knew they would, and Durzu seemed delighted. The crowd that had been rounded up to witness the day's events was sullen but there were four regiments of Durzu's guards around the square and in the castle, with another one patrolling the streets and guarding the warehouses full of slaves. The front rows were made up of Kottermani officers from all the regiments, as well as the prominent citizens of Berry. Right where everyone could keep an eye on them. There was a short ceremony to go through with the Emperor and then the spectacle of Fallon being tortured to death. This, truly, was his day.

"Are you ready?" Durzu asked. "Is my father ready?"

"Of course," Swane said. "Give him the scroll you want read out and he will tell everyone that you are heir."

He saw Durzu smile and look towards the Emperor, who stood like a statue, surrounded by his guards. "He does not look well, does he?" Durzu remarked.

"It looks like the strain of campaigning was too much for him. I would not be surprised if he passed away peacefully in the night one day soon," Swane agreed.

Durzu held out his hand. "You have been a good friend," he said. "Without you, I would not have got this far."

"Nor would I," Swane agreed. "It has been a profitable partnership. We make a good team."

He saw Durzu's head nod, but the Kottermani Prince's eyes were focused on a spot over Swane's shoulder, while his hand tightened on Swane's.

Swane had been expecting this. Behind him, he heard a series of thuds, gasps and a long gurgle that ended in a throaty groan but he didn't need to turn around to see what had happened. He could read it on Durzu's face. The Kottermani Prince let go of his hand and staggered backwards, his face looking suddenly gray.

Swane glanced over his shoulder and saw Durzu's guards lying in spreading pools of blood on the cobbles, the weapons they had produced still in their hands. The Emperor's guards, the surviving pair of them anyway, stood over the bodies. Swane shook his head.

"You retrieved the quarrels that Fallon loosed at me? Now that is underhanded," he said disapprovingly. "And yet inventive. I could almost admire it."

Durzu fumbled out a dagger but, while it looked as if he knew how to use it, Swane already knew the hilt was wooden.

"I can see why you were never the Crown Prince," he said conversationally. "You did not think things through. Did you think

I would be happy with just Gaelland? After all the power I have been granted by Zorva? Of course I had to get rid of you and I needed a way to do that. You had to try to kill me but you needed more, far more, than this pitiful attempt at a trap."

As he spoke, he watched Durzu slowly recover himself and prepare to at least go down fighting. Swane locked the Prince's legs, making the leather of his boots stick to both the skin of his legs and feet but also to the cobbles. Durzu cried out as he froze in place, and then Swane raised his hand, making the wooden hilt of the dagger copy his every movement. Durzu could do nothing to stop the dagger rising towards his throat.

"Wait! You need me! You cannot rule without me, my people will never accept you!" he cried desperately.

"I will simply issue my orders through your father. And, in a year or two, they will have become so used to me that I can dispose of him," Swane said with a smile. He paused with his hand just inches from his own throat.

"Wait a moment," he said, watching hope bloom on Durzu's face. Then he slashed his hand across the air.

"That looked so funny!" he chuckled as he released Durzu, letting the Prince topple to the ground and thrash for a few moments until he bled out.

"Clean this up," he ordered the guards. "Get some servants here."

He walked over to the Emperor and plucked Durzu's scroll out of the man's unfeeling hand, replacing it with one of his own. "Read this. It is much more entertaining," he told the Emperor. "Well, at least to me."

He walked past a file of servants returning with the guards to clean up the bodies. The Kottermanis would be told that Durzu had attempted to kill the Emperor after finding out he wouldn't be named as heir and then had cut his own throat from shame when the attempt failed. As long as the Emperor said it, they would swallow anything. With Durzu dead and Kemal soon to follow, there were no voices that could be raised against him.

Dina had pretended all this was difficult. But, to him, it was all too simple.

CHAPTER 79

Fallon did not even bother to resist as the Kottermanis dragged him into a cart and tied him to a stake in the back, in such a way that he could only move his head. It was the same sort of stake that had been used to burn women accused of being witches, before he had caught the Snatchers and ended that terror. Around him, he could see that Kemal and the others were being loaded into more carts. The message was clear. Once he was dead, they would follow.

The carts ambled to the castle gates, where they then waited just behind it. Fallon felt like telling the Kottermanis to get a move on. Waiting to be tortured to death in public seemed to be worse than what was to follow – even though he knew that was impossible.

But it seemed Swane still had other plans. He was giving a speech to the people, his voice magically enhanced so Fallon could not avoid hearing it. First Swane announced that Gaelland was now part of the Kotterman Empire and they would have to submit to the Emperor. A cheer followed this, the sort of cheer that people made when soldiers were pointing weapons at them.

Then someone droned on in Kottermani for what seemed like an age. Fallon could see Kemal out of the corner of his eye and the Prince's face was beyond fury. Swane finally spoke again and all was explained.

"I thank the Emperor for anointing me as his successor and swear I shall not take this honor lightly. To be responsible for all the peoples of the Empire is a heavy task and one I shall live up to," Swane announced, his voice magically booming around the castle, and Fallon smiled humorlessly at what that would mean for Kotterman.

"It is a tragedy that so many of the Kottermani nobility were killed in the cowardly attack by the traitor Fallon and his rebellious scum a few days ago in the castle."

Fallon's head snapped up at that. What was Swane blithering on about?

"Worse, it is a tragedy that the Emperor's own son, Prince Durzu, attacked the Emperor and killed himself out of shame when he failed. Truly it is a pity, but I pledge myself to serve the Emperor as I served my own father." There was a long pause and then another half-hearted cheer.

Whips cracked and the pair of horses pulling the cart jerked into life, pulling it past the castle gate. But the cart did not go straight to the stage where Swane stood. Instead it took a longer route, through the crowd that filled the square and watched from the windows. Even though Fallon refused to look to either side, there were many faces he recognized as the cart rumbled through the crowd. Some he had fought; some had fought for him. Most looked away rather than meet his eyes. The square stank of fear.

Around and throughout the crowd stood Kottermani soldiers, men in bright helmets and dark armor, making sure there was no trouble, making sure the crowd knew who had won the war. The square was silent despite the people packed into it. There was still a faint smell of blood etched into the cobbles and nobody wanted to speak and have their own blood stain the ground. The only noise was Swane as he hectored the crowd, telling them this was the fate that awaited anyone who even thought of defying him.

"Look upon this man and pray you do not suffer his end! Anyone who does not obey my every order will suffer even worse. You all stood by and let this traitor kill my father, King Aidan! You are lucky I do not kill every child under the age of five to punish you. As it is, taxes will be doubled for the next five summers and one in twenty will be shipped to Kotterman as slaves."

A whisper of horror went through the crowd, which faded as Swane shouted again, his voice magically booming over the square.

"Lift one finger in protest and it shall be double taxes for ten summers and one in fifteen sent away! You are animals that must be whipped back into line and I do not care how many have to die to make my point!"

Fallon let Swane's voice wash over him and fixed his face in an expression of contempt. These fools had let Swane back in and now they were going to pay.

Finally the procession was over and rough hands untied him and dragged him up the makeshift stairs to the stage they had built for his execution. It was taller and wider than the one Brendan had knocked up for Aidan's death and was hung with bright fabrics.

"Let this be a lesson for all of you! Those who defy the Crown will meet the same fate!" Swane screamed from the side of the stage.

Even though he knew what waited for him, Fallon could not keep the bitter smile from his face. The people had been so terrified that witches haunted their streets and now something far worse would sit on the throne. And they had let it happen.

The Prince stormed across the stage and grabbed a handful of his hair. "There'll be no last words for you. No fine memory for those sheep out there to tell their filthy little children. We're going to make you beg for mercy until they shudder when they say your name."

"You mean the way they do when they speak yours?" Fallon said.

The Prince's face darkened and he raised his hand ... before letting it drop and forcing a chuckle.

"Good try. Hoping to make me so angry I'll kill you quick. But after what you did to my father, you deserve to linger. Get him ready!"

Fallon glared hatred at Swane as rough hands dragged him towards the bench they had set up, where they would make the last few heartbeats of his life as painful as possible.

He whispered a quick prayer to Aroaril, his stomach lurching at the sight of the sharpened tools lying there, and wished with all his heart he could see Bridgit and Kerrin one more time. He was slammed down onto the bench by Kottermani guards, the breath wheezing out of his lungs. As he lay there, fighting for breath, acutely aware that he did not have many more left, he looked up at the castle tower. Surely it was just his imagination, because it looked as if Bridgit and Kerrin were standing there. Then his view was obscured by a Kottermani with a knife. Fallon could not even cry out as the knife plunged down.

CHAPTER 80

THREE DAYS EARLIER

The ship was silent as a grave as they sailed out of Berry and turned south. Men, women and children sat around, head in hands, or stood at the rail, weeping. Others could not bear to look at the distant land and went below. Nola had been one of those, disappearing before Bridgit could talk to her. Instead she turned to Riona, but her friend simply fled below, her eyes streaming.

"They'll be happier when they know what's going on," Kerrin said.

"I hope so, son," Bridgit said. She walked up to where Gallagher stood alone at the tiller. She was still five paces away when she saw the tears on his face.

"There is still chance of a miracle. We just have to trust in Aroaril," he said.

But she could tell there was no conviction in his voice. "Listen, it is time to stop blindly trusting in Aroaril. The only thing that will save us now is ourselves. I need to know you can do what I ask. Do you want to save our friends?"

Gallagher cuffed the tears from his face. "What do you need me to do?"

"I need you to trust in me for the next few days. Now head south."

"South? But I thought—"

"I'll explain it all later. Just have a little faith."

He looked shocked, then nodded. Bridgit turned away and put her arm around Kerrin.

"I'm scared, Mam," he said.

"We both are," she replied softly.

She wanted to tell her friends of her plan, tell everyone. But she felt she could only say it once. She summoned over one of Padraig's wizards, feeling a sharp pain that her father was not there. She nearly lost control then but kept her face impassive.

"Tell me as soon as the other ships are sighted," she ordered.

"Other ships? From where?"

"Get some birds up and find them. Sailing from the south," she said shortly.

The young wizard looked more confused by her explanation but she could say no more. Not yet. She had to get control of herself first. It was all a gamble – a mad, crazy risk that could cost all their lives, or win the day. She had seen immediately that Fallon's poisoned quarrel plan was hopeless. He might have killed Swane but that would still leave a massive Kottermani army in Gaelland. Even without a puppet prince, they would not leave. Not without ships full of Gaelish slaves and every last coin that Gaelland possessed. But if Fallon's plan failed and Swane took his revenge on the people, it would create a real opportunity. A perfect diversion, in fact.

"How long do we have to wait, Mam?" Kerrin asked.

"As long as we have to," she said.

She went below with Kerrin, found somewhere quiet for them both and allowed herself to weep for her father. He had not been the best father but she had always known that he loved her and that was enough. His final act was to try and keep Fallon alive, by any magical means possible, until the magic ate him up from the inside. No matter what happened to the rest of them, Padraig was not coming back. And yet he had done his duty with a smile. Then she wept for Fallon, and for Brendan, Devlin, Gannon, Bran, Casey, and Fitz and all the others who might pay the price for her plan. It did not matter that they had volunteered, she had to honor their sacrifice.

She had managed to wipe her face clear again by the time the young wizard found her.

"A fleet is approaching, my lady," she said breathlessly. "Kottermani ships."

Bridgit forced a smile. "Excellent. Summon the other ships in close and tell Gallagher to take us right at them." She saw the bewildered expression on the woman's face and almost told her what was going on. But, seeing as she had not told Fallon, let alone Nola or Riona, that was not going to happen.

"Tell me," she asked instead, "what is your name?"

"Laura," the wizard replied.

"Then stay with me, Laura, for I have more tasks for you."

She finally walked out on deck to find people beginning to notice a cluster of sails moving towards them. But even that was not enough to get them out of their devastated silence, until the ships were so close they could actually see armed men aboard.

"Get the children below and then every man and woman is to come up on to the deck," Bridgit ordered.

That led to a whole host of questions but she ignored them, instead walking up the stairs to the higher aft deck, along with Kerrin and the wizard Laura, where they joined Gallagher and Rosaleen. She sent Jason and a squad of his Lunstermen to block the stairs so none could follow her, so a scared and angry crowd looked up at her. The other ships nudged closer as well, until wherever she looked there were people staring up at her.

"We need to turn and run!" the grizzled old fisherman Donnchadh bellowed from the deck, which received a roar of approval.

Bridgit crossed to the rail and looked down on them. "We will do nothing unless I say so!" she shouted and they quietened down. "If you trust me, then be silent and I shall explain all soon."

There were a few doubtful looks but they rapidly closed the gap on the dozen Kottermani ships.

"Drop all sails!" Bridgit ordered and, a few moments later, the Kottermani ships followed suit, so the two fleets eased towards each other. Now they could see most were filled with Gaelish people – not prisoners – but Gaelish armed with a motley variety of weapons.

The leading ship, however, had just Kottermanis. This one slipped alongside Bridgit's ship, her people backing away from the rails. Bridgit and Kerrin, however, hurried down to the side, where a woman and two young boys were waving.

"Tie us up!" Bridgit ordered.

Men rushed to obey and then Feray, Asil and Orhan stepped across to their ship, where the two women embraced and the boys grinned at each other. Bridgit signaled to the young wizard and turned to see everyone aboard all the ships waiting and watching expectantly, a mixture of confusion and fear on many faces.

"I lied to you," she said, her voice booming across the water with the wizard Laura's help, which quietened them instantly. "We are not running and hiding. We shall not live in fear, waiting to see if Swane will come for us. Swane thinks he has won. He thinks the world is his. He thinks he can sacrifice children to his foul god and all will bow before him. He is wrong!" She paused and could feel them hanging on her every word. "We are going back to kill Swane, rescue our friends and take back Gaelland!"

The answering roar made the ships tremble and she had to wait because it never seemed to die down.

"Princess Feray and the Kottermanis who fought against us in Berry are now on our side. They have brought many of our people from Lunster, who have tasted life under Swane and are willing to die rather than see that again!"

Again the crowd roared their approval, swearing they would not stop while Swane still lived and she let them cheer until they finally calmed down.

"We shall wait here until Swane lets down his guard and then we shall make him pay. Just be ready to follow our orders!"

She left them cheering madly and signaled to Feray, and to her friends. There, that was the plan, she thought, as her friends gathered around. Now she had to make it happen.

"When were you going to tell us?" Nola demanded.

"When I was ready," Bridgit replied evenly. "I could not risk anyone back in the city knowing, for they could be made to reveal it. And then we are all dead."

"But—" Riona began, only for Bridgit to cut her off.

"I made you suffer and weep and I apologize for it. But remember, my husband is in the city also. Now, are we going to bicker or are we going to save them?"

"Save them, of course. Tell us everything," Rosaleen said.

Bridgit looked over at her Kottermani counterpart carefully. They had used the birds to communicate but had not really talked. Their sons were friends and that was a good start, though the fact that both their husbands would be killed unless they worked together was a better finish.

"Well, it will not be like the stories of old. Here, the women have to come riding to the rescue," Bridgit said. "First, Feray, we will rely on you to get us into the harbor without a fight."

"My people will always obey orders if they think it is coming from rank," Feray said. "We can pretend your men are slaves and then we are in the city."

"Good. Swane will want to sacrifice Fallon and any other prisoners in front of everyone. He'll be unable to resist it. That is our chance," she said, placing her palms flat on the table. "Feray and I will take the castle from the rear. Then we shall free the prisoners and capture Swane and the Emperor. Kemal and Feray will order the Kottermanis to lay down their arms and it will all be over, just like it was in the first battle of Berry. It is all about using a diversion to distract them and striking when they do not expect it, as we originally intended to do."

She looked around the cabin and was met with silence.

"But what if the men are already dead? What if they are not taken prisoner?" Nola whispered.

Bridgit bowed her head. "If that happens then the plan is the same. Only we kill Swane and his allies in revenge for our menfolk," she said harshly. "And if something goes wrong on the day then we die fighting with them. I know Fallon set great stock in Cavan's island but I will not run away and hide from evil."

This time when she looked around they all met her eyes, and nodded grimly.

"We shall use the birds to watch what happens," she said. "Once we know for sure, we shall make our move, one way or the other."

"That's if our foolish husbands haven't killed each other before we get there," Feray added with a wry smile. Then it faded. "But what happens afterwards? I have not spoken to Kemal properly since he tried to destroy you. You could be exchanging one enemy for another."

"Well, let's save their skins and then worry about it," Bridgit said. "If Kemal still wants Gaelland after all we have been through, he is welcome to it. All that matters is stopping Swane."

"It is risky," Gallagher said.

"How many risks have we taken to get here?" Bridgit asked.

Feray laughed. "Too many to number!"

"Then what is one more? There is no other way. Victory or death."

"Well, I know which one I prefer," Feray said.

*

The flotilla of ships stayed clustered together for safety, off the coast, waiting to see what would happen in Berry. And while that was hard for everyone, it was torture for Bridgit. The wizards kept a steady stream of birds circling over Berry. It let them see Fallon's poisoned quarrel plan had failed – she did not tell anyone how she and Kerrin had secretly loosened the flights on Fallon's quarrels because Swane had to live for her plan to work. They heard how the Kottermanis had taken the castle after a bitter fight but there was no way of knowing how many had survived the battle, or who they were.

That was the worst day. She had to put on a brave face for everyone else, especially Kerrin, but inside she was dying, waiting for news. She had done many terrible things but being the first to see who had lived and died was easily the equal of every child she had lost. She insisted nobody else could be around to receive the news, not even Kerrin. This was something she had to bear alone.

"Touch the raven's head and close your eyes," the wizard Laura said uncomfortably. In Padraig's absence, Bridgit now called for her. "It will be as if you are there."

Bridgit took a deep breath and did so. Instantly she thanked Aroaril she was sitting down, for it felt like she was flying. The castle of Berry swam into view and she began to circle it, seeing scores of bodies hanging from the walls. She felt her heart skip a beat then the bird went in closer and she could see faces, see the hideous wounds that had killed each one. Although her eyes were shut, tears streamed down her face as she recognized man after man. The sight of Fitz made her gasp aloud. But when she saw her father hanging there, it was as if she had been stabbed in the heart. The other men had followed Fallon to their death, but Padraig had gone there at her own request. She gritted her teeth and pressed on, going around not once but twice until she was sure Fallon, Devlin, Brendan and Kemal were not there. She let go of the bird's head but kept her eyes closed.

"Are you all right, my lady?" Laura asked.

"I shall be. Leave me, please Laura," Bridgit said, amazed she could even speak. "Send in my friends."

Riona and Nola were waiting outside and rushed in, looking as bad as Bridgit felt.

"They are alive," she told them and only then did she let herself go, sob out the fear and relief with her friends. He was alive! They were alive! Her mad gamble could work.

By the time she was ready to face the others and pass on the good news, she had also learned the Kottermanis were rounding up Gaelish men and women as slaves and stealing, beating and raping indiscriminately. And while that was hard to watch, she knew it was also playing into their hands and when reports came back that Swane was building a stage outside the castle, she allowed herself to relax, a little. Her time was taken up with constantly refining their plans, based on the information they were getting from the magicked birds.

Gallagher was now to free the slaves being held at the food warehouses, and arm them. Between them, the ones who had escaped Berry and the ones who had arrived from Lunster, they would have thousands of angry men.

Both Gaelish and Kottermani had to work together if they were to overthrow Swane and it was a mark of how desperate things were that everyone seemed to accept the alliance, even though both sides had fought against each other only a few moons ago. Feray's officers, Nazim and Mahir, and her spymaster Abbas were more than happy to work with the Gaelish.

With the execution stage now built, it was obvious they had to strike immediately, for surely Fallon and the others would be killed on the morrow. Bridgit ordered all the ships to come in close, where she could speak to the people. There she told them they could fight and win, or fight and die. It was up to them. The thought of rescuing their friends and stopping Swane had them fired up and their cheers rocked the ships.

Early the next morning, the first part of the plan went well, with Feray using bluff and arrogance to take the fleet of Kottermani ships into the Berry harbor. It helped that almost all the officers had been ordered up to the castle square and the handful of junior men left behind thought it was merely a fleet of slaves – until those "slaves" and their "guards" turned on the Kottermanis who were guarding the harbor and stripped them of arms and armor before tying them up and locking them in an empty warehouse.

Bridgit helped organize everyone into groups, except for a few dozen of the oldest men and women, who would stay behind on the ships to watch the children. Every man and woman carried a weapon because they had to fight, or die. That was the choice. Yet Bridgit could not bring herself to bring the children into a battle. Even Kerrin, although he complained bitterly, had to be left behind.

*

There was no gate at the back of the castle but the wall was low enough that it was not a true barrier. There were a score of Kottermani guards posted there but they were looking out for trouble from the Gaelish, not for a company of perfectly dressed Kottermani archers to march in impeccable order up to the wall and calmly begin to form pyramids and clamber over.

At first bemused, and then confused, the guards shouted questions but were told by Nazim, unquestionably a Kottermani corbaci, that they had orders to do this. By the time the bewildered junior officer in charge decided he should sound an alarm, it was too late and they were swiftly overpowered. A couple of soldiers who tried to run were picked off by expert archers and then Nazim waved the all-clear. Feray, Bridgit, Nola, Riona and Rosaleen trotted out of cover and across to the wall, where Kottermani soldiers gently helped them up and over.

"Remember, you find Kemal and get him out, then take over the whole castle, so Swane has nowhere to run if he escapes us in the square. You have to be ruthless. If anyone stops you, they must die," Bridgit said.

"We know what is at stake," Feray said calmly. "We will not kill ordinary soldiers unless we have to, because they are just obeying orders. But nothing will stop us."

Bridgit nodded and waved to the two score of archers that were her escort. They were the best bowmen Nazim had, and had honed their skills providing food during a harsh Gaelish winter. They had better not miss Swane this time, she prayed. Her plan had already cost her father his life – although he had given it willingly enough – and she could not bear to lose Fallon as well. The archers did not speak Gaelish but she had a couple of Abbas's men with her, who did speak some.

Together they flooded into the castle grounds. Mahir led companies in through the kitchen garden entrance, while other officers rushed into the stables and storerooms and the buildings outside, flushing out anyone and making it safe. The main doors to the castle had been shattered in the earlier battle and the four sentries there stood no chance against Nazim's men, who swept them aside and rushed into the castle.

"The prisoners," Bridgit cried, spotting Brendan looming above the others in the cart. She could hear Swane bellowing at the crowd, his voice echoing back over the castle, and knew Fallon had to be out in the square. There was still time to save him. All was going to plan – the men up on the walls were all watching the crowd in the square and no alarm had been raised. Swane had lost the castle behind him and he did not even know it. All that remained was to free the prisoners and snap up Swane and victory was theirs.

"I'll save Kemal, you get to Fallon," Feray ordered.

Feray raced across the courtyard with Nola, Riona and Rosaleen, while Bridgit took her group and headed up to the wall. But then it all started to go wrong.

*

Kerrin led Asil through the back streets easily enough. These were the streets where he had run and trained with the first recruits and he remembered the way. The streets were deserted. The people were either at the castle square or hiding, while the only Kottermanis they saw were either dead or tied up and they watched mutely as the two boys ran past. Escaping the ship had been child's play, thanks to Orhan distracting the few adults left to watch the children.

"How do we get into the castle?" Asil asked, panting, as they reached the rear wall.

"That's up to you," Kerrin said. "I don't speak Kottermani."

"Let's just hope neither of our mothers has left orders to arrest us," Asil said, then threw back his shoulders and strode out towards the soldiers pretending to guard the wall, Kerrin a step behind. "If we can get inside, do you know where to go?"

"Leave that to me," Kerrin said confidently. "I know that castle like the back of my hand."

Asil glanced at him. "What in Aroaril's name does that mean? You have an enormous hand?"

Kerrin smiled. "Gaelish expression. Get us into the castle and I'll take it from there."

*

There was a guard tower at the top of the stairs. They must have seen what had been happening in the castle for their swords were ready and the two groups of Kottermanis tore into each other. There was no room for bows, just swords and daggers and fists and boots and even teeth.

Bridgit cursed as her men suffered because they did not have armor but they did have the advantage of numbers and the last of the guards were cut down.

"We have no time to help the wounded. Leave them and hurry," she ordered.

Nobody did anything so she looked around impatiently for her interpreters. To see them both lying in pools of blood on the stone.

She could hear Swane still ranting, but she could feel time slipping away as the Kottermanis looked at her doubtfully.

How could she make them understand what she wanted when none of them could speak her language?

*

Kemal glowered down at his Kottermani guards, who would not look up at the cart and meet his eyes. The Gaelish prisoners had been bound and gagged. The only concession to his former status as Crown Prince was to avoid the gag. He knew there was no point in shouting at men like this so he kept silent, until he caught sight of something across the courtyard. He stood up, with some difficulty, as his hands were tied.

"Do you know you serve Zorva? Did you not hear that speech by the Emperor? How could that Gaelish Prince be named as the heir to the Elephant Throne?" he challenged them.

None would answer but an officer stepped forwards, wearing the emblem of the Emperor's personal guards.

"You will be silent, or I shall gag you," he threatened.

"How long have you served the Emperor?" Kemal demanded.

"Long enough to obey his every order without question," the officer snapped back.

"Have you not seen the change in my father? The Gaelish have possessed him. It is the work of evil and—"

"Get me a gag," the officer ordered his men.

"Look at me," Kemal shouted. "Listen to me. Or you will regret this day for the rest of your lives."

"We serve the Emperor. We have no doubts," the officer retorted. "For Aroaril's sake, if none of you have a gag then I shall cut out his tongue to keep it silent."

The officer took hold of the side of the cart to climb up – but then an arrow punched into his back, driving him down to the cobbles. His men gazed at him in shock, began to turn, and then went down under a hail of shafts. Kemal grinned at the sight, then danced back as an errant arrow sank into the wooden cart near his leg.

The rest of the prisoners were all watching in disbelief as Kottermani soldiers rushed across the courtyard, surrounded the cart and finished off any of the guards who lived.

"What's going on?" Devlin called.

Kemal laughed. He could not answer, could not find the words, just laughed as he saw Feray running towards him.

"What are you doing?" he asked.

"Saving you and destroying Swane," she replied breathlessly. "Want to help?"

Kemal stopped laughing and went down on one knee to kiss his wife.

"You are a vision from above," he told her. "I never thought I'd see you again. What is the rest of the plan?"

Feray produced a knife. "No time to explain. Just follow my lead," she said, and began to saw at his ropes.

*

Nola and Riona rushed through the carts, looking for their husbands – and found them sitting together.

A few strokes of the knife and Devlin and Brendan were freed and the four of them embraced.

"I am sorry, I am so sorry," Brendan sobbed helplessly. "I never want to fight again."

Nola drew back. "What happened to you?"

But he could not answer her.

"Neither of us can do more fighting," Devlin said, wincing as he cradled his wounded arm. "We're not much good anymore."

"No," Nola said, holding her husband's head and looking into his swimming eyes. "You are better."

*

Bridgit could hear Swane threatening vengeance and torture on Fallon and her heart was in her mouth, worrying she was going to be too late. Without her interpreters, she could not explain her plan to the Kottermani archers. It was not a matter of just running down the wall and hoping they followed her. She needed them to pretend they were part of the castle garrison and running from attackers. The castle garrison had seen Feray's men free the prisoners and they were now loosing arrows down. The prisoners had all been freed and were now sheltering from the arrows behind the carts. They were safe enough but trapped. She was supposed to save them but just running out there could get all her men killed – and then what would happen to Fallon? She took a deep breath. She would have to do it anyway and hope.

"Mam!"

She had never been so happy and simultaneously so furious to hear Kerrin's voice. She whirled to see Kerrin and Asil race up the stairs into the guard tower. A dozen things to say crowded into her mind but she bit back on them.

"You two!" she snapped, then controlled herself. "Asil, I need you to translate what I say. And then I'll deal with you both later!"

Asil looked shocked but quickly understood her idea and snapped out orders to the Kottermanis that were with her. The men quickly pulled on the dead men's cloaks to disguise the fact they were not wearing armor, then raced along the wall towards the corner towers, shouting and pointing over their shoulders.

Bridgit, Kerrin and Asil ran at the back of the group, wearing cloaks to disguise themselves. Bridgit's legs were shaking and her heart was pounding and the fear she was too late was only a part of that. The child was heavy within her and a winter of enforced inactivity had hardly helped. She used the boys' energy to pull her along.

The ruse worked long enough for her Kottermanis to close in on the castle guards. By the time they realized something was wrong, her men were among them, stabbing and cutting without mercy. A winter of struggling to survive had brought these Kottermanis closer together it seemed, for they worked as a team, while their opponents were more scattered and were left screaming and bleeding on the stones. Bridgit was horribly aware all this shouting and screaming and fighting had to be attracting attention and things could fall apart very quickly. She could hear the crowd out the front now, calling for mercy. Her Gaelish in the crowd were leading the cry to try and cover any noise that might be going on in the castle, but it sounded thin compared to the sound of fighting. Surely Swane must realize things were not as he had imagined.

"Asil! Tell half of our men to hold these doorways, the rest with us. Go!"

The tower was not tall, just two stories above the wall, but the stone stairs seemed to go on forever. They burst into the first floor guard room to find more Kottermanis waiting for them. These soldiers were prepared, however, and now they had the advantage. There was little room for either side, men shoving and stabbing and snarling at each other and the wounded not even having enough space to fall.

"Tell them to keep going! We have to get to the top!" Bridgit shouted into Asil's ear.

But getting orders across in that cramped space was impossible. Asil shouted and shoved but only three of her Kottermanis broke off and raced up the next set of stairs, the rest still impossibly locked in the fight with the tower guards.

"Come on, Mam!" Kerrin spotted a gap and slithered through, Asil a heartbeat behind. Bridgit was not going to leave them and ducked under a wild sword thrust, scraped her back along the rough stone wall and then kept going, her burning thighs driving her up the last set of stairs.

Emerging into the weak Gaelish sunlight made her eyes blur, and then she clutched for her forgotten sword as she saw the three bodies of her men on the ground, one thrashing as he died, the other two already dead. They had taken care of four of the Kottermanis they had found up there but the last, a giant of a man with a bloodied sword, stood ready. He seemed momentarily thrown by the appearance of two boys and a woman, but he shook off his surprise and advanced on them, sword held high.

Bridgit forgot her burning legs, the struggle to draw in breath, her worry about Fallon, everything except the need to protect Kerrin.

"Hey!" she cried, circling away from the boys, trying to draw the guard to her, hoping one of her Kottermanis was only a moment or two away. The guard went for her and she held out her sword, wondering how in Aroaril's name she was going to stop him.

Asil was shouting something in Kottermani but the guard ignored him. Bridgit backed away until she could feel the battlement behind her and decided to duck away to her side, away from his sword arm, the moment he swung. She just wished her legs did not feel as though they were made of pease pudding.

"Mam!" Kerrin screamed, but she was focused only on the guard and when he was about to swing.

Then Asil raced forwards. The guard reacted lightning fast, swinging his sword around viciously, but Asil slid on his knees, the blade hissing more than a foot over his head. In the boy's hands were two sharp daggers and, as he slid past the guard, he slashed out with both, cutting wounds into the man's ankles.

The guard threw back his head and howled with pain. He tried to turn and cut down Asil but his damaged tendons would not support him and he staggered. Bridgit reacted instantly, jumping forwards and locking her arm and shoulder, driving her sword into the angle of his neck. There was no time to think and she did not waste an instant of it. She had to save the boys. Hot blood sprayed out and she cried out in disgust and horror, spitting it clear of her mouth.

Choking now, the guard pulled himself off her blade, tried to stop the crimson flow from his neck, tried to raise his weapon but failed. His wounded ankles gave way and he collapsed to the stones, making a horrible choking noise.

Bridgit let her reddened sword drop and grabbed Asil by the arm, dragging the boy clear. Both lads were watching the Kottermani guard's painful death, their eyes wide and horrified. She wanted to comfort them – but there was no time.

"Kerrin! Your dad!" she snapped and his eyes cleared. She made Asil turn away, shielding him from the sight with her body.

"There!" Kerrin pointed downwards, to the stage set up almost below them.

She could see Fallon and her heart leaped. Kottermani guards held his arms, while Swane was holding his head up by the hair, hissing something foul at him. She glanced back but there were no archers coming up the stairs. There were bows and arrows but she was under no illusion she or the boys could hope to draw one, let alone think to hit anything below.

Kerrin produced his small Kottermani crossbow. "I can hit Swane from here," he announced.

"It's all right, we just need one archer," she replied confidently, as much to herself as to the boys.

But, as they watched, the Kottermanis dragged Fallon back across the stage, to a bench, where he was lifted and crashed down onto it. She could see his back arch in pain, and then the guards held him down, one gripping his legs, two more holding the arms, while a fourth produced a long knife from a rack of evilly sharp implements and advanced on Fallon.

"Mam!" Kerrin cried.

Bridgit looked over her shoulder desperately but still no archer was in view. And, even if they raced up now, there would be no time. She looked again at Kerrin and quailed at the thought of the responsibility falling onto his shoulders. It might almost be easier to take the boys away from the wall and not watch, rather than have Fallon's death on Kerrin's shoulders. They were almost over the top of the torture bench and she wondered if she should simply throw swords down there to distract them.

"I can do this, Mam," Kerrin said softly and she looked at her son and saw the rock-hard certainty in his eyes. It was the same look she had seen in Fallon's eyes, many times, and it cleared her mind. Better to try and miss than stand here and hear Fallon die.

"Ignore Swane. Take out the man with the knife," she said calmly, as if she were asking him to clear the table after dinner.

Kerrin was only just tall enough to lean out of the embrasure, but that was actually an advantage, because he could rest his arms on the broad stone. The crossbow looked impossibly small but it was aimed down, and the distance was little more than fifty yards. Anything thrown from this height would at least distract, though that would be ample warning of what was going on and would probably bring all Swane's magical fury onto them. But who cared, if it worked. She hefted her sword and Asil clutched his bloodied daggers.

"We throw when Kerrin looses," she said, her voice belying the fears raging inside her.

Kerrin leaned out, took a breath and then, in the gap between taking another, loosed his crossbow.

CHAPTER 81

Fallon felt the tip of the knife just brush his chest as his filthy tunic was sliced open. He kept his eyes closed, bracing himself for the pain, but then someone howled in outrage. It took him a few moments to realize it wasn't his voice and he opened his eyes to see the guard with the knife pawing at the back of his neck, a small quarrel flapping away in response to his actions, the head only just inside the skin. Fallon and the other guards gazed at him for a moment, then a knife and sword bounced off the stage, making the Kottermani holding Fallon's left arm let go.

The shouts of the crowd were rising now, while Swane was bellowing something that Fallon ignored. There was only one person using that size crossbow that Fallon knew about. Kerrin. Which meant Bridgit had to be here, which meant ... he did not bother trying to follow that thought any further. He swung his free left arm over and drove his fist into the throat of the Kottermani who knelt to his right, freeing his other arm. The guard holding his feet looked up as Fallon sat up and slapped his cupped hands over the man's ears. Eardrums burst with a pop and the man reared back, screaming.

Fallon rolled to his side, towards the rack of torture implements, as the guard who had been holding his left arm drew his sword and thumped it down into the bench where he'd been lying a moment before. Fallon snatched up the guisarme they'd been planning to haul out his guts with: a combination of a spike with a wickedly hooked blade on the end of a pole the length of his leg. It wasn't quite the shillelagh but it was good enough. He feinted towards the guard's eyes, then slammed the hilt into his stomach and belted him over the head with the hooked blade, ripping clear a huge chunk of skull.

The man he'd punched in the throat was getting up onto his knees so Fallon lifted his own knee into the man's face, smashing his nose and sending him slumping over again. The man with the quarrel in his neck tried to draw his sword but Fallon rammed the spike on the end of his guisarme into his throat and shook his body off the end.

"Come on!" he challenged Swane and the others.

He glanced out towards the square where scores of fights were breaking out, as groups of Kottermanis were being swamped by men and women who were producing weapons out of nowhere. He grinned at Swane. Bridgit obviously had some sort of plan and if they could but bag Swane now, then it would all be over. He jumped onto the bench and advanced on Swane, heedless of the man's magic. A pair of guards tried to stop him but he used the spike at the top of his guisarme like a spear, jabbing the first in the eye, then using both ends of the weapon to strike down the other.

The old Emperor stood unmoving at the side of the stage but Swane was backing away. Fallon felt a surge of confidence – but then Swane signalled and a pair of the Emperor's guards advanced on him. From their dress and silent advance he recognized them as the same type of warrior that had terrorized Berry on Aidan's orders, masquerading as child snatchers. And, carefully, he backed away, hoping that Bridgit had another part to this plan.

*

When Fallon freed himself, Gallagher exploded into action.

Waiting in the crowd, watching his friend being dragged out to die had tested him to the limit. Although getting there had been easy enough until that point, going exactly as Bridgit had planned. A mixed force of Gaelish and Kottermanis had hurried through Berry, overpowering Swane's patrols as they went. Then Bridgit and

Feray had led the Kottermanis in one direction and he had taken the Gaelish down to the slave warehouses and freed the people held there, before they all headed to the castle square. The sun was out but it was a typical Gaelish spring day, so everyone was wrapped up warm, which meant they could hide weapons under their cloaks. They had split apart into small groups and eased close to Kottermani soldiers, ready to attack when Fallon was freed.

The tension had risen until Gallagher had felt like he had to do something or he would lose his mind. When Fallon fought his way clear of the torture bench, he released a bellow and charged towards the nearest Kottermani soldier.

"That's it! Let's go!" he roared.

The Kottermani soldier two paces away turned and glared at him, drawing his sword but Gallagher was on him before he could get it clear of the scabbard, sinking his long knives into the man's neck. The man's comrade turned but as he opened his mouth to shout, Donnchadh struck off his head with a huge blow.

Gallagher raced at the rest of the Kottermani squad, grabbing another and slitting his throat. "Kill them all! Kill them before they kill you!" he roared.

All around the square, the Gaelish were springing into action, stabbing and killing, then melting back into the crowd. Kottermani soldiers, not understanding the chorus of calls in Gaelish but understanding all too well that they were being attacked, drew swords and began hacking indiscriminately at anyone near them.

Gallagher picked up a Kottermani shield and used it to block a blow that would have killed a young girl, then stabbed the soldier. As the Kottermani collapsed, he kicked the sword over to the girl's father, who clutched his family close.

"Want to save your family? Pick up the sword!" he challenged.

The man, a dock worker from the look of his clothes, gazed at him in shock.

"Come on, man!" Gallagher shouted. "It's them or us!"

Another Kottermani rushed in, bloodied blade swinging, and Gallagher was forced to block desperately against the furious attack. He could not see an opening for his knife and, from the look on the Kottermani's face, this soldier thought he was moments away from victory. Then the soldier gasped in shock, blood spilling out of his mouth. The docker ripped his borrowed blade out of the soldier's lungs and nodded at Gallagher.

"Someone pick up this sword. Get the bastards!" Gallagher shouted.

Men stared back at him blankly but then a vaguely familiar figure stepped out of the crowd. It took Gallagher a moment to place him. Turlough, the Greeter from the Bank Guild.

"Citizens of Berry! Fight for your lives! Fight for your children! Fight for Aroaril! Stand up now or forever live in shame!" he roared, his beautiful voice rolling over the people. Almost like magic, they responded to his words, sounding as they did like the orders from a noble. Gallagher shrugged. He didn't care how they fought, just that they did. Turlough smiled at him and led a charge of townsfolk at the Kottermani soldiers.

Shouts and screams filled the square as Gaelish fled in all directions from furious soldiers, while every time a Kottermani turned away, another group of Gaelish attacked. With their officers all up by the stage and split into small groups, the Kottermanis were unable to work together, while the Gaelish did not wait for orders, just came together to overwhelm small groups of soldiers, steal their weapons and move on. Although the Kottermanis were not able to fight as they wanted, there were still four regiments of them and they did not care who they killed. People fled in all directions as bodies began to clog the square and screams of wounded and dying joined the shrieks of fear from women and children.

*

Bridgit had been caught up watching Fallon spring to life and help free himself but she whirled around as feet clattered on the stairs. She breathed again as half a dozen of her Kottermanis raced onto the roof.

"Asil! Tell them to protect Fallon and put arrows into everyone else on that stage!" she cried.

*

Fallon decided to tackle the guard on his left first. There was no reason to it, he just decided to take one of them with him and that one looked uglier than the other. He drew back his guisarme and prepared to commit to the attack, hoping that Kerrin and Bridgit would turn away.

But a volley of arrows thumped down and he jumped away as the first landed with a splintering crash in the wooden stage. The guard he had been focused on took a pair of shafts through the chest and collapsed, while the other swung his swords like a man possessed and darted from left to right, blocking some arrows and dodging the others. In a couple of heartbeats he was over Fallon's side of the torture bench and smiled triumphantly at having escaped the arrow storm, now too close to Fallon for them to risk any more shafts.

Then a small quarrel dropped down and struck him in the eye and his grin turned to an agonized howl as he tried to pluck out the shaft. Fallon didn't need a second invitation and stamped his foot forwards, ripping the guisarme's blade across the guard's throat.

"Swane!" he shouted over the choking guard. "I'm coming for you!"

But Swane wasn't even looking at him. Instead, he was red-faced and shouting, pointing out at the square. He could shout orders all he wanted; Fallon could see there was no way anyone was getting control of that confused battle. Still, while Swane was occupied, Fallon liked the idea of sinking his spike deep into his evil heart.

But a noise behind Fallon made him whirl to see a group of men trying to get up onto the stage. Merchants and the like – they were Swane's Gaelish supporters who he had hunted while he'd been Lord Protector. They'd come to do Swane's bidding yet again.

*

"It's safe to go now. Bridgit's men have cleared the wall of guards. We get to your father and then free him from the dark spell that he's under. Then we can order everyone to stop fighting," Feray said to Kemal.

"I have to help the wounded first," the Gaelish priestess protested.

519

"No," said a giant Gaelishman. "I will look after them."

"But Brendan, don't you want to fight?" the priestess asked.

"Not anymore. I shall just help others," Brendan said.

Rosaleen turned back to Kemal and Feray. "Then I am ready to help you. We shall need to protect people from Swane's powers and I fear I am the only one strong enough to do it."

Kemal glanced over at the rest of the former prisoners. Half were wounded but a score of them had accepted weapons and they were a fearsome-looking bunch. He wouldn't want to fight them.

"The rest of you?"

"Oh, we are ready to fight. We have a score to settle," a bald giant said fiercely.

Kemal patted him on the shoulder with one hand and accepted a sword with the other.

"This time we turn the tables on our enemies," he said. "And I too am ready to get some revenge."

*

Fallon knew his one chance to drive the merchants away was to try and scare them. They were not warriors and maybe he could persuade them that coming up the stairs to the stage would require them selling their lives, rather than selling over-priced goods.

But as he snarled at them, ready to smash the first person who made it up, they waved their hands at him, showing they were unarmed.

"Fallon, we are with you!" one shouted.

He paused for a moment, unsure whether to believe them, then recognized Lorrissa, one of the few Guild heads he had thought trustworthy.

"Swane is mad. We must destroy him!" she cried.

He stepped back, still keeping his guisarme up across his chest, ready to defend himself if one or more of them proved treacherous.

"Get a weapon and help," he invited.

Lorrissa led a rush to the rack of torture implements, while others picked up the swords the dead and wounded Kottermanis had dropped.

"Shall we get Swane?" Lorrissa asked.

Fallon waved them forwards. "Let's kill the bastard," he said.

*

Bridgit leaned back over the wall. "It looks like he is safe at last, thank Aroaril," she breathed.

"Shall I go for Swane now? I hit the other two I aimed at," Kerrin asked eagerly.

Bridgit gathered the two boys into her arms, hugging them tight. She felt like crying but bit down on that hard. There was too much that still needed to be done.

"Are you all right, Mam? Is Dad safe?" Kerrin asked awkwardly.

"Yes," she said, releasing them a little, and breathing out heavily.

"What shall we do now?"

She tightened her grip on them both. "You will stay here and not move a muscle, nor look over, nor show yourself. The fact you saved your dad might just save your hides. But, for Aroaril's sake, don't disobey me this time!"

She grabbed the archer and pushed him towards the stairs. "Follow me," she ordered, then pointed at Kerrin. "And you two, don't move!"

*

Swane did not know where to look. There were four regiments of Kottermani soldiers out in that square, but it was almost impossible to tell because of all the confusion. Some companies were in good order and had formed small squares, throwing back any attacks, while others had split apart to chase fleeing civilians and were now being picked off by men with swords. Where had the attackers come from? What was going on?

On the other side of the stage, Fallon and a motley bunch of merchants were fighting with the last of the Emperor's guards. It looked like the guards would hold but he did not like the way Fallon was getting closer to him. He should be dead by now! It was time to do this properly. He pointed at Fallon and summoned

Zorva's power, ready to stop his heart – but nothing happened. It was as if there was something blocking him. He let his arm drop, feeling a touch of fear.

"What do we do, sire?" Finbar asked.

"Back into the castle. We shall get safe and then send for more regiments. We'll just keep feeding them in here until all these traitors are dead," he snapped, feeling better about that idea.

"And Fallon?"

Swane hissed in anger. Fallon must be protected by one of Aroaril's filthy priests. But he could not escape. The city was surrounded by Kottermani regiments, loyal to the Emperor, and the Emperor would do whatever Swane said.

"Later," he spat.

He turned towards the castle to see Kottermanis marching out. "Good!" he exclaimed. "The officers must have heard what was happening and decided to come to our aid."

But even as he raised an arm to wave them over, Finbar grabbed him and dragged him back.

"Sire, they are not ours – look, the foul priestess is out the front, with Fallon's Gaelish rebels."

"More traitors!" Swane cried. Well, he knew what to do with them. He had the Emperor and thousands of Kottermani troops. He would surround this city and destroy every last person inside of it. What was Gaelland to him, now that the Empire was at his feet?

He pointed to Finbar. "Rally the Kottermanis to us. We shall cut our way out of the city and then crush Berry."

Finbar nodded and the Kottermani Emperor began bellowing orders in a voice that magically echoed across the square, calling all Kottermanis to him, ordering them to die to protect their Emperor. Then, with Finbar on one side and Swane on the other, they hurried the Emperor off the platform, away from the approaching priestess and towards safety. A pair of Gaelish rushed at them – ragged, angry men carrying Kottermani swords. He reached again for Zorva's power and this time they were unprotected. He could grasp their hearts and drop them dead at his feet. The surge of power as it left his body left him gasping but that extravagant act had done its job. Other Gaelish backed away and the first Kottermani companies closed on the three of them, creating a wall of steel and wood.

A group of Gaelish stood in their way and he ordered them slaughtered, although they cried and begged as they fell.

"Sire, that's Munro and his men you are killing!" Finbar exclaimed.

Swane watched his informers die without a flicker of emotion. "They didn't warn me of this. They deserve to pay. And if Berry is to die, what need have I of them? Get us to the gate. Give the orders through the Emperor."

Finbar gulped and hurried to obey. More Kottermanis were arriving every moment, under the Emperor's direction, and Swane began to relax. Soon he would be safe and then there would be no mercy for anyone in this city.

*

Fallon jerked his guisarme out of a guard's chest and cursed as he saw Swane make his escape. Kottermanis flooded up onto the stage and he prepared to fight them, only for them to slaughter the last of Swane's guards instead. He held his guisarme protectively until Rosaleen rushed to his side and he saw Feray and Kemal behind them, as well as Gannon, Bran, Brasso and a score of his men.

"Where's Bridgit?" he gasped, suddenly feeling the effects of fighting after two days of no food.

Rosaleen glanced up towards the castle. "Well, you're still alive so she must be up there somewhere. But we have to get the Emperor – we can't let Swane get out of the city."

"And what do we do when we get to the Emperor?"

"That's where we come in," Kemal said. "We free my father and end this."

Fallon mustered a tired grin. "Then what are we waiting for?" he asked.

But it swiftly became obvious that their plan was going to be difficult. The fighting in the square was bitter and confused. More than a thousand Kottermanis had chased townsfolk into the surrounding streets and now there were nasty brawls going on in every alleyway. Many of the other Kottermanis were dead or dying in the square but the best part of two regiments had managed to form a thick circle of swords and shields around the Emperor and Swane. Inside there they were as safe as houses. Even Fallon's best men could not break that circle apart. Instead it marched across the square, driving irresistibly towards the east gate.

Bran and Gannon were sent around to join Gallagher and the bulk of the trained men as they tried to stop the Kottermani progress. But while they could slow things down, there was no stopping the Kottermani advance. They formed a wedge and, without shields and armor, the Gaelish could not hold it back. The freed slaves and the ordinary men and women who had picked up weapons and stabbed Kottermani soldiers in the back were almost useless here, swept aside like annoying little children if they tried to stop the wedge of Kottermanis.

Fallon and Kemal led an attack on the rear, but while they could take down a couple of Kottermanis, the others kept moving and any gaps were sealed instantly by big men with shields. The wounded were left behind and the only thought of the marching Kottermanis was to protect their Emperor. Unfortunately this also meant they were protecting Swane.

"We have to try something different," Fallon gasped, every muscle aching.

"Looks like you need help," a familiar voice said.

He turned to see Bridgit. Behind her was a group of Kottermani archers, but he hardly looked at them. He opened his arms and held her. She embraced him fiercely.

"You weren't supposed to come back. But thank Aroaril you did," he whispered.

"Thank Aroaril you are still alive. If I had not got there—" and then her voice failed.

Kemal cleared his throat. "As happy as I am to see you back together, we have to get Swane," he said loudly.

Fallon did not want to move but Bridgit pushed him gently away. "We have risked too much to let Swane escape now," she said, trailing her fingers down his face as she did so.

Fallon tried to clear his mind and think. "We need to use archers, wizards, anything we have to slow them down. Then get men ahead of them to block the gate and attack them from all sides," he said.

"Do it," Kemal agreed.

*

Swane fretted at their slow progress. An enormous army waited outside the city and all he had to do was get there.

"Send a message to the officers outside the gate. They must march two regiments in to meet us and keep the gate open for our escape," he told Finbar.

The wizard stepped closer to the Emperor, then stopped as if he had run into a wall.

"What is it?" Swane demanded.

"Fallon's wizards," Finbar warned, pointing.

Swane looked back. A crush of Gaelish pressed hard after them, picking off any wounded and stragglers and forcing the rearguard to fight as they walked backwards, with any stumble instantly fatal. Then, to his horror, the back row of Kottermanis went down as magic shattered all their shields. As the soldiers stared in shock, the Gaelish fell on them like a pack of ravenous wolves on a flock of sheep. Scores went down but the rest of the column sealed up a new line of shields, sacrificing the rest of the shield-less men but stopping the Gaelish attack.

"Stop them! That must not happen again," Swane shouted furiously.

Before Finbar could even reply, arrows began to fall into the center of the formation, striking down officers and men, slowing the advance. Worse, as they moved out of the square and into the streets, Gaelish hurled things down on them from surrounding houses, everything from knives to the contents of chamber pots.

"Protect us!" Swane roared.

Finbar just looked at him. "Sire, I cannot do everything," he said. "You must choose."

Swane felt himself on the edge of losing control but dragged his temper back in time. Finbar was his link to the Emperor.

"Stop those wizards. And get the Kottermanis to use their shields against these cursed arrows," he decided.

Finbar nodded solemnly and the Kottermanis formed a shelter around Swane and the Emperor, their shields raised to protect against the constant rain of arrows. At Finbar's direction, the Emperor called out encouragement and the Kottermanis stiffened their lines. Swane looked back to where the rear rank was watching their shields stretch and return to their old shape as Finbar battled against Fallon's wizards. It was time to gather more power, he decided.

With shields up around him, most of the Kottermanis could not see what he was doing and, besides, they were facing outwards, watching for Fallon's men as they attacked out of every cursed alleyway and street they went past. There was no shortage of wounded and men falling from random arrows. He did not have the beautiful obsidian knife that had been Brother Nahuatl's but he had his bone knife, which was more than sharp enough for the task. A fire would have been perfect for the sacrifices but his God would understand. A wounded soldier, his chest split open, lay in the street, his life leaking away. Swane ripped the wound wider with his knife and then tore out the heart, muttering prayers to Zorva as he did so. It was not the huge surge of power that he had felt when Durzu died but it still made him gasp. He tossed aside the bloody heart and hurried over to the next wounded man. This heart gave him even less power than before and he hurled this heart away angrily. He needed power and he needed it now! Then it struck him. There was little life left in these dying men. He needed something fresh.

"Finbar!" he shouted.

The wizard staggered over, his face gray and his eyes red-rimmed. "They are tiring, but so am I," he croaked.

"I need the power to speak Kottermani, so I can make the Emperor give out orders," he said irritably.

Finbar's eyes widened. "I cannot give you much time, sire," he warned. "I am exhausted."

"Give me all you can and I shall do the rest," Swane said irritably.

"And what happens to me?" Finbar asked.

"You will collapse soon anyway. Help me and I shall order you carried. Hesitate for another heartbeat and I shall slit your throat myself," Swane snapped.

Finbar closed his eyes and Swane felt his throat grow warm. He was about to strike back with his own power when it stopped.

"It is done. And I am too," Finbar groaned and slumped to the ground.

Swane turned to the nearest soldiers. "Carry him," he ordered.

The pair of them immediately sheathed their swords and picked up the fallen wizard and Swane nodded happily to himself. He understood the words and they did also. He smiled at the unconscious Finbar but his smile was quickly wiped away by screams from the back of the column, where magic was being used to drag down the rearguard.

"Emperor! Order your men to let me cut out their hearts!" he commanded.

The Emperor nodded and pointed at a pair of soldiers. They looked shocked but their officers echoed the order and some of their comrades hauled off their armor and pushed them down to their knees. Swane hurriedly prayed and then used his bone knife to tear out their hearts.

This time he felt the ecstatic surge of power and laughed with delight, heedless of the fact he was splattered with blood and holding quivering hearts, or that the surrounding Kottermanis were looking on in horror.

He turned to where the Gaelish were tearing into the Kottermani rearguard and pointed up at the nearest houses. Like all of Berry's terraces, they were solid brick on the first story and then grew more rickety and unstable as they reached higher. The fourth floor on both sides of the road was a sloping wooden construction that looked as if it had nearly fallen in winter. Swane used his power to bring first one side and then the other down, falling both on Kottermani and Gaelish.

"Hurry now! They will not follow us!" he shouted, heedless of the casualties he had inflicted on his allies. After all, there were thousands more of them outside. The important thing was, pursuit had been stopped.

"More hearts!" he called.

The surrounding men began to edge away but when their Emperor issued the orders they reluctantly obeyed. Swane bent to his task, chuckling as he did so, anticipating the power that would soon be his.

*

"He's killing his own men and using the power to stop us," Rosaleen announced.

Fallon lifted a fallen beam up to let Gallagher drag one of his men out, howling at his broken leg. "Really?" Fallon asked sarcastically.

"We cannot let him get away," Rosaleen insisted.

"Don't you think we know that? If he gets outside then he brings the rest of the army in. We have to get to the Emperor," Fallon growled. He waved at his men, who were hurriedly clearing a path through the debris so they could follow the retreating Kottermanis. Any wounded they found were dragged clear, although it was obvious there were more under the rubble and it was taking too long.

"We'll use the roofs. We can overtake him that way," he said.

"Wait!" Bridgit grabbed him and kissed him. "Don't get killed, not after I saved you."

*

The Kottermanis still had arrows, crossbow bolts and slingshots raining down on them from all sides, as well as small companies of men attacking them from side alleys. Some enterprising townsfolk had even dragged a wagon across the road as a barrier and fighting swirled around it as the Kottermanis tried to break past. Fallon looked down to see they were overtaking the Kottermanis. He had a mixed group of men, old faces from Baltimore, his best recruits who had been captured with him, as well as Kemal and some of his men and a handful of both Padraig's wizards and Rosaleen's priests.

They raced over the rooftops, jumping the narrow gaps between the houses. Fallon pushed his legs onwards, feeling his muscles shake in protest at the lack of rest and food he had put himself through over the past few days. But then he looked down to see Swane magically pick up the wagon and smash it into smithereens and he told himself to forget about exhaustion. He could rest later. Then they struck a road that was too wide to cross on their above-ground path.

"Get down, we're ahead of them now," Gallagher said. "That's too far for us to get across."

"But the wall is so close," Fallon said, looking longingly at it.

"I have some of my priests over that way. I can get them to hold the gate against Swane until we get there," Rosaleen said swiftly.

Fallon could feel time slipping away. "Do it," he said, then used his boot to smash in a nearby window. "The rest of us, get down fast."

*

Swane could feel the thrill of triumph coursing through his veins. Though it might have just been the thrill of the power he was getting from Zorva. Either way, it was intoxicating. The nearby soldiers were watching him with something close to terror on their faces. They were more afraid of him than the arrows and other missiles landing from above. Only those carrying Finbar were safe from him and so the wizard had a dozen men holding him, with others trying to help.

Swane did not care. The power he had taken made him unstoppable. Gaelish rushed out of an alleyway, howling cries of hate and fell onto his right flank but he simply clapped his hands together and a gust of wind picked them up and tumbled them back down the alleyway.

"Keep moving! Get me outside and then we shall go back and kill everyone!" he bellowed. The hilt of his bone knife felt sticky with blood and he had to grip it tightly. He was tempted to use it again on another Kottermani, just for the feeling it gave him – then he saw the gates ahead and thrust it in the air.

"Stop for nothing!" he roared.

Then the screaming began.

*

Fallon leaned against the wall as the alleyway seemed to revolve around him. His legs felt shaky and his arms weak. But, considering he should have had his intestines pulled out and limbs chopped off by now, things could be worse.

"Are you all right?" Gallagher asked.

Fallon rubbed his eyes and pushed himself upright.

"Let's get that bastard," he said, taking a deep breath. Finish this and then he could eat, and sleep. At least it gave him much more sympathy for what wizards went through. That made him think of Padraig, and Caley, and he used that anger to spur him on.

The Kottermanis were hurrying past, a solid wall of shields. But Kemal had two score of archers, and a volley of arrows peppered Swane's Kottermanis, punching holes in their lines and turning their retreat into a shambles. Beyond the chaos, Fallon could see Swane's head and felt hatred feed his body.

"Now!" he howled and led a fevered rush down the street to crunch into Swane's Kottermanis. Kemal's men stayed back, loosing arrows over the top so as not to get caught in the confusion. Fallon had Gannon at one shoulder, Gallagher at the other, and Bran right behind, powering him forward every time a Kottermani tried to check him.

A soldier with an arrow in his shoulder tried a feeble thrust but Fallon smashed him aside and hurdled his body. The street around him seemed to blur and it felt as if he were back in the castle, surrounded and outnumbered, watching his men die, as well as in Baltimore, fighting off the raiders and protecting his family, yet also here, trying to stamp out Swane's evil once and for all.

He hooked his guisarme under a shield and reefed it up, allowing Gannon to thrust his blade into the soldier's chest. He jabbed with the spike, time and again, aiming for eyes and faces. He either made Kottermanis duck down and away, where they were easy prey for Gannon and Gallagher, or they died where they stood, the sharp steel slicing through eyes and mouths and into their brains.

He raked his hook across, the edge catching a Kottermani's mouth and ripping his cheek open. The man let out a bubbling scream as the force of the blow spun him around, and then Fallon lunged, the spike lancing into the back of the man's neck and dropping him instantly. He looked up over the man's body to see Swane and the Emperor just paces away.

Swane was screaming something in Kottermani but Fallon ignored that. The foul Prince's hands and forearms were covered in blood and spatters were across his chest and face, while his eyes were wild. There did not seem to be anything human in there.

A group of Kottermanis carrying the limp form of Finbar dropped the wizard and rushed at them but a group of Baltimoreans, led by Craddock and Donnchadh, met them and the two sides shoved and hacked at each other. Fallon stepped around them – and then a figure flew through the air at him. He tried to bring his guisarme around but a boot slammed into his chest and sent him flying.

*

Kemal hefted his sword and hurried after Fallon and his men.

"High One, is this wise? It is hard to tell who is who," Mahir warned.

"Wise? Of course it is not wise. But now is not a time for wisdom," Kemal snorted and charged forwards.

He sensed his men were at his back but he did not care. He could see his father and Swane through the press of fighting men. Just get to them and he could end this senseless slaughter.

Then he saw the Emperor's guards attack Fallon. One kicked Fallon backwards, a blow that was too good, for Fallon flew, avoiding the second's killer strike.

Kemal did not think twice. He jumped over Fallon's fallen body, standing between him and the pair of deadly guards. A heartbeat later, Mahir was beside him and then a line of his men. The guards hesitated, instinctively looking back to make sure they protected the Emperor.

"Father! Stop this! You are controlled by evil!" Kemal bellowed, seeking to be heard over the clamor of the fighting.

The Emperor stood, unmoved.

"Release him, foul one!" Kemal shouted at Swane. Swane gestured and Kemal felt his heart lurch but then it steadied and he caught sight of Rosaleen pointing at him, her power blocking Swane.

"Give up, Swane! Let my father go!" he cried, feeling a surge of triumph.

"Fool! He obeys only me, doing whatever I say!" Swane roared back.

Kemal smiled. Swane had forgotten he was speaking Kottermani.

The struggling soldiers instantly pulled back, while the guards looked at Swane.

"Kill Prince Kemal and the rest of them!" Swane ordered.

The Kottermani soldiers did not move and Kemal held out his hand to the Gaelish. "Hold! They want to come to our side and destroy Swane's evil!" he called in Gaelish.

The Emperor repeated Swane's words, pointing at Kemal and, while most of the soldiers just stood their ground, two guards raced forwards. One jumped high but Kemal was waiting for that and rammed his sword upwards, slicing open the guard as he came down. The other slipped past a thrust and struck back with an open hand, snapping back Mahir's head, then pivoted and elbowed Gannon in the head, knocking him away. Kemal lunged but had his blade knocked away, then a knife appeared in the guard's hand and he ducked, expecting to feel sharp steel slicing into him at any moment. But, just as the guard was about to throw, his leg was jerked by Fallon and his dagger flew upwards as he slipped. Before he could steady himself, two of Kemal's men jumped in and stabbed him.

"Now let's finish this," Fallon said, clutching his side as he pushed himself to his feet with his guisarme – the same one he had just used to hook the guard's foot.

Kemal glanced at him. "Thank you for my life," he said.

"Thanks for mine," Fallon replied. "Now let's take Swane's."

Swane watched the Emperor's guards go down with fury. Could nobody do what they were told? He had the Emperor order the nearest soldiers to kill Kemal and Fallon. But these soldiers, who had watched him slaughter eight of their fellows on the retreat down the street, simply shook their heads and backed away.

"Fools! I shall watch you all die for this!" Swane snarled. He clapped his hands together, creating a thunderclap that sent Fallon and his friends tumbling backwards.

They came to their feet, many of them gingerly, and he swiftly knelt and slapped his hands against the cobbles. These rippled, as if they were made of water, the ripples growing bigger as they surged towards Fallon and Kemal. It was not the slow death he had planned for them but it was still a death.

Then a priestess in white appeared, placing her hands on the cobbles. The waves Swane had created stopped as if they had struck a barrier, bursting up before falling down again, thumping into the dead and wounded who had been lying there.

Swane cursed. He wanted to destroy this priestess, take her heart and give it to Zorva but he could not trust the Kottermanis. They might try to attack him while he was fighting her. So he grabbed the Emperor's arm and hauled him down the street.

"Stop! Do not touch the Emperor!" one of his erstwhile soldiers cried, and three of them made to block his escape.

Swane pointed at them and the metal discs on their armor began to glow red, then smoke, as they burned through the leather backing and through to the skin.

The trio collapsed, screaming in agony as they burned to death, but Swane just hustled the Emperor away past them. "The Emperor is in danger! Save him!" he shouted.

There were still plenty of Kottermanis who hadn't seen what was going on and now they sealed the street behind him, allowing him to hurry towards the gate. Finbar was lost and that was a shame but he would find some Kottermani who spoke Gaelish and replace him. He did not need the man's power anymore. He could feel his own growing with every sacrifice he took.

A handful of townsfolk trying to stop their progress were swept aside and then the gates were before him, held open by two companies of Kottermanis. He dragged the Emperor onwards, heedless of the shocked glances he was getting from the Kottermanis around him. Outside, ten thousand Kottermani soldiers waited.

One order from the Emperor and they would smash Berry into dust.

CHAPTER 82

Fallon groaned as he rolled back onto his feet. His ribs were shrieking with pain now and even his hatred could not summon up more energy. Kemal offered him his hand and he took it gratefully.

"Swane's losing the Kottermanis. Now's the time to take them back from him," Fallon said.

"My thoughts exactly," Kemal said grimly. "We have to stop him before he's completely taken by Zorva. Though every time he uses his powers he drives my people away from him, I'd rather he did not have them."

Fallon looked around and waved over one of Padraig's wizards. The closest one had a familiar face – a woman who had risen in the Guild through sheer ability and persistence, rather than her skills at playing politics with the Guild leaders. But it took him a moment to remember her name.

"Michelle," he said. "The country rests on your shoulders now. You have to make it so every Kottermani in this street can hear Prince Kemal."

"That is not a problem," she assured him, then nodded to Kemal.

*

Kemal took a deep breath. He knew he didn't need to shout, because his words would echo across the street and he was more concerned about the words he needed.

"Soldiers of the Empire. It is your Crown Prince Kemal speaking to you. The Emperor is a prisoner of a creature of Zorva. The Gaelish Prince Swane is covered in the blood of your comrades that he has sent to the Dark God. My father cannot speak for himself but if you have any love for the Empire or want to live up to the oath you swore, then stop Swane. Make him let go of my father, your Emperor."

The closest Kottermanis had all stopped fighting and now went down on one knee to Kemal. He waved them upwards and the two sides, who had been tearing into each other just a short while ago, looked at each other doubtfully.

At that moment Bridgit, Feray, Gallagher and the rest of the Gaelish arrived, having cleared the street.

"So they are obeying you now?" Bridgit asked.

"Getting there," Kemal said. He pointed at his new men. "Swane is the enemy. We must stop him!"

He signaled down the street and they saluted and ran down the street after Swane, the Gaelish alongside them.

*

Swane cursed as Kemal's voice boomed down the street. The Kottermanis who were around him had already been looking doubtful – now they were almost hostile.

"He lies! He is the traitor! I am the new heir to the Empire and he is jealous!" Swane shouted. He let go of the Emperor's arm. "Hear it from your Emperor's own mouth." He lowered his voice. "Tell them that I am to be obeyed at all times and am saving you from Kemal the traitor."

The Emperor stood there dully, unmoving and unspeaking.

"Talk, curse you!" he hissed at the man. "Repeat my words!"

"He will not do that any longer, creature of darkness," someone shouted in Gaelish. "We are stopping you."

Swane turned to see a pair of white-robed priests of Aroaril step out from a side street. Their words were foreign but the Kottermanis recognized the robes, the same ones their own priests wore, and they stepped away from them.

"Priests of Zorva! Kill them!" Swane shrieked.

But none of the Kottermanis moved to obey.

Swane smiled. Enough of this deception. It was time to show the world who he really was.

"Run now, or you will die," he told the priests, forcing himself to say it in Gaelish. He reached out with Zorva's magic. These two did not have anything like the strength of the priestess. They would be easy to overpower.

"We are not afraid of you," the shorter of the two priests said scornfully.

Swane smiled. "You should have been," he said.

"Don't you mean we should—?" the priest began, but blood burst from his nose, ears and eyes and he fell to the ground, twitching. The other began to pray in a loud voice but Swane snuffed him out like he would a candle, bursting his heart with a gesture. It was just a shame he had not dedicated their deaths to Zorva. Imagine the power that would have flowed then!

He turned away from the priests and back to the Emperor. "Now tell them: I am your heir and Kemal is the traitor," he ordered.

The Emperor threw back his head and shouted out those orders and Swane looked around triumphantly. But the Kottermanis were looking, if anything, more hostile.

"Your Emperor has given an order! Obey it!" he barked.

"Step away from the Emperor. We do not know what you are but nobody who can slay priests of Aroaril like that can be good," a Kottermani officer declared. "Kneel down and we shall take the Emperor into a church and hear his words then."

"They will be the same," Swane rasped.

"Then it will be my head. But that is a risk I will take," the officer said flatly.

Swane smiled ruefully, then flung out his hand and the officer was picked up and thrown backwards, smashing into a building with a sickening crack.

"Out of my way, or you will join him," he ordered the Kottermanis.

Instead of fading away, they moved to block his way out.

"So be it," he said with a shrug and reached up towards the gate. The stones on the wall were in poor repair and it was a simple matter to send them crashing into the packed ranks of Kottermani soldiers, sending men flying or crushing them. The screams were never-ending. He grinned as he worked, his body singing with the ecstasy of the power. Destroy them now and get the Emperor outside and try again. These fools might be against him but the rest of the army would obey whatever the Emperor said.

He expected the Kottermanis to run – but instead of running off, they ran at him. He flicked them away as if they were ants, until the survivors cowered among the rubble. He prepared to use the last of it to clear his path to the gate when he felt his power being blocked again. He whirled to see Kemal, Fallon and a new army of Gaelish and Kottermanis arriving – with the priestess at the front.

"Stop now, Swane. Stop now and throw yourself on Aroaril's mercy before you do this world any more damage!" the priestess cried.

Swane glared at them. All his enemies in one place. It was time to finish this. He whipped out his bone knife and turned to the Emperor. "Bow down and bare your chest to me," he ordered. Out of the corner of his eye he saw Kemal racing at him but he snapped his fingers and sent the prince flying.

The Emperor fell to his knees, dragging his silken shirt open. Swane summoned a chunk of stone, bouncing it across the cobbles until it scraped to a stop beside them. He grabbed the Emperor by the shoulder and bent him backwards across the stone. Then, in a practiced move, he slashed the Emperor just below the rib cage. As the surviving Kottermanis cried out in horror, he reached in and up and tore his beating heart free as he prayed to Zorva.

The surge of power he felt as he raised the Emperor's heart made him shake. With his bloody trophy still in his hand he turned to face them all, ignoring their cries of horror and protest.

"Now you will all die," he promised.

CHAPTER 83

Rosaleen had stopped Kemal being thrown to his death and now the Kottermani prince struggled to his feet, waving at his surrounding men. "Arrows!" he snapped.

"Crossbows! Spears!" Fallon shouted.

A hail of missiles flew out at Swane but they all missed, veering off in all directions, some to clatter harmlessly into buildings, others to crunch into the surviving Kottermanis around the gate.

"My turn now!" Swane cried and reached upwards.

Instantly the houses along the street began to crumble – but as fast as he tugged at them, Rosaleen and the various wizards pushed them back into place.

Swane laughed at them. "I can do this all day," he boasted. "Can you?"

Rosaleen glanced around to see the wizards looking shaky. Bridgit appeared by her side, her face drawn.

"He is right. We cannot hold him much longer. You need to try something different," she said.

"I shall confront him. Aroaril's power will defeat Zorva," Rosaleen said confidently.

Bridgit grabbed her hand. "He has already killed two priests," she warned.

"I have no choice. I have to face him," Rosaleen said.

"Use fire," Gallagher called.

One of the wizards picked up a chunk of broken spear and handed her the makeshift torch, holding his hand over the top until it sparked into flame. Rosaleen drew back her arm and hurled it at Swane, the missile turning into a roaring ball of flame as it flew.

Swane reached up and sent the missile flying past him, to smash into a merchant's shop with a thunderous blast that sent chunks of timber and brick cartwheeling across the street.

"Metal. He can't do anything with metal," Fallon said. "Get the heads off arrows and spears, anything we've got."

While Swane bent over the bodies of wounded men, doing more foul work with his knife, men and women hurriedly stripped the metal heads from shafts.

"Throw them now!" Rosaleen called and while Swane was too far away for most of them to even reach him, let alone do any damage, a hail of metal objects flew down the street. Yet, instead of falling to the ground, they picked up speed as they flew, a deadly hail all aimed at Swane.

But Swane slapped his hands on the ground and cobbles rose like a sheet, the metal assault bouncing off his stony shield.

He pointed at them and the wounded men he had been working on rose and began shambling towards them, their eyes dull, each with a hideous wound just below their ribcage, yet all carried swords. Behind them, Swane was already kneeling beside more.

"Aroaril, not these again," Fallon groaned. "Only fire can stop them."

"You take them. I'll stop Swane," Rosaleen said firmly.

Fallon tightened his grip on his guisarme. "Take out their legs and then their hands. Once they're down, the wizards will have to burn them up."

"What about Rosaleen? She needs all the magical help she can get," Gallagher growled.

"So do we. If we don't stop him, every one of us will end up in his army and this will become a city of the dead," Fallon replied. "Now, are we going to stop him or are we going to talk about it?"

Nobody answered and he pointed at Gallagher. "Carve her a path through them. Keep them off her and give her a chance."

Gallagher clasped his wife's arm. "None of them will touch you," he swore, then beckoned to the others. "Come on!"

*

Rosaleen walked down the street, feeling as if she was in a nightmare. There had been no need to give orders to the Kottermanis; they had seen the shambling horrors lurching towards them and reacted instantly, hacking and chopping at their former comrades.

The creatures of darkness veered towards her but the men around her fought viciously to keep her clear. Pieces of the creatures littered the street but even when they were down, even when arms were parted from bodies, they still clawed and grasped.

Behind them, Swane was creating new ones as fast as the old ones were being cut apart. Each time he bent life to his evil and prevented souls from finding release felt like a whip to her heart.

"Swane! Enough!" she screamed.

Swane turned to face her, blood dripping from his hands, his eyes like the burning pits of Zorva.

"You cannot stop me. None of you can. I will go on and on until this city is under my control and the whole world will bow down to me or be destroyed!" he cried, his voice cracking with madness.

She hated and despised everything about him and reached up with all of that, praying for the power to end this evil. She imagined Swane burning in a holy fire, his filth cleansed from the world. She pointed at him, expecting to see him wither in a blast of her power.

But he merely laughed at her and slapped his hands together. A huge burst of wind rushed down the street, knocking over the living and undead alike. Rosaleen struggled against it, fighting to stay in place, but with another surge from Swane, a gust picked her up and sent her tumbling along.

She hit the cobbles, felt skin scrape from her shoulder and back and the wind blast from her lungs and she lay there, gasping for breath, her eyes burning with tears. She had given him everything she had and he had laughed at her! How in Aroaril's name could they hope to stop him?

A hand reached down and took her arm, pulling her into a sitting position and cradling her while she whooped breath back in. She looked up gratefully to see a grim-faced Bridgit and nodded her thanks.

"Can you see a weakness?" Bridgit asked quietly. "Can you beat him?"

Rosaleen coughed and shook her head. "I wanted to wipe his evil from this street but it was as if I was a child. He is holding too many souls now, the power within him is beyond imagining."

Bridgit looked away, down the street. There were screams as men were falling prey to Swane's creatures, or at least parts of them, while Swane himself was hard at work creating more.

"You can't fight hate with hate. The opposite of hate is love. Use that," she said.

Rosaleen looked at her, wondering if these hideous images had caused Bridgit to lose her mind but her friend's eyes were alight with her idea.

"We must take away his power," Bridgit said. "The souls he has will only find peace when he dies. If you give them that peace first, then he won't have them anymore."

Rosaleen opened her mouth to say that was impossible, but then she closed it. With a heave from Bridgit she stood and walked again towards Swane.

Again, the creatures converged on her but the living fought even harder to keep them away. She dropped to her knees and bowed her head. She was dimly aware of Gallagher smashing at a creature with a fallen length of timber, of Fallon and Kemal fighting back-to-back against a pair of them, of Bridgit calmly pointing out targets for the handful of other wizards still on their feet. As for Swane, he was carving up more bodies, seemingly intent on creating a foul army of the dead. Then she shut all that out and reached out for Swane with her mind.

There was a thunderstorm of hatred there, ready to rip her apart if she dared to enter but she waited outside, not attacking but calling instead. She reached not upwards but inwards, calling on what she knew and what she had experienced.

She started with what was freshest in her mind, the love between a woman and a man. Everything she felt about Gallagher she sent into that thundercloud. Almost immediately it began to shrink, and in her mind's eye she felt a sense of peace as souls were freed from Swane's slavery, using her memories of love to slip the chains of evil fastened around their spirits. Then she turned to her memory of her happy childhood, sending out the love of a child for its mother, a simple, heartfelt emotion. She could feel the thundercloud shrinking every moment and pressed on.

She was vaguely aware that the creatures were now crazed in their desperation to get to her but while her protectors fought just as furiously, the creatures were moving slower. Some had stopped.

Yet there was still a dark heart to the thundercloud that was Swane's power and she instinctively knew she needed more. "Help me!" she cried. "Hold my hands!"

She raised them up and the first one she felt was Bridgit. With a surge that made her convulse, she took Bridgit's love of a mother for their child, the longing and regret for children lost and the overwhelming need to protect a baby and sent that out at the cloud.

"More!" she cried.

Next came Feray and she took not just love for husband and children but the love for a people and for fairness and justice. From Gallagher came a love for the sea, for his friends and, in a wave that warmed her, for herself.

From Kemal came the love of Kotterman, of its landscape and sun. Other hands touched her and she took their love and sent it into the cloud. Love between men, between women, for pets, for sunrises, for food and more, much more, she took and sent.

In her mind's eye, that thundercloud was almost gone. There was just one, small cloud but it was still as black as sin and ready to tear her apart. It was, she sensed, the bedrock of his power. She could not find anything else within her, or within the people touching her, but then Fallon's hand pressed on her shoulder.

She gasped and raced through love for wife and child, for village and friends and found, buried deep down, his love for Prince Cavan. Nothing happened but she pressed on, using Fallon's regrets and determination to wipe out the evil deed he had been tricked into, his agony at what he had done and his desperation to make up for it.

The cloud burst apart and she opened her eyes.

She could barely see down the street because there were so many people touching her but the creatures had all fallen. And while Swane was still standing, he seemed different somehow.

"I have done all I can. He is all yours," she said. She felt like she had run some enormous race and sagged back into Gallagher's gentle hands.

*

Fallon winced. He had been using the guisarme to bring down Swane's creatures for Kemal to chop and his broken ribs were agony. But he felt strangely better. It was as if Rosaleen had taken some of the darkness out of him when she had taken on Swane. He looked around cautiously. The creatures had battled ferociously to get at Rosaleen and although they lay all over the street, in various pieces, Fallon could see he was not alone in thinking they might come back to life. When nothing stirred, he looked further down, to where a strangely shrunken Swane knelt, whimpering.

"Quick, before Swane does anything else," Fallon said.

Next moment there was a mad rush down the street to grab Swane, strip him of his bone knife and pin him, two men to each arm, holding him on his knees.

Fallon followed a little slower and looked down at the Prince. His face had changed again. No more did he look like some perverted version of Cavan. Now he had a shifty cast to his face, his eyes darted left and right, seeking to escape, and while his jaw had shrunk, his teeth seemed to have grown too large for his mouth.

"This is not the end!" he snarled. He tried to struggle but there was no real strength in him and the two Gaelish and two Kottermanis who held him controlled him easily.

"It has to end here. How should he die? By fire?" Kemal asked.

"We should do it in front of everyone, like he tried to do to us," Gannon said fiercely.

Fallon shook his head. "He does not deserve it. The people know what he is really like now."

"Then how shall he die? I have many men who would be delighted to do it, after what he did to their comrades," Kemal said.

Fallon hefted his guisarme. "No," he said. "I killed his brother and I killed his father. Now I will kill him and it will all be over."

Swane opened his mouth to say something but, after what Fallon had heard from Aidan, he had no wish to give this bastard a chance to curse him. He lunged, the steel spike driving through Swane's right eye and deep into his brain, scraping against the back of the Prince's skull.

Swane convulsed, then went limp and Fallon pulled the weapon out and threw it away. There was none of the satisfaction he had thought he would feel. In fact he felt like he needed a bath.

"Burn his corpse and that will be an end to it," he said tiredly, slumping to the ground. Kemal extended a hand and he allowed himself to be pulled to his feet.

"What now?" Kemal asked.

Fallon groaned. "Food. Then sleep," he said. "After that, do you want Gaelland? Want to make your empire complete? Do you want to keep fighting?"

Kemal grinned and held up his hand, which was smeared with blood. "We're blood brothers now," he said. "And after all we've been through, do you think I want to fight you?"

"You would have done anything to kill me a few moons ago."

"True," Kemal admitted. "But I was a different man then. As were you. A few moons ago you offered me a deal. Now I would like to offer you one, a treaty of peace that will guarantee your freedom and give you the money you need to rebuild."

Fallon smiled, then winced at the pain in his side. "It sounds good but I am no longer the Lord Protector of Gaelland. I need to talk to my wife first."

"Well, if she's going to lead the country then I am very glad we are going to be at peace." Kemal grinned and patted Fallon on the shoulder. "Go and see her, my friend."

Fallon clasped hands with Kemal and then stumbled down the street to where Bridgit and Feray were lecturing a contrite-looking Asil and Kerrin.

"Hey!" he shouted.

Instantly Kerrin raced across to him, thumping into him around the chest, making him groan as much from the cracked ribs as from the feeling of holding his son again.

"You did it. You saved me, just as you said you would," he said into his son's hair. "I am so proud of you."

"Are you going to stay with us now, Dad?"

"For the rest of my life," Fallon swore. He gripped Kerrin's shoulder. "Mate, Caley's gone. She died saving me, attacking Dina."

Kerrin looked up at him, his eyes shining. "I knew she would. She and grandpa were going to keep you alive. And then we could save you, Dad. Mam told us how. She's the best, isn't she?"

"More than you could ever know," Fallon said, looking up at Bridgit.

*

Bridgit paused to take a breath from telling Kerrin he had disobeyed her *again* by leaving the tower and coming to see what had happened. Kerrin had seized his chance, rushing down to throw himself at Fallon. She watched the two of them embrace and took a deep breath. How would Fallon react? She had used him as bait and risked his life, while he had seen many of his men, as well as Caley and Padraig, die.

Then he looked up from hugging Kerrin and smiled at her and it was as if the hourglass was spinning in reverse, throwing them down the years. She strode towards him. In saving him, had she lost him?

*

Fallon hugged Kerrin once more and then lurched over to Bridgit, holding her as he thought he could never do again. Finally he looked down at her.

"You planned all this?" he asked hoarsely.

"Not like this," she said. "I thought we would grab them at the castle and end it there."

"But Padraig? Even Caley? Were you planning this when I told everyone about my poisoned quarrel?"

She looked into his eyes and he saw the iron in there. Like raw metal in Brendan's forge, she had passed through trials of fire and water and turned to steel. "Yes," she said. "It scared me, I hated it, but it had to be done. I am sorry if—"

"You have nothing to be sorry about," he said thickly. "I am the one who is sorry. You saved Gaelland and destroyed Swane."

"You are not angry at how I used you, lied to you, didn't tell you?"

He kissed her, breaking free only reluctantly. "I feel like I have reborn. I feel like all my anger is gone," he said. "And I feel like I can see clearly now. You are a better ruler than I am. All my life I have searched for a leader worth following. I thought I found one in Cavan but it turns out I actually married her – she just needed to find herself."

She pulled away a little. "Did you take a knock on the head?" she asked.

"Several times," Fallon admitted. "But these were ones that did me good. I still feel regret for killing Cavan, but what I shall do is work each day to make it better. Work with you to make Gaelland better, if you want it. Or we can walk away, go back to Baltimore."

*

Bridgit looked into his eyes and could see the truth there.

"You would step aside, obey me?" she asked.

He chuckled. "I started doing that the day we married!"

She smiled and looked up and down the street, to where people were looking to her for guidance, for orders. It sounded like a choice – and one the old Bridgit would have run from. But, to the new Bridgit, there was no choice.

CHAPTER 84

Bridgit walked around the throne room, which was filled with tables and people. The first of the spring crops had come in and the food was decent, although no better than what thousands of families around Gaelland were sitting down to and a far cry from the decadence of the previous year, under King Aidan.

She smiled at everyone, even the new councillors who had arrived from distant counties. After having a Kottermani force in every coastal town, it seemed even the most pro-Aidan county had discovered an enthusiasm for the new rule and she had been elected as First Minister unanimously. She had accepted it with only a little reluctance. She had never wanted this position but, as Fallon said, that meant she was perfect for the job. Besides, after she had saved the country from Swane's evil, she could not just turn away from it. That decision, to use Fallon as the bait in a giant trap for Swane, had sealed her fate, it seemed.

She lingered longer at tables of old friends, embracing Nola and Riona, although it was hard to pry them from the arms of Brendan and Devlin.

"How is Baltimore?" she asked.

"It grows," Devlin said. "Not everyone returned but Ely and her family are a welcome addition, as are some of the other former slaves that Kemal sent back from Kotterman."

"It grows but you still don't," Brendan said with a wink.

Bridgit joined in the laughter, enjoying seeing Brendan without a haunted look on his face. She had heard that he had begun to use a small hammer again, working the iron he loved so much.

"It is almost as it was," Nola said, her hand settling comfortably on her husband's big forearm. "I know you have a few things to do here but we could always find a place for you."

"Well, we might have to put it to a vote," Riona said with a wink.

Bridgit slapped her friend lightly on the shoulder and moved on to the table of Kottermanis. Kemal and Feray were unable to be there, because there was so much to be done back in their country. They were negotiating a score of treaties that would see the Empire break into its original countries, while also freeing the slaves across the vast land. They were ruling as co-Emperors, which had created almost as big an upheaval. Luckily they had the new church on their side, and priests rich in Aroaril's favor, which helped the people accept what they were doing was right. It would be a work that might need to be finished by Asil and Orhan, but they had sent their warmest wishes for today and a delegation bearing gifts. While they were using the Empire's vast stores of gold to smooth the way to ending the Empire, they had still found enough to pay Gaelland reparations for the havoc the invading army had wreaked. They had also returned more than a hundred slaves who had been secretly shipped to Kotterman over the years. Work was underway around Berry to repair the damage from the battle, as well as what had been done in other towns. Kottermani gold was paying for that but the workers were the black marketeer merchants who had grown fat off Aidan but now grew thinner repairing the damage his son had caused.

The Kottermanis also provided a fine gift of more than a hundred silver-backed mirrors, better than anything in Gaelland. They had been used to line the large cell for Duchess Dina. She had grown fat on a diet of enforced inactivity and stodgy food, while her new wardrobe was a selection of dirty, sack-like rags. Now, wherever she looked, all she could see was her scarred face, unwashed hair, her lumpen body and her rough clothes. It might have been more merciful to kill her but Bridgit was in no mood to be kind to Dina.

Her duty to the Kottermanis done, Bridgit moved on. It truly felt as though this country was made up of her children and there was no end to the task of nurturing them. Although, as today showed, that task was getting easier. Having been shown the face of true evil, the people were eager to embrace the new Gaelland and its fairness for all.

Her musing was interrupted by Rosaleen and Gallagher, resplendent in white robes. They were easy to see because all bowed in respect to them as they passed, a tribute to how they had defeated Swane and also to the way they had helped rebuild the people's faith in Aroaril afterwards.

"Ah, there you are!" the Archbishop smiled, embracing her. "But where is the real guest of honor?"

Bridgit felt a moment of alarm. "Don't tell me they're in trouble again," she muttered, looking frantically around the room.

A moment later she exhaled as Kerrin and Fallon appeared. "She was crying a moment ago but she's happy now," Kerrin announced, holding up his baby sister for Bridgit to see.

"It was an unusual name at today's Naming Ceremony, but a pretty one," Rosaleen commented.

"Cavana," Bridgit said with a slight smile. "Don't think there were a few conversations about that."

Fallon embraced her, kissing her gently. "Would you have preferred Swania?" he whispered.

She slapped him lightly on the chest. "Would you prefer being sent to Kotterman as a slave?" she murmured back and gave him a wink.

His eyes had cleared and he looked ten summers younger to her. Or maybe her eyes were getting worse. Whatever, that little girl had put the sparkle back into their lives and there were times she even thought this made all those dark times worth it, that coming out the other end after all they had been through had made them happier.

"Mam," Kerrin said. "I think she's done it again."

Bridgit let go of Fallon reluctantly and looked down as Kerrin held up the perfect little girl. It seemed her work really never ended.

Then Fallon reached down and took her. "I'll change her," he said. "This is one mess I know I can handle."

THE END

Acknowledgments

Even though my name is on the cover, there are many people who helped – either to make this book a reality or to make the story, the characters and the words better. Without them, it would be a lesser work and I thank them deeply for what they added to the book.

To my beta reader Belinda, who always has good suggestions; my agent Jo Butler at Cameron's Management; the team at Momentum – Joel, Patrick and Michelle; to copy editor Tara Goedjen, whose brilliant work made me think about every aspect of this book and made my writing look better; to the fantastic proofreader Chrysoula Aiello whose eagle eyes were very much appreciated.

If you enjoyed this book, then you deserve my thanks as well.